LILY
OF THE MANOR

LILY

a novel

OF THE MANOR

ANITA STANSFIELD

Covenant Communications, Inc.

Cover image: © Ildiko Neer / Trevillion Image

Cover design © 2017 by Covenant Communications, Inc.

Published by Covenant Communications, Inc.
American Fork, Utah

Printed in the United States of America
First Printing: July 2017

23 22 21 20 19 18 17   10 9 8 7 6 5 4 3 2 1

ISBN-13: 978-1-52440-294-5

For Alia Alexandria

Chapter One
THE TUTOR

Northern England—1807

FREDERICK WOODSTONE HAD EXPECTED THE walk from the village out to the manor house of his destination to be long—but not this long! He felt as if he'd walked for hours. Well, he *had* walked for hours. His feet were certainly complaining, and he frequently recalled the faithful horse he'd owned for years, an animal that had been as much a pet as a means of transportation. But old Sully had finally let go of this world, and Frederick simply hadn't possessed the funds to replace the animal. And so he'd taken to walking the distances where hired carriages would not take him without charging amounts that were not within his meager budget. He didn't *mind* walking—most of the time anyway. Walking cleared his head, and he often used the silence to engage in some form of conversation with God. Such conversations, even if they were most often very one-sided, kept him going on this journey of life that currently had no specific destination.

Frederick wished he had packed more food and an extra flask of water, and he could only hope that upon his arrival at the elaborate home of the Broadbent family he might be offered sufficient refreshment to get him through the necessary return walk to town. If this interview didn't go well and he didn't acquire the employment he was hoping for, the remainder of the day could be very unappealing.

When it began to rain, he was glad to have an umbrella, but he quickly realized his shoes were getting very muddy. His hopes of arriving at this appointment looking his very best were dwindling quickly. He gave in to the temptation to lift his face to the sky and allow rainwater into his mouth, which refreshingly eased the dryness of his tongue and throat, but he knew that bathing his face and hair in rain made the umbrella mostly irrelevant. He'd wanted to show up at the door looking clean and dapper and respectable. As it was, he would look more like a lost vagrant or beggar.

But as Frederick kept walking, he reminded himself that he'd done his best and the long walk and bad weather were not his fault. If these people could not overlook such things and give him a fair interview, they were not likely the kind of people he wanted to work for. And yet he needed work so desperately! He still couldn't find any logic or reason as to why he'd come to this particular area searching for work. It had almost seemed to be calling to him, which might sound crazy to some people. But for a man like himself, who firmly believed that his life was in God's hands, he couldn't deny the way his instincts had brought him here once he'd realized he needed a fresh, clean start with people who didn't know him.

Frederick was relieved to see the majestic house come into view— although it could more accurately be described as something between a house and a castle. With the time it took him to actually get to the groomed gardens surrounding the house, he was struck by how very large it was. The distance had made it seem smaller.

The rain had stopped by the time Frederick came to the main door. He closed his umbrella and set his bag at his feet before he attempted to smooth his short-cut brown hair by pressing his fingers through it. He straightened his suit and tie, cleared his throat, squared his shoulders, and used the elaborate brass knocker to alert those inside that a stranger had arrived at their door. A stranger with hopes so high that he feared this would end up being all wrong, and he had no idea how to find the strength—or the means—to keep looking for work that was suitable to his knowledge and disposition.

Frederick had expected the door to be answered by a formal-looking maid or butler, but it was a blond-haired boy of about ten or eleven who pulled it open, exchanging an inquisitive gaze with Frederick before any words were spoken. The boy was well-groomed, and his clothes were clean and pressed. But they didn't look like the clothing that would be worn by the child of someone who lived in a house like this, and Frederick couldn't imagine the child of a servant being allowed to answer the door.

When the boy didn't speak, Frederick asked, "Is this the Broadbent house?"

"It is," the boy said, and with those two syllables Frederick knew that this child had not been raised with education or refinement. In the course of his profession, he'd developed a fascination with speech and how it defined people and the lives they'd lived. He'd worked very hard himself to improve his speech skills so that he could be considered worthy of teaching the children of wealthy people.

Frederick decided to treat this boy as if it were normal for him to have answered the door. "My name is Frederick Woodstone. I have an interview scheduled with the head of the household. If you could please—"

He was interrupted by the sound of a woman's voice in the distance, bellowing in alarm, getting louder as she came closer. "Young Master David," she called. "I've told you and told you to come for me or Mr. Ingham when callers come."

The boy eased back from the door, looking sheepish but not at all frightened. He looked more proud of himself for having gotten away with something mischievous, and Frederick had a difficult time keeping a sober expression when the woman with the bellowing voice finally came from around the door, blocking his view of the boy with her stout body and scowling face. Her hair was gray, and most of it was tightly concealed beneath the little cap on her head.

"Forgive the child, sir," she said. "I dare say he has ambitions of being a butler one day. He just might be able to do it if he learns to mind his ways."

"Nothing wrong with a little ambition," Frederick said, wondering how best to converse with this woman. He couldn't discern whether she was scowling because of the boy or because of her assessment of *him* as she took in his appearance, all the way from his muddy shoes up over his wet clothes to his disheveled hair. But her scowl disappeared behind a warm concern.

"Did you walk all the way from town?" she asked, astonished.

"I did, yes," he said. "I believe my first order of business should be to remove my shoes and—"

"Indeed it is," the woman said, now behaving like a mother hen as she picked up Frederick's bag and motioned him inside. "And we must get you warmed up. Some tea and biscuits wouldn't go amiss."

Frederick breathed in a hearty helping of relief over the woman's kindness and insight while he bent over to remove his shoes, aware of the woman now giving the boy orders to pass on to three different people. Rather than just leaving Frederick's shoes by the door, she picked them up and gave them to the boy to hand off to someone who would see them properly cleaned. She also handed the boy Frederick's umbrella.

Once the boy had hurried away down a long hall, Frederick stood to face this woman, trying not to feel uncomfortable in his stockinged feet, especially since he was well aware that there was more than one visible hole where his toes peered out.

"Now," the woman said, setting down his bag, "you must be the young man interviewing for the tutor position."

"I am, yes," he stated, relieved to not have to explain his reason for being here.

"We've had a bit of an uproar here this morning which has set us all back a little, but that should give you some time to warm up and have a bite to eat." Frederick nodded, very glad to hear it. Not only was he cold and hungry, he desperately wanted to be able to gather his wits and get his thoughts straight. He was far more nervous about this interview than he cared to admit, and he certainly didn't want to allow his nerves to show.

"Come with me," the woman said. He picked up his bag and followed her. "My name is Mrs. Pilfer. I'm head housekeeper here, although," she chuckled, "I've never worked in a house like this one. You won't find much of anything conventional here, young man. If you're looking for work that's conventional, you've come to the wrong place." She chuckled again. "But I dare say you'll still be needing to be fed and warmed up before you go out looking for the right job."

Frederick wanted to say that he wasn't necessarily fond of convention and he hoped with all his heart this *was* the right place for him. But he didn't know how to say it without sounding either patronizing or desperate.

He followed her into a parlor where a fire was already blazing, and he gravitated toward it while she was telling him that tea and biscuits would be brought straightaway, and she even told him the location of a room where he was welcome to freshen up. She estimated it might be nearly an hour before his interview might take place, and she would come and get him.

"Thank you . . . very much," Frederick said. "You've been most kind."

Mrs. Pilfer smiled and started to close the door, but she stopped and said, "Bless me! I've not even asked your name. I can't very well go and tell my employer you're here if I don't know your name."

"Frederick Woodstone," he said, and she repeated it as if to make certain she'd heard correctly.

The door closed, and Frederick was left alone with the fire and the relief of feeling warm and safe. He moved closer to the warmth of the flames and prayed it would last, that the interview would go well, that he might be found appropriately unconventional enough to be a full-time tutor for the children in this household. And if he might be blessed enough to become employed immediately, he wouldn't have to walk back to town in the rain, and he would have a place to sleep that was much better than what meager accommodations he could afford.

A tray of tea and biscuits was brought in by a young woman who introduced herself as Mary. She was kind but shy, and he guessed she couldn't have been more than fourteen or fifteen. After she left, Frederick sat down and indulged in the savory warmth of the tea and the heavenly array of biscuits and little sandwiches laid out prettily before him. He was glad to be alone when he realized he was much hungrier than he'd wanted to admit and he would have found it difficult to eat politely. He was sure he should feel embarrassed by the way he ate every morsel of what he'd been offered, but instead he just offered gratitude to God for providing him with such decadent nourishment.

Frederick went to where he'd been told he could freshen up. He took with him a comb that had been in his bag, and he returned to the warm parlor feeling much more prepared for his interview—except for his feet being covered only by hole-ridden stockings. But as he moved close to the fire once again, he was pleased to see his shoes there, looking cleaner and more polished than they had since he'd purchased them, which was too long ago to remember.

Once he had his shoes back on, Frederick noticed the tea tray had been taken away, but a carafe of water and two glasses had been left in its place. As he poured himself some water, he wondered who the other glass might be for. He'd barely swallowed the refreshing liquid his body needed before he heard the door coming open, and he set the glass down as he stood, expecting Mrs. Pilfer, who had promised to take him to the room where the interview would be held. Instead he saw a younger woman enter the room and close the door behind her. As she turned to face him, he felt so taken aback that he momentarily lost his breath. He had never seen any human being with such striking features or unusual coloring. He guessed her to be about ten years older than he, even though his first impression from her hair color was that she had to be much older. Her hair, in fact, was white. He had to think the words again to be assured it wasn't some kind of illusion. Her hair was *white.* Not blonde, not gray, but white—which made it very near the color of her pale skin. Her facial features had a sharpness to them that almost made her look undernourished, except that she had a vibrancy about her that made it immediately evident this was not the case. Her pink lips and startling blue eyes created a stark but fascinating contrast to her pale complexion. The dress she wore was simple, perhaps even old-fashioned, and nearly the same blue as her eyes. He might have wondered if she too was a servant in this unconventional household, except that her hair was styled too elegantly for a servant, and she wore a necklace that no servant would ever own; and even if she did, she never would have worn it while working.

Frederick realized he'd been staring, and he looked down, clearing his throat slightly.

"There's no need to feel embarrassed, Mr. Woodstone," she said in a voice that was as unusual as her appearance. It was completely feminine but had a richness to it that was almost melodic. "I've not once in my life met someone without having them wonder what to think about the way I look. I'm quite accustomed to it." She walked past him toward the fire as if she had been cold before coming into the room. "Some people have gone so far as to conclude that my appearance is perhaps an indication that I'm some kind of freak." She laughed softly. "A ghost, perhaps, or maybe even a witch." She turned her back to the fire. He surmised that she was slightly taller than average for a woman, and he was a little less than the average height for a man, which made him only slightly taller than she was. "What is it about people that they immediately assume when a person's appearance is strange and unfamiliar, it somehow equates with that person being unholy?" He heard in her words some kind of declaration that she wanted him to look past her appearance and not jump to any conclusions regarding her character. He couldn't tell someone he'd just met that he wasn't the kind of man to judge, but it seemed she'd become accustomed to needing to make such declarations upon meeting new people.

"People can be difficult to figure out," was all he could think to say, wishing he knew to whom he was speaking. The advertisement for the job had simply said he would be interviewed by the head of the household. He'd assumed it would be a man. Was *she* the woman in charge of Broadbent House? "If you're interested in my personal opinion . . ." He purposely hesitated, knowing it was proper for him to speak his mind only if asked to do so.

"I'd be *very* interested," she said.

"I don't know you well enough to know anything about you; we've only just met. I admit that your appearance is striking, but many of God's creations are." He saw a subtle intrigue in her eyes, so subtle that he suspected she wasn't given to showing her emotions easily. "My mother had a very distinctive and rather large birthmark on her face. She was a beautiful woman, but she was often treated badly because of the mark. I believe she was often referred to as *unholy.* And yet she was the kindest and finest woman I have ever known."

"By the way you speak of her, I assume she has passed on."

"She has, yes."

"I'm guessing it was not so very long ago; you seem to still be affected by her absence."

"Do I?" he asked, taken aback by her perception. She only tipped her head slightly, and he added, "It's been more than a year, but we were very close. Yes, I am certainly still affected by her absence in my life."

"But you believe her spirit still lives on?" she asked.

"Is this part of the interview?" he countered, wanting to know where he stood in this conversation but not wanting to come across as impolite or inappropriate.

"Actually, yes," the woman stated. "The person I hire to live under my roof and teach my children must hold to certain beliefs. It's not enough for that person to simply teach whatever I might require. Children learn much by example; they see through falseness. I believe that every person has the right to believe whatever they choose to believe. It is also my right to hire someone who has similar beliefs to my own so that I know my children are being taught in a way that does not conflict with what *I* teach them."

"That is perfectly reasonable," Frederick said, even while he realized that she was expecting him to state his beliefs without having any idea what she required in the person she chose to hire. Of course, she would be looking for integrity. Her stating that children could see through falseness made it evident that she was capable of doing the same. He simply had to state his beliefs and hope that his being here now was not simply a waste of precious time and energy.

Frederick put his hands behind his back and turned just a little in order to face her more directly. "I'll just tell you a little about myself and my beliefs, and then you may ask me anything you'd like to know that I might have missed. While I've had a great deal of experience with some people looking down on me due to certain aspects of my background, I prefer to be completely honest as opposed to trying to hide anything about myself that might be misconstrued." He saw her nod slightly as if she approved, and he forged ahead. "I was an only child. I don't remember my father. According to my mother, he was a violent and distasteful man. She left him when I was still a baby in order to protect us both. She changed our surname and raised me on her own, working as a seamstress for our support. She took me to church every Sunday, we read together from the Bible every day, and we prayed together morning and night. She guided me in religious matters with the clear understanding that I needed to search my own soul and determine my own beliefs, that I should not rely on her convictions—or anyone else's. Following her advice, I came firmly to my own convictions and became a vicar when I was barely twenty. I enjoyed the opportunity to assist and guide people through the challenges of life, but found I was not very good at giving sermons. After striving earnestly for a few years to become better at it, I finally accepted that I was more suited to teaching. The best part of being a vicar was the opportunity to teach the children. I sought out more education so that I could formally pursue teaching. I sent you my accreditations in that regard."

Again the woman nodded, and Frederick moved toward answering the original question. "I believe that every child is known and loved by God, and that if each person could understand that one thing, the world would be so much a better place. I believe that education is vital in order to not just survive in this world but to thrive and make a difference for good. To learn to write and read and speak well is mandatory to having doors of opportunity opened. To learn maths and understand its application opens more doors. I also believe that it is equally vital to realize that all we are given comes from God, and only accepting and respecting that as truth can lead to real happiness. Therefore, a spiritual education is equally as important as an academic one, and the two should go hand in hand. And yes, I believe my mother's spirit lives on. I believe she watches over me and guides me in my life. I believe she guided me here today, but I'm not certain if she simply wanted me to get some exercise or if this is where I belong. That will be up to you."

Once Frederick had stopped speaking, he could hear the pounding of his own heart. He could only hope his boldness had not turned her opinion against him. She increased his nervousness when she didn't speak; she only walked to the window and looked outside, pulling the curtain aside with her pale hand.

When the silence became excruciating, Frederick said, "May I be so bold as to ask your name? I fear I am at quite a disadvantage. You know much about me, yet I know nothing about you."

"Forgive me," she said, still gazing out the window. "I am Mrs. Broadbent. I should not have assumed that my identity was obvious."

"And Mr. Broadbent?" he asked, wondering if her husband had simply put her in charge of this duty or if there was some other reason for her conducting this interview.

"Is deceased," she stated.

"I'm very sorry for your loss," he said with a sincere compassion that had come naturally to him long before he'd become a vicar. He'd surely learned it from his mother.

"Thank you," she said. "It's been several years. I've become accustomed to his absence."

She said nothing further, but she hadn't dismissed him, so he asked what he thought was obvious and appropriate. "Could you tell me about the children?"

Mrs. Broadbent turned to look at him and smiled in a way that offered him hope that this was going well. His hope increased when she said, "Why don't you come with me and you can meet them?"

Frederick felt a little breathless. Surely she wouldn't be taking him to meet the children if she considered him obviously unsuitable for the position. He wanted to think that he'd passed the first stage of the interview, and perhaps now she wanted to observe how he interacted with the children. He knew he just needed to be himself; she would see through falseness. But that didn't worry him because he'd never attempted to be anything other than what he was. And children didn't intimidate him; he'd softened a number of fairly difficult ones. It was more the parents' perspective that made the difference. If a parent believed their child could do no wrong but the child was spoiled and prone to misbehaving, it was always the teacher who got blamed for any problems. He hoped she was the kind of mother who had taught her children to respect adults appropriately and that she would work *with* a tutor on guiding their discipline and behavior, as opposed to either giving him the entire responsibility or, perhaps worse, not allowing him any responsibility in that regard whatsoever.

Frederick followed Mrs. Broadbent up a lofty staircase, grateful he was actually wearing his shoes—and they were clean. He hoped he got a chance later to thank Mrs. Pilfer for her insight and kindness. He couldn't help noticing the litheness with which the lady of the house moved as she ascended the stairs just ahead of him.

"The children are somewhat out of control since the last tutor left. Nellie, the governess, does what she can, but she's easily overwhelmed." Mrs. Broadbent laughed softly. "Nellie is excellent in managing the morning and evening routines of the children, but she's not as good at lessons or structured activities. But then, we all have the things we're good at, don't we?"

"Indeed, we do," Frederick said and followed her to the top of the stairs, down a short stretch of hallway, and up another set of stairs.

"The tutor's job would be to keep the children engaged with lessons and activities during the daytime hours six days a week. You would have your evenings and the Sabbath to do as you choose."

Frederick's heart quickened at the implication that he was being seriously considered for the job, and he already liked the schedule.

"On the Sabbath, we attend church, and you would be welcome to attend with us, but that is up to you. We then spend time together as a family, so as I said, that day would be your own. If you ever need a weekday off to deal with any personal matters, that can be arranged. If you need any personal items from town, that can be arranged with Mrs.

Pilfer, who sends someone twice a week for supplies, and the cost of your purchases can be taken from your salary. She's very excellent at keeping track of such things."

Frederick didn't want to sound presumptuous about assuming this meant he had the job; until she actually told him he was hired, he had to behave as if she were just giving him information regarding the *possibility* of him being hired. So he simply said, "That all sounds more than fair and very efficient."

She laughed softly again. "The responsibility of tutoring my children is an enormous undertaking, Mr. Woodstone. I suspect you will very much need your time off, and if you manage them well, you will very much deserve it. I fear our last tutor fell rather short of being able to manage his expected responsibilities."

Frederick felt a little nervous over that comment. He wondered how many children she had and how spoiled they might be. He thought of how hard he'd prayed for this to work out, and in his mind he heard his mother saying, *Be careful what you pray for.* At that very moment, Mrs. Broadbent stopped walking and put her hand on a doorknob, but she hesitated and turned to look at him. He could hear the ruckus of children playing on the other side of that door, but he was more distracted by the increased intensity in her eyes, as if she were about to tell him some great, mystical secret.

"Mr. Woodstone," she said in a somewhat hushed tone, "before you go into the playroom, you need to know that these children are all mine, but I did not give birth to them." He felt confused and knew she could see evidence of that from his expression. "For reasons that are not important at this time, I have been drawn to children who have been cast aside and left without the most meager essentials in this life. I have legally adopted all of these children; they all carry the name Broadbent, but not one of them came into my home prior to the death of my husband."

Frederick felt intrigued, in awe, overwhelmed, and full of questions. But he didn't have time to consider any of those things before she opened the door to the most magnificent room he'd ever seen. The playroom was bright due to the number of large windows; even with cloudy skies outside there seemed more than ample light in the room, as if it might have been emanating from some internal force that wasn't visible. There were tables with games and puzzles, surrounded by chairs painted in different bright colors. There were more toys than Frederick had ever seen—even in a toy shop. And there were at least ten children of varying ages in the room; he couldn't get an accurate count because some of them were moving around far too much with an indoor version of a game of tag. He was just trying to take it all in when Mrs. Broadbent loudly said one word in a kind tone: "Children!" They all became immediately still and attentive, but he saw no fear on their faces. They respected her, and they admired her. He could see it in their eyes, in their expressions. He wondered what kind of magic had taken place here, and in that moment he wanted desperately to be a part of it.

"This is Mr. Woodstone," she announced. "He's thinking he might like to be your new teacher." There was some clapping and a few cheers, but the children quickly quieted down again to hear what was being said. "I would like each of you to introduce yourselves to Mr. Woodstone and talk with him privately for a few minutes, and then we'll discuss the matter later on." She motioned to the boy Frederick recognized as having answered the front door. "David," she said, "since you were so eager to meet our guest earlier, you should go first. The rest of you can play until it's your turn, but do so quietly, please."

A minute later, Frederick was seated across from David at one of the tables. The other children had returned to their playing—a little more quietly than before, but not much. Mrs. Broadbent was seated on a small sofa on one side of the room, and he suspected it was a common spot for her. She appeared to be very comfortable there, observing this roomful of children she had taken on. Frederick's mind was still trying to catch up with the concept of this situation. He'd never imagined anything like it.

Not having expected to be interviewed by the children, it took him a moment to know where to begin. David was obviously waiting for him to say something. He began with the obvious. "Tell me about yourself, David."

"Like what?" David asked.

"I'm guessing you're about . . . ten years old?"

"That's right. Very good."

"What do you like best about school?"

"I like learning to read," he said. "I didn't know how before."

Again the boy's speech gave away the fact that he'd likely had no education at all before coming here, and it seemed he hadn't been here terribly long.

"Reading is great," Frederick said. "I love to read myself." He looked around. "Do you like it here?"

"Oh yeah," David said but didn't expound.

"Do you think *I* would like it here?"

"You'd be a fool not to," David said as if he were ten years older.

Frederick found the comment interesting and wanted to press the boy on what he meant exactly, but Frederick sensed it was better to keep these interviews simple. He asked, "What's your favorite time of day?"

"When Mama reads to us before bedtime," he said, and his eyes became brighter.

Frederick considered what that implied about Mrs. Broadbent, but he just smiled at David and said, "I like a young man who can appreciate the value of a good book."

David seemed pleased with the compliment before he stood up and said, "I'll get Lucy; it's her turn next."

"Thank you." Frederick then proceeded to have a similar conversation with Lucy, who was nine. She was shy, and it took a little more prodding to get her to answer simple questions, but she was as enthusiastic as David had been about her favorite time of day being when their mother read stories at bedtime. Frederick spoke with Virgil, also nine; Anne, age thirteen; and Wilfred, who was five. There was Trudy, age seven, and Stanley, age twelve. Hugo was eleven, Alec was six, and the youngest of the group was Matilda, who had just turned four. The last child he spoke to was Blaine, age eight—which made eleven children in all. They ranged from dark hair to blond and some in between. Some were shy, others precocious. Their personality differences were evident already—at least those they were willing to show to a stranger. But they all had very clear commonalities. They were all very grateful to be here, which was evidence that they had come from situations that had been much less favorable. They each had a subtle haunted look in their eyes, evidence that they'd all seen too much of the real world for children so young. They all clearly adored this woman they referred to as their mother, and they agreed unanimously that when she read stories to them before bed, it was their favorite time of day. It was evident that no tutor or governess could ever replace whatever it was this woman gave these children. Frederick felt so deeply moved that he couldn't even imagine being told he wasn't suitable for the position and would need to leave.

After he'd met all the children, Mrs. Broadbent asked him to come with her, and they left together. Frederick didn't want to leave the play-room, truly feeling as if it were a magical place, but he followed the lady of the house into what she called the schoolroom, and he caught his breath. He had taught children in the basement of a church and a room over a pub. He had tutored a few children in their homes. But he'd never imag-ined a room like this. Just as in the playroom, there were many large win-dows. The room had more than enough desks and chairs for every child and a fine desk at the front of the room for the teacher. There were charts and maps adorning the space, and the alphabet and numbers had been painted decoratively on the wall opposite the windows. There were shelves of books and stacks of paper and an ample supply of pencils and paints.

Frederick felt like a child himself as he stood in the room and slowly turned in a circle, just taking it in. He was startled to remember he wasn't alone when he heard Mrs. Broadbent say, "I'll be back in a few minutes, Mr. Woodstone. Make yourself at home."

He nodded, and she left the room; he wondered if she was going to go and ask the children what they thought of him. He figured his conversations with them had gone relatively well, but in truth he had no idea what this woman's priorities were—at least in regard to finding a tutor for her children. He'd come here expecting to teach two or three children, maybe four. But eleven? Eleven children, each of whom likely had trauma in their lives that could cause behavioral issues. He could understand why the previous tutor—or perhaps there had been more than one—would have left. It was indeed a daunting undertaking. But Frederick didn't feel intimidated. His experience as a vicar had exposed him to some pretty traumatic things. In his heart he believed he was right for this position and it was right for him. He felt fascinated by the very principles behind this situation, as well as the woman who had chosen to use her wealth to care for these needy children.

Frederick's mind went wild with the possibility of lessons catered to the different ages and reading levels of the children; with all the resources available, he could do such great activities with them. He cautioned himself to not get his heart set on something that might never be his, but he concluded it was too late. If Mrs. Broadbent didn't hire him, he would leave here heartbroken.

She returned much sooner than he'd expected, but instead of giving him a verdict, she ambled around the perimeter of the schoolroom and asked, "So what do you think?"

"Of what, exactly?" he asked but didn't wait for her to answer. "I think this is the most beautiful schoolroom I've ever seen, and the idea of working here fills me with joy. I think these children are very blessed to be in your care, and I would feel very blessed to be able to work with them. What do *you* think, Mrs. Broadbent?"

"Well . . ." she drawled and showed a hint of a smile, "the children like you. And I can't think of a single reason not to give you the position."

"Really?" Frederick asked with a little laugh, hoping his overt enthusiasm wasn't inappropriate. But since she also laughed lightly, he figured it was all right.

"Really. How long before you can start? If I had my way you'd just stay now and start in the morning. They've been without structured lessons for weeks now. But I'm certain you have other matters to take care of, and—"

"Actually," Frederick said, bursting with gratitude at the realization that his every prayer had been answered, "everything I own is with me, and there is nowhere I need to be. It would save me a long walk in the rain if I just stay."

"Truly?" she asked as if she shared his gratitude. Perhaps her prayers had been answered too. He liked the idea of being the answer to someone's prayers.

"Truly," he said.

"Then let's discuss the details." She motioned to one of the children's desks, and he sat down. She sat at another desk nearby, turning her chair toward him. When she told him what the salary would be—on top of his room and board—he had to fight for self-composure. He'd never imagined making such a fine wage—especially for doing something he loved to do. She told him some of the house rules, which were very few and not terribly strict. Her focus was on the children's well-being, and it seemed the household revolved around them more than anything else.

After they had talked for a while, he expected her to take him back downstairs and have one of the servants show him where to find his room, but she took him there herself. He was being given a room larger than the home he'd grown up in, and there was a sitting room next to it that was also his. She suggested he might like to rest, and she would have his bag brought up by Mr. Ingham, the head butler. She also said she'd send one of the servants up around seven to show him the way to the kitchen, where he would have supper, since she didn't want him to get lost.

Frederick thanked Mrs. Broadbent for everything and added firmly, "I won't let you down."

"If I believed you would, I wouldn't have hired you," she said with a confidence that inspired him.

She left the room and closed the door behind her. Frederick turned to survey his new bedroom more closely, unable to believe this was real. It felt like a dream—the kind of dream his mother would have wished to come true for him. Perhaps she *had* guided him here. He concluded that he *did* feel the need to rest. It had been a long walk and an emotionally strenuous day. But now he felt nothing but relief and hope, and the worries that had kept him awake the previous night no longer existed. Before he climbed into the huge, luxurious bed, Frederick knelt beside it and offered his gratitude to God for every step of his life that had led him to this day. A warmth filled him as he concluded his prayer, kicked off his shoes, and climbed between the smooth, clean sheets. He felt as if he'd stepped into his destiny.

Chapter Two
BELONGING

LILY BROADBENT RETURNED TO THE playroom once she knew that Mr. Woodstone had what he needed. She felt an enormous burden lifted off her shoulders to finally have a tutor for the children here in the house. She'd liked Mr. Woodstone the moment she met him and had been convinced he was the right man only a couple of minutes into his little oratory about the way his mother had raised him, his convictions and beliefs, his time serving as a vicar, and his coming to know that teaching was the place he felt most comfortable. For a man so young, she admired how conscious he was of his own strengths and weaknesses and how comfortable he could be in talking about them.

The children were full of questions about Mr. Woodstone, and they were all excited with the prospect of finally having a tutor again, although a couple of them were not very fond of school lessons and would prefer to just play. She helped them remember the rules and the schedule for school hours, and she cautioned them to all be patient and kind toward Mr. Woodstone. "If there are any rules broken or any unkind behavior," she cautioned, "there will be consequences." The children were well aware of the privileges they might lose if they didn't adhere to the rules. One of the first privileges to go was not being allowed to participate in reading together in the evenings. Lily knew the children would try very hard to be good in order to be present for that.

Lily stayed with the children until the maids brought supper into the playroom for them. Lily always ate breakfast alone—since she never felt prone to wanting to eat at the same time as the children. But she always had lunch in one of the dining rooms with the children, which was a meal where each person had an opportunity to talk about anything they wanted to share. The children ate their supper in the playroom with the governess, since Lily preferred to share one meal a day with adults.

With the children eating supper and being closely supervised, Lily went to her room to freshen up before going downstairs. She sat at her dressing table with three mirrors that showed every angle of her face. She felt no need to straighten her hair; it was so tightly pinned in place that it had lasted beautifully through the day. Had her husband been alive, she would have changed into a finer dress for their evening meal. It was a tradition he'd grown up with, and she had honored that as his wife. But under the present circumstances, getting dressed up for dinner seemed a silly waste of time. So Lily just contemplated her reflection, aware of the little clock ticking on the dressing table nearby. She was ready to go and had a few minutes before she needed to set out on the trek from her rooms to the kitchen.

For the first time in many months, Lily took more than a moment to consider her appearance. She'd become well accustomed to its strangeness due to her white hair, and she'd long ago stopped caring what anyone else thought about the way she looked. Her husband had been indifferent to her appearance; he never said a negative word about it, but neither had he ever said she was beautiful or lovely. Perhaps that was simply his tendency to be honest to a point that had often made him abrasive to other people. Bernard Broadbent was one of the most decent men she had ever known, and what they had shared had given them both a great deal of happiness and fulfillment. He would have done anything for her, and she knew it. But he also knew the same of her. His death had been a shock that she'd only been able to ease by seeking out a way to use the fortune he'd left to her for the benefit of those less fortunate. She knew she couldn't save every ailing child—even though she wanted to—but she could make a difference to those she had felt specifically drawn to, and she was grateful every day for the resources available to her to make such a dream a reality.

Lily dearly loved the life she was living; she had no desire to change it in any way. And now she would have this fine young man here to help guide and educate the children toward greater learning and subsequently greater understanding. She found him endearing in ways that were diffi-cult to pinpoint, but recalling their initial meeting earlier and his obvious shock at her appearance, she was now drawn to studying her reflection for long minutes, when she normally gave her mirrors hardly a second glance. She recalled how she had been taunted as a child and how even as an adult she could hardly go into town without receiving odd stares and glares of disdain. She'd grown accustomed to it and had convinced herself that it really didn't matter. And in her heart she sincerely believed that was true. Now, today, for reasons she couldn't decipher, she wondered what it might be like to have a normal complexion and normal hair color. She couldn't recall ever encountering anyone who remotely resembled her. She had always assumed that her parents had very normal appearances, even though she had been raised in an orphanage and had never known them. But the reasons for her strange coloring had remained a mystery. To the best of her knowledge, neither of her parents showed even a hint of it. She asked herself why she might suddenly be so somber regarding her strange appearance, and when the answer came, she didn't want to accept it. The only thing that had made today different from any other day was the appearance of Frederick Woodstone. She had long ago let go of any regard over what people might think of her. She was neither naive nor pretentious. But as she sat gazing at her reflection, she wondered what Mr. Woodstone thought of her. And the notion was ridiculous. She went down to supper and put all thoughts of him aside—except for the miraculous fact that tomorrow he would begin lessons with the children, and she couldn't wait to observe what magic he might spin in the classroom.

* * *

Mr. Ingham himself came to take Frederick down to dinner. Except for the way he was dressed and his fine manners, he was not at all what Frederick might have expected of a butler. He was not rigid or stiff in any way, and, in fact, he engaged Frederick in friendly conversation until they came to a plain dining room with a very long table that was just off the kitchen. Frederick knew this was where the servants ate their meals. Generally in such a household, the servants would have their evening meal after the family had eaten and all had been cleared away, and he wondered if Mrs. Broadbent had already been given her dinner. He honestly didn't know if there were any other relations in the house with whom she might dine. But he couldn't help wondering where she might be and what she might be doing. He just couldn't get her striking appearance and melodic voice out of his head.

Frederick was made to feel welcome by everyone present. He'd already met Mr. Ingham and Mrs. Pilfer and Mary. Now he met the cook, Mrs. Maddox, and her assistants, Jane and Lora. Max and Willy took care of the stables and the animals residing there, and they also cared for and drove the carriages and wagons. Abigail was also a maid who apparently shared some kind of romantic involvement with a young man named Luca, who worked as an underbutler. Zed too was an underbutler, and there was Levy, who worked as a houseboy—although his title seemed contradictory when he was obviously no longer a boy. He—along with some of the other servants in the household—likely had little or no education, and having such employment in this kind of situation was the very best they could ever hope for. Frederick looked around the room at their faces as the meal was being put on the table, and he felt a desire to form friendships with these people. Perhaps he could even help some of them improve their literacy. At this point he just hoped he could remember their names. He was grateful for his experience as a vicar and as a schoolteacher where he'd often needed to connect people's names with their faces and be able to recall them so as not to offend anyone with whom he interacted.

When Mrs. Maddox announced that everything was ready, everyone was seated, and Ingham guided Frederick to the chair he should use. As the highest-ranking male servant in the household, the butler held an unofficial patriarchal role with these people, and Frederick was pleased with the way Ingham initiated a blessing on the food. Everyone held hands around the table until the amen was spoken. As bowls and platters of food were passed around, Frederick couldn't recall the last time he'd enjoyed so fine a meal. The tender venison, boiled potatoes, and steamed vegetables soothed his spirit as much as they filled his stomach. While they were eating, he was asked questions about himself, and he repeated his background much as he'd told it to Mrs. Broadbent earlier. Some people around the table remained very quiet while others were more active in the conversation, but everyone was polite and cordial.

About halfway through the meal, Frederick noticed a place setting and an empty chair at the head of the table. He was about to ask who was missing when Mrs. Broadbent herself came into the room and sat there.

"Forgive me for being late," she said, and the food was passed down the table in her direction. "We had to finish the chapter before they would settle down."

"We all know how reading time can drag on," Mrs. Pilfer said, handing the lady of the house the boiled potatoes. "We just don't want you having to eat your supper alone."

"You're very kind, as always," Mrs. Broadbent said with a smile toward the housekeeper, "but I'm certain I would survive. With any luck, Nellie can get the children settled down soon."

Frederick recalled that Nellie was the governess—the one he'd been told about who supervised the children through their morning and evening routines. By listening, he learned more about the household routine and who did what—especially regarding the children.

Frederick ate slowly, savoring every bite along with the conversation. He was glad when his being the new addition in the household lost its novelty and he could just listen as opposed to being the center of attention. He liked listening to people and learning more about who they really were. Some of the servants ate quickly and left the table to see to their responsibilities or to get to bed since they had work to see to very early in the morning. Others lingered at the table and visited, and the lady of the house did the same. Frederick's fascination with her deepened as he noted that she was well acquainted with the personalities and circumstances of each one of these people who worked for her. She chose to eat with them as opposed to eating alone and being waited on.

Less than half of the servants were still at the table when Nellie arrived to report that the children were all tucked in and settled down. She appeared to be near his own age and not necessarily pretty but with a natural radiance that made it evident why Mrs. Broadbent had put her in charge of caring for the children—although they obviously worked closely together since Mrs. Broadbent had already made it clear from a number of comments that the children were the center of her life, and she likely wouldn't be out of their sight for very long.

Even though Nellie had eaten supper with the children, it was evidently her habit to come to the kitchen and enjoy some adult conversation as supper there was winding down. Nellie was pleased to meet Frederick, and they quickly got into a conversation about the children through which he was able to learn more about their personalities and what might be challenging for him as he taught them. They discussed how their schedules would complement each other, and it became evident that one or the other of them would be in charge of the children almost continually—except for Sundays when they were solely in the care of their mother for the majority of the day. Mrs. Broadbent remained a part of their conversation, and it was evident that she would commonly come and go throughout the days; she didn't want to disrupt the children's routine, but she always wanted to be involved with what they were doing.

When the conversation began to lose momentum and Frederick realized he had a big day ahead of him, he excused himself and managed to find his way back to his room; he only had to retrace his steps and make a different turn three times. The house was enormous, but he'd worked in such houses before. The difference was that he'd never lived in one. He'd always been a visiting tutor who had come on certain days and times for lessons, and he'd occasionally been given a meal. When his mother had been alive, he'd lived with her in the tiny home they'd shared for as long as he could remember. After her passing, he'd had to sell that house to pay off the debts that had been incurred through the years of his mother's health struggles. He'd moved into the vicarage until he'd made the decision that such a life was not right for him. Since then he'd rented lodging in a few different places, but his income had been minimal and the places he could afford had been meager.

Trying to fall asleep in his new bed, he could hardly fathom that this day had begun with only the hope that he might find steady and suitable employment in this new part of the country to which he'd felt drawn. Now he had officially become part of a household so unique and intriguing that his mind was still trying to catch up. He'd never met anyone like Mrs. Broadbent, and her startlingly unusual appearance was only the beginning of how very different she was from other women of her class. In the hours he'd known her, he'd already seen staggering evidence of how freely she gave of herself and her resources to make life better not only for the children she had adopted but for the people to whom she had given employment. She was providing a home, a purpose, and security to every person here—and now he was one of those blessed enough to be a beneficiary of her goodness. He silently thanked God once again for granting him such a privilege and asked for divine assistance in being able to do his best work on behalf of these children and to be sensitive to their individual needs and challenges. He finally slept in spite of being as nervous as he was excited to begin his new life.

* * *

Lily was one of the last to leave the kitchen—as she usually was—but not until she'd expressed her genuine appreciation to those who had worked to provide yet another fine meal. She followed her typical evening routine of wandering slowly through the house. She knew the servants would make certain the fires were cared for, the doors locked, and the lamps extinguished. Her need to traverse the halls and staircases and peer into certain rooms was more an act of affection. This grand house was all that remained of her deceased husband and, in fact, the entire Broadbent family line. It had ended with him, and he had died without progeny. Her husband's deep sense of integrity was one of many things that had made her love for him grow over time, and her love had not diminished in the years he'd been gone. She had worked hard to use all he'd left to her in the best possible way. But he'd never known the children who were now in her care, and only a few of the servants had been here prior to her arrival as a new bride. It was the house that remembered her sweet Bernard. It had witnessed his entire life, from his infancy to his adulthood and beyond. It had witnessed his birth and his death. She had lived a good life with him in the rooms of this house, and it was only in idly traversing these hallways when they were silent and dark that she could feel close to Bernard at all. The more time that passed, the more difficult it became to hold on to the memories. But the house seemed to understand. She was a rational person and knew the house itself had no sentient powers. Still, it had felt a part of her since the very first day she'd come here, and it had certainly been a part of the life she'd shared with Bernard. She felt less lonely when she walked the halls. She might not ever be able to rationally explain to herself or anyone else the reasons for that. It was simply how she felt.

Lily finally ended her evening walk by coming to her own room, where a fire was burning to ward off the chill of the ongoing rain. She set down the lamp she'd been carrying and proceeded to get ready for bed. It was her habit to sit in bed and read until she became too sleepy to hold up her head, which prevented her from thinking too much while she was trying to get to sleep. But tonight she found it difficult to focus on reading. Her mind kept straying to the new young tutor she'd hired today. She had a good feeling about him. He'd done well in his interactions with the children, and he'd fit in comfortably with the staff. She hoped the coming days would prove him capable of being able to handle the demands of the job he'd been hired to do. But she didn't feel worried. She believed he would adjust with time, and she was always willing to give people time to adjust.

* * *

Frederick spent his first day with the children trying to assess their individual needs according to their current ability to read and write. Ironically, some of the younger children actually had more education than a few of the older ones. He found them to be fairly well behaved—most of the time. But he quickly got a feel for which of the children might tend to pick fights or misbehave, and he simply kept reminding them of the boundaries and rules that applied to everyone and of what the consequences would be for breaking those rules.

The first time Mrs. Broadbent slipped into the classroom to observe, he felt nervous. What if she didn't approve of his teaching style? Or his methods of discipline? But he quickly managed to just ignore her presence and proceed as he normally would, figuring if she had any complaints or concerns, she would let him know. He already knew her to be a reasonable, levelheaded woman; surely she would come to him with any concerns if she had them.

On the second day, Frederick took the children out to the gardens for a lesson on nature. After a couple of days of rain, the ground was wet and the spring air cool, but they were all dressed appropriately and went on an orderly excursion through the well-groomed bushes and shrubs and flowers, most of which had not yet bloomed with the onset of spring. But the children could see the sprouts of tulips, daffodils, and iris bulbs coming up through the ground. And the rose bushes were turning green, and little buds were starting to form on the branches, as was the case with other bushes that were just waking up after a long winter and showing the promise of beautiful blooms yet to come. Frederick told the children they would come out to the garden once a week all the way through summer and autumn to observe the changes in the plant life there.

After they returned to the classroom, he passed out paper and pencils and asked each child to draw a simple sketch of one of the plants they'd seen and what it had looked like in its current stage. They each wrote their names on their completed sketches, which were tacked to the back wall of the classroom with plenty of space to add other drawings that would document the garden's progress in the coming weeks.

Mrs. Broadbent came in while the sketches were being hung up, and she expressed her pleasure and approval, taking a moment to offer a specific comment to each child. Frederick told the children to gather their materials to practice penmanship, and they scattered to their desks to do so.

"This is very nice," Mrs. Broadbent said to him while she looked again at the sketches. "What a lovely idea."

"I believe it's important to pay attention to God's handiwork," he said, and she smiled, which he assumed meant that she agreed. While he had the chance, he hurried to add, "I assume if you observe any challenges—or anything I do with which you disagree—that you will talk to me about it so I can improve."

"Of course," was all she said before she moved to her usual chair in one of the back corners of the room where she could observe.

As with much of the work in the classroom, Frederick needed to give each child an individual assignment and guide them according to their own level of understanding. No two of them were at the same stage or were capable of moving at the same pace. The result was that portions of the day were spent with the children at their desks while he remained on his feet, moving from one student to another to offer guidance and encouragement. The routine was diversified by interspersing desk time with what he called rug time, when they all sat on the big rug at the front of the classroom while he taught them about many different things and allowed them to ask questions. Sometimes they did games or activities to help the lessons make more sense, and on sunny days he always took them outside at least once to do something physical or get some fresh air.

Saturday evening brought the first week to a conclusion, and he had been teaching the Broadbent children for four days now. All things considered, he felt like it was going fairly well. Mrs. Broadbent had not offered any criticism; in fact, she had said very little to him at all. But that was likely a good sign.

Frederick had come to know the children and every member of the household by name, and he felt comfortable in his interactions with these people who were now such a big part of his life. He enjoyed sharing breakfast and supper with the adults in the kitchen as much as he enjoyed having lunch with the children in the playroom.

As Frederick stood to leave the supper table Saturday evening, Mrs. Broadbent asked if she could speak to him.

"Of course," he said, wondering if now she would tell him she'd prefer him to manage the classroom differently in some way.

"Walk with me," she said and ambled slowly out of the kitchen and down a long hall. He fell into step beside her.

"From what you've told me about yourself," she began, "I assume you will want to attend church tomorrow."

"Yes, very much," he said. "I meant to ask about that, but I've been preoccupied with other things."

"Your preoccupation with teaching my children has been very impressive, Mr. Woodstone. I had a good feeling about you; I'm glad to see that you're not proving me wrong."

"I'm glad for that too," he said on the wake of a nervous chuckle, taken off guard by her compliment.

"It's my hope," she went on, "that you might be willing to accompany me and the children to church. Nellie and Mrs. Pilfer accompany us as well. A few of the others attend; some don't. But it's Nellie and Mrs. Pilfer who help me look out for the children. Of course, we need three carriages in order for all of us to go anywhere together at the same time." She laughed softly. "And the vicar has graciously given us three pews at the very back of the church, which makes it easier to take one of the children out if they are misbehaving. A few of them have difficulty being still for long—as I'm sure you have noticed."

"Indeed," he said lightly, knowing exactly which children she referred to.

"Nellie does well with the girls, but she is not so confident with the boys. And Mrs. Pilfer is getting on in years and is not so capable of taking charge of children with so much energy. I know that I told you Sundays would be a day off for you, so I realize I'm imposing on you to ask this, but—"

"It is no imposition whatsoever," Frederick assured her. "It would be a blessing to me to not have to attend church alone, and I'm glad to help in any way I can."

Mrs. Broadbent smiled. "I'm very glad to hear it. I was hoping you'd feel that way. Given the fact that you once served as a vicar, I believe you might have some experience in understanding the importance of church attendance for children but also the challenges in helping them learn to grasp that importance."

"I believe I do, yes," he said.

"Some of these children had never entered a church before they came to live with me. A couple of them had religion held over them as a means of frightening them into submission, and their only experience with God is the belief that He will smite them to an everlasting hell if they don't do as they're told. I want them to learn that God loves them and will bless their lives, but such a desire is easier said than done when so much damage has already occurred in their young lives."

"I understand what you mean," he said, feeling a new level of compassion for these children and a new level of respect for the woman who had chosen to be their mother.

She stopped walking and turned toward him. He stopped as well, wondering what she might want to say that was of such importance. "Of all the things that a child can be taught, Mr. Woodstone, there is nothing more important than the understanding of God's love. From what you've told me, I believe your mother taught you that lesson well; therefore, I believe you understand what I mean. When children have been abandoned and treated cruelly, it's difficult for them to even believe that God exists at all, let alone that He could be a loving God. I chose you to help teach these children because I believe you understand that."

"I do, Mrs. Broadbent, and now that I know the strength of your convictions, I will be mindful of that continually."

She smiled slightly and took his shoulders into her dainty hands the same way he'd seen her do with the older children. "Thank you, Frederick . . . for taking this on and taking it seriously. You can never know what it means to me."

Frederick was taken aback by the severity of her words along with the use of his given name. He nodded in response as opposed to trying to speak, suddenly overcome by an unfamiliar surge of emotion he preferred to keep to himself.

The moment ended, and they continued walking as she said, "We leave for church about an hour after breakfast. I'll see you in the morning."

"Good night, Mrs. Broadbent," he said. "Sleep well."

"And you," she said and turned a corner that went in the direction opposite to where he needed to go. He watched her for a long moment, then headed toward his rooms, wondering what adventures he might encounter while attending church with the children. But he felt more glad than unnerved by the prospect, and he couldn't deny that it felt good to be needed. For years his mother had needed him, and since her death he'd found ways to give of himself. But this was the first time since her death that he truly felt as if his presence in someone else's life genuinely mattered. And he was glad for it.

* * *

While Frederick was eating his breakfast, it occurred to him that getting through church with the children was likely only part of the challenge. Wondering what it might be like to get them all cleaned up and dressed properly for a Sunday meeting, he headed upstairs to the three adjoining bedrooms the boys shared. He wasn't surprised to find a certain amount of chaos with the older boys left in charge of helping the younger ones get into their Sunday clothes. He quickly got their attention, asked some questions, and gave them specific assignments and directions in order to hurry the process along. He was told that Nellie and their mother were helping the girls get ready.

"Even though there's only four girls and seven of us," Virgil reported, "girls need their hair fixed all pretty and dumb stuff like that."

"Someday," Frederick said to *all* of the boys, "you won't think that the stuff girls do to look pretty is dumb at all."

The boys giggled or scoffed—depending on their age—then Blaine told him that once they were ready they were supposed to wait at the top of the stairs for the girls to join them and then they'd go down together to where the carriages would be waiting. Frederick sat on one of the top steps with the boys, asking them questions to try and discern how each of them felt about church, and what they'd been previously taught about rules regarding their time in church. It was easy to see which ones their mother felt the most concern for, but Frederick mostly listened and didn't comment.

When they heard the girls coming, Frederick stood and said quietly to the boys, "A gentleman should always stand when a lady approaches."

"They ain't no ladies," Blaine muttered. "They're just a bunch o' dumb girls."

"Mama's a lady," Stanley declared, and the boys all quieted down.

"Oh, you're all ready!" Mrs. Broadbent said with pleasure. "I assume Mr. Woodstone had something to do with helping you along."

No one answered, but Frederick got a slight smile of appreciation from his employer before they started down the stairs.

Frederick rode in a carriage with all seven boys. They had fought over who would get to ride with him, which he figured was an indication that they enjoyed his company. It had been concluded that they could all fit in the carriage if they squeezed together a little, and Wilfred—the youngest and smallest of the boys—could sit on Frederick's lap. Trying to anticipate how it might be difficult for them to sit through a church meeting—some of them more than others— Frederick told them how he had once been a vicar, which seemed intriguing to them; at least it made them all quiet down for a few minutes. He didn't bother sharing his beliefs about God and prayer and angels; he figured there would be better times for such conversations— and he certainly needed to get to know them better before treading into such territory as personal spiritual beliefs. But he did tell them how difficult it had been to be the person who had to stand up in front of all those people and give a sermon when he knew that some of them didn't even want to be there, and others were disruptive. He suggested that out of respect for the vicar, if nothing else, they might consider the idea that remaining still and quiet—even if it was difficult—would show respect for the vicar. He got no response beyond some odd grunts, but a few of them seemed to be taking in what he'd said.

Once they arrived at the quaint little church building at the edge of town, Frederick noted that the vicar seemed pleased to see Mrs. Broadbent with her brood of misfit children and the servants who came with her to church. He was kind to Frederick when Mrs. Pilfer introduced them, and he teased the boys a little before they all made their way to the designated pews and sat down. Mrs. Broadbent sat with the four girls, Mrs. Pilfer, and Nellie on the pew in front of the boys, where Frederick sat in the middle of them, purposely seating closest to him those most likely to misbehave. Some other servants from the household sat on the pew behind them.

They got through the meeting with very little disruption, which Frederick attributed to his little talk in the carriage combined with a few subtly stern stares he aimed toward a boy if he began to show signs of getting noisy. The moment the meeting was over, Mrs. Broadbent turned around and said with a pleased smile, "You boys were so very good in church today! I think we must surely have extra helpings of dessert!"

The boys were excited by this, but it only took a quick "Shhhh" from Frederick to remind them they were still in the church building, and they all comically expressed their enthusiasm with great silence. Wilfred asked Mrs. Broadbent, "Can Mr. Woodstone have Sunday dinner with us?"

Frederick felt immediately awkward, knowing it was not considered appropriate. He hurried to say, "I'll be having dinner with the servants. Your Sunday dinner is for family, I'm sure."

"But Nellie eats Sunday dinner with us," Matilda protested, leaning over the back of the bench toward the boys but looking up at her mother.

"Yes, she does," Mrs. Broadbent said directly to her youngest daughter. "Because she is your governess she is very much like family, like an aunt or a cousin; we've talked about that." Frederick figured that would be the end of it, but she then turned to Wilfred and said, "Mr. Woodstone also spends a great deal of time with you. If you want to invite him to Sunday dinner, you are welcome to do so." He heard quiet noises from some of the children to indicate they were pleased. Still, he felt a little embarrassed, thinking he should politely refuse somehow, but Wilfred turned to looked at him and asked, "Would you like to come to Sunday dinner, Mr. Woodstone?"

Frederick glanced at Mrs. Broadbent and said quietly, "You needn't feel obligated, truly. I can—"

"The children will be very disappointed if you don't come. We eat at two. It's the biggest meal of the week, so come hungry."

She stood to leave, and the children followed her like a little flock of geese falling in line behind their mother. He realized that Nellie and the other servants had already gone outside. He followed after the gaggle of children, surprised to observe stares of disdain from other churchgoers, along with some whispers and discreet pointing of fingers accompanied by judgmental expressions, aimed at Mrs. Broadbent and the children. He wanted to stand between these people and the Broadbent family and tell them in his most firm voice that they were all blind if they could not see the love and goodness parading before them. The vicar in him was reminded that he should not judge even those who were judgmental. Mrs. Broadbent pretended not to notice, even though he knew she did, and he wondered if such attitudes toward her were commonplace. He figured they likely were, but he just followed her example of dignity and grace and left the church, guiding the boys back into the carriage in order to return home. *Home.* It already felt like home to him, and he'd quickly grown to feel some responsibility for these children. He marveled that a week ago he'd been praying for a decent job; now he not only had a job, he had a home, a purpose, and many new friends. For the first time since his mother's death, he felt as if he truly belonged somewhere.

Chapter Three
THE LILY

FREDERICK FOLLOWED THE BOYS DOWNSTAIRS FOR DINNER a few minutes before two. Since they were meant to eat in the formal dining room—which he'd never seen before—he likely would have gotten lost without their guidance. The girls were already there, along with Nellie and Mrs. Broadbent. As the children were moving to their usual seats at the table, Frederick was surprised to have Mrs. Broadbent invite him to sit at one end of the table, which was directly opposite of where she sat at the other end, with Nellie and the children lining the sides of the table. He felt a little uncomfortable initially, knowing this was where her husband would have once sat. But she simply declared that it evened out their places at the table since Nellie and the children used up six chairs on each side.

Mrs. Broadbent also asked if Frederick would say grace before they began their meal, and she told the children it would be very nice if he would do so since he had once been a vicar. The boys all spoke up to tell their mother that he'd told them about that in the carriage, as if their knowing before the girls did was some kind of triumph. Their mother calmed them down, Frederick spoke a simple blessing over the food, and the meal began.

While they were served slices of cold beef and lamb, thick slices of bread and butter, a variety of cheeses, and some fresh berries, Mrs. Broadbent went through what was obviously a routine of asking each child to talk about what they'd most enjoyed about the previous week and what they had learned in church that they might not have known before. Frederick couldn't help being pleased to hear that the children were enjoying their lessons with him and that they were glad to have him there. The children all struggled to answer the question about church, but their mother didn't seem at all impatient over that; she just listened and moved past it very delicately. When the children were finished, she also asked Nellie the same questions, which made Frederick realize that he too would be asked to share. He had no difficulty saying how much he was enjoying his new job and how grateful he felt to be in their home and to spend his time with such a great group of children. He told them that one of the things he'd thought about at church was how good it was to make the effort to devote that little portion of time each week to attend a Sunday meeting and that it was a way to let God know you had faith in Him, even if it was sometimes difficult to believe He was there.

Mrs. Broadbent responded by saying, "Thank you, Mr. Woodstone. That was very insightful."

"And what about you, Mrs. Broadbent?" he asked. "Might you tell us about the highlights of *your* week? And what you might have learned today in church?"

A rare silence at the table let him know that this had never happened before. Apparently the Sunday ritual did not normally extend to the head of the household. But he believed that it should; he believed the children needed to see that their mother was more than a mother; she was a woman with her own feelings and experiences. He'd been taught to recognize that about his own mother, and it had served him well.

For a long moment Frederick feared she would skirt around the question, but she finally said, "Well . . . since you asked, I would have to say that the highlight of my week has been having Mr. Woodstone come to join our household. I think he's going to fit in very nicely." Everyone made sounds of agreement, and she went on to say something she had observed in the past week about each and every person at the table that had given her joy, making it evident that she'd been paying attention to what they were doing. Frederick marveled at how skilled she was at making everyone in the room feel important and valued.

When it came to talking about her experience in church that day, Mrs. Broadbent said, "I was reminded today that God loves each of His children equally, but that's not something new. However . . ." she drawled with a smile that implied she intended to say something very important that the children should pay attention to, "I did learn *one* thing that was new today. I learned that you boys are *much* better behaved in church when Mr. Woodstone is there to keep you in line."

This made all of the children laugh, and Nellie too found it amusing. Frederick couldn't help joining in their laughter, again feeling more at home than he had since his mother's death.

They enjoyed pie for dessert, and then Frederick marveled once again as he saw an activity unfold that he never would have imagined. Everyone at the table took their own used dishes to the kitchen, where hot dishwater was waiting; one sink with soap in it for washing and one sink with clean water for rinsing. Each person—child and adult alike—washed and rinsed their own dishes, then dried and put them away. Everyone was then required to spend ten minutes helping to clean up the kitchen, which included washing the dishes that had obviously been used by the servants for their Sunday dinner. Nellie whispered to Frederick that this was the way it worked every Sunday. The meal they'd eaten had mostly been prepared the previous day, which was why it had consisted of foods that were either not perishable or had been served cold. Teaching the children to help in the kitchen on Sunday helped them learn to show respect for the people who worked hard for them throughout the week and made it possible for the servants to also enjoy some time off on Sundays.

"Of course we have to eat," Nellie whispered while they both dried some freshly cleaned serving dishes, "and so a certain amount of kitchen work has to be done on the Sabbath, but Mrs. Broadbent insists that the work must be equally divided, and it should not be any more than absolutely necessary."

"Incredible," Frederick whispered in response. "Thank you for explaining."

"Of course," she said. "It took me some time to catch on to the lady's way of thinking, but I believe you know what I mean when I say I feel very blessed to work in such a household."

"Indeed," Frederick said, aware of the children, each engaged in his or her task with an efficiency that indicated how frequently they had participated in this routine.

Once the kitchen was declared to be in order, Frederick followed Nellie's lead when she let him know that Sunday afternoons were set aside for Mrs. Broadbent to spend time alone with her children. Frederick went to his own room, where he read from the Bible until he got sleepy and took a nap. He decided he liked Sundays here at

Broadbent House, although he knew he couldn't expect to eat Sunday dinner with the family each week. Still, he enjoyed the company of the other servants, and eating with them in the kitchen would be enjoyable as well.

The new week began with some unexpected challenges in the classroom. Frederick recognized from his previous experience with children the signs of having his boundaries tested. Now that the children had become more comfortable and at ease with their new teacher, some of them apparently had the need to exhibit bad behavior—perhaps just to see if they could get away with it. Frederick knew how to handle it by following through on consequences that had already been clearly explained to them on the first day of school. But some of the children were more stubborn than others at accepting the consequences for their behavior, and Frederick could clearly see signs that these children had come from very difficult circumstances. He was seeing more vividly now their fears and insecurities and how those were being manifest either in extreme shyness at one end of the spectrum or outlandishly bad behavior at the other. He sometimes felt more like an athletic referee than a schoolteacher as he broke up fights, intervened in arguments that were pushing the more tender children to tears, and enforced firm consequences for unkind or destructive behavior.

Frederick had felt especially anxious the first time there was an outburst between two of the children while Mrs. Broadbent was in the room. But he sensed that the boys who seemed intent on getting into a brawl were testing him even more severely with their mother on hand, wondering if he might back down in her presence. He handled the situation the way he would handle it whether she was there or not. That day, after the children had been turned over to Nellie, Mrs. Broadbent found him in the classroom and simply said, "You do well handling the difficulties with the children. Thank you."

She left the room before he could even think of an appropriate response, but he felt some relief and validation to know that she approved of his methods. He also felt more exhausted than he had since he'd started this job. Perhaps this was why the last tutor had left. He wondered how many there might have been before him. But he felt blessed to be here and even more blessed to realize that he had the experience and knowledge to be able to handle the situation, and he would not give up on these children. They needed people in their life who were committed to their well-being, and he was glad to be one of them.

* * *

Spring settled in more fully with a warming of the temperature outside and a continual progression of the flowers and plants in the garden, which was documented by the children's excursions there and the simple drawings they did afterward to be hung on the wall. Frederick settled in as well, growing comfortable so quickly that after only a month at Broadbent House, he found it difficult to remember how he'd ever managed without knowing these people and being a part of their lives. He was glad to have successfully navigated through the bad behavior that had come with the children testing their boundaries. Now that they knew rules had to be kept and consequences would be enforced, they had all relaxed more, and a mutual trust and respect had begun to grow in their teacher-student relationships. He'd grown to know the children as individuals, and he'd become accustomed to their challenges as well as the remarkable qualities that were evident in every one of them. And he couldn't deny that he'd grown to love them. He looked forward to his time with them each day and was glad that he could spend time with them on Sundays as well. He enjoyed attending church far more since he didn't have to go alone, which he had been doing since his mother's death. And he was surprised but not disappointed when Mrs. Broadbent let him know that he should always plan to share Sunday dinner with the family. Her implication was that she wanted him and Nellie to be involved with this portion of their family time, since the two of them worked so closely with the children.

As an added bonus to feeling like a part of the family, Frederick also found comfortable acquaintance and friendship among other members of the staff. After making certain it was all right with Mrs. Broadbent, he made an offer one evening at supper to teach reading and writing to any who were interested, and a few of them responded eagerly. A specific schedule was set up for three times a week, and he quickly came to enjoy these lessons almost as much as he enjoyed his time with the children. Mary and Abigail were among his students, and he grew to like them very much. Mary was only fifteen but had been working here for years since she'd run away from an abusive home; she was shy but very kind and full of sincerity. Abigail was more forthright and confident and a few years older than Mary, although the two of them were the best of friends and did well in working together. Luca, a fine young man in his early twenties, was also an eager student. Abigail and Luca were very much in love, and everyone knew it; they had plans to marry—perhaps in the autumn, they told him—and Frederick knew that Mrs. Broadbent was all in favor of the relationship and their forthcoming marriage. Becoming friends with these people made Frederick feel more and more a part of the household. He kept extremely busy with all of his responsibilities, but the satisfaction he felt in his work and the new life he was living far outweighed any inconvenience.

Frederick was more often than not exhausted at the end of a teaching day, and he knew well enough that he needed his time to rest and recuperate so that he could be fully engaged with the children during the days. Still, the end of a school day, when the children were put into Nellie's care, often felt disappointing, and he was sad to see them leave. He usually remained in the classroom for at least an hour after they left, going over his lesson plans for the following day and making certain everything was in order, but he didn't like the silence, even if he could appreciate that he needed it in order to concentrate and get his work done.

On a particularly warm day near the end of April, Frederick took his little flock out to the garden for their usual excursion. Today he knew the grass would be dry, and he'd asked the children to bring their drawing paper and pencils along, as well as a book that would give them a hard surface on which to draw. The assignment was to choose a flower or plant and sit on the grass and try to draw a more detailed picture by actually looking at the subject, as opposed to just remembering it. He'd given the class some basic drawing instructions during the course of their usual lessons, and he'd made it clear that drawing came more naturally to some people than others, and it was okay to have their drawing skills be whatever they were. But he'd taught them that drawing pictures—even simple ones—was a way to help preserve memories, and it was a good skill to acquire.

In the garden, he ambled slowly around, looking over the children's heads to see what they were drawing, and making himself available if they had any questions or struggles with what they were doing. While they sat in the spots they had chosen, with some distance between them, they were all remarkably quiet and focused on their work. When he paused to see what little Lucy was doing, the nine-year-old expressed with glee, "Look, Mr. Woodstone! It bloomed! I've been drawing pictures of it every week and waiting for it to bloom, and it did!"

Frederick squatted down beside her to focus on the object of her excitement, which was a single white lily in full bloom, looking magnificent in the sunlight. "Oh, it's beautiful!" he said. "Do you know what kind of flower this is?"

"It's a lily, like Mama."

Frederick took careful notice of the delicate beauty of the flower and how its color was very much like Mrs. Broadbent's unique hair color. He agreed with enthusiasm, "Yes, it is very beautiful, just like your mother."

He took notice of Lucy's drawing, which was actually quite excellent for a girl her age, and he told her so, which made her smile before she went back to drawing the details of her precious lily.

Back in the classroom the new drawings were tacked to the wall, and there was quite a lengthy discussion as they looked at the progression of nature that had been documented. The children seemed pleased with the project, and Frederick was pleased to see evidence of their finding fulfillment and satisfaction as they were learning about a wide variety of things.

When school time ended, Nellie came to collect the children as she always did, and Frederick exchanged a few words with her as they went through the routine of shifting responsibility for Mrs. Broadbent's gaggle—as the two of them had come to quietly call them.

Once he was alone, Frederick sat at his desk going over his plans for the following day, then he leaned back in his chair to read through the brief writing assignment he'd given to the children so that he could see how they were doing with their grammar and punctuation, as well as their ability to put their perspective into written words. He heard a knock on the open door and looked up to see Mrs. Broadbent.

"Forgive me for interrupting," she said as he stood to greet her.

"It's no problem," he assured her.

"There's something I'd like to talk to you about, but it's so lovely out I wonder if you would mind if we took a stroll in the garden while we talk. If now is not a good time, then—"

"Now is fine," he said, "and it certainly is a perfect day for taking in as much fresh air as possible."

"Indeed," she said, and they walked together out of the room and down the stairs, toward the door that exited closest to the gardens. They shared simple talk about the weather and the success of Mrs. Maddox's venison and pigeon pie they'd enjoyed for supper the previous evening. She asked how the children were doing, and he shared what he felt were his most pertinent observations in that regard. He had a few mild concerns, which she agreed to be aware of during her time with the children, but overall he believed they were progressing nicely. And she agreed, which helped boost his confidence in the work he was doing. He considered it a great blessing to enjoy his work so much, but he felt even more blessed to know that his employer approved of his methods and was pleased with his performance.

The gardens looked especially lovely in the late-afternoon sun, and they strolled at a slow pace between two long rows of rosebushes covered with buds that were about to burst open.

"This will be exquisite in a few weeks," she commented. "And the fragrance when the roses are in bloom is surely straight from heaven."

"I will look forward to that," he said, realizing more every day how much he enjoyed her company and how very comfortable he felt with her. He recalled other parents in the past who had employed him to teach their children, and his experiences with them had led him to believe that it wasn't possible to share such an amiable relationship with an employer. But then, he'd never known anyone quite like Mrs. Broadbent. He'd been living here for weeks, and he still felt intrigued and fascinated by her in ways he couldn't quite define. He only knew that he appreciated any opportunity he had to spend time with her.

When silence settled around them as they continued their leisurely stroll, Frederick felt compelled to say, "I want to thank you, Mrs. Broadbent, for everything. I truly love working with your children, and I have been treated so well in your home. I couldn't possibly ask for better employment."

"I'm very glad to hear it," she said, smiling at him. "But you must call me Lily when others are not around."

"Lily?" he repeated, as surprised by her request as he was by the realization that he honestly had not even known her given name. He also recalled clearly what Lucy had said earlier. "Lily," he repeated as it settled in, and he laughed softly.

"Is it funny?" she asked, not sounding offended but rather curious.

"Not at all. It's a beautiful name. I just . . . didn't know, and . . . only today Lucy was drawing a picture of the first lily that has bloomed in the garden. She said it was like her mother; I assumed she meant because it's white . . . the same color as your hair. Now I understand."

"Dear Lucy," she said and was silent a long moment as if she just had to think about the child and relish the love she felt. She sighed and added, "My husband had the lilies planted in my honor when we were married."

"What a lovely gesture," Frederick said.

Lily cleared her throat as if she wanted to change the subject, and she did. "I hope you don't think it inappropriate for us to use given names when we are alone. I know that formality is more appropriate, and I want the children to learn respect for their elders so that they will be able to succeed within the society where they are growing up. But personally, I prefer less formality . . . Frederick."

"I agree," he said.

"You agree with much of what I say. I've come to know that you don't say something you don't mean; otherwise I might think you were only patronizing me. As it is, I just have to see the situation for what it is."

"And what is that?" he asked.

"We think very much the same about a great many things."

"Yes," he said. "I suppose we do . . . Lily." He liked saying it aloud, and he liked the way she smiled when he did. He wondered if continually being referred to as Mrs. Broadbent might feel tedious for her; perhaps bearing her husband's name was a less-than-pleasant reminder of his absence in her life. He could only guess based on little comments she'd made about the man.

They turned a corner and walked along a row of neatly trimmed shrubberies, and she became silent again. He wondered when she might get to the point of whatever it was she wanted to talk to him about. He was about to ask when she said, "I wonder if it would be too much of an inconvenience for you to postpone whatever your plans may be with the children tomorrow. I have other plans for them."

"They're your children, Mrs. Broadbent," he said out of habit. She looked at him sideways, and he corrected himself. "Lily. I'm happy to do whatever you feel is best for them. May I ask what you have in mind?"

"Certainly." She offered up that soft little laugh of hers. "And I'm afraid this doesn't mean you have the day off, because I'd like you to come along with us; the boys are much better behaved when you are with them."

Frederick responded with a little laugh of his own. "I'm very glad to hear that I can make a positive difference. And if you must know, a day off sounds terribly boring and lonely. I'd be glad to accompany you. Is there anything I should know in advance?"

"One day a week I indulge in an activity that I used to do with my husband, and I've continued the practice since his death. I go to visit families here in the valley. Some of my visits are simply meant to be sociable; I believe a community needs to be connected so that if challenges arise, people are comfortable enough with each other to be able to help when help is needed. I try to do my part in facilitating such connections. I visit and try to be sociable, even though it's not necessarily in my nature."

"Not in your nature?" he echoed, not certain what she meant.

"I'm more comfortable in my own home . . . in an environment I can control, I suppose. I know that many people consider me strange—both because of my appearance and my lack of convention in many matters. Therefore, I've tended to avoid social interaction throughout most of my life. But my husband insisted that I accompany him on these visits, and I quickly grew to appreciate the value and importance of the practice. I've come to find that when good, humble people have the opportunity to get to know me, they lose their prejudice, and many have come to welcome me into their homes. I too have overcome some of my own prejudice toward others as I've realized that not everyone is critical of the unique family situation I've created."

Frederick took in what she was saying and wondered if it was possible for him to respect and admire her even more. She continually amazed him by her innate selflessness and her desire to do good. He only said, "It sounds like a very admirable endeavor. It would be an honor to accompany you. I assume you have a particular goal in mind as far as including the children?"

"I do, yes," she continued. "I've generally had Max and Wally accompany me. Of course, I need someone to drive the carriage, but I also feel more confident having the men there to make certain that nothing goes awry. And people tend to consider it improper for a woman to engage in such activities without a proper chaperone; therefore, Max and Wally have graciously become accustomed to being my escorts. However, it has occurred to me that the children should understand the principles of why I do this. I believe they have learned many social skills simply by having to get along with each other, given that there are eleven of them of such varied ages and personalities. But in order for them to be prepared to get by in the world, they need to have their horizons expanded. I know my little brood can be overwhelming, but there are a few families in particular who also have many children, and I've spoken with them about the possibility of bringing the children to visit. They are prepared and even enthused about meeting them. I think it will be good for everyone."

"I would agree."

"Hence, I was thinking we can leave at the time lessons would normally begin, and visit two households in the morning. I'm hoping for favorable weather so that we can take advantage of a perfect spot for a picnic. Then we can visit one more home after lunch and return around the time the school day normally ends."

"It sounds like a delightful day," Frederick said with the enthusiasm he felt. He loved the idea of having the children get away from their routine and experience new things. And he couldn't deny that he enjoyed Lily's company, and the prospect of sharing such a day with her was inviting.

Again they walked in silence. They were some distance from the house now, but she didn't seem keen on heading back, so he just walked beside her, wondering if there was anything else she wanted to talk about. He was completely unprepared to hear her say, "Nellie is very fond of you, you know."

Not certain if she was only referring to their working relationship or if the implication was something else, he replied, "I'm very fond of her as well."

"Not in the same way, I think," she said, sounding mildly delighted, as if she were a schoolgirl teasing him.

"What do you mean?" he asked and actually stopped walking, as if that might better help him take in what he was being told.

Lily stopped as well and turned to face him. "I've noticed the way she looks at you . . . the way her face brightens when you enter the room." Frederick was stunned beyond words and grateful when she spoke and filled the gap of silence. "But it is as I suspected. You have *not* noticed."

"I'm afraid I haven't," he said, glad he felt comfortable enough with her to be completely honest. "I mean . . . am I so oblivious to such things?" He answered his own question. "Apparently I am."

"Which, I suppose, is why I felt that I should tell you," Lily said. "And I wondered how you might respond. I wondered if you would be pleased or . . . not. It seems you are *not* pleased."

"I . . . I . . . I think Nellie is a fine woman, and I'm flattered by her interest, but . . . I don't see her . . . in that way." He considered his own feelings carefully before he declared them. "I know myself well enough to know that I never could see her in that way or feel anything for her beyond a comfortable working relationship—friends at best."

"I suspected that might be the case," Lily said and continued walking, so he did the same. "I hope I didn't speak out of line, given that it's a personal matter for you. But I also didn't want you to end up in an awkward situation and be caught off guard."

"I'm glad you told me," he said. "I'm just . . . not certain what to do about it."

"You must talk to her . . . respectfully and with honesty . . . as I know you will. A woman deserves to know where she stands. Well, a man does too, certainly. But if you kindly tell her your feelings—or lack of them— she might feel hurt initially, but she will quickly get beyond it and be able to focus on a good working relationship with you rather than being distracted by romantic notions that will never transform into anything when they are without foundation."

"You're a wise woman, Lily. I'm grateful for your advice."

"And I am grateful for *yours*," she said.

"Mine?" he countered, unable to recall ever giving her advice; he wouldn't have thought it appropriate to do so.

"Not in words, exactly," she clarified. "But observing you with the children has taught me a great deal about how to handle some issues I had been struggling with. If I may return the compliment, you are a very wise man, Frederick, and you are clearly gifted in your abilities with children. You seem to have an extra sense about them . . . about what they're thinking, how they're feeling, what makes them behave the way they do. I surely could never find a better person to help guide my children."

"You're far too generous in your adulation, Lily," he said, still trying to become accustomed to using her given name—even though he liked it so much better.

They exchanged more trivial conversation as they slowly worked their way back toward the house. Not far from the edge of the gardens, Lily sat down on a bench and declared that she wanted to sit alone for a while. She thanked him for his time, and he went back inside and up to his classroom to finish what he'd been doing. But he found it difficult to concentrate. He kept thinking about Nellie and wondered why he had been so oblivious to her apparent interest in him. He felt concerned about being able to communicate with her suitably and not embarrass her, and he offered up a silent prayer over the matter. He knew Lily's advice was correct; if the matter was ignored, it would surely only cause bigger problems. In spite of his concern over Nellie and not wanting to hurt her in any way, he found himself far more distracted by a strange lingering mood that seemed to be clinging to him from his time spent walking in the garden with Lily. *Lily.* He had to say it aloud since he was alone. "Lily." How could he describe or possibly understand the way she affected him? Given the nature of their relationship and their obvious age difference, he could only come to the conclusion that they *did* have much in common; he respected and admired her greatly, and he was glad to think they could be forming some kind of friendship in addition to their working relationship.

Knowing he had to read through all of the children's assignments and attend to some personal things before supper, he forced his mind away from both Nellie *and* Lily and focused on his work, smiling to think of the outing that was scheduled for the following day with Lily and the children. He had to be sure and *not* call her Lily when others were around. It had felt so strange at first, but he'd quickly formed a lovely attachment in his mind between her name and her face, and it now felt awkward to think of her as Mrs. Broadbent.

* * *

That evening during supper, Frederick kept thinking about the situation with Nellie. He wished she was here so he could observe her and decide for himself if there was any truth to what Lily had suggested, but she always shared breakfast and supper with the children; occasionally she would come to the kitchen near the end of the meal if the children were settled in, but not always—which meant the only meal they ever shared was Sunday dinner. Beyond that, their only interaction was twice each day when they traded the responsibility of the children. He tried to recall things she might have said or done to indicate some personal interest in him, but he truly had no recollection of any such thing.

The following morning, the children came to the classroom as usual, but they were full of excitement since their mother had told them they would be having an outing today. He told them to find something quiet to do until their mother came to meet them there, then he realized that Nellie was hovering in the classroom. He recalled then that she often did; she was usually hesitant to leave, and he'd believed it was due to her affection for the children and wanting to drag out her time with them for a few more minutes. She certainly loved the children and enjoyed her time with them, even though they often frustrated her and could leave her frazzled; however, it only took a quick glance toward her now to see evidence of what Lily had said. Nellie's true reason for loitering had nothing to do with the children. She was discreetly watching *him,* and very attentively. She was practically blushing. Had he been so blind? Yes, obviously he had! His heart quickened with nervousness, and he felt his own face turn warm with some measure of embarrassment. He knew he had to clear this up as quickly as possible.

Seeing that the children were fairly well occupied, he impulsively decided to just do it now and have it over with, as opposed to dreading it. As Lily had said, Nellie might be hurt at first, but she would know where she stood and would be able to move on. More than anything he wanted this awkward strain to be gone from between them. Now that he'd become aware of it, he didn't know how he could bear living with it. He could only hope that she would take it well.

"Children," he called, and they all looked toward him. "I need to speak with Nellie in the hall for just a minute. I trust you'll all behave yourselves." He added lightly, "And I will be able to hear you!" He shook a comical finger at them, which made them all smile, then they turned their attention back to what they had been doing.

Nellie looked pleased as she followed him into the hall, and he wished he had something to say that would warrant her anticipation. *Just say it and get it over with,* he told himself, calling on his experience as a vicar telling people difficult things they had often not wanted to hear.

"Nellie," he said gently, "forgive me if I'm being . . . insensitive or . . . unkind, but . . . I've just recently sensed that . . ." Wanting to keep Lily out of the situation, he thought it best to avoid bringing her up. He cleared his throat a little too loudly due to his nervousness, which increased when he noted the expectation in her eyes. "Well . . . I didn't realize until just yesterday that . . . correct me if I'm wrong, but . . . I get the impression you might have feelings for me that are not feelings I can reciprocate." He paused to let that sink in and felt sincerely saddened by the way her eyes widened with realization over what he was saying, and her expression faltered. He could see that she was trying not to cry, and he hurried to add, "Nellie, listen to me. I don't want you to be embarrassed, and I certainly don't want any awkwardness or difficulty between us. We must never be ashamed for what we feel or don't feel. We must only have the courage to communicate our feelings properly and to act on them the same way. I admire and respect you, Nellie, and you've been a good friend to me. I want very much for that friendship to continue. You are a lovely and wonderful woman. I simply do not feel any kind of romantic inclinations toward you, and I know my feelings won't change. I don't want any tension between us if you're expecting something from me that I cannot give. I hope that you will forgive me, and again, I sincerely don't want you to feel ashamed or embarrassed. I want us to be friends—good friends. Do you understand?"

She nodded stoutly, and he could see that it was becoming more difficult for her to hold back her tears. He took her shoulders in his hands and looked directly at her. "It's okay to cry, but please don't waste away your sentiments on me. Cry if you need to, but . . . can we move forward as we have been? Can we still be friends?"

Tears leaked out of her eyes, but she nodded again. "You're very kind, Frederick," she said with a quivering voice. "Forgive me for assuming that . . ."

"You don't need to apologize for your feelings, Nellie. Just as I cannot apologize for mine. We simply must be honest with each other—and with ourselves."

She managed a smile even while she wiped at her tears. He gave her his handkerchief, and she dabbed her eyes with it. "You must have been a wonderful vicar."

"I don't know about that. I think I'm much better at teaching than consoling those who are seeking spiritual guidance."

"I think you do well at both," she said and sniffled. "Thank you for being honest with me. You're a good man, Frederick. You can't blame a woman for seeing that." She chuckled awkwardly. "I would be honored to continue our friendship as long as you promise me that we can put this behind us and not allow it to create any strain."

"Of course," he said, but he could tell she was much more upset than she was letting on, and he felt horrible—even though he knew he'd done the right thing.

"I hope your day out goes well," Nellie said and hurried away. He let her go, knowing there was nothing else he could say. He imagined her crying all day and wished he could somehow change the outcome. But he couldn't force himself to feel a certain way simply to avoid hurting someone else. He prayed that she would be all right, and he believed that, with time, she would. He would demonstrate to her each day that his feelings of friendship were real and sincere, and in time she would heal and move on. If Nellie was a woman who needed that kind of love and companionship in her life, then he hoped she would find it. For himself, he wasn't sure he needed anything but the gratification of making a difference to the children he had the opportunity to teach. He wanted only to be able to keep this job until all of these children were old enough to no longer need him, and then he hoped to be able to find work elsewhere that would see him through to the point in his life when he could no longer work, but he could easily have saved enough money to live on comfortably. For him it felt like a good, solid plan, one that would make him happy and content.

* * *

The outing with the children went well for the most part. It was difficult for them to contain their excitement at times, but they were fairly well behaved as they visited the families that had been expecting them. Frederick enjoyed observing the children interact with other children besides their adopted siblings, and he kept an eye on them, wondering if any of their less-than-admirable qualities might manifest themselves while they were in unusual surroundings, interacting with new people. But he only had to offer gentle reminders a couple of times, and the Broadbents did very well overall.

Frederick also enjoyed observing Lily as she interacted with the families they visited. She was obviously comfortable in their homes, and she knew them well. Her dignity and grace seemed all the more accentuated by the way she expressed genuine kindness to everyone she encountered.

The picnic turned out to be one of the most delightful events Frederick had ever experienced. The hampers of food prepared by the kitchen staff were full of a variety of little sandwiches, fresh fruit and vegetables, and pretty little cakes that were a reward for everyone who ate the required allotment of healthy food first. Frederick loved watching Lily interact with the children; he enjoyed the way they teased each other, and he admired her genuine interest in each one of them. After they'd eaten and had each helped to clean up and put the hampers and blankets back into the carriages, they played some games in the meadow where they'd picnicked. They'd brought a ball along, and Frederick wondered if Lily would ever stop surprising him when she initiated a simple ball game they had obviously all played together before. Everyone had to hold their hands behind their backs, and they could only move the ball with their feet. They were divided into two teams, a mixture of boys and girls of varied ages. The girls' dresses, which always hung just below their knees, left their feet free to easily access the ball, but Lily's dress was another matter, and she was obviously at a disadvantage. He was pleasantly surprised by the way she hiked it up slightly and tied it around her waist with a long ribbon that she'd brought with her, clearly having this activity in mind. She still had very little of her lower legs exposed, but nevertheless proved to not be hindered by the limitation. She was quick and agile with the ball, and Frederick—being on the opposite team and the only other adult—found he had to genuinely put in his best effort to try and help his team keep up. In the end, Lily's team won, and she cheered wildly along with her teammates. He clapped his hands respectfully as an example of good sportsmanship, and then everyone was rewarded with more cake and an abundance of water for replenishment following their vigorous exercise.

Their afternoon visit to another home went even better than the morning visits had gone, and they returned to Broadbent House just a little bit later than the time when school would normally end. Nellie came out the door to greet them, appearing completely fine and genuinely thrilled to see the children. After the gaggle of eleven followed the governess into the house, Frederick found himself standing alone next to Lily. The carriages drove toward the carriage house, and Frederick said, "That was a lovely day. Thank you for including me."

"No, I must thank *you*," she said. "I can assure you that your presence makes such an endeavor go much more smoothly. In fact, I've wanted to do this for a long time but wasn't certain I could manage the children on my own. As I've said before, they behave much better in your presence—not because they fear you but because they respect you."

"If they respect *me*," he countered, "then they certainly respect you far more."

"Perhaps," she said lightly, "but they also know how to take advantage of me. I fear I have many soft spots, and my children are well aware of them."

Frederick laughed as he admitted, "I'm certain I took advantage of *my* mother's soft spots. Perhaps that's just the way mothers are."

"Perhaps," she said.

Silence implied that they should say their farewells and go into the house, but she remained standing there, and he took advantage of the opportunity to say, "I want to thank you for alerting me to Nellie's feelings. Once I actually thought to pay attention, I could see that you were right. I would never want there to be any misunderstanding or awkwardness that might get in the way of our working together."

"And you're certain that such feelings could never be reciprocated?" she asked, sounding concerned.

"Absolutely certain," he said.

"Then addressing the situation will be difficult for you."

"I already did," he said, glancing toward her to see surprise in her expression. "I didn't want to keep anticipating it with dread; I talked to her this morning before we left. She was upset but very kind; of course, she's always kind."

"As are you," Lily said.

"She took it as well as could be expected."

"And with time I'm certain she'll be fine." Then, after a thoughtful pause, she added, "You look as if you don't believe me."

"I believe she'll be fine, certainly better off for having the situation clarified. I just . . . wonder why she would feel that way about me at all. It feels . . . strange."

"Strange?" She let go of one of those soft laughs of hers. "Have you never had a woman fall in love with you before?"

"Not that I know of," he said, then added more lightly, "but perhaps I missed it; apparently, I can be oblivious to such things."

"And you've never felt that way about a woman?"

"Only once, but it didn't last. I can see now it was a very . . . naive and immature kind of feeling, which I'm certain is what Nellie was experiencing."

"Perhaps," Lily said. "Of course, you are still so very young. Who knows what the future will bring for you?"

Frederick wondered from the way she'd referred to his age if she might have the same misconception that many other people had had in the past. It had come up a great deal when he'd been serving as a vicar and many members of his congregation had believed he simply couldn't be old enough to hold such a position. "It's been my experience that I tend to look much younger than I am; perhaps I'm not as young as you think. You didn't ask about my age when you interviewed me."

"How old *are* you?" she asked, more out of curiosity than an apparent concern.

"Twenty-nine," he said.

Her response was an immediate little laugh. "Truly?" she asked.

"Truly," he said, smiling at her. "How old did you think I was?"

"Twenty-two, perhaps."

He laughed himself. "And that would have made me a vicar at . . . fifteen or sixteen?"

"I see your point now."

"It's always been that way. When I was in my teen years, people thought I was still a child. I tried growing a beard once to make myself look older, but . . . it only made me look . . . shall we say . . . less respectable. Some men can wear a beard with dignity. I'm not one of them."

She laughed again but far more than he thought was warranted by the comment. "Is it that funny?"

"Yes. I mean not *just* that. It's just . . . ironic."

"How so?"

"I fear I have the opposite problem. Perhaps it's the color of my hair; perhaps it's the way my face looks so thin no matter how much I eat. And I do love to eat! But I've always been mistaken for being much older than my age. As a child I was believed to be in my teens but small for my age. And when I became a woman, people always believed me to be older than my years. My husband was several years older than I, but people believed we were very near the same age."

"So how old are you?" he asked, then hurried to add, "Or perhaps that's a completely inappropriate question to ask a lady. And I would never presume to guess a lady's age—especially after what you just told me."

"I am not offended by your asking. I've never understood why some ladies consider their age a delicate secret to be locked away. I've lived each of my years; I'm happy to take ownership of them."

"Well said. I like that." He turned to look more directly at her. "So . . . ?"

"I was married at nineteen. My husband passed when I was twenty-three. I began adopting my children when I was twenty-five. And I am now thirty-one."

Frederick smiled at her and saw her smile back. He felt something—however subtle—change between them as they looked at each other and realized they were not nearly as far apart in age as they had believed. She felt more like an equal to him rather than his superior—although he was still keenly aware that she belonged to a different social class, and she was still his employer. Still, the friendship that had been evolving between them made more sense to him now, and he was all the more in awe of her wisdom and courage, given that she was only a couple of years older than himself.

"Perhaps we should go in," she said, still looking at him. "There are some things I must attend to while Nellie is with the children."

"And I must do some preparations for school tomorrow."

"Thank you for a lovely day, Frederick."

"Thank *you*, Lily," he said and watched her walk into the house while he wondered about the source of a sudden quivering in his stomach.

Chapter Four
QUIETLY SHARING

THE FOLLOWING TUESDAY AT THE end of a busy school day, Frederick was told that Mrs. Broadbent wanted to speak with him in the library. He had to ask how to get there; given the short time he'd lived in this house, there were many rooms he'd never seen. The house was so large he figured he only knew how to navigate through about one-quarter of it.

Frederick paused at the closed library door and wondered if there might be some problem with one of the children or with how he might have handled something. He took a deep breath and knocked. Hearing her call for him to come in, he stepped into the library and got a quick glance at its enormity before he turned to close the door.

Lily looked up from the book she was reading and said, "Oh, good. It's you."

Frederick was momentarily distracted by how lovely she looked and by the way his heart quickened a little by just being in the same room with her. He pushed away any attention to his reaction, certain he should remain focused on his reasons for being here.

"Please sit down." She startled him from his thoughts and motioned to a sofa that faced the one where she sat.

"Thank you," he said and seated himself. "What can I do for you?"

"First of all, I would like to know how the children are doing with their lessons."

Frederick had become accustomed to their somewhat regular meetings where she simply wanted an update concerning each child: how they were progressing with their skills in all of the standard categories of learning, but also how they were doing socially and emotionally.

After he had sufficiently reported his views on the current status of each child, Lily said, "They are all moving along very well, I think."

"I believe so," he said, sensing there was something else she wanted to talk about. He was relieved when she came straight to the point.

"I would like to ask a favor. And you are certainly not obligated, but I thought I should at least ask."

"Of course. Ask me," he said eagerly, unable to imagine her asking anything that he might consider too much of an obligation.

"I generally set aside one evening a week—well, I generally leave late afternoon so I can be back for bedtime reading and supper—to call on one or two families that might be experiencing some particular difficulty or challenge. Some visits—like those we made with the children—are more for the purpose of socializing, even though they would help me be aware of any special needs. But the purpose for these visits is focused more on meeting needs that are outstanding. I try to be discreet about my intentions because I don't want people to misunderstand, and I certainly don't want to draw attention to what I'm doing; that would defeat the purpose entirely. The thing is . . . there is a particular situation that has been difficult for me because I simply don't know quite what to say or do. It's a dear man, a farmer who lost his wife some years ago; more recently, one of his children passed from a sudden illness. His grief is understandable, of course. I've taken Max and Wally with me on my visits, but neither of them hardly makes a grunt when it comes to talking of such things. It occurred to me that with your experience as a vicar—and, of course, your being a male—you might be able to offer this good man some kind words or insight that could help him feel more at peace."

Lily took a deep breath, as if she'd found it exhausting to say all she'd just said. He wondered if she had actually been nervous about having this conversation. She went on. "I know it's a great deal to ask, Frederick. And if you are not comfortable with the expectations I've put upon you, I certainly understand. Just tell me so, and we'll not give it another thought."

"I'm not certain I can say anything that will make a difference," Frederick said, "but I'm very glad that you asked. I will certainly try. I don't believe God would want us to do nothing if there's even a small possibility of giving some aid or comfort."

Lily smiled and let out a huge sigh of relief, which implied she *had* been nervous. "And once again there is evidence of how very much you and I think alike."

"Yes, I suppose we do," he said, considering how much of her time was spent serving others and giving of herself.

"Oh, I'm so glad you're willing to come and at least try!" she said with enthusiasm. "We will set out tomorrow as soon as you turn the children over to Nellie."

"I'll be ready," he said. "Is there anything else?"

Lily laughed softly. "Not unless you might feel inclined to discuss Shakespeare." She held up the book she'd been reading to show him that it was *Hamlet*. "I'm terribly fascinated, but I often wonder if I really understand what he's trying to say. I consider myself fairly well educated in spite of my upbringing, but I still get very lost sometimes in trying to comprehend the depths of literature."

Frederick wondered what she meant by *in spite of her upbringing*. He wanted to ask but decided to let it pass for the moment. He simply said, "I've studied Shakespeare a fair amount, but I'm not certain I have any better understanding of it than you do."

"I suspect differently," she said with a slightly comical sideways glare, as if she were accusing him of keeping secrets from her. "I'd love to hear your thoughts on the story. Unless you have somewhere else you need to be . . . in which case we could talk about it another time, perhaps."

"I have nowhere else I need to be," he said, knowing that grading papers could be done anytime. And he admitted in all honesty, "I'm always up for analyzing literature." He *didn't* admit to how very much he enjoyed her company, more so with each passing day. "It's one of my favorite pastimes, although I've rarely had anyone to actually talk to about what I read."

Lily's eyes lit up eagerly from his comment, and for the first time since he'd come here, it occurred to him that she was lonely. She made conscious efforts to be social, she interacted a great deal with those who worked for her, and she was very much involved in her children's lives. But he wondered if there was anyone in her life that she could call a true friend, someone with similar interests with whom she could just share conversation. As the thought settled into his mind, he realized the same thing applied to him. He spent few hours a day alone, but that didn't mean he wasn't lonely. And just because he'd gotten used to it didn't mean he necessarily liked it. Was this yet one more thing they had in common?

Frederick lost track of the time while they discussed Shakespeare, occasionally laughing together over things that weren't necessarily very funny. The chiming of a clock in the room alerted Frederick to the fact that he had work he needed to do before supper, since he'd promised the children he would read through their writing assignments and have their maths assignments graded. And he knew how important it was to keep his promises to them; they had to know they could rely on him to honor his word.

He excused himself regretfully and was pleased when she told him she hoped they could have such a discussion again soon. Setting to work back at his desk in the classroom, Frederick found that his mind kept wandering to Lily. He was grateful to be developing more of a friendship with her, and he didn't allow himself to even wonder over anything beyond being friends.

* * *

Lily paced the foyer, impatient for Frederick to arrive so they could leave. Given that school would have only officially ended a few minutes ago, he wasn't at all late, but still she felt nervous. Or perhaps anxious was more accurate. She had been comfortable in his presence from their very first interview, but over time she had come to enjoy his company more and more. Following their time together in the library the previous day, she'd found it difficult to not think about him, and she wasn't certain how to interpret the fact that she had come to feel far from indifferent about any opportunity to spend time with him—and her feelings had nothing to do with the children.

Lily's heart quickened when she heard the clicking of his shoes on the stairs, descending at a hurried pace. She turned to watch him as he came into view and wondered how a woman could reach her age and never have felt what consumed her now. But how could she ever express such feelings without compromising the treasured friendship they'd come to share? She knew well how society would frown on even the appearance of any kind of relationship between them, and while she didn't care a whit about what anyone thought of *her*—she was already regarded as strange and was mostly ostracized from polite society—she did care about how such a thing might affect Frederick. She could not selfishly act on these feelings and put him into any kind of difficult or awkward situation. He worked for her, and she had no reason to believe that he could ever see anything in her beyond being his employer, a woman with whom he shared a comfortable friendship and common pursuits.

Frederick smiled at Lily as he reached the bottom of the stairs, and Lily smiled back, hoping he didn't notice any sign of how deeply affected she was by his smile. Just being in his presence put her every nerve into a heightened sense of awareness.

"I hope I didn't keep you waiting," he said.

"Not at all," she said. "Is everything all right with the children?"

He chuckled. "We had some typical bickering to contend with, but nothing Nellie won't be able to handle." He offered his arm in a gentlemanly way. "Shall we?"

"Of course," she said and tucked her hand around his arm, wishing she could dare hope it was possible for them to share such endeavors for the rest of their lives. She forced herself to simply enjoy *this* endeavor and to remain focused on the moment.

In the carriage, they talked about the children, and she marveled—as she always did—at how he knew each one of them so well and how he could effortlessly report their strengths, their struggles, and even humorous anecdotes that had occurred throughout the day. Their conversation moved on to Shakespeare but only lasted a couple of minutes before they arrived at the home of Mr. Topp, who was the focus of this little excursion.

Frederick stepped out of the carriage and offered his hand to help Lily descend. He kept hold of her until she found sure footing on the moist ground, still not dried out from a recent bout of rain. Max and Wally hung back near the carriage, which was more comfortable for them; waiting for her was something they'd become well accustomed to, and they knew she had no problem with their waiting inside the carriage should the weather become a problem or even if they simply preferred the comfort of sitting rather than just standing about.

On their way to Mr. Topp's door, Frederick asked Lily, "I assume you will make the introductions and let him know why you've brought me along? Or do you need me to—"

"Of course," she said. "I'll try not to make this any more awkward for you than necessary."

She was surprised by the way he put a hand on her arm to stop her so he could look at her when he said, "This is not awkward for me, Lily. I'm glad you asked me to come with you. I've never felt awkward with trying to help someone in need—even when they're not eager to receive what I have to offer."

Lily took a deep breath, continually surprised by his genuine goodness. She nodded, glad for his clarification, but she simply said, "I appreciate your efforts."

They moved on to the door, where Frederick knocked. Two young children—a boy and a girl—appeared after they had apparently been racing to see who could answer the door first.

"Hello, Mrs. Broadbent," the little girl said.

"Hello there," Lily replied. "Is your father at home?"

The door was opened wider, and the boy said, "He's sitting by the fire."

Lily knew that he was quite often just sitting by the fire, due to the fact that he was so caught up in his grief that he rarely found the motivation to do much else. He was a responsible man and had taken care of all the spring planting on his land, and he always made certain his children were cared for. But if something didn't need his urgent attention, he was most often lost in his sorrow.

"Mr. Topp," Lily said as she approached him with Frederick at her side.

Topp stood and looked mildly embarrassed—as he often did. Then his eyes moved to the man standing beside Lily, and he looked confused as well as embarrassed.

"I hope this is not an inconvenient time," Lily said. "I'll come straight to the point. You and I have shared many conversations about the difficulties you've endured, and I know how difficult the loss of your wife and child have been for you. I hope I've not overstepped my bounds in bringing Mr. Woodstone to meet you. He is my children's tutor, and he does so well in working with them—especially in being able to understand the challenges these children have faced. Before he decided that teaching suited him well, he served as a vicar. He's dealt with grief many times, Mr. Topp. I've asked Mr. Woodstone if he would come with me today, thinking he might have some helpful insight that might not have ever occurred to you or me. Would you be willing to visit with us? If not, we completely understand."

Mr. Topp looked slightly sheepish, but Lily knew he was not a proud or stubborn man. He motioned toward the available chairs and said, "I'm certainly not opposed to hearing about something that might help. Please . . . sit down." Once they were all seated, Mr. Topp humbly admitted, "I confess, Mr. Woodstone, that I've kept taking the children to church, believing it was the best thing for them, but I've not been so comfortable with God since He took my little Sally away from me. Losing my dear wife felt like too much, but I kept going—mostly because the children needed me. But when we lost our dear Sally, I just . . ." Mr. Topp hung his head and let out a quivering sigh.

Lily wondered if she should speak, but Frederick was quick to say, "If I may offer some of my own beliefs on such things, Mr. Topp, it seems evident to me that this life is filled with many difficulties that are impossible to understand. From the teachings of the Bible and my own observations, I've come to believe that while we often have very little control over the challenges that come to us in this world, we have the opportunity to know that God gave us the gift of His Son so that all could be made right in the end."

Mr. Topp looked intrigued, and Lily marveled that Frederick had only been talking for a minute and this man was already showing the first glimmer of anything beyond sorrow that Lily had seen since his daughter had passed.

"While some hold to the belief," Frederick continued, "that our eternal situation with God is based solely on our choices in this life, I personally believe that God is far too loving and merciful to not give us further opportunity for understanding and progress once we leave this world, where so much is confusing and most often unfair. If our Lord and Savior gave everything that we might have what He Himself calls a 'peace that passeth all understanding,' then the miracle of His gift to us is surely something we cannot comprehend."

Lily observed as Frederick leaned his forearms on his thighs so that he could look more directly at Mr. Topp, who returned Frederick's gaze, almost entranced by what he was saying. She knew her instincts about Frederick had been right; he *did* have the ability to help this grieving man, just as he'd been the right man to help her children heal and achieve their greatest potential.

"The more I have studied the teachings of Jesus, Mr. Topp, the more I have come to find a pattern of the perfect hope He promises to those who believe in Him. It's my firm belief that His sacrifice for us includes the promise of miraculous healing and peace beyond this life, but that miracle is also accessible in this life to some degree." Frederick then reached out and put his hand over Mr. Topp's, where it rested on the arm of his chair. "I can't begin to explain how it works, my good man, but I can say for certain that our Lord and Savior knows and understands fully every heartache that we experience. His sacrifice was not only to wash away our sins if we are but willing to accept His grace, but it was also to give us peace and comfort in the midst of our present grief and sorrow. What do *you* think, Mr. Topp? I have no wish to inflict my beliefs on others, only to perhaps offer a new perspective that you might not have considered before."

"I need to give it some thought," Mr. Topp said. "But . . . it's true that I've never looked at it that way before."

Frederick nodded toward a large Bible sitting on a little table nearby. Lily had been here many times and hadn't even noticed it. "May I?" Frederick asked.

"Of course," Mr. Topp said.

As Frederick picked it up and blew dust off the cover, Lily realized it was a classic family Bible and probably the most valuable possession in this humble home. They were not necessarily easy to come by, but they were considered a great treasure not only because of the scriptures contained on the printed pages, but because births, deaths, and marriages in the family were also recorded inside.

While Frederick was thumbing through pages, searching for something, he recited from memory, "As it states in John, chapter fourteen, *'Peace I leave with you, my peace I give unto you: not as the world giveth, give I unto you. Let not your heart be troubled, neither let it be afraid.'* I would like to challenge you, Mr. Topp, to read some of these passages, keeping in mind the idea that they have been left for us to help us through this very kind of trial." He set the open book on Mr. Topp's lap and pointed to the page. "This is a good place to start, I think. Remember, they're not just words in a book, my good man; they are meant to give us understanding and hope. I believe that if you pray to gain that understanding as you read, you will be led to the messages that can help you move forward and find happiness and peace with these beautiful children who are left in your care until the time comes when you will be reunited with those you love who have crossed over."

Mr. Topp nodded as he looked down at the Bible in his hands. He sniffled and wiped a hand quickly over his cheeks to brush away tears. "I will," he said.

Frederick leaned more toward him and put a hand on his shoulder. "I sincerely believe that God understands why it's been difficult for you to turn to Him, but when you're ready to resume the relationship, you will find that He is there for you, that He always has been."

Mr. Topp nodded again, and Frederick suggested they read a few passages together. Lily sat in silence and observed as the conversation continued and deepened, and she could almost see Mr. Topp's countenance softening already. He'd always been a humble man, and his heart had been open and ready for a moment such as this. He'd only needed the guidance and encouragement that someone like Frederick Woodstone could offer. And Frederick's ability to offer those things so naturally left Lily all the more in awe of him.

While Lily contentedly observed the interaction between the two men, she couldn't help noticing that Mr. Topp's children were sitting on the floor in a discreet corner of the room, absorbing what was taking place. She uttered a silent prayer that this family would find healing together. Perhaps now they had some kind of method for knowing how to move forward.

As Lily and Frederick were leaving, Mr. Topp asked if they might come and visit again soon.

"I would enjoy that very much," Frederick said. "Thank you for letting us come into your home." He smiled toward the children and added, "You have a beautiful family."

In the carriage, Lily said to Frederick, "I think I just witnessed a miracle."

Humbly Frederick replied, "I'm only the messenger, Lily. I just think that . . . people get so focused on their pain that it's difficult to see beyond it to the very thing that can help them, often the thing that's been in front of them all along. I also think that even many of the most devout Christians have never made the effort to fully understand the true messages of the Bible."

"You must have been an extraordinary vicar," she said.

"Now you're just trying to embarrass me," he said with an awkward chuckle, but he still didn't seem put off by the comment. "As I've told you before, I far prefer teaching, and I think I can do more good by quietly sharing the word of God, as opposed to giving weekly sermons—which I was *not* good at, I can assure you."

Lily tried to think of something to say, something to express her gratitude and her appreciation for his unique gifts. But no words came to mind that wouldn't likely make the conversation more awkward. She felt the need to respect his humility and not make too much of a fuss over what a huge difference she knew he had just made in the life of Mr. Topp and his children.

Lily was relieved to have the silence broken when Frederick nodded toward a basket on the seat beside her. "Did we forget to give that to Mr. Topp?"

"No, that's for someone else. Our stop won't take long. Mr. Sawyer is far too cantankerous to tolerate an actual visit. He's getting on in years and his health isn't good, so I try to leave something for him every week. He would never admit that he needs what I give him or that he appreciates it, but that's not really relevant, is it?"

"No, I wouldn't think so," Frederick said with a smile.

The carriage halted, and they stepped out in front of a dilapidated farmhouse. Evidence of neglect was everywhere, and Lily wondered how the house was still standing. But Mr. Sawyer had refused any offers of help. He would never let her or anyone else through the front door, but she still wanted him to know that someone was aware of his needs and willing to help—if only in some small way.

As she and Frederick walked toward the house, he glanced over his shoulder and noticed that Max and Wally were right behind them. "Is there some reason," he asked, "that they stay close to you when you visit Mr. Sawyer . . . as opposed to your visits anywhere else?"

"I don't believe he would hurt me," Lily said, "but he is *very* mean and cranky, and it's not unusual for him to greet visitors with a gun in his hand."

"Good heavens, Lily!" Frederick said and put a hand on her arm to stop her. Max and Wally stopped too, and Frederick didn't seem to care if they overheard him. "I admire your ethics in doing good for others; truly I do—far more than I can say. But you cannot put yourself in harm's way. Send someone else to make your deliveries if you must. This is not—"

"Frederick," she interrupted, touched by his obvious concern for her well-being, "I believe it's important for *me* to do this. He won't hurt me. Max and Wally have simply insisted they accompany me."

"We *are* properly armed," Wally said, moving aside his coat to reveal the pistol tucked into his belt. "We'd not let anything happen t' the lady."

"That's somewhat comforting," Frederick said, more directly to the men, but he didn't seem convinced.

"This will only take a moment," Lily said and moved on toward the porch.

She knocked at the door, but no one answered. After trying a few times, she left the basket on the porch, and they were moving back toward the carriage when Lily heard something strange and stopped abruptly. All three men stopped walking when she did.

"What is it?" Frederick asked.

"Did you hear that?"

"Hear what?" he asked.

"A child," she said, her heart pounding. "I could have sworn I heard a child . . . crying out. And I heard pounding!"

"I wasn't payin' attention," Max said, and Wally grunted as if to agree.

"Shhh," Lily said, putting her hand up to keep them quiet. She heard it again and saw evidence that all three men heard it too. "How can that be possible? Mr. Sawyer's wife and child died years ago."

"Perhaps it's none of our business, m' lady," Wally said, but Lily felt overcome with panic.

Before she could even consider what to do, Mr. Sawyer appeared seemingly from nowhere out of the trees, on a horse that looked as old and grizzly as he did.

"What are you doin' here?" he snarled, his attention on Lily. "I told you not t' come back here . . . ever."

"I just . . . left some things for you," she said and searched for words to ask about the possibility of there being a child in the house.

As if Frederick had read her mind, she felt him take hold of her arm firmly as he whispered, "Leave it alone."

"Good day, Mr. Sawyer," Frederick said to the angry old man. "We intend no offense."

Frederick hurried Lily into the carriage, and they were on their way, but Lily's panic over what she had undeniably heard only increased. "If he is hiding a child in that house . . ." she muttered, breathless over the very idea, "we must . . . we must . . ."

"We must what?" Frederick asked. "I know enough about the law that I can tell you with certainty there is nothing that we can legally do. As unfair and horrible as it is, Lily, a man has the right to treat his own children any way that he chooses, and the law cannot interfere. If you try to interfere, *you* are going to get into trouble with the law, or you are going to be in danger of Mr. Sawyer's wrath."

Lily took in what he was saying, but it was impossible to hide how upset she felt. "And what if it's *not* his child? His own child supposedly died of the same illness that took his wife years ago."

"Is there some child missing from the area? Has there been some report of a kidnapped child during the years you've been here?"

"No."

"Is Mr. Sawyer the kind of man that would travel any farther than to town and back? He doesn't appear to have the means to even go that far! So where might he have kidnapped a child? And why? The most likely explanation is that his child did *not* die. And if that's the case, there is *nothing* we can do! Are you hearing me, Lily? You have to let it go!"

"How can I?" she muttered, still breathless with growing rage. "How can *you*?"

Frederick leaned toward her the same way he'd done with Mr. Topp, making it impossible for Lily to avoid his gaze. But it was fury in his eyes now. "I grew up hiding, Lily. I told you this when we first met. My mother took me away from my violent father and changed our surname, and she raised me with a very clear knowledge of how we would have *no* choice but to go back and live with him if we were ever found. She had tried every possible means of figuring out a better choice for us, but the law was not on our side. It makes me *sick* to think of a child suffering like that, *any* child. But life has taught me there are some things we simply cannot control and cannot change. For you to even *consider* putting yourself at risk for the sake of that child is ludicrous. What would that mean for the other children? If you put yourself in danger and get hurt, where would that leave them? If you are imprisoned for interfering with a man's legal rights, where would that leave them?" He took hold of both her hands and said more softly, "I know this is impossibly difficult, Lily, but you have to let go of this. You cannot sacrifice the well-being of your children and those in your household who depend on you. Perhaps there's something that can be done, but we need to think about it rationally and take some time to consider every possible repercussion. Do you understand?"

Lily nodded but was unable to speak. She was grateful for Frederick's ability to keep his senses about him when she was obviously unable to do so. For now, she could only pray that the means might present itself for her to be able to help this child. She didn't know how she could ever get through another day without being haunted by what she'd heard.

The manor house had come into view out the carriage window before Frederick broke the silence by asking, "Are you all right?"

She looked at him and weighed her answer carefully, coming quickly to the conclusion that she could be completely honest with him. "No, I don't think I am."

"Nor am I, if you must know," he said, which made her feel a little better . . . until he added, "but you must trust me when I tell you there's nothing to be done. The possible repercussions are unthinkable."

"I'm not certain they would be any more unthinkable than living with the decision to do nothing," she countered and was relieved to have the carriage come to a stop near the door of her home. She didn't wait for anyone to open the carriage door or help her out; she just did so on her own and hurried inside, needing some distance from Frederick's protest that was such a direct contradiction to everything her instincts were screaming. Once alone in her room, she paced frantically and prayed for guidance, eventually calming down to the point where she could sit and breathe normally. She couldn't deny that Frederick was considering her best interests, and he had made some good points regarding the protection of herself for the sake of the other children and those in the household who relied on her. But she couldn't comprehend that taking some action to help this child might possibly bring on such drastic results as he was implying. And surely nothing was more important than the well-being of a child—*any* child!

Lily finally concluded that she needed to give the matter some time. She would continue to make it a matter of prayer and not act rashly, but in her heart she already knew that she could never rest peacefully while the cries of a child were haunting her continually.

* * *

Throughout the evening, Lily forced her thoughts away from her dilemma so she could spend time with the children and not let on that anything was wrong. She chose to have supper in her room, not certain she could mask her agitated state in front of the adults—and certainly not with Frederick present.

Bedtime was nearing when Abigail came to Lily's room to collect the dinner tray and see if Lily needed anything else. While they were chatting, Abigail mentioned that she'd heard some of the other servants talking about the Barker family having some children who were ill.

"Chicken pox," Abigail reported. "Doctor's been there, and they should all be fine, from what I hear. But you always said to tell you when we hear of such things. I suspect you might be wanting to take them one of your baskets. Mrs. Maddox said she can have one put together in the morning if that's what you wish."

"Yes, that would be perfect," Lily said. "Thank you. I appreciate your insight."

After Abigail left the room, Lily tried in vain to sleep while the cries of a suffering child resonated over and over through her mind. When she did drift into slumber, it was fitful and frequently interrupted by bad dreams in which this child was calling out for her. She finally gave up on trying to sleep and tried to read from the Bible, which only seemed to add weight to the idea that she could not ignore this situation—no matter the risk. At her core she regarded herself as a Christian woman— above all else. What kind of Christian would she be to ignore such a situation? She knew that Frederick too was deeply Christian in his beliefs, but she could understand why his fears might taint his perspective. She concluded after praying again about the matter that she would have to do everything in her power to make certain every concern was addressed as feasibly as possible, and then she had to do everything in her power to help this faceless, nameless child whose cries she could not ignore.

* * *

Frederick began his day with the children, having had very little sleep to sustain him. Lily had not appeared for breakfast, which meant he hadn't seen her since they'd disagreed in the carriage. He felt deeply concerned for her and had a hovering suspicion that she would not heed his warnings, that she would defy all logic and try to rescue this child. He could understand her wanting to do so; he felt torn over the matter himself. In the hours since he'd boldly told her that she could not defy the law and put herself at risk, his own heart had been drawn to this hidden child, and he could feel himself leaning more toward Lily's stand on the matter. Still, practicality shouted loudly inside his mind. As a child he'd been taught that the law was often less than fair to those who were the true victims in this world, and as a vicar he had counseled with people in prison—people who were there for ridiculous reasons. He had seen their suffering and the deplorable conditions. The thought of Lily ending up in such a situation made him literally sick to his stomach. And yet he knew her determination, and he feared that one way or another this was going to turn the household upside down.

Frederick felt a keen desire to shadow Lily's every footstep, wanting to be certain that if she chose to do something irrational, he could at least do his best to help her remain safe. Knowing he could *not* be with her each waking moment—if at all—he prayed that he might know if he was needed and that she wouldn't do something irreparably foolish.

Frederick was surprised to have morning class time interrupted by one of the maids bringing him a sealed note from Lily. Since the children were occupied with their individual reading, Frederick sat down at his desk and broke the seal, wishing he had any idea where her thoughts were in regard to the reasons they'd disagreed yesterday—and the fact that he had so boldly expressed his concerns to the woman he worked for.

He unfolded the paper and read: *Mr. Woodstone, It's come to my attention that the Barker family has some children who are ill, and I am intending to pay them a visit later this morning. It is my hope that you might be able to accompany me. Perhaps you could ask Nellie if she would look after the children while we're gone. It shouldn't take long. Let me know if this would work for you. Lily*

Frederick felt some relief that she wanted his company for something unrelated to the child she wanted to rescue, and perhaps they would have a chance to talk about the situation more calmly than they had yesterday. He left Stanley and Anne—the oldest of the children—in charge of the classroom, as he did occasionally, and went to find Nellie. He knocked at the open door of her sitting room, where he could see her reading, a common pastime for her when the children were not in her care.

"Hello," she said when she looked up to see him there. She smiled, and he felt slightly less uncomfortable than he had since he'd told her the truth about his feelings—or rather the lack of them.

"Hello," he said. "I have a favor to ask of you—at the request of Mrs. Broadbent."

"Of course," she said, putting her book aside. "What is it?"

Frederick handed her the note and let her read it. She did so and said, "Your visit to Mr. Topp's house must have gone well if she wants you to go with her again."

"Apparently," Frederick said.

"Or," Nellie drawled with a sly smile, "she just likes your company. Or maybe both."

While Frederick was trying to figure out the apparent hidden meaning in what she'd just said, Nellie added, "For being such an insightful man on many matters, Mr. Woodstone, you are terribly oblivious to certain things."

"Am I?" he asked, having no idea what she was talking about.

Nellie stood up and handed the note back to him. "First, let me say that I'm glad you told me how you really feel in regard to me, and I want you to know that I'm all right; I really am."

"I'm glad to hear it," he said, feeling some relief in that regard.

"I can see now that my admiration of your excellent abilities with the children and your fine character drew me toward feelings that had no substance to them. I suppose one of the drawbacks of working in such a household is that it can be very limiting to one's perspective in social matters." She sighed loudly. "That's all, really. I just want you to know that I'm fine; that *we* are fine."

"Thank you, Nellie. I value your friendship. I don't want any awkwardness between us. But . . . what did you mean about my being terribly oblivious to certain things?"

"You had no idea how I felt about you, and now you are equally oblivious to the reasons Mrs. Broadbent enjoys your company."

Frederick took in a deep breath and couldn't let it out as he perceived the implication of Nellie's words. His inability to breathe heightened when she added, "And in my own opinion, you are also oblivious to the reasons that *you* enjoy *her* company. I can look back now and see that you never felt for me the way I temporarily felt for you, but such is not the case with Mrs. Broadbent." She smiled. "I just thought you should know what I believe everyone in the household has been able to see—except you."

Frederick forced himself to let out a breath and draw in another—rather than getting light-headed right here in front of Nellie. He put on a stoic face, ignored the pounding of his heart, and simply said, "Thank you for your observations, Nellie, but . . . I'm sure you're wrong. She just . . . I just . . ."

"What?" she asked when he couldn't finish.

Frederick turned and left the room, saying over his shoulder that he would see her at the time they had agreed upon to leave the children in her care.

Chapter Five
HIDDEN CHILD

BEFORE FREDERICK RETURNED TO THE classroom, he had to find a quiet place to be alone for a few minutes and try to comprehend what Nellie had just told him. He'd tried to tell her she was wrong, which had likely only made him look like a fool. Attempting to acknowledge what she'd said as opposed to pushing it away as a ridiculous possibility, his breathing sharpened, and the pace of his heart quickened once again.

"Heaven help me," he muttered and pressed both hands over his heart as if he could will it to somehow feel differently. In a matter of seconds he reminded himself of all the reasons he could not and should not have such feelings for the woman he worked for, a woman who belonged to an entirely different social class. He told himself that it was likely only the kind of trivial infatuation that Nellie had felt for him. But something powerful and overwhelming burst forth from the deepest part of his soul, alerting his every nerve to an absolute truth he had been trying to ignore. And what had Nellie said? He was oblivious to something that everyone else in the household could see? "Heaven help me," he muttered once again. If that was the case, trying to pretend it wasn't true seemed futile. But what was he supposed to do about it? And even if Nellie believed that Lily had feelings for him, he wasn't so sure he agreed with her. He looked again at the note in his hand, struck by the way she'd signed her given name, even though she'd addressed him as Mr. Woodstone. Was it possible? Was it really possible?

The idea was too enormous and frightening to take in, and the children were on their own, waiting for him. He forced the entire conundrum to the back of his mind and hurried to the classroom, wishing his heart would stop quickening its pace every time he glanced at the clock and found himself counting the minutes until he would be accompanying Lily to the Barker home.

* * *

Lily once again waited at the foot of the stairs for Frederick to join her. She told herself once again that her biggest reason for asking him to accompany her—even though it meant interrupting his usual work day—was his ability to be so kind and compassionate to people in need. But she was well acquainted with the Barker family, and she had no reason to believe that the children being afflicted with the chicken pox was a reason for any serious concern. The illness was known to be miserable for children, but it was simply one of those things most children had to endure. She anticipated that her visit to the Barker home would be brief and likely uneventful. Therefore, her reasons for impulsively writing that note earlier, requesting that he join her, were beginning to sound more and more flimsy as she considered how she would explain her desire to have him come along. Hearing his shoes on the stairs, she knew truth was the only option. He was too sharp to accept anything less, and she needed to be honest with him.

* * *

Frederick slowed his pace as he came to the bottom of the stairs. He was still trying to adjust his thinking to the idea Nellie had suggested. More accurately, he was trying not to think about it at all, but he hadn't been able to think about anything else. Initially attempting to convince himself that it was ridiculous and absurd quickly disintegrated beneath the truth he couldn't deny. And now that he'd been shocked into facing his true feelings, seeing Lily standing in the foyer with sunlight shining down on her from a high window, he suddenly found it difficult to breathe, let alone move. He stopped on the bottom step and held tightly to the bannister as she turned to look at him.

"Thank you for joining me," she said. "I apologize for the short notice. I hope it didn't cause you too much inconvenience."

Seconds of silence alerted him to the realization that he was staring at her. "No inconvenience," he said. "Nellie was glad to look after the children. They have assignments to complete while I'm gone."

More silence made him realize that *she* was staring at *him*. Was it true—as Nellie had implied—that Lily had feelings for him to which he'd been completely oblivious? Her expression was difficult to read, but her eyes betrayed a message that she seemed to be trying to hide, and now that he was looking for evidence, he could see it all too clearly.

Fearing he would make a fool of himself when he'd barely had moments to even consider what was happening, Frederick looked down and cleared his throat before he stepped toward her and offered his arm. "Shall we?" he said, and she put her hand on his coat sleeve.

Once they were inside the carriage, she said, "You're very quiet. Are you still upset with me?"

"Upset?" he echoed, honestly unable to think of what she meant. He was distracted by other thoughts.

"We disagreed yesterday," she said as if he didn't know. He'd certainly forgotten.

"I'm not upset with you, Lily," he clarified. "I'm only concerned for your well-being. You're very passionate about your convictions, and I admire that, but you must not compromise your safety."

"Your concern is very touching," she said. "Only one other person has ever shown such concern for me. Perhaps I'm not acquainted with how to respond."

"Your husband," Frederick stated, considering, from an entirely different perspective, the relationship she'd shared with him. He wanted to know how they'd met, how he'd treated her. Had he loved her? Had she loved him?

"He was very kind to me," she said before she sighed loudly and looked toward the window. "There's something I need to tell you. I confess I wanted some time alone with you so I could say what needs to be said."

Frederick wondered if she would admit to her feelings or if this was about something entirely different. He was not at all prepared to hear her say, "I met with my solicitor this morning. He's a good man. My husband trusted him with every legal and financial matter, and I have done the same. What you said to me yesterday, about what might happen to the children if something happened to me, it troubled me deeply. I sent word to him very early this morning, and he's come and gone. I have updated my will. It's all taken care of."

"*What's* taken care of?" he asked, wondering if this was a bizarre kind of preparation for her to carry out some foolish plan in regard to the child she wanted to rescue.

"If anything happens to me, you will be the legal guardian of the children." Frederick couldn't manage to even utter a sound before she added, "Everything I have will be yours so that you can care for them properly. Now I know that all will be well . . . should anything ever happen to me." She finally looked at him, as if to gauge his response, but he still couldn't speak. He couldn't believe what he was hearing. "I'm not implying that anything *will* happen. It's a prudent and wise thing to do . . . for a person to make certain that affairs are in order."

Frederick finally found his voice. "Yes, Lily, it's a prudent thing to do, but . . . me? Why me? Why would you do that? Why would you do it without talking to me first?"

"Would you have told me no? Would you have refused to take responsibility for them?"

"No, of course not, but—"

"It's all settled, Frederick. You needed to know, but we never need to speak of it again."

Frederick wanted to speak of it a great deal, but they had arrived at the Barker home, and he had no choice but to step out of the carriage and help her do the same. Anything he said now would be overheard by Max or Wally.

* * *

Lily felt hesitant to let go of Frederick's hand after he'd helped her find sure footing. She wondered if she'd felt him trembling. Or was that her? Perhaps both. Something was different about him since they'd disagreed on their return to the manor yesterday. Was he simply so concerned about the situation? Or was it something else? For the moment she put her attention to the purpose of this excursion. Wally handed her the basket of food and medicine that Mrs. Maddox had assembled prior to their leaving.

Lily handed the basket to Frederick and walked ahead of him toward the house. The door was opened by one of the children who was apparently *not* ill. Lily stepped inside, aware of Frederick coming in behind her, and she quickly introduced him. Mrs. Barker nodded in greeting toward Frederick before she quickly reported that three of her five children were ill, and in the same sentence, she thanked Lily for her visit and for the basket, expressing great appreciation.

"I'm glad to help in some small way," Lily said and reached out to take the crying two-year-old from Mrs. Barker's arms. The woman was clearly exhausted.

"Wait," Frederick said, putting a hand on Lily's shoulder. "Have *you* had chicken pox?"

Lily looked at him, puzzled. "I would assume," she said, well aware of the fevered warmth of the child in her arms, not to mention the little oozing blisters on his skin. "Doesn't every person contract them in childhood?"

"Usually," he said, a concern in his voice that startled her to a sudden uneasiness. "But not always. I just think it would be wise to avoid contact if you haven't had the illness."

"Indeed you should!" Mrs. Barker said and took the baby back from Lily abruptly.

"Well, I remember having the chicken pox," Frederick said, clearly attempting to ease the tension while he assisted another of the ailing children who was asking for a drink of water. "I recall it well." He sat down and put the child on his lap, helping him sip from a cup. "And it's terribly miserable; is it not, my boy?"

The little boy nodded up at him and muttered, "It's so itchy!"

"Indeed," Frederick said. "You just rest and drink lots of water and do as your mother tells you, and it will all be over in a week or two."

Frederick insisted that Lily keep her distance from the afflicted children while he helped Mrs. Barker with a few simple tasks. Then they were soon on their way. In the carriage, he said with no hint of anger but certainly with great concern, "In the future, I think it would be wise for you to not be so eager to meet those who are ill until you know what you're dealing with. The pox only come once in a lifetime, but there are other illnesses for which that is not the case. I admire your commitment to helping those in need, and I support you in that endeavor completely. But you must consider your own health and the fact that you have so many people depending on you."

Lily felt a little startled to realize how *this* conversation had so much in common with the one they'd had yesterday. But one thing had nothing to do with the other, and she gently protested, "You sound as if I've just put my life in danger. The chicken pox is known to be very miserable, but it can be managed."

"If you did *not* have the chicken pox as a child and you get it now, it is much more difficult for adults to get through without complications."

"And you know this because . . . ?"

"Being a vicar forced me to become educated on a great many ailments the people in my care endured. I had far too many conversations with the local doctor about such things. And I also had the chicken pox at the age of nine; my mother got it from me, and she became very ill. I don't wish to see the same thing happen to you."

"But I've probably already had the illness . . . as a child."

"And yet you don't remember, so you don't know for certain," Frederick said, once again with that edge in his voice that she knew was concern, but it bordered on sounding angry. And then he asked a question that she'd been dreading. "What of your parents, Lily? You've never talked about them. Is it possible to write and inquire over whether or not you—"

"I never knew them," she said abruptly, and his surprise was evident. She decided to just get the rest out of the way. With as comfortable as she'd come to feel with him, she didn't know why she hadn't brought it up before. "I was raised in an orphanage until I ran away when I was thirteen."

"Lily!" he said breathlessly. There was shock in the way he uttered her name, but also compassion. "And then what? What happened after you ran away?"

"I found work . . . here and there. I lived on the streets some. I met my husband when he was in London for business, and I was begging. He took me home and gave me proper work, and in time . . ." Lily studied his eyes, fearing some kind of disapproval or reproach. But she saw nothing but kindness and perhaps . . . sorrow. "

It certainly explains a lot," he said, and she didn't know if that was meant to be a compliment or an insult until he added, "about the children, I mean. But I never would have imagined that such a fine lady could have come from such an upbringing. You are even more remarkable than I had believed."

Lily looked away, unable to bear his gaze any longer. Trying to distract herself from feelings that consumed her and words that were threatening to jump out of her mouth and embarrass her, she thought of their visit to the Barker home. She had to admit, "I don't remember having the chicken pox, Frederick."

"Then I pray you had them when you were too young to remember," he said grimly, and she couldn't help feeling afraid.

"But I barely touched the child," she protested, even though she knew well enough that her contact would have been sufficient for an illness to be passed. She didn't want to admit to her own feelings of discomfort, but neither was she willing to succumb to illness. A part of her desperately wanted to believe she had a choice; she chose to focus on believing that she had surely already had chicken pox as a child and that there was nothing to worry about.

"It's *very* contagious, Lily," Frederick said, not making her feel any better. "As I understand it, if there is a fever or open sores, it's even more contagious." He sighed, and Lily could feel him trying to calm his own fears. "But what's done is done. It could be several days before we'll know. I can only pray you will not get ill."

"I will pray for that as well," Lily said, even while she knew well enough from personal experience that no amount of prayer could take away the inevitable consequences of a person's choices, even if those choices were made in naïveté or ignorance—or with the best of intentions.

Following a stretch of strained silence, she couldn't keep herself from saying, "At least I know the children will be left in good hands."

Frederick looked at her as if she'd spoken blasphemy. "That is not even a little bit funny."

"It was not intended to be," she said firmly. "You should know how implicitly I trust you with their care."

"And you should know how thoroughly empty life would be for each and every one of us if we lost you!"

Lily considered the evidence of his anger and responded in a soft voice. "I have no intention of leaving this world, Frederick. I have much to live for."

"I'm very glad to hear it," he said more calmly. "I would hope, then, that you will cease putting yourself into dangerous situations."

Lily couldn't say anything; she couldn't make any promises on that count, given what she was planning. But with any luck, everything would go smoothly and all would be well by tomorrow.

Wanting to distract him as much as she ached to hear some evidence of what she was sensing, she pushed herself past a carefully placed boundary and spoke in a light voice that she hoped would lighten the mood. "Are you speaking for the children, Frederick? The staff? Or are you admitting that *you* would find life thoroughly empty if I were gone?"

His gaze became so intense that it startled her, and then he admitted, "I would never be the same." But as soon as he said it he looked away, and she could feel a barrier between them. She wanted to ask if she had misread him or if he would find it impossible to bridge the many gaps between them—none of which made any difference to her. But how could she tell him that without sounding forward and presumptuous?

Lily was still wondering how to dispel the tension between them when the carriage arrived back at the manor and they both went inside, barely saying a few more polite words before he excused himself to get back to the children.

* * *

When suppertime came, Frederick opted to have a tray brought to his room as opposed to risking the possibility of having to sit at the same table with Lily and wonder if everyone in the room could sense what he was feeling. According to Nellie it had already happened. But now that he had acknowledged his own feelings—and given all of the weighty conversation he'd shared with Lily earlier—he wasn't certain he could manage to get through a meal and not embarrass himself.

Frederick ate very little and felt far too restless to get ready for bed. He tried to read but ended up pacing his room while bits and pieces of many conversations flitted through his mind and combined with his recollections of the way she'd looked at him earlier today. Added upon all of that was the absurdity of this change she'd made to her will. And if that weren't enough to burden his mind, he had to worry about the possibility of her becoming ill. Even worse in some ways was his suspicion that she had not let go of her concern over the child they suspected was being held hostage by Mr. Sawyer. He knew the matter had not been dropped, and his instincts felt on high alert that she might try to do something that could land her in trouble.

Frederick prayed as he paced, asking for guidance in knowing what to do, what to say to her, how to help her stay safe and healthy. In the midst of his prayer, he felt drawn to the window and looked down to see a sight that made his heart pound. The carriage was parked at one of the rear doors of the house with Max and Wally lingering close by, clearly waiting to go somewhere.

"Lily," Frederick muttered and grabbed his jacket before he hurried out of his room and down the back stairs, glad he'd not changed for bed. He knew what she was doing; he didn't even have to wonder. And he felt so overcome with fury that he could hear his pulse pounding in his ears as he ran and prayed he would get to the carriage before it left. The fact that he'd been drawn to the window at the very time the carriage was waiting there seemed evidence that his prayers were already being answered.

Frederick hurried out the door into the brisk night air, breathlessly relieved to see the carriage still parked there, and Max and Wally chatting as if they had all the time in the world. Their jobs seemed to involve a great deal of waiting, and they were quite comfortable with it.

Now that he'd made it in time, Frederick almost felt light-headed from how fast he'd been running, and it took him a good minute to get his breath back. He put his hands on his thighs to lower his head while he leaned back against the wall of the house.

"Are you all right, Mr. Woodstone?" Wally asked.

"Fine," Frederick managed and put up a hand to indicate he needed a moment before he would be able to speak further. When he *was* able to speak, he demanded, "What are you doing here this time of night?" Max and Wally glanced at each other a little sheepishly, and Frederick added, "Allow me to venture a guess: Mrs. Broadbent has come up with some crazy scheme in which she has enlisted your aid, and it includes breaking the law."

"As I see it," Max volunteered, "sometimes the law just isn't in favor of the common good of the people, and the people gots t' find a way t' work around it."

"Is *that* how you see it?" Frederick asked. "And what if some harm comes to her? What then?"

"We won't let that happen," Wally said with conviction. "It's us against one weak and ornery old man, and this time o' night he's likely t' be drunk and even more likely t' not even be at home."

"And how do you know that?" Frederick asked.

"We goes to the pub many evenings when the lady's not in need of our services, and Sawyer is there—like clockwork, he is." Wally nodded toward Max. "Max here will go t' the pub and keep an eye on the old man. We gots a signal worked out in case the old man starts headin' back. But it's a good chance he won't even be at home."

"And then what?" Frederick asked. "Has she even thought through the long-term results of this?"

"That's not a question you should be askin' us, Mr. Woodstone," Wally said.

"We would do her bidding t' the ends of the earth," Max added.

While their devotion was impressive, Frederick couldn't help feeling alarmed. When Lily came out the door, wearing a hooded cloak and pulling gloves onto her hands, she was clearly surprised to see him.

"What are you doing here?" she demanded, sounding more authoritative than she ever had. "I didn't want you to be involved with this."

"As opposed to what, Lily?" he responded in the same tone of voice, not caring that Max and Wally were standing right there. "What if something happens to you? What if you get hurt . . . or worse?"

"Nothing will happen," she insisted while Max helped her into the carriage. "We have a carefully devised plan, and we will do nothing if Mr. Sawyer is anywhere nearby."

"And when he realizes the child is missing?" Frederick took hold of both sides of the carriage doorway and leaned his head inside. " Do you not think he will suspect it was you? You're the only person who dares to come onto his property at all. And you take in needy children. You are the first person he'll suspect."

"And as illegal as what I'm doing might be, I can't believe the law would shine favorably on what *he* is doing. Do you honestly think he will go to the police and report that his child is missing when he's led the entire community to believe that the child had died? Now, we must hurry. Are you coming or not?"

"Fine," Frederick said and flung himself into the carriage, sitting on the seat opposite her, as he always did. If she was going to get herself into trouble, the least he could do was be there to try and keep her as safe as possible. They suddenly had nothing to say, and he wished he could see her face better in the darkness. He assumed the lack of lamps on the carriage was an attempt to remain more discreet. As the silence grew taut, he felt torn between wanting to yell at her and wanting even more to just kiss her. In his distorted imaginings, he wished that kissing her would help her calm down, convince her to see reason. He wanted to believe that such an act might allow his own thoughts and feelings to somehow travel into her, that she might be able to see how risky this was—not just the actual act of trying to take the child tonight but everything it would mean in the future.

Trying to be calm and rational, Frederick asked, "So if you actually manage to get this child away from his home, then what? Will we keep him or her hidden away as well?"

"If necessary. It's a big house. The difference is that we can give him safety and daylight. We can feed him well, teach him respect and trust, give him love. We can give him an education."

"Him?"

"Of course I don't know. I just . . . feel like it's a boy. It sounded like a boy's voice to me. I suppose we shall soon see. Max has ridden ahead to the pub. We will know soon if the child is alone. Think about it, Frederick. We heard cries for help when it was evident Sawyer wasn't at home. As soon as the old man came back, yelling and shouting as he always does, the child became quiet."

"I pray with all my soul that you know what you're doing," Frederick said.

The carriage came to a halt, but they didn't get out, and they had nothing to say to each other. After waiting for what seemed far too long, Wally called out. "I see the signal. All is well."

Frederick got out of the carriage and helped Lily step down. "What signal?" he asked Wally, who pointed in the direction of town. There was a distinctive lantern burning with a blue glow.

"Max hung that in a tree at the edge o' town. Blue means Sawyer is at the pub. Red means he's on his way back, but that horse o' his don't go very fast. As soon as it turns red, we'll still have some time. Max'll watch out for the old man. Sawyer does love his drink."

Wally then lit two lanterns, handing one to Lily and carrying one himself as he led the way. They went carefully around the perimeter of the house to make certain there wasn't an outside entrance to a cellar. They found the front door locked, but the back door was *not* locked. They crept quietly into the house with Wally leading the way and

Frederick following Lily, silently praying for this to be over quickly and without incident.

"Hello?" Lily called. "Hello? Mr. Sawyer is gone. We're here to help you. Are you here?" Silence was the only response. "You don't need to be afraid," Lily called. "We were here before and heard you calling out for help. If you need help, we will help you. That's why we came . . . when we knew your father would be gone. Is he your father? Please answer me. Please believe that you can trust us."

A cry of help and a distinct pounding could be heard. Lily looked in alarm toward Frederick and then Wally, saying quietly, "We must find the child. Hurry."

The house was small, and it didn't take long to find the cellar stairs, which were behind a door that had to be unlocked. Thankfully the key was hanging on a string near the side of the door. Frederick remained close to Lily while she remained close to Wally as they descended the steep, narrow stairs into a damp, musty room. When their lanterns shed light over the room, they were all momentarily stunned into silence. Huddled in a corner on what could barely be called a bed, was a boy that Frederick guessed was nine or ten. He had brown hair and large, frightened eyes, but there was hope in his expression. And Frederick suddenly felt regret over how he'd tried to talk Lily out of helping this child. The goodness of her heart was stronger than her fear, and he was awed by her courage and grateful for her determination.

Lily handed her lantern to Frederick and inched closer to the child, kneeling on the floor near the bed while Frederick glanced around the room, noticing that it had the basic amenities, and it didn't appear to be as dirty as he might have expected for a cellar. But it was still a cellar, and it had been locked. For a child to be living this way was unconscionable.

"You mustn't be afraid," Lily said to the boy. He retracted slightly, but there was distinct hope in his eyes. "We want to take you away from here . . . if that's what you want. We'll take good care of you. You'll have your very own room with big windows, new clothes, plenty to eat, and everyone there will be kind to you. I realize you have no idea who I am, but I hope you can believe that we want to help you and that you can trust us. Do you understand what I'm saying?"

The boy nodded.

"Can you tell me your name?" Lily asked.

"Danny," he said with a shaky voice that sounded nothing like the shouting he'd done to get their attention, the shouting that implied he *did* want to be rescued.

"Danny," Lily said gently, "will you come with us?"

"Papa . . . find me," the boy muttered, and it was immediately evident he'd had little opportunity for speaking. He almost stuttered as he added, "Papa hurt me more . . . if run away. Papa hurt you, too."

"We're being very careful, Danny. We will work together to figure out the best way to keep you safe. But we must go now before he comes back." Lily held out a hand to him. "Will you come with me now?"

The boy tentatively reached out his hand and touched Lily's fingers, then he gripped her hand hard, as if she might save him from drowning. He then leapt to his knees and threw his arms around her neck. "Take me away," the child pleaded. "No let . . . Papa . . . find me."

Frederick wanted to cry like a baby when Lily looked up at him over the top of the boy's head. "We must go," Frederick said, and the boy looked up at him. "Will you let me carry you?" he asked.

Danny hesitated only a moment before he reached out for Frederick, who gave Lily the lantern he was holding in exchange for the boy. Wally led the way up the steps, and once they were all out of the cellar, Lily locked the door again and returned the key to its place in an effort to make nothing appear disturbed. With any luck, Sawyer would come home drunk and sleep it off, believing his son was still in the cellar, and it would be hours before he even realized the child was gone.

Frederick hurried toward the carriage, mindful of the way Danny's arms were holding tightly around his neck, clinging to him desperately. Wally and Lily were right behind him, and he noticed with a glance that the lantern in the distance was still blue. It was starting to rain, and Frederick hoped that meant any sign of carriage wheels, horses' hooves, and footsteps would be washed away before morning.

In the carriage, Frederick held Danny on his lap as they moved away from the unthinkable life this child had been living. Lily sat next to Frederick rather than across from him. She tucked a blanket over the boy, and he realized she had come prepared with a few things. Danny snuggled down beneath the blanket, and Lily offered him water from a flask and also a piece of bread. He ate and drank a little, but there was no indication that he'd been without food or water, even though he was very thin.

Rain began pounding on the roof of the carriage with more force, which helped Frederick feel better about leaving no evidence of their little kidnapping scheme. A few minutes into the ride, Danny began muttering about his fear that his father would find him. Both Lily and Frederick kept reassuring him they would do everything they could to keep him safe. Danny didn't necessarily seem convinced, but he was eager to accept their help as well as the hope they were offering.

Back at the house, Frederick was surprised to find Mrs. Pilfer, Abigail, and Mary all waiting for them. Lily had clearly let them in on her plan, but it was evident she didn't want anyone else in the household to know. It was easy for Frederick to surmise that these were the servants she trusted to not only keep her secret but to be capable of acting skills sufficient to make this endeavor believable. They obviously couldn't take care of an additional child in the house without help from some of the staff, but Lily had worked everything out very carefully.

While Wally took care of the horses and carriage, Mrs. Pilfer led the way up the back stairs, declaring that Abigail and Mary would be following them with heated water and clean clothes they had found among the vast supply of clothing for the other children. They'd rummaged through the clothes that had been set aside due to the fact that they currently didn't fit any of the children at the present time, and the women had found something in a number of sizes that could be ready.

They went to a spare room that Frederick realized was next to Lily's. He heard Mrs. Pilfer say that this was the room each child had used when they'd first come here and had been traumatized by the change. Eventually they had been integrated into sharing rooms with the other children. Frederick wondered if that would ever be possible for Danny; was he meant to be kept a secret until he was old enough to set out on his own?

Danny took to Mrs. Pilfer right away, and he agreed to allow the housekeeper and the maids to help him bathe once they'd promised not to look as long as he promised to get himself properly clean. "And that means between every toe and behind your ears, young man," Mrs. Pilfer said, and the boy nodded.

Mrs. Pilfer commented that Danny was actually rather clean—especially in contrast to some of the other children Lily had brought home with her. Frederick realized this wasn't the first time Lily had arrived at a late hour with a child in need. But as far as he knew, all of the other children were here legally.

Lily held Danny on her lap while the bath was being prepared, and she spoke soft reassurances to him, some of which Frederick couldn't hear as he paced the room, his thoughts and emotions tumbling together into a whirlwind that tore at his heart in more ways than he could assimilate.

With hot water in the tub, and soap and shampoo at hand, Mary and Abigail spoke kindly to Danny, urging him to get cleaned up. Mrs. Pilfer said to both Frederick and Lily, "The two of you smell terribly of whatever musty place you got him from. I'll have clean water sent to both of your rooms as well. We'll take good care of the boy while you get cleaned up."

Lily spoke kindly and plainly to Danny about leaving him in the care of these women while she took care of some things, but she promised to return within the hour. He seemed initially hesitant to let her out of his sight, since she was the one who had rescued him, the one who had promised he would be cared for and safe. But the other women were kind and managed some mild teasing that helped soften the mood.

Frederick felt an aching urge to speak with Lily; there was so much he wanted to say—needed to say—but she hurried into her bedroom and closed the door. He had no choice but to return to his own room, and within minutes, buckets of warm water were brought to him. He figured that every bit of stove top in the kitchen had been filled with pots of water in anticipation of this very thing. He got cleaned up and put on fresh clothes as quickly as he could manage. He could barely push a comb through his wet hair while his mind was still spinning with all that had happened—and how it had made him feel. And he believed the only way to make sense of his inner turmoil was to share those feelings with Lily. Perhaps if he could verbalize his feelings, he might have some hope of understanding them himself.

Frederick returned to Danny's new room to find him bathed and dressed in clean, warm pajamas. He was surprised to find a doctor sitting on the edge of the bed, asking the boy questions about the situation he'd been living in and about his daily habits of eating and hygiene. Frederick realized that once Max had known they had gotten safely away with the boy, he had been instructed to go and get the doctor Lily had called on for years, a man who had become a trusted friend through all of the times he'd come to the manor to treat the children and members of the staff for various maladies and minor injuries.

When the doctor had finished examining Danny, Lily's bedroom doors were still closed. But he spoke quietly with Mrs. Pilfer in the hall, and Frederick hovered nearby, glad not to be told to leave. Mrs. Pilfer seemed to accept that he was in on all of this, and the doctor didn't question his presence once the housekeeper introduced them.

"He's clearly traumatized, which is understandable," the doctor reported, "and his language skills are sorely lacking, which is also understandable." He sighed and added, "He's also undernourished and in sore need of some exposure to sunlight. From what he managed to tell me, I believe he's suffering from a deficiency that has been proven to be caused by an extended deprivation from the sun. We don't understand how it works, but it does, so I'm not going to question it."

"And how might we expose him to sunlight," Mrs. Pilfer asked, "if we are unable to take him outdoors—at least for the time being?"

"Windows, my dear woman," the doctor said with a little smile. The two of them obviously knew each other well. "My official suggestions are a good diet, exposure to sunlight, and a great deal of tender care."

"None of that will be a problem," Mrs. Pilfer said.

"I knew it wouldn't be," the doctor said. "I'll be off now. Send for me if I'm needed. Reassure Mrs. Broadbent again that her secret is safe with me. She knows I'll do just about anything to ease the plight of a child."

"And for that we thank you," Mrs. Pilfer said and left to escort the doctor out.

Frederick quietly opened the door to Danny's room and was surprised to find Lily sitting on the edge of the bed and Danny sleeping soundly. It seemed that once he'd known all was well, he had quickly succumbed to exhaustion. The lamps had been extinguished, and Frederick could only see a vague outline of Lily against the windows behind her, through which he could see that rain was still falling. Her hair was down, and she appeared to be wearing some kind of dressing gown.

"Is he all right?" Frederick asked in a whisper.

"He will be, I think," she said and stood up, kissing the boy's brow before she walked through a different door than the one Frederick had just entered. He followed her, then realized they were in her bedroom; he was relieved when she kept walking through another open door into a sitting room. There were no lamps burning, and she didn't light one; she seemed to prefer the darkness. Despite the rain, there was a faint light coming through the windows, which gave the room a bluish glow. As Lily moved toward a window and looked out, Frederick could see that her wet hair was hanging down her back, almost to her waist. He'd never seen it any other way than carefully pinned up and styled. Now it was as white and flowing as a waterfall. The light-colored dressing gown she wore gave her the overall effect of looking the way he imagined an angel might look if they were visible to mortal eyes. He was alone with her now, and there was much he needed to say, but he hardly knew where to begin.

Chapter Six
EQUAL IN STRENGTH

"ARE YOU ALL RIGHT?" FREDERICK asked, considering it an obvious question and certainly a necessary one.

"I'm better now than I have been since I first heard him crying out for help and was unable to give it."

With that she gave him the perfect opening to say what was most important. "I owe you an apology, Lily. And you should know me well enough to know that I don't say something I don't mean; if anything I might get myself into trouble by speaking my convictions too freely." She turned more toward him, and he sensed a softening in her countenance. Had she been believing he'd be angry with her for rescuing Danny—and for getting him involved?

"I suppose that's yet another thing we have in common," she said.

"Perhaps." He cleared his throat and took a step closer. "Forgive me, Lily. I can see now that I was allowing my fears to overrule the obvious ethical decision. To see Danny here . . . now, and to consider how he's been living . . . I can't even imagine what made me think that leaving him there was all right, no matter the repercussions. I've always believed we should do what God would have us do to serve others—even if it meant sacrifice and discomfort—but you have put me to shame with your courage. I can see now that I haven't always lived what I've believed." He cleared his throat again as if to signal that he'd concluded his statement.

"Apology accepted," she said. "It takes a great deal of courage and humility for a person to admit they were wrong. I respect you for speaking your convictions freely, Frederick. And I must confess that you were not wrong. The things you said made me think deeply on my responsibility to the children—and to the household—and how important it is that I not put myself or them at risk. I handled the situation with more planning and care than I might have if you'd not said what you did. Otherwise I might have been foolish enough to confront Mr. Sawyer directly or indulge in some other foolhardy measure, and I really could have gotten us all into trouble."

"Well," Frederick drawled, "it seems we should strive to communicate openly, and perhaps we can help each other keep a more proper balance."

"It seems we should," she said, and Frederick felt a distinct tension descend between them as they stared at each other in the bluish luminescence of the room.

The silence became strained, and Frederick knew that if he were any kind of gentleman he would not expect a woman to force him to acknowledge what was so obviously evolving between them. Just as with the rescue of Danny, he had a long list of reasons he should be afraid and why the possibility of their mutual attraction could never be socially acceptable or come to anything good. But they couldn't reasonably consider the potential challenges if they never acknowledged the truth of their feelings. And he needed to come up with enough courage to take the first step.

With that thought, he literally and metaphorically took another step toward her, then another. Being closer, he could now see her face more clearly, and the expectancy in her eyes bolstered his courage. He lifted a trembling hand to touch her face, knowing that such a gesture could never be construed as anything but romantic, and there was no turning back. She closed her eyes and leaned her face into his hand—a response that also could never be misconstrued.

"Lily," he whispered, "I have to tell you how I've been trying very hard to talk myself out of feeling this way—the same way I was trying to talk you out of rescuing Danny."

"Then you must realize by now," she said, putting her hand over his and opening her eyes to look at him, "that we must not be ruled by any social expectations or by what others might deem right or wrong. We must do what our hearts tell us is right."

Frederick leaned slightly closer, and she responded by doing the same. He could do nothing now but kiss her, even though the pounding of his heart made him wonder over his ability to remain standing upright if he did so. He felt more than heard her take in a trembling breath just before their lips met. For a moment he imagined her to be like a wild bird, and he was trying to get close enough to touch her without frightening her away. He drew back to look into her eyes; even in the shadows he saw approval there and kissed her again. No longer afraid that she might withdraw, he took her face into his hands and attempted to express the feelings that he'd been trying to deny. Her hands took hold of his shoulders while he kissed her yet again. He then just gazed into her eyes as if he could silently communicate feelings that words could not express. She let out a contended sigh as if she fully understood before she pressed the side of her face to his shoulder and he wrapped her in his arms.

"Oh, Lily," he murmured and pressed a kiss into her damp hair. "I don't know what I'm doing. I have no experience with women."

"How refreshing," she said and pressed her hands to his back.

"Well," he chuckled, "I had a crush on my teacher, Miss Wingham, when I was sixteen. But it never came to anything. And I did kiss Harriett Milner after a church social once." He tightened his embrace. "Does that count?"

"Not really, no," she said with a soft laugh, "but I prefer it that way." She looked up at him, and he saw a seriousness come over her expression. "You see . . . I have very little experience with men."

"But you were . . ."

"Married? Yes. He married me to protect and care for me, to make certain that my needs would always be met. We were friends, and in public we were every bit husband and wife. We loved each other in our own way. But there was never a private marriage relationship. I never fully understood why he wanted it that way, but he was so good to me in every other way that I never questioned it. I kept my loneliness and my desire for children to myself."

Frederick took all of that in but didn't know what to say. He simply asked, "And now what, Lily?"

"Now I think we are both very tired and in much need of some sleep. If the children and the majority of the staff are not to know of our secret endeavors, we must be up early and appear as if everything is normal."

"Yes, I suppose we must. And what of you and me? Are we to keep that a secret as well?"

"I don't think it would be possible," she said with a little smile, and he knew its implication.

"According to Nellie—who was kind enough to alert me to what a blind fool I have been—the entire household already knows."

Lily kissed him as if she relished being able to do so. She smiled again and said, "Then I will see you at breakfast. And perhaps if everyone is focused on the scandal of my being romantically involved with the tutor, they won't notice other strange happenings in the house."

"An excellent plan," he said and kissed her once more before he forced himself to walk out of the room. Now that they'd crossed this line, he never wanted to be away from her again.

* * *

Lily stood where she was for an unmeasurable length of time after Frederick had left the room. She was only aware of the rain sliding down the windows and the tingle of his kiss on her lips. She'd convinced herself years ago that such feelings—and such experiences—would not be a part of her life. All she'd survived throughout her youth had been grandly compensated for by the kindness and generosity of her husband. They'd shared a common purpose and a comfortable friendship, but her loneliness was something she'd come to accept long before he'd suddenly taken ill and died.

Lily had found herself with an unfathomable fortune at her disposal and a deep desire to ease even a little bit of suffering in the world—the kind of suffering she'd endured in her own childhood. Since that time, she had focused her life only on the children she'd brought into her home, those who worked for her, and those who lived on her estate. She believed that along with the great wealth she'd inherited came a great responsibility. Her husband had lived with an entirely selfless attitude in regard to those who looked to him for their living, and she strove to honor him—and more importantly to honor God—by giving of herself and her resources to change lives for the better. But she'd long ago stopped thinking about the possibility of her own life being blessed with the companionship of a good man. She surely could have lived a full and complete life by caring for her children and serving others. She knew that. But Frederick had awakened something in her she'd never felt before and therefore could not have imagined possible. She felt so thoroughly elated that she feared crashing down into some kind of harsh reality where she would discover it was all too good to be true. Not willing to even consider such an idea, she focused only on the memory of his gentle words and his tender kiss. And she held them close to her heart.

Exhaustion swept over her suddenly, like a wave, and she checked on Danny to find him still sleeping peacefully. She sighed with deep contentment to know the child was now in her care; she knew she'd done the right thing. Now she could only pray that no further harm would come to him or to any of those caring for him. Putting the matter in God's hands, Lily kissed the boy's brow and went to her own bed, sliding between the sheets, feeling more completely satisfied than she ever had. She prayed that this abundance of hope and peace would last.

* * *

Frederick awoke to an awareness that rain was still falling, and he had the sensation that he'd been dreaming. Then it all came back to him, and he knew that no dream could have ever felt so real. He truly had helped Lily rescue a child from a life of horror, and he truly had kissed her and held her in his arms. The evidence that they shared these feelings for each other heightened his senses and made his nerves tingle. As tired as he felt, he hurried to get ready for the day, wanting to see how Danny was doing and even more so to see Lily.

Frederick wasn't exactly certain about where to find Lily, and he wasn't sure if it would be appropriate for him to knock at her bedroom door. He was relieved to come across Abigail in the hall, who told him that Mrs. Broadbent was in Danny's room. He knocked lightly at the door and heard her call for him to come in. He entered and closed the door behind him before he turned to see Lily sitting in a big chair near the window, her hair still down, wearing the same dressing gown she'd been wearing last night; in daylight he could see that it was pale blue. Just seeing her took his breath away, and she met his eyes in a way that reminded him once again that he'd not dreamed what had transpired between them. After sharing a long gaze, they both turned their attention to Danny, who was curled up on her lap as if he were much younger than his age. Without the support of the large chair with its wide, soft arms, she wouldn't have been able to hold him like that.

"I wanted to see how you're both doing," Frederick said, and Danny turned at the sound of his voice.

"This is Mr. Woodstone," Lily said gently to the boy. "He helped us last night. Do you remember?" Danny nodded. "I told you about him. He's the teacher. During the day, he teaches the other children their lessons, and they all like him very much. I was thinking that until it's safe for you to have lessons with the other children, perhaps Mr. Woodstone could spend some time with you in the morning and late in the afternoon—before and after school—to help you learn to read and write. Would you like that?"

Danny made no response, and Lily said to Frederick, "Danny has told me that he would like to learn to read and write, but . . . I think it frightens him." She looked down at Danny. "Does it frighten you, Danny?" she asked. "It's all right for you to tell us how you feel. We can trust Mr. Woodstone."

Danny nodded again and buried his face against Lily's shoulder. Lily looked at Frederick with a deep concern in her eyes that was completely disguised by her positive tone of voice when she said, "Danny, is it all right if I tell Mr. Woodstone what you told me? He is my dearest friend. I trust him with my life. I trust him with yours, too. May I tell him?"

Danny nodded his head again but kept his face hidden.

"Apparently," Lily said, and Frederick sensed that she was much more emotional than she was letting on, "Danny's father was very unkind to Danny's mother about her wanting to read and write. He's afraid . . . for that reason. Did I say that right, Danny? Is that how you feel?"

Again the boy nodded without looking up.

Frederick moved closer and knelt down near Lily and Danny. He took Lily's hand and squeezed it to offer silent reassurance while he said with gentle encouragement, "There's nothing to be afraid of, Danny. We will keep you safe."

Both Frederick and Lily were startled when Danny lifted his head abruptly and snapped, "You . . . can't promise! You . . . you . . . can't promise! Papa . . . find me. He find me!"

Frederick exchanged a glance with Lily in which she silently expressed her hope that he would know how to answer. He kept hold of Lily's hand and put his other hand carefully on Danny's arm. "We will always be honest with you, Danny. I promise you that. And you're right. We can't promise that something bad won't happen. We don't know what your papa will do when he realizes you're gone. But we can promise you that all of the people who know you're here are very good at keeping secrets, and we all want more than anything to keep you here where you can be safe, and we will do *everything* we can to make that happen. Do you believe me?" Danny nodded, seeming less afraid; he clearly needed complete honesty, and knowing they were realistic about what might and might not happen made him more willing to trust them.

"For now," Frederick said, "let's take it one day at a time. Every day that you're with us will be a good day, and we won't worry too much about the next day. Does that sound fair?"

Danny nodded, and Frederick realized that for all of the boy's limitations in speaking, he had no troubling understanding what was said to him. "And whatever happens," Frederick went on, "learning to read and write is a grand thing, and we will keep it a secret if you like. No one ever has to know you can read or write if you don't want them to. What do you think? Would you like to start this afternoon?"

Danny nodded again—not with enthusiasm, but there wasn't any hint of fear.

A moment later Mary arrived with a breakfast tray. Lily asked Danny if it was all right for Mary to sit with him for a few minutes while he ate his breakfast so that she could step into the hall. Eagerly distracted by the food, the child nodded before he moved to sit at the little table where Mary was setting out sausages and eggs, warm scones, and two kinds of jam. Frederick's last glance at Danny before he went into the hall showed the boy's complete disbelief over such an abundance of food. It broke Frederick's heart and at the same time filled him with joy. Once again he felt ashamed to think of how adamantly he had tried to stop Lily from rescuing this child.

Lily followed Frederick out of the room and closed the door behind her.

"How are you?" he asked. "You look exhausted."

They'd been up half the night getting Danny settled in, but she confirmed it was more than that when she said, "He had nightmares. It was dreadful, but he's not the first child I've brought into my home with such a challenge. I believe it will get better with time. I'll get some sleep later. Mrs. Pilfer suggested that we simply pretend I am ill, which would explain the doctor's visit last night. And I'll be able to just remain near Danny until he can feel more at home . . . more safe. Since I'm ill," she smiled subtly, "I should be able to get some rest sometime today."

"It sounds like an excellent plan," Frederick said. "You've told me how you are physically, but . . . this can't be easy for you."

"Nor for you," she said, looking at him with eyes that hinted of her deeper feelings for him.

"But I wasn't up with him in the night trying to soothe away horrible dreams." He touched her face with the back of his hand. "How are you really?"

"Oh, Frederick," she muttered in a shaky voice and leaned her face against his shoulder, at the same time pressing her hands to the front of his waistcoat. "It's so terribly awful. I don't understand how people can be so cruel to children—to anyone for that matter, but especially to children."

"I don't understand it either," Frederick said, putting his arms around her. "But he's here now, and we're going to keep him safe. He will recover from this, Lily; he will. Thanks to you."

She looked up at him. "But what if his father *does* find him here? Do you really think we can keep him hidden safely enough?"

"I think we should pray a great deal for God to make up for whatever way we might fall short in our endeavors on Danny's behalf. God knows each of His children; surely He would want us to keep Danny safe. We will do exactly what I told Danny we would do; we will take it one day at a time."

Lily nodded, seeming assured by his confidence. He prayed his confidence and their combined prayers would see them all safely through this.

"I fear I should have spoken to you first about helping Danny before and after classes. Perhaps I should not have just assumed that you would—"

"I'm glad to help in any way I can; you know that. In truth I had the very same thought."

Lily smiled and put her head on his shoulder, easing her hands around to his back. "You are very good to me, Frederick. I can't imagine what I ever did before you came here."

"I have trouble imagining that myself," he said and pressed a kiss to the top of her head.

"Tell me everything will be all right," she murmured, and he was taken aback by the evidence that she was not as thoroughly confident and unafraid as she generally let on. But her willingness to show her vulnerabilities to him touched his heart, and he wanted nothing more than to be there for her and to protect her and everything she cared about.

"It will be as all right as we can possibly make it, Lily," he said. She looked up at him, and he added, "I will be at your side no matter what happens." Not wanting to sound presumptuous, he added, "If that's what you want."

"More than anything," she said, and he wanted to ask her exactly what that meant. Was she implying that they should abandon every concern for what were considered proper social barriers? He wanted to ask her, but now was not the right time. They'd barely acknowledged their feelings for each other not so many hours ago; they had plenty of time to work out the details. Right now, keeping Danny safe and helping him adjust to the changes in his life were most important above all else; planning the future would have to wait. But Frederick couldn't help but hope with all his heart and soul that what he was coming to share with Lily would last forever. Now that they'd come this far, he couldn't imagine any other possibility.

* * *

Over the next few days, Lily kept close to her rooms under the guise of feeling ill, and no one in the house seemed at all suspicious that anything was out of the ordinary. Those who had been entrusted with the knowledge of Danny's presence so they could help with his care were doing well at behaving normally. And the way they managed to sneak extra food from the kitchen without anyone else noticing had become somewhat of a game that was a source of amusement, especially for Abigail and Mary.

Danny was becoming more relaxed and comfortable with those who interacted with him, but he was especially attached to Lily. He'd already taken to her as a mother figure, and Frederick was once again amazed at her uncanny ability to be so perfectly loving and kind. She'd not even known of this child's existence a week ago, and now it was as if she'd been caring for Danny from his infancy.

For those who were aware of Danny's presence in the house—and the means by which he'd been taken from his home—there was a mutual concern about repercussions from Danny's father. But nothing happened that caused them any alarm. Max had reported that he'd seen Mr. Sawyer at the pub—as he often did on his regular evening visits there—and the old man had given him a hard glare that seemed to imply some kind of suspicion or anger. But Max had ignored him, pretending not to notice, and he'd immediately reported the incident to Lily, who had then discussed it with Frederick. They agreed that Mr. Sawyer might be able to lay legal claim on his son if he got the law involved, but it was highly likely that he wouldn't want the law to know he'd been hiding a child in his cellar. Even though Frederick knew from some past experiences as a vicar—and as a teacher—that there were no laws that protected a child from abuse or neglect by a parent, certain judges and barristers could assert their influence one way or another, and he believed that something as overt as hiding a child for years would be frowned upon and Mr. Sawyer could be in trouble for it—but not necessarily. Frederick knew they were walking a fine line having Danny in their custody, but Mr. Sawyer probably knew the same about his own behavior regarding the child. For now, they were simply grateful that the police hadn't shown up, and they hoped that if that happened, Danny could remain safely hidden. If Mr. Sawyer suspected that Lily Broadbent had anything to do with the disappearance of his son, it didn't seem likely he could do anything about it. They could only pray that was the case.

Frederick worked with Danny for an hour or so every morning and every afternoon—with the exception of Sunday—and enjoyed the time they shared, even though Danny's limitations were challenging. It quickly became evident that Danny's father had done a lot of talking, which was Danny's only exposure to *any* human being and any conversation—except that it had mostly been one-sided since Danny hadn't been allowed to speak much more than answering questions or spouting responses that would keep his father's anger to a minimum. Still, Danny was eager to learn, and within just a few days, Frederick could see him opening up more and responding well to what he was learning. Frederick just had to look past the reasons for Danny's challenges and try not to think about it; if he allowed himself to think even for a minute about the monstrous behavior of Danny's father, he became utterly incensed. He focused instead on the indications of Danny coming out of his shell of fear; and every little step Danny made toward behaving more like a normal child warmed Frederick's heart.

Frederick managed to get a little bit of time alone with Lily each day, usually late in the evening after Danny had gone to sleep. They had begun a habit of sitting close together on a sofa in her sitting room while they talked about the day, the children, and each other. It had become comfortable and natural to hold her hand or to put his arms around her. And even to kiss her. Although becoming comfortable with their growing closeness and affection did not make him at all unappreciative of how remarkable it felt to be sharing such a relationship with Lily Broadbent. In the days since they had crossed this boundary, he had contemplated deeply where he stood and how he felt, even though so much of his time—and Lily's—had been focused on Danny, as well as keeping everything else in the house as normal as possible, especially for the other children. He and Lily had not discussed their feelings for each other; each evening they both reached a point of exhaustion before they'd even fully expressed their concerns and observations about the children—most especially Danny. But as Frederick sat close to Lily with his arm around her shoulders and holding her hand, he noticed they had less to say about Danny, mostly because he was doing fairly well.

"Lily," he said and kissed her brow, "I think we need to talk about . . . us. So much has been going on, but . . . we can't just assume that we know each other's thoughts . . . and feelings in regard to . . . this situation."

Lily eased back to look at him. "Of course," she said. "We should talk. Say whatever you need to say, Frederick. As in all things, we must be completely honest with each other. I know the situation is . . . unusual, but . . . none of that matters, does it?"

"None of *what* matters?" he asked, hoping to assess the temperature of her thoughts on the possible future of their relationship. He knew well what he wanted, and he didn't have to question whether or not it was right—at least for him it was right. But it was her feelings that mattered most to him.

"What others might think," she said. "Any . . . expectations or . . . imaginary divisions that have been made up by people for generations that really have no meaning—at least to me they don't matter."

"What are you saying, Lily?" he asked and touched her face, offering a silent inference of his own opinion on the topic.

Lily leaned her face against his hand. "I'm saying that I don't care about any of that; it's what you and I feel that matters, what you and I want."

Frederick looked into her eyes and tried to hear his own thoughts over the sound of his beating heart. Their future could very well be hanging in the balance of this conversation, these decisions. And, oh, how he wanted a future with her! He couldn't imagine any other possibility. But in spite of all she'd said—and his agreement with it—he still couldn't quite get past the fact that he worked for her, and while she might have grown up even more poor and lowly than he had, she had married into great wealth, and with it she'd become a very powerful woman. He didn't feel intimidated by her wealth *or* her power. He respected her deeply for the way she used both with courage and strength of character. But he was finding it difficult to reach beyond the established barriers between them to say what he knew a man should be saying.

"What *do* you want, Lily? What do you feel? Ask anything of me, and I will do it for you. Anything!"

"Then marry me," she said, and he took in a ragged breath. He searched her expression for some sign of humor but found none. "Give me one good reason we shouldn't get married, Frederick. You must forgive me if I'm being too bold or forward, but I have pondered the situation between us and my feelings for you a great deal, and I fear that in spite of the equality we share in our personal relationship, you might be hesitant to ask for my hand."

Frederick couldn't deny that she was right. He'd hoped that marriage would be the outcome of all that was blossoming between them, but he had sincerely wondered how he would cross that line with her and not be seen as trying to take control of her fortune. He knew other people would see it that way, but it was how Lily felt that mattered. Given the brief number of days that had passed since they'd acknowledged their deeper feelings for each other, talk of marriage seemed ludicrous. But in reality, he and Lily had been close for months, and they knew each other well. There was no part of him that doubted this was the right course for his life.

While Frederick was trying to find the best words to answer her question, he was startled by the way she moved away from him and stood abruptly. She walked to the window and moved the curtain to look out, as if she might be seeing some kind of escape.

"What's wrong?" he asked and followed her.

"I fear I've done it again," she said.

"Done *what*?" he asked, studying her profile in the dim light, wishing he could read her thoughts. "Talk to me, Lily."

"I can tend to become overbearing when I want something." She sighed and put a hand to the window, leaning her weight against it. "Mr. Broadbent observed this about me and brought my attention to it, and I knew he was right. He told me he found it endearing, but others might not see it that way. I believe he was right about that as well."

Frederick was ready to tell her that she should never apologize for the facets of her character that made it possible for her to do all the good she did. But she turned to face him, and there was no apology in her countenance, only confidence and determination. "I had to learn to take care of myself in order to survive, Frederick; I had to learn to declare my needs and desires and never to expect someone else to simply guess what those might be. I cannot deny that Mr. Broadbent saved me in many ways when he brought me here and gave me work. And when he chose to marry me, my life became richly blessed. But that doesn't mean I wouldn't have found a way to survive if I'd never met him. And he knew that. He respected me for that. He told me I should never let go of those qualities in myself and that I should never let him or any other man tell me how to make my decisions; he told me I should strive to live up to my full potential as a woman and as an equal human being to him and to every individual of the human race—no matter their social station. I know he was right, Frederick. I've tried to live that way. But I know that as human beings, sometimes our strengths can also be our weaknesses. And I've never been in a situation such as this; I've never felt this way before. I would never want to offend you; I would never want to say or do anything that made you feel anything less than my equal in every way. I need the strength of a man in my life, Frederick, and I want to be the kind of woman that can offer a man all that a woman should. But I can't change who I am in here." She pressed a fist over her heart. "I want to share my life with you, Frederick. This is not impulsive or irrational; it's quite the opposite. But in spite of every practical reason that I believe this is a good decision, I also cannot deny that I have never felt such . . . passion . . . over anything or anyone. I never understood why love could make people behave in ways that were completely rash and senseless. Until now. I've had to work very hard to make certain I'm thinking rationally, but I know that I am. I know what I want, and now you know it, too. So tell me, Frederick. Do you want what . . ."

Frederick pressed his lips to hers and felt her take in an astonished breath.

"Lily," he whispered when their lengthy kiss was finished, "I agree entirely with Mr. Broadbent. He surely must have been a very wise man. And I'm so grateful to him for bringing you here and making it possible for *me* to come here and be a part of your life. I do *not* see you as too forward or overbearing. I admire your strength, Lily. And it would be nothing but an honor to stand at your side through the rest of this life and into the next. Your ability to speak your mind and to step forward to try and right the wrongs in this world are two of the many, many things I love about you." He heard her gasp softly. "And I do love you, Lily. I love you in a way I never knew it was possible to love. I too believe there is every practical reason we should be together, but I also believe that the way I feel about you could make me abandon *all* reason just to spend my life with you."

"Oh, Frederick," she murmured and pressed her lips to his. "I love you as well." She took his face into her hands. "I cared for my husband, and I know he cared for me. But it was never like this. It was not even close to this. I have never felt this way before, and I think I would be a fool to believe I could ever feel this way twice in a lifetime. You are everything I could have ever hoped for."

Frederick put an arm around her waist and drew her closer, smiling before he kissed her again. "Then we have yet one more thing in common," he muttered close to her lips and kissed her again. "I've lost count of all the things we have in common."

"Practically everything, I think," she said and urged him to kiss her again.

Frederick felt that passion she'd referred to sparking to life inside of him and knew that he needed to be cautious and never give her any reason to feel like he didn't respect her. He stepped back and took her shoulders into his hands. "The answer is yes, Lily; yes, I will marry you. And you're right, I would have found it difficult to ask, but I would have come to it eventually. This is the conversation I've been wanting to have." He touched her face. "I feel nothing but grateful, Lily. I love you so much."

She sighed and smiled and closed her eyes, putting her hand over his. "That's exactly what I wanted to say," she murmured, and he kissed her once more before he hurried out of the room, knowing he'd reached his limit on how much time he could spend with her alone, late at night—especially given the topic of conversation. He figured it went without saying that they would discuss plans and arrangements for their marriage and their future at the next possible opportunity. He'd never felt so happy and so hopeful in all his life.

* * *

Lily had barely finished sharing breakfast with Danny when Mrs. Pilfer informed her that her solicitor had just arrived and needed to speak with her. The household—including the children—had been informed that Lily was doing better and would soon be able to resume her normal routine. Her feigned illness was becoming less necessary now that Danny was adjusting and feeling more comfortable in the care of Abigail or Mary, who had each spent a great deal of time with him. And he also had time every day with Frederick. The hours between Danny's lessons with the tutor were filled with doing the reading and writing exercises he'd been assigned, and already his improvement had given him the zeal to enjoy his progress, along with the excitement of actually being able to read books on his own. He'd also been given some toys to play with and some puzzles which he particularly enjoyed. Frederick had also allowed him stewardship over a large atlas filled with maps of many places in the world, and Danny loved to look at it for hours. The child was beginning to comprehend life beyond a dark cellar.

Lily left Danny studying the atlas intently, with Mary close by to keep an eye on him. She tried not to be nervous about whatever her solicitor might want. She was determined not to appear—or even feel—guilty for any reason. Her conscience was clear with God; she only wished she could know that the law would support her with the same measure of ethics. She went to the drawing room slowly as she held to the pretense of recovering from an illness.

Lily entered the room to find Mr. Key pacing near a row of large windows. His demeanor put her on edge, but she forced a calm facade, certain he could have no idea about the situation with Danny.

"This is a surprise," she said, closing the door behind her.

"Forgive my coming unannounced," he said and stopped his pacing to face her. "And for the early hour. Something's come to my attention that I felt you should know about right away, and I must leave later today in order to represent a client in London. I'll be away for several days and didn't want this matter to wait."

"Of course," she said and sat down, motioning for him to do the same. "Tell me."

Mr. Key took a seat, and Lily felt a renewed gratitude to have this man she trusted implicitly dealing with matters over which she had very little understanding. Her husband had worked with him for years, and she'd become fond of Mr. Key long before Mr. Broadbent's unexpected death. It had been Mr. Key who'd informed her that she'd inherited the entirety of her husband's fortune, and he had encouraged her to use it well and wisely in worthwhile endeavors. He had helped with the legal facets of each one of the adoptions of her children, and he'd gone out of his way and put in far more effort on her behalf than his fees would have required. She admired and respected him, and she knew he would always have her best interests at heart. In truth, she believed he would completely understand her reasons for illegally taking Danny into her care, but she had no intention of telling him about it unless the matter became public and she needed his help to keep Danny safe. For now she simply exhibited calm curiosity over what he might consider to be a problem worthy of his unexpected visit.

"The matter is regarding the recent changes we made to your will," he said, and she breathed in some relief. "It might be nothing, but I felt it was important for you to know exactly where it stands."

Lily prepared herself to hear what her solicitor might say while her thoughts were preoccupied with the children upstairs, all of whom she loved so dearly. And the man who had claimed her heart in ways she never thought possible. She only wanted to be certain that everything would be all right for all of them.

Chapter Seven

THE SOLUTION

"As ALWAYS, I AM APPRECIATIVE of your extra efforts on my behalf," Lily said to Mr. Key.

"On a hunch I decided to recheck the laws in regard to your specific concerns—about the care of the children and the management of the estate—should anything happen to you. I'm afraid it's one of those matters that is open to some amount of personal interpretation. In spite of your wishes being made specifically clear, there is a terrible chasm in the law when it comes to a woman's rights concerning property—and the care of children. Because these children have no living relatives—at least none who would lay proper claim to them—I cannot guarantee that your wishes would be heeded, my dear. Turning everything you have over to one of your employees is something a judge may not deem appropriate or suitable. I don't agree with the law in that respect, but it's one of so many things beyond my ability to control. I always hate saying this, but I have to say it, Lily. If you were a man this would not be an issue."

"I see," she said, trying to suppress her fury beneath the longtime understanding she had that it would do her no good. "So if I were a man, I could will my property and the care of my children any way I might choose? But as a woman, even the legality of my being the children's adoptive mother could be in question."

"I'm afraid so. We both knew when you took the children in that such would be the case. But you're young and healthy, Lily. I don't think either of us has had any cause for concern that you might not be able to care for the children until they were adults." He looked at her through narrowed eyes. "Is there something you're not telling me? Some reason for this sudden concern?"

I could be arrested for kidnapping, Lily thought immediately. But she kept that thought to herself and instead shared her other source of concern. "Last week I inadvertently exposed myself to chicken pox when I visited a family with ill children, and I don't ever recall having the illness as a child." She saw his brow furrow with concern but pressed on. "I understand it can be much more serious when contracted as an adult. Apparently it can take a couple of weeks to know if I've got it, and it's only contagious while symptoms are present, but . . ."

"Well, you needn't worry about me; I clearly remember having the pox when I was a child. Dreadfully miserable. What of the children? The rest of the household? If you become ill, are any of them—"

"The household is aware of my exposure, and everyone here knows they've already had the illness, which makes them immune." She left out any mention of Danny, knowing he couldn't be spoken of at all. Danny had no recollection of ever being ill, but then he'd never been in contact with other people at all. She felt concerned that he too might become ill but had discussed it with Frederick, and they believed that as soon as she felt any symptoms—*if* she became ill—she just had to stay away from Danny. Although there was the disconcerting fact that if Danny didn't get the illness as a child he would likely get it eventually and be worse off in facing higher risks.

Lily forced her mind away from thoughts of Danny and focused on the present conversation with Mr. Key. "Even the youngest of the children have had the illness, so that's a blessing. But you can understand how the possibility of my becoming severely ill would cause me some concern. Of course, a proper will should be in place regardless. We never know when something unforeseen might happen. Given the present circumstances—on the chance I might become ill—I want to know everything is in order."

"Well," Mr. Key said while removing his glasses so that he could rub his eyes with a thumb and forefinger, "I think your concern is warranted. I hate the idea of your becoming ill, Lily. But we must have the faith that you'll get through it. Still, you're right. We must do everything we can to ensure the care of the children . . . and we certainly don't want your staff to be suddenly without work or a home. If the estate falls into the hands of the government, which it would if there's no legal owner, it could be tied up in legalities for . . . who knows how long."

A silence fell between them, which was typical when a problem needed to be addressed and they were both thinking about possible solutions. Lily uttered a silent prayer, as was her habit, and was so startled by how quickly an idea appeared clearly in her mind that she actually gasped.

"What is it, my dear?" Mr. Key asked with concern.

She looked at him firmly while she allowed the idea to settle in with more certainty before she dared speak it aloud. She felt so amazingly comfortable—and comforted—with the solution that her vision became blurred by the mist of tears clouding her eyes. But Mr. Key had seen her cry many times, and she certainly wasn't embarrassed.

"Talk to me, Lily," Mr. Key said, putting a fatherly hand on her arm.

"If the law puts high favor on the rights of a man," she began, "then I simply need to know that everything that matters to me is in the care of a man I trust completely."

"Which is exactly what you said to me when we made the changes to your will, my dear. But I'm afraid simply willing everything to this Mr. Woodstone is not sufficient to be absolutely certain that—"

"But when a woman marries, everything she owns legally becomes the property of her husband—which we both agree in most cases is a travesty—but . . . if he's a good man, a trustworthy man, a man who truly loves the children and—"

"What are you saying, Lily?" he asked, and she felt an increasing gratitude for their comfortable relationship and the many years he had assisted and sustained her.

"Oh, Mr. Key," she muttered and took hold of his hand, both to keep her own from trembling and to get his full attention, "it's a miracle. God's hand is truly in my life."

"I don't understand."

"Mr. Woodstone," she went on. "I chose to will everything to him because I *do* trust him, because he *is* a good man, the best of men. But Mr. Key . . . I love him and he loves me. We've told no one, but just last night we discussed the possibility of marriage . . . eventually. But why not now? He and I both know it's inevitable. We simply must get married before anything can happen to me." She tightened her hold on his hand and intensified her gaze, trying to measure the reasons for his astonished expression and how he might respond. When he didn't speak, she asked, "Would that not solve every legal problem?"

"Um . . ." He looked away as if to think more clearly. "Um . . . I believe it would, Lily. Socially, it's a disastrous step, but I know you don't care about that." He looked at her again with a severity she had rarely seen. "Are you certain? Are you absolutely certain?"

"I've never been more certain of anything! You know the deep conviction I felt over each of the children, how I just knew when I found the ones that were meant to be mine. What I feel for Frederick is all of that and more. And he has proven over time the depth of his integrity . . . and his goodness."

"Then perhaps it *is* a miracle, Lily. And a very timely one. Heaven forbid that you should leave this world for any reason before your time. I want you to live long enough to become a grandmother, to see these children settled into lives that are successful and independent. But when it comes to helping people settle their affairs in a will, I know the power that peace of mind can bring to a person. Beyond that, Lily, it would do my heart good to know that you're not alone. To think of the children actually having a father is . . . well . . . it might make an old man cry if I were to think about it too long."

"No need for tears," she said and kissed his cheek. "All will be well. I just need to know that every possibility is taken care of so that I *can* have peace of mind. Now, I need you to tell me, if I get married while you are away . . . and something happens to me before you are able to make any further changes to my will . . . might I be assured that—"

"If you are legally married, Lily, I can make certain your husband has control of all that you might leave behind. It would only take some simple paperwork for him to legally become the adoptive father of your children as long as he is your husband."

Lily leaned back and sighed, letting go of his hand to press both of hers to the sides of her face as if that might help her take in the enormity of what all of this meant. She heard the laughter of joy and relief before she realized it had come from herself. She talked with Mr. Key a short while longer, discussing the most practical way to go about seeing her plans through, making certain that everything was legal and proper—and to ensure that it could all be taken care of before she might become ill, given that it was a distinct possibility.

After Mr. Key left, Lily slowly wandered the halls of her enormous home, pondering all she was feeling, and praying that she would be guided along the right course for her future—and that of everyone else involved. The timing of her conversation last night with Frederick and Mr. Key's visit today were far too uncanny for her to believe they were anything but evidence of God's hand in her life. She'd seen such strange timing before in regard to other things in her life—mostly the way she'd been guided to each of the children now in her care. The timing of events combined with the distinct warmth she felt in her heart could not be ignored.

When she had settled firmly on how she felt and where she stood, she went to the classroom and took a deep breath before she entered quietly through the door at the back, where she often went to observe. For a long moment, before the children became aware of her presence, she met Frederick's eyes across the room. His love for her shone so strongly from his countenance that she was overcome with a quivering that started deep inside her chest and radiated out through her entire body. She smiled at him, hoping he could feel her silent expression of love for him. The children all turned at the same time to see the reason for their teacher stopping in the middle of a sentence. Then they all flocked toward her, full of laughter and excitement since she'd not seen any of them for days. She'd missed them terribly, but in order to properly pretend she was ill—for Danny's sake—she'd needed to stay away from the children. She laughed as she knelt down in order to be closer to their average height, and hugged each of them tightly in turn. A glance toward Frederick made her insides quiver again to see him leaning casually against his desk, his arms folded over his chest. He was wearing an expression of delight and contentment as he observed her interactions with the children.

Lily took a few minutes to let each of the children tell her a little of what they'd been doing. They asked if she was feeling better and told her they'd missed her.

"I've missed you too," she said. "Every one of you. But I will be there this evening to read with you before bedtime—I promise." She glanced at Frederick and added, "I need to speak privately with Mr. Woodstone for a few minutes. Do you think you can each be good and work quietly on your reading while I do? We'll be just out in the hall, so we'll be able to hear if you get up to any nonsense." She winked as she said it, and they all laughed. Her heart felt so filled with the love she'd come to share with these children that she could hardly believe how it had expanded to be filled again with the love she'd come to feel for Frederick.

The children all went back to their desks with some nudging and encouragement. Lily stepped out into the hall, and Frederick followed her, closing the door behind him.

"Are you all right?" he asked, taking both her hands into his.

"I am," she said and was indescribably relieved when he kissed her.

"Oh, so am I!" he said with a smile, and she laughed softly. With more seriousness, he said, "Mary told me Mr. Key had come to see you. Is something wrong?"

"Nothing that isn't fixable," she said. "It had nothing to do with Danny."

"Oh, good," he said with overt relief, and she knew he shared her concerns. "I couldn't help wondering."

"If anything legal *does* come up about Danny, I know Mr. Key will do everything in his power to help us. The problem is that he is controlled by the law—as we all are."

"Yes," Frederick said soberly. "So what *did* he come to talk to you about so early in the morning?"

"It was about the changes to my will," she said, keeping hold of his hands. "He's concerned that it might not hold up legally—given that I'm a woman and women have so few rights in regard to property. And he's concerned about the fact that with my children being adopted, the absence of another parent might not necessarily make those adoptions hold up if something were to happen to me."

"Nothing's going to happen to you, Lily," he said as if saying so might make it true.

"Except perhaps the chicken pox," she said gravely. "Or I could get arrested for kidnapping."

"I don't want to even think about either possibility," he said, sounding almost angry.

"And yet they are both possibilities," she said, squeezing his hands. "And neither of us can afford to be impractical enough to deny that fact."

"I know," he said and let go of her hands to wrap her in his arms, as if he could protect her from anything bad *ever* happening to her.

Lily looked up at him and decided to just get to the point and say what needed to be said. "It occurred to me while I was visiting with Mr. Key that there is an obvious solution to these concerns. I was praying when the answer came, Frederick, and I've been praying about it since he left. I know in my heart it's right. But you have to know it for yourself. You must never make any decision based on my opinions and beliefs, just as I know you would never expect me to make any decision based on anything but what I know for myself."

"Of course," he said, his brow furrowed with confusion. "What decision do you mean, exactly?"

"Frederick," she said and pressed her hands more tightly to his back, "the law dictates that a man has many more rights in regard to the ownership of property—and the adoption of children. That's why I changed my will to give all of those rights to you. But Mr. Key fears the will is not enough. The solution is obvious, is it not?"

"Is it?" he asked, still confused.

"Once we are married, Frederick, everything I have will legally be yours." She felt him take in a sharp breath and knew that he understood the enormity of what she meant. "Mr. Key assured me that if we are legally married, the estate and all matters pertaining to it will be yours. And he told me it would only take some paperwork for you to legally become the adoptive father of the children, and there would never be the fear of having them go back to the lives they left behind."

"I . . . don't know what to say, Lily," he murmured quietly. "It's what I want . . . I mean, what I want is to be your husband and to be a father to the children. I want that more than anything. But I feel so unworthy of the wealth . . . and the responsibility of the estate, and—"

"Which is exactly how I once felt. But no one is more worthy than you, Frederick. You would honor the responsibility with integrity and compassion; you would use what we have been blessed with for good, just as I have tried to do." She sighed and made a point she knew was important. "I believe marriage is inevitable for us, Frederick. Do you feel the same? Be truthful with me."

"I will always be truthful with you, Lily. And yes, I believe it is inevitable. I can't imagine my life without you."

"Then we only need to take that step soon rather than waiting."

"Soon?" he echoed. "What are you saying?"

"I'm saying that we need to go to Scotland and get married before I get ill . . . on the chance that I might get ill."

"Lily." Her name came through his lips on the wake of a trembling breath. "I . . . I . . . don't know what to say. I can't bear the thought of you getting ill."

"That is out of our control, and it is not the point of what I'm proposing. It's a factor in the timing, but it is not the point. We must also consider the possibility that there *will* be repercussions for bringing Danny here. We don't need to talk about that because it's impossible to predict what will happen. But I need to know that everything is taken care of. I need that peace of mind, Frederick. You are an answer to my every prayer, my darling. Please tell me you understand. Please . . . help me make this possible. Share your life with me . . . whatever that life might entail . . . and for whatever amount of time God allows me to stay in this world."

Frederick pressed a hand to her face before he smiled. "Yes, Lily. Yes, of course. The sooner, the better as far as I'm concerned."

Lily laughed and held to him tightly. He laughed as well and wrapped her in his arms, briefly lifting her feet off the floor. After he'd set her back down, she reminded herself that the children couldn't be expected to be on their best behavior for too long without supervision. She looked up at Frederick and hurried to tell him her plan. "As soon as the children are down for the night, we will have Max drive us to where we can take a hired coach to Scotland. If we travel through the night, we can be married in the morning and come straight back and be home in time for supper if all goes well. Everything will be legal and proper, and we both know there isn't a person in this house who wouldn't be thrilled."

Frederick laughed softly. "It sounds too good to be true," he said. "If you're certain it's what you want, I will do everything in my power to make you happy . . . and to honor your trust in me."

"I know you will," she said and lifted her lips to his. "And I will do the same for you. God willing, we will have a long and lovely lifetime together."

"God willing," he repeated and kissed her again.

* * *

Lily quietly made arrangements with each staff member that would need to take on extra work while she and Frederick were gone. Max was more than happy to drive them to the nearest location where a public coach could be hired, and those who helped care for the children and were aware of Danny's presence in the house were more than happy to take over. Rather than trying to keep any secrets in regard to the marriage, Lily and Frederick sat down with the children before supper to explain their plans and their reasons for needing to take care of the matter quickly. They were all thrilled with the prospect of Mr. Woodstone becoming their father as long as he could continue to be their teacher too. Being told about the possibility of Lily becoming ill with chicken pox, the children all expressed their concern, but Lily and Frederick answered their questions in a straightforward manner, both feeling it was best to be honest, which would better enable the children to get through any potential difficulties.

Frederick and Lily also sat down to talk with Danny and explain everything to him. He seemed a little nervous to be without either of them for a full day, but he was easily reassured that Mary and Abigail would take very good care of him, and he also knew that Max and Wally and Mrs. Pilfer would all help keep him safe.

They both spoke to Nellie when she arrived to take over the care of the children after Lily had read them their story and tucked them into bed. She was pleased and declared with a smile, "Didn't I tell you so?" She winked at Frederick, who looked mildly embarrassed as he admitted that she'd been right. Lily could only feel grateful that Frederick's affections were for her and not for Nellie or any other woman. She hoped Nellie would find love in her life, but no one was more perfect for Lily than this man who had become the center of all that mattered to her.

With the children and their governess all informed of their plans, Frederick and Lily went as usual to the kitchen for a late supper with the servants. Frederick made the announcement that they were going to be married. Everyone cheered and applauded, but no one seemed terribly surprised. Lily felt certain that neither of them had been very good at concealing their feelings. Together she and Frederick explained one of the reasons for their belief that they should be married right away. No one liked the possibility that Lily could become ill, but they had all been aware of the possibility since she'd questioned them to see who might be susceptible to the chicken pox soon after she'd been exposed. They were all not only supportive of Lily's decisions, but each and every one of the people who worked for her wished her well, and she knew they genuinely wanted her to be happy. They all felt like family to her, but it was heartening to realize that they shared the same feelings.

After supper Frederick went with Lily to check in on the children to make certain they were all sleeping. She kissed each of their heads as she did every night, and was warmed by the way that Frederick did the same. He had already stepped so naturally into the role of being a father to them. They went together to check on Danny and also found him sleeping.

"I suppose it's time we were off," Lily said as they stepped into the hallway, and Frederick quietly closed the door.

"Lily," he said and took her hands, "are you absolutely certain this is what you want? We can find another way to protect the interests of the children. Don't marry me just because you are afraid that—"

"I want to marry you because I love you," she said fervently. "I know there is no better course for my life than this. But I can understand why the situation could be challenging for you. If you prefer to wait or to—"

"I don't want to wait, Lily, and I don't want anyone but you. Marry me now or marry me in a year; my feelings won't change. If our marrying now gives you peace of mind . . . if it helps the situation, then I am all in favor of it. I just want you to know that I'll support you in caring for the children . . . and the estate . . . in any and every way I can, whether you marry me or not. Just tell me what you want."

"I want to marry you, Frederick," she said, easing closer to him. "I pray that I don't become ill, and I'm glad to know that even if I do no one else in the house will get it. But if I *do* become ill, I want you nearby . . . I *need* you to get through whatever may come. I don't want to bring hardship into your life, Frederick, but if you're not my husband, it would hardly be proper for you to be with me while I'm ill."

"I *want* to be with you whatever happens. I'm tired of being alone, Lily." He pressed his forehead to hers. "I didn't even realize how lonely I felt until . . . until I fell in love with you and I wanted to be with you every possible minute. Nothing could make me happier."

Lily laughed softly and moved her head to his shoulder. "Then I suggest you go and pack a few things." She drew back and looked at him. "I'll meet you at the carriage in half an hour."

"I'll be there," he said as he kissed her quickly, then hurried off.

Lily took a deep breath and tried to calm the quickened pace of her heart before she went to her bedroom to find Mary already packing her things.

"I don't need much," Lily told her. "We're not staying anywhere."

"No, but you'll want to at least freshen up and change before you get married," Mary said and turned from the wardrobe to display a dress she'd just taken out. It was mostly white with some blue trim, and Lily had only worn it once to a social she had felt obligated to attend a very long time ago. "I thought this would be a good choice. I hope you agree. I've aired it out, and the fabric is not the kind to wrinkle too badly when it's packed."

"I think it's perfect, Mary," Lily said. "Thank you. I honestly hadn't even thought of such a thing, but you're right. I appreciate your foresight."

"May I hug you?" Mary asked, and Lily felt surprised, knowing they'd hugged before.

"Of course," she said and opened her arms.

They shared a tight, sisterly embrace before Mary drew back and wiped tears from her cheeks. "Forgive me. I just . . . I'm so happy for you. I don't know if I've ever told you how much I love working for you. And I so want you to be happy; you *deserve* to be happy."

"Thank you, Mary." Lily took her hand. "That means so much to me. You'll take good care of Danny for me; I know you will. And the others."

"Of course. They'll be fine. And you'll be back before you know it." Mary turned to carefully fold the white dress and place it on the top of a few other items in a portmanteau before she closed it. "I hope you can get some sleep in the carriage. But either way you can catch up on your rest when you get back. We'll take care of everything."

"Thank you," Lily said again and hurried to be ready for a long journey.

* * *

Frederick paced near the waiting carriage while Max and Wally hovered nearby, teasing him about having the nerves of a prospective groom. Even though Max would be driving the carriage, Wally had helped harness the horses and was there to see them off. Frederick appreciated their humor since it actually helped ease his nerves. He simply felt anxious to get away and have Lily safely in his care. He didn't want anything to go wrong before they could follow through on this impulsive and wonderful plan to begin their lives together.

Frederick heard the door, and his heart quickened, but it was only Mary bringing a portmanteau, which she handed to Max. "It hardly weighs a thing," she said to the men. "But I insisted that she at least needed a proper dress to be married in."

"Indeed," Max said. "I'll take good care of it."

Mary smiled and nodded toward Frederick, who returned the gesture before she went back into the house, saying over her shoulder, "She'll just be a moment."

Less than a minute later, Lily appeared wearing a dark cloak that was a stark contrast to her pale skin and hair illuminated by the moonlight.

"I'm ready to go," she said loudly enough for Max and Wally to hear, but she was looking directly at Frederick.

"Shall we, then?" Frederick asked and took her hand to help her into the carriage after Wally had opened the door. A minute later the carriage was in motion.

They sat across from each other, and minutes passed in silence until Frederick asked, "Are you all right?"

"I'm extremely all right, Frederick. And you?"

"Oh, very, very all right," he said, and they both laughed softly.

"I confess to being very tired," she said. "I don't think I've slept very well ever since we brought Danny home."

Frederick loved the way she talked about Danny now being *home*. He prayed it would stay that way. "It would be wise for us to both try and get some sleep, I believe." He motioned to some pillows that had been left on both seats and added, "Apparently Mrs. Pilfer anticipated that and wanted us to be comfortable."

"Oh, how lovely," Lily said and fluffed one of the pillows as she curled up on the seat and lay down, pulling her cloak over herself like a blanket. Frederick followed her example and attempted to get comfortable on the other seat. He was barely a little taller than Lily, but she was thin and delicate, and the carriage seat accommodated her tiny frame more easily than it did his own. Still, he was able to eventually find a position that felt relaxing. When he became still, he saw the shadow of Lily's hand reaching toward him through the darkness. "I love you, Frederick Woodstone," she murmured.

"And I love you . . . my precious Lily."

He squeezed her hand before she let go and tucked her hand beneath the pillow on which she'd lain her head. He doubted that he could actually sleep, but the movement of the carriage had a soothing effect, and the next thing he knew he was coming awake to the realization that the carriage was stopping. They would be moving into a hired coach now. The transfer was made within minutes, and they both considered it good fortune that they did not need to share the coach with other travelers. Keeping hold of Mrs. Pilfer's pillows as they went from one coach into another while their minimal luggage was made secure, they soon got comfortable once again.

Once again Frederick didn't believe he could sleep, but he did. His next awareness was that daylight had altered the atmosphere inside the coach, and he had a clear view of Lily sleeping on the opposite seat. She looked so beautiful that it took his breath away. He wondered what miracle had brought him into her home and into her heart. The very idea that she loved him and wanted to share her life with him was something he'd still not been able to comprehend. He could only thank God for blessing him so thoroughly and pray that she would remain safe and healthy and they might be able to share a long and full life together—with their brood of a dozen children. He smiled to think of them at home, imagining their routine for the day and what it would be like when he and Lily returned as a married couple—hopefully in time to tuck their children into bed.

The coach slowed down significantly, and Frederick glanced out the window to see that they were on the street of the town which he assumed was their destination; he realized he hadn't even known exactly where they were going. Max had made the arrangements, and apparently it wasn't terribly uncommon for people in England to go to Scotland to be married, where the laws were different and it was possible to avoid the waiting periods required in England. Lily came awake at the change of the carriage's rhythm and sat up sleepily. She smiled when she saw him.

"Good morning, my love," he said. "Did you sleep?"

"Better than I expected to, which is certainly good. And you?"

"The same," he said and crossed the carriage to sit beside her, wrapping her in his arms. She rested the side of her face against his chest, and he pressed a kiss into her hair. "It's our wedding day, Lily. Nothing will ever again be the same for either of us."

"Everything will be better," she said and eased a little closer, if that were possible.

The coach left them at an inn, where they were offered accommodations sufficient to freshen up, change their clothes, and eat a good breakfast. Apparently this was a place accustomed to assisting those who came and went very quickly in order to be married. The people were kind, the atmosphere pleasant, and the food delicious. When Lily appeared wearing white, the reality of their situation settled in a little more, and Frederick felt both giddy and solemnly reverent regarding what would take place between them today. Her dress was more elegant than what she normally wore, and he suspected it had been made for a social event. It was trimmed with blue ribbon—a blue that was very near the color of her eyes.

"You look beautiful," he said and meant it before he kissed her quickly, then he helped her with her chair so they could share breakfast before they would walk the short distance to where they would be married. While she'd been changing, he'd made certain all the arrangements were complete and that everything was in order.

"This is lovely," she said, glancing around at the little room with large windows where the innkeeper's wife had brought them to have their meal. It had obviously been built this way to accommodate people coming or going from hasty weddings, since it offered some privacy from the noisy dining room of the inn, and it was also decorated to create a more pleasant atmosphere than the plain practicalities of a typical pub.

"It is indeed," Frederick said. "We must thank Max for sending us to the right place."

"He's very social and quite sharp," Lily said. "It seems he always knows what's going on, and he knows people who know people who can get just about anything done."

"That's good to know," Frederick said, and they shared their delicious meal mostly in silence, except for some speculating about how the children might be doing, assuring each other that the little ones were in good hands and all would surely be well.

After they'd filled up on the more than ample breakfast, they both freshened up and left their things at the inn. They walked, holding hands, through the pleasant air of late summer, pausing only long enough for Frederick to purchase a bouquet of flowers in a variety of colors from a delightful woman who treated them as if they were the only bride and groom she had ever encountered; however, it was obvious that she created her bouquets for this very purpose and that the location from which she sold them had been carefully planned.

Lily took the flowers from Frederick and held them close to her face, closing her eyes to inhale their fragrance. She opened her eyes to look at him as if she were absorbing each moment of this day into her memory. "Thank you," she said. "They're beautiful; they're perfect. Everything is perfect."

"Yes, it is," he said, and they walked on.

The ceremony was brief but not lacking in the importance and solemnity of what it represented. Frederick found it difficult to hold back the temptation to cry while their vows were being spoken, but he saw the glisten of tears in Lily's eyes and knew she felt the same. When they shared a tender kiss to seal their marriage, he felt as if they had just crossed a bridge together into a magical world that neither of them had ever visited but they both knew was the best place they could possibly go, and they were going there together. He wasn't naive enough to believe that marriage would magically make life easier or that it would prevent difficulties from occurring. But he did believe that sharing his life with Lily would make it better, and he knew she believed it too. Together they could take on life's challenges more effectively, and they would never have to be alone. He simply refused to believe that anything or anyone could ever take her from him. Their reasons for getting married quickly were something he chose not to think about; if she *did* become ill, he would be certain she had the best possible care, and he had to believe she would come through it just fine. And as far as her meddling in Danny's life, he believed that if Mr. Sawyer hadn't come forward by now with any accusations, he likely never would.

In that moment, Frederick believed that everything would be all right, and he chose to push away any foreboding concerns about the possible difficulties that might lay before them. In that moment, he also chose to think only of all that was good, and he could almost tangibly feel what it would be like decades into the future with Lily at his side, the children grown and doing well, and he and Lily having all that was good and sharing that bounty with others at every possible opportunity. It was just as Lily had said: everything was perfect.

Chapter Eight
TAKEN

LILY FELT LIKE A COMPLETELY different person as she walked back to the inn with Frederick's hand in hers. After the newlyweds changed back into their traveling clothes, the innkeeper's wife provided Frederick and Lily with a basket that was apparently part of the services they had paid for, designed specifically for people who came to this place to be married and quickly be on their way to some other destination. In the basket were some lovely baked goods, fresh fruit, and a variety of cheeses, all arranged prettily around a bottle of wine and two pewter goblets with the name of the inn carved into them, meant to be a memento of their visit to this quaint place—which would always be a treasured memory.

The journey home felt entirely different to Lily. It wasn't the obvious difference of it being daylight now instead of traveling in the dark of night. And it wasn't that they were now wide awake as opposed to attempting to get what sleep they could. Just knowing she was now Lily Woodstone made her feel more hope and contentment than she'd ever known. Her previous marriage had given her security and protection; her husband had been kind and very good to her. He had taught her how to be a lady and had given her opportunities she never could have imagined in her previous life. But he'd made it clear from the beginning that it would be a marriage in name only. In many ways she had been relieved about that, but as she'd grown increasingly comfortable in the company of her husband, her loneliness over such a boundary had settled in. She'd often felt as if something was wrong with her that had made him not want to share an intimate relationship. He had often held her hand and offered mild gestures of affection—but he'd treated her more as a very close friend than a wife. She'd admired and respected Mr. Broadbent—

and she always would. And she had certainly grown to love him. But she'd never *been* in love until she'd met Frederick. And she was more glad and grateful than she could ever say to no longer have to be called Mrs. Broadbent. She was Mrs. Woodstone now. And she'd never been happier.

Her happiness erupted in a spontaneous burst of laughter, and Frederick laughed with her before he searched her expression, silently asking the reasons. "I'm just happy," she said.

"So am I," he said and kissed her. With their kiss she eased more fully into his arms, sensing a difference in the way he held her. She was his wife now, and there was no reason to hold back or keep their passion within boundaries that no longer existed. She couldn't define any exact change in the affection they shared or the way they clung to each other, but it was undoubtedly different, and she relished the thought that they would never have to be apart.

An hour or more passed while they did little but just look at each other; they held hands and held to each other, and occasionally he kissed her. They had nothing to say, but it seemed necessary to just gaze into each other's eyes and silently assess the changes taking place in their lives. It occurred to Lily that a traditional marriage was preceded by complicated preparations and followed by grand celebrations. She didn't feel the need for any of that; she'd experienced it before, and it had not made her marriage to Mr. Broadbent any more meaningful. In fact, it was quite the opposite. The brevity of the ceremony she'd shared with Frederick had already impacted her heart and spirit too deeply to comprehend. And yet it *had* been so brief. She could easily imagine that this quick trip to Scotland would become very dreamlike in her memory—and perhaps in his. Even in the present it nearly felt like a dream, a strange separation from their everyday lives. Perhaps all the ceremonious things that generally surrounded a marriage were meant to help the bride and groom—and those who were a part of their lives—take the matter more seriously. But she knew that would not be a problem for her and Frederick. For different reasons, they had each come to this day with a rich need to love and be loved, to be a part of something bigger than living their individual lives separately and alone. They were one now, as the Bible said: one flesh. They were also now one heart, one mind. She knew that marriage didn't necessarily equate to such a union, but with Frederick, being one in all things felt completely possible to her; if not, she never would have had the desire to be married to him. As it was, she could only feel hope and peace and a tender anticipation of all they would share from this day forward.

The basket of food provided them all they needed to get through the hours of traveling until they arrived home. The coach only stopped twice for the sake of necessities and so they could replace the tired horses with fresh ones. They arrived only a few minutes behind schedule to the place where Max had left them the previous evening, and he was there waiting for them.

"Mrs. Woodstone," Max said with a little smirk as Frederick helped her step down from the coach.

"Oh, I like the sound of that," Frederick said and squeezed Lily's hand before he let it go.

"As do I," she said with all the enthusiasm she felt over her new name and the new life it represented. She winked at her husband, then asked of Max, "Is everything all right at home?"

"As good as it ever was," he said. "But o' course the children all miss the both o' you. I doubt they'll be going t' sleep without seeing you—especially young Danny."

"Then we should hurry," Frederick said, and they were quickly on their way home.

In the carriage, Lily's mind turned to the practical matters of returning to the manor as husband and wife. She said to Frederick, "I asked Zed and Levy to move your things to my rooms. I hope that's all right."

Frederick smiled. "Of course it's all right," he said. "I had just intended to take care of it myself. I don't need to be waited on."

"I know that," she said. "I just knew we would likely be tired from the journey, and we'll want to spend some time with the children."

"Of course," he said.

Lily took a deep breath and encouraged herself to say something else that she knew needed to be clarified. "I know there are things that likely go without saying, but I don't want there to be any miscommunication between us . . . therefore I believe it's better to be clear."

"Of course," he said again, this time more fervently. "I would never want you to hold back anything that you feel needs to be said; and I know you would expect the same of me."

"Yes," she said. "I just want you to know that you *are* the head of the household now, and it's important for you to behave accordingly. You know well enough that in our home all people are treated with respect and equality, but I came to learn that I could never forget it was still my home and I had to be a leader and an example to those who work for me and those who lease land on my estate. It's *our* estate now, *our* home. We have the wonderful privilege of providing a home and a living for many people; they deserve to be treated fairly and with kindness, but that doesn't change the fact that they work for us—and it needs to be that way. They need someone to look up to, and they need guidance and direction in their work and sometimes in their lives. I realized a long time ago that I do not need a man to survive or to make important decisions for me. I know you respect the equality between us or we would not be having this conversation. But you *are* my husband now, Frederick. I know we will continue forward with the same routine; the children need you to be their teacher as well as their father. But if decisions need to be made, if you need help with something—anything—you must not shrink from asserting the authority that is now legally and rightfully yours."

Lily took in his stunned expression, even though she could barely see it now that darkness had settled in again. "You seem . . . unsettled over what I just said. Talk to me, Frederick."

"I suppose I just never looked at it that way," he said. "From the start, I've been well aware of the burdens you've carried in regard to the estate and the household. But everything's happened so fast I confess I find it difficult to think of myself in the position of master of the house." He said the last phrase with mild sarcasm. "You know my personality is of a quiet nature, and—"

"You must never alter your personality, Frederick. You must always remain who you are inside; that is the source of your greatest strength and the reason I fell in love with you. I know exactly how you must feel; when Mr. Broadbent died, it was Mr. Ingham and Mrs. Pilfer who helped guide me into filling my role as lady of the house in a way that was proper and necessary. It took me time to adjust, but just as a family needs parents, an estate such as ours needs leadership. As a vicar you had people looking to you for guidance and direction; just consider this a new occupation with similar requirements."

Lily heard him take in a deep breath and let it out slowly. "I suppose I can do that."

"If we'd had this conversation before we went to Scotland, would you have still married me?"

He laughed gently, sounding immediately more relaxed. "Oh, Mrs. Woodstone, nothing and no one could have stopped me from marrying you. No sacrifice is too great, and no task required of me will make me change my mind about that."

Lily laughed with some relief. "I'm glad to hear it. And there's one more thing we need to be clear about."

"What's that?"

"I absolutely love being Mrs. Woodstone. It's the best thing that's ever happened to me."

He laughed again. "Better than being rescued by Mr. Broadbent and given a good life? Better than inheriting a fortune?"

"I will never cease to be grateful for those events in my life," she said with deep sincerity. "Nevertheless, I stand by what I said. Becoming your wife is the best thing that's ever happened to me."

"I'm very glad to hear it," he said, "because I'm in complete agreement." He kissed her in a way that had become comfortable between them, then he kissed her again, and she felt an unfamiliar passion creeping into his affection. She felt almost dizzy as she pressed a hand into his hair and eased closer to him.

"Our wedding day is almost over," he whispered.

"So it is," she whispered back and urged him to kiss her again.

"Do you know what's good about that?"

"What?" she asked, unprepared for the answer he gave her.

"It means that it's nearly time for us to share our wedding *night*."

"So it is," she said again, hearing a dreamy quality in her own voice that accurately represented the tingling she felt all over when he kissed her yet again.

The carriage slowed down as it approached the house, and Frederick eased away from her, chuckling as if he might have been doing something mischievous. As husband and wife, their being engaged in amorous kissing certainly *wasn't* mischievous. But she loved the affection between them and the feeling that they shared a great secret no one else would never know or understand. Her anticipation of all they would yet share made it difficult to breathe, but she turned her thoughts toward her excitement to see the children, and she hurried into the house and up the stairs with Frederick's hand in hers.

Frederick checked his watch and returned it to his waistcoat pocket as they ascended the stairs. "It's almost story time," he declared, and they laughed realizing they shared the same delight over spending time with the children.

Together they went first to check on Danny, knowing he was the most fragile and his isolation had likely made their absence more stark. He was very glad to see them and hugged them both tightly, but he didn't seem at all upset or disoriented by their having been gone. Mary and Abigail had obviously been taking good care of him. They spent a few minutes with him, answering his questions about their having gotten married and reassuring him that everything would continue on as it had, only better.

Lily and Frederick then went to find the other children all gathered for story time, already dressed for bed. Nellie was just trying to get them settled down so she could read to them. When they saw Frederick and Lily come through the door, their excitement could have brought the roof down. They were both assaulted by a wave of hugs and laughter and questions that made the newlyweds laugh heartily as they embraced every child and offered reassurances that all their questions would be answered once they had quieted down.

The children finally settled into their usual places on the carpet with the blankets and pillows they'd brought from their beds. Lily sat on the small sofa where she always sat to read to them, and Frederick sat close beside her, putting his arm around her shoulders. Eleven pairs of eyes focused on the couple, and Lily said, "Instead of reading from a book tonight, we're going to tell you about our adventure while we were away, and you can ask us any question you want."

"We might not answer them," Frederick said lightly, and they all laughed. "But you can ask."

Lucy's hand popped up immediately, and Lily pointed to her. "What is it, Lucy darling?"

Nine-year-old Lucy looked directly at Frederick with the eyes of a child who had known abandonment and severe neglect. "Must we still call you Mr. Woodstone, or may we call you Papa now?"

Every single child spoke up, indicating they also wanted an answer to that question. Lily felt near tears, thinking how desperately they each wanted a father in their lives. She had given all she had to give as a mother to these children, but she could never personally make up for the absence of a father. The children had grown to love Frederick, to look up to him, to respect him, and to enjoy his company. He had long ago earned their trust. She looked at her husband as he glanced at her, as if seeking her approval. She only nodded slightly to indicate that it was entirely up to him how he answered Lucy's question, which she had asked as the self-appointed voice for the entire group.

Frederick looked at the children, meeting each of their eyes for a moment as if to make certain they all knew that what he had to say applied to every one of them. "I will still be teaching you your lessons, and all of the same rules will apply. However . . ." he drawled dramatically and laughed in a way that implied he felt a kind of happiness he simply couldn't hold inside. The children all laughed briefly, as if his laugh had been infectious—even if they didn't know the reasons for it. "However," he repeated, "becoming your father is one of the greatest things that's ever happened to me. I think it's an amazing miracle that I could marry your mother, and just like that," he snapped his fingers, "it makes me your father. It's like a caterpillar popping out of its cocoon to realize it has become a butterfly." More seriously he added, "I want you to know that once some paperwork is taken care of, I will legally be your father in every way, and I will do everything I can to take care of each and every one of you as a father should. In my heart, I've felt like your father for a long time already. It's up to each of you whether or not you feel comfortable calling me that."

The moment he had concluded what he felt he needed to say, the children responded with an apparent need to once again assault both Frederick and Lily with hugs and laughter. They left their pillows and blankets behind and rushed into an awkward yet perfect bundle of little bodies, all wrapping their arms around their parents and each other, clustered together like the flowers in Lily's wedding bouquet. Amidst a variety of voices telling Frederick they wanted to call him Papa from now on, there was a sweet melody of laughter that filled Lily in a way she'd never imagined possible. She couldn't be any happier.

* * *

By the time Frederick and Lily had been able to answer all of the children's questions and get them settled into bed, it was very late, and they were both exhausted from such a long day. To Lily it seemed as if being in Scotland early that morning had been a dream, and Frederick agreed as they walked slowly toward her bedroom—the room they would now share. A short while later, when she felt her way through the dark and climbed into the bed where she'd slept alone for many years, she found Frederick there. He took hold of her hand beneath the covers, and tears tingled in her eyes. A joy too deep to comprehend flooded through her to simply not be alone during the night when the darkness and quiet had a way of amplifying her loneliness. He let go of her hand to put his arm around her, urging her head to his shoulder. He kissed her brow but said nothing except, "I love you, Lily."

Lily eased closer to him in response, fearing that if she spoke, her voice would betray how close she was to tears, and she didn't want to start crying now. She might have expected this moment to be filled with immediate passion, but for now the contentment between them felt relaxing and absolutely perfect. She heard him sigh before he kissed her brow again, and she fell asleep, silently thanking God for the miracle of being Mrs. Woodstone.

* * *

Frederick awoke in the night and momentarily felt disoriented, then he felt Lily shifting in her sleep beside him, and all the pleasant memories of a dreamlike day flooded into his mind, making him smile. He resettled himself to get as close to Lily as he could without waking her, and drifted back to sleep, blanketed in the hope of a bright future with this amazing woman into whose life he had been guided.

When Frederick woke again, the room had just a hint of predawn light, but it was enough for him to see that Lily was awake, watching him with a fascination in her eyes that he believed mirrored his own.

"Good morning," he said and rolled onto his side to look back at her.

"Good morning." She smiled and touched his face with gentle fingertips.

"How long have you been awake?" he asked.

"Only a few minutes," she said. "Almost long enough to believe this is real. Sometimes it feels too good to be true."

"I know what you mean," he said and touched *her* face. "But it *is* true, Lily." He eased closer and kissed her, embarking on an experience he had feared might be awkward or strange, given that neither of them had ever previously been involved in an intimate relationship. But everything they shared was wondrous and beautiful in a way that only strengthened his absolute belief that this cherished facet of marriage was surely one of God's greatest gifts to His children. As a vicar, he had taught the principle that great blessings would come when people chose to preserve intimacy within the bonds of marriage, but he never could have comprehended how great those blessings would be! And yet he knew that all they shared was only beginning; they had a lifetime to live as husband and wife, and he found it difficult to comprehend the full depth of his joy. He chose not to even think about the possibility that anything bad could ever come between them.

They were both careful to not be late in beginning their usual daily routine, not wanting any attention drawn to the fact that in all practicality they should have been somewhere far away on a honeymoon. Of course, all of the adults in the house would understand that and know the changes that had taken place in their relationship now that they were married, and they would be nothing but respectful about it. Still, Frederick and Lily agreed that what they shared privately should remain private. They also knew it was best for the children if their schedules and the dynamics of their lives remained the same. Each one of them had some measure of fragility, and consistency was important in helping them feel safe and secure. Lily was their mother, and she had become the center of that security to them. And now Frederick had become their father, and he needed to become accustomed to assuming that position in their lives, to make it clear to each one of them that they could rely on him to be there for them and to keep them safe, the same way Lily had proven herself to them since they had come into her home. *Their* home, he reminded himself. This was no longer a place where he worked; it was home, and it always would be.

Frederick was surprised by how little time it took to feel completely comfortable in his new role with the children—and in the house. Within a few days he'd become accustomed to the children calling him Papa, and the staff all made it very easy for him to not feel awkward about being in a position to make certain decisions and to be seen as Lily's equal in matters regarding the estate. He spent some time with his wife in the office where all of the book work, important documents, and historical records affiliated with the estate were kept. He knew he had much to learn, but she taught him enough that he felt that he could manage to get by if he had to. The fact that they had an efficient and knowledgeable staff helped immensely— not to mention the fact that they could be trusted. Lily told him that Mr. Ingham and Mrs. Pilfer—the two with the most authority in the house—were well versed on important matters, and they had been in Mr. Broadbent's employment for many years before Lily had come to live here. In the event that Lily became ill or anything else happened, she assured Frederick they could guide him. They also had an excellent overseer, who kept track of the farms and properties that were leased, and he too could be trusted to act on their behalf for the best interest of their tenants.

Frederick had difficulty even imagining that anything bad could happen to mar the blissful life he'd quickly settled into with Lily. He counted the days since she'd been exposed to chicken pox and considered all he knew about the illness, and he felt certain she had likely passed the point where she would have gotten sick if she was going to.

And that very evening she told him she wasn't feeling well. They'd planned for the possibility, and each of the servants knew what was expected of them in helping with the children and making certain Lily would have the best possible care. Still, when Frederick realized that Lily actually had a fever, he was overcome with panic. Mrs. Pilfer and Abigail helped keep him calm with their own matter-of-fact approach to making Lily comfortable and reassuring both her and Frederick that they would get through this.

Mrs. Pilfer said with firm kindness to Lily, "You must remember that not one of us in the house will become ill because we've all had the pox— except for little Danny, but we'll take very good care of him. I know what to watch for—and so do the girls," she said, referring to the maids who worked closely with Lily. "The moment something seems suspicious we'll be sending for the doctor, and we'll take very good care of you." She directed her next remarks to Frederick. "You need to be getting your rest and not wearing yourself out with worry. The children need you to be there for them while Mrs. Woodstone is down ill."

Frederick nodded, appreciating her clear thinking and sound wisdom, and feeling a little distracted by hearing Lily referred to as Mrs. Woodstone. He loved knowing that his name was now hers, but he still hadn't quite gotten used to it. He looked at Lily, who had been made comfortable in their bed, and he could already see evidence that she was not well. He resisted the temptation to give in to the fear threatening to overtake him and instead turned his mind to prayer, knowing already that without being able to pour his heart out to God, he would never get through this.

* * *

Lily had trouble falling asleep with how achy she felt, and then there was the shivering that came and went, which was evidence of her fever. She woke up in the dark and felt a little better, and she had the strong urge for a hot cup of tea. Certain she could manage to get down to the kitchen to make it on her own so she wouldn't have to disturb anyone, she eased carefully out of the bed and put her feet into her slippers. She checked to be certain Frederick was asleep. Glad she'd not disturbed him, she put on a warm dressing gown and slipped quietly out of the room. She lit a lamp that was on a table in the hall and carried it with her down the back stairs and to the kitchen, going slowly and keeping one hand firmly on the bannister and then against the wall, knowing she was weak, but not so much that she couldn't see to her own needs. She knew her symptoms were likely to get worse before she got past this illness, but for the moment she appreciated being able to manage on her own. She found the teapot already filled with water, ready to be heated for morning.

While trying to light the stove, she heard a strange sound that made her momentarily afraid. She turned to look around her, holding the lamp high to try and see if anything was amiss in the huge kitchen. Seeing nothing and hearing only silence, she set the lamp down again and once more attempted to strike a match to light the stove. But another sound—much closer—startled her, and she gasped. The lit match fell from her hand, extinguished before it hit the floor. Only a second later a strong, dirty hand came over her mouth, suppressing the scream that erupted due to her pounding heart and strained breathing. As weak as she was, she had little energy to exert in fighting against being dragged out of the kitchen and toward the door, more afraid than she'd ever been in her life. She'd feared becoming ill, and she'd entertained the possibility of having to face legal consequences for taking Danny away from his father. It had only vaguely crossed her mind that Mr. Sawyer might actually do something to harm her—especially since so much time had passed and nothing had happened. But she had honestly never imagined *this* scenario. She couldn't believe it! But as she was gagged and blindfolded and literally carried out of her home, she wondered what he might do to her, and she had trouble believing she would ever see Frederick or the children again.

* * *

Lily came awake with an awareness of pain at the back of her head. It took her a minute to recall that she'd been struck and had obviously lost consciousness. Now she was in total darkness, lying on a dirt floor, and she was cold. A distinct smell in the air was familiar, and she knew exactly where she was—the cellar from which she had rescued Danny not so many days ago. Her sorrow on Danny's behalf heightened to consider that this had been the reality of his life before she'd ventured to remove him from this horrible place. Sorrow tightened into fear as the reality took hold that she was at the mercy of this horrible man and she had no idea of his intentions. If he'd had the audacity to hide a child from the world for years—leaving the child afraid and undernourished—what might he do to Lily if he believed she was responsible for taking the child from him? Clearly, he'd been more cunning than she'd expected. And now what? How would she get away from here? Despite all her planning to be certain everything would be taken care of in her absence, she felt only panic at the idea of not being with the children—and Frederick. She wanted a lifetime with him, not just a few days! This wasn't right! She had to get out of here!

Lily forced herself to remain calm and shifted her focus to practicality, figuring she should get some idea of her surroundings and what might be available to her that could aid in her escape. But it was so dark! As soon as she attempted to move, she realized her wrists and ankles were bound. She managed to sit up and lean against the stone wall behind her. There was nothing to prevent her from screaming, but she knew that no one but Mr. Sawyer would hear her, and she preferred not to draw his attention. When she realistically considered the possibilities of what he might do to her, she wondered if death might be preferable. Of course, she would prefer returning safely to her home and family. But if that was not an option, she would sincerely rather die than be a victim to this horrible man's warped vengeance. Then it occurred to her that Frederick would quickly realize she was gone and he would know exactly where to find her. He would enlist the aid of Max and Wally, and all three were strong and capable men. They wouldn't leave her here to suffer; she only had to endure this nightmare for a number of hours. She had to hold to the determination to survive no matter what else happened so she could go home to the people she loved—the people who loved *her* and would not abandon her.

Fighting to push fear out of her mind and focus on realistically getting out of this alive—and hopefully unscathed—Lily knew that for the moment she could not depend on anyone else or wait to be rescued. It gave her hope, yes, to know that people loved her and would miss her—a hope that Danny would have never experienced. But she had no idea what was actually taking place or how long it might take for her to be found. For the moment, she had to take matters into her own hands as much as possible.

Assessing the situation more rationally, she realized that her wrists were tied in front of her, leaving her hands unfettered; and she was actually able to reach to where her ankles were tied. In the darkness, she carefully felt her way around the knots in the rough rope and began to loosen them. The knots were tight and complicated, and it was tedious, but she kept her mind focused on all the reasons she had to live and return home: Frederick, the children, every member of the staff—all of whom were like family to her. They would miss her, and she needed to take care of them. She realized then that for all her efforts to make certain Frederick would legally—and emotionally—see that everyone was cared for in her absence, the loss of the people she loved would be stark and painful for her because she knew they loved her. It was strange that she'd never thought of it that way. Already the imminent threat of serious danger had made her realize that she'd always been more concerned about caring for others and taking responsibility for the estate and the children she'd taken into her home. But now it occurred to her how much Frederick and the children and the staff would miss her as well if she was gone. She was swallowed by tears in concert with a warmth inside of her as she accepted in a way she never had that she was truly loved; it wasn't just about giving people employment or giving children a home. It was about the love she gave to each one of them; she'd never thought about it because it came so naturally. And growing up as she had, she wasn't accustomed to thinking of herself as having much value in that regard. Mr. Broadbent had made it clear that his life was made better for having her in it, but their relationship had been a strange one in some ways, and she didn't think she'd ever felt that he truly needed her. It felt more like he was good to her because she had needed *him*.

Lily's thoughts wandered through the changes in her life since her first husband's death, enhancing her desperate need to be reunited with her loved ones. As she tugged at the knotted rope in the dark and attempted to untangle the complicated way in which she'd been tied up, she began to feel a deep aching in her body and the slight shivering that came with a fever. Only then did she recall that she'd been feeling ill when this had happened. She felt certain that something in her body was giving her a surge of strength as an instinctive response to her need to survive. But realistically that could only carry her for so long. What if she became too ill to fight him off? What if being in this cold, dark place without proper care made her more vulnerable to having the illness take greater hold of her?

She began to panic and forced her mind away from such thoughts, even though she could feel her body giving in to the symptoms that were becoming less impossible to ignore. She felt triumph as she was finally able to free the rope from around her ankles, but being able to untie her own hands was another matter entirely. The rope around her wrists wasn't terribly tight, which had given her some ability to use her hands in untying her ankles. She carefully felt her way around the darkened room a little to try and assess her surroundings, hoping desperately that there might be something—anything—available that she might be able to use to her advantage when the chance came. She found a small wooden table with nothing on top of it; she experimented enough to know that she could pick it up, even with her bound wrists, and it might give her one possible blow against her captor. She also a found a dirty blanket, which couldn't be used as a defensive weapon, but she wrapped herself in it as much as possible once she'd crawled around a bit more, finding nothing else in the room. She was glad for the slippers on her feet, thinking that it wasn't uncommon for her to go down to the kitchen in the night with nothing on her feet at all. If that were the case, her feet would be far colder than they already were.

When Lily heard movement in the house above her, the fear of facing the fiend who had done this to her pumped the blood through her veins with greater force, making her more aware of her weakness and the aching illness consuming her. She was also certain she had the signature itchy blisters of chicken pox coming to the surface. She could feel something on her face when she touched it, and there were itchy spots on her back and belly and legs beneath her nightgown and robe.

The cellar door opened, and a vague light descended into the little room. Lily hurried to kneel beneath the blanket she was wrapped in, thereby concealing that her feet were free. She also made certain the discarded rope was concealed beneath her. Any chance she had at taking him off guard would be to her advantage.

If Lily had held on to any doubt about the identity of her abductor—or his motives—the appearance of Mr. Sawyer made everything very clear. He carried a lamp that illuminated his evil face, and he sneered at her with self-satisfaction as he set the lamp on the floor. He stared at her with pure malevolence before he began pacing and ranting about how thoroughly evil she was, calling her a witch who had moved into the valley and taken over, meddling in everyone's lives and poking her nose where it wasn't wanted. He shouted and screamed and called her horrible things, words she hadn't heard since she'd been surviving on her own in the streets of London, barely managing to remain safe and unscathed. Lily thought of Danny being subjected to this and felt a temptation to throw up. Being ill heightened her nausea, but she managed to suppress the urge, not wanting to make herself any more vulnerable than she already was.

Lily noticed that Mr. Sawyer was holding a pair of scissors, and her fear heightened. Did he intend to stab her through the heart with them? Or did he have some other wicked intention? She considered just running toward those cellar stairs and imagined getting out of the house and running into the trees where she could hide. But her physical weakness—in contrast to his obvious strength—made it clear that such an attempt to escape would be futile. She likely wouldn't even get out of the house before he caught her, and even if she did, with the severe illness overtaking her, she could never survive the walk from here to her own home.

Lily's fear heightened when Sawyer began looking at her more directly as he rambled in his anger, justifying that Danny was *his* son and insisting she'd had no right to take the boy from his father.

"And what makes you think it was me?" she countered, trying to sound brave.

"Oh, don't you go thinkin' you're so clever, missy. You might have the rest of this valley fooled by your meddling in their lives, but I know the likes of you. I've wooed more than one woman like you; too bad they're dead and gone now. It'd make things a lot easier if I still had someone to be doin' the cookin'. Maybe *you* could do the cookin'." He pointed the scissors at her.

"I'll not be staying, Mr. Sawyer, and certainly not doing your bidding."

"We'll just see about that," he snarled, and she felt certain he was delusional. Did he honestly believe that people wouldn't come looking for her? And that they wouldn't know exactly where to find her?

"First things first," he said and moved toward her, the scissors still pointed at her like an intended weapon. In the flash of a second, Lily considered his possible intentions. Would he attempt to violate her? Cause her injury? Would he actually *kill* her? The fear she felt was all-consuming, and combined with her physical state, she could well imagine herself passing out at any moment. And she wondered if this would be how her life would end.

Chapter Nine
THE TRUE LILY

LILY WAS COMPLETELY STARTLED—AND surprised—when Sawyer took hold of her hair with one hand and lifted, pulling so hard that she could no longer sit on her feet while she knelt. She could barely remain on her knees, and yet she couldn't manage to get to her feet—especially without alerting him to the fact that her ankles were no longer bound. The way he pulled her hair hurt so badly she wanted to scream, a desire that was enhanced by her fear over his possible intentions. She gasped when he took the scissors to her hair and cut off the portion he was holding in his hand, close enough to the scalp that she could feel the scissors move against her head. He took another handful and did the same, then another. Lily tried to tell herself it was only her hair and it would grow back, but she began to sob, feeling violated and demeaned in a way she couldn't begin to comprehend while it was actually happening. She'd never considered herself beautiful; her features were sharp, and her coloring was unusually pale. She knew that. Her long, thick white hair was the only thing that had ever made her feel even the slightest bit pretty when she would look at herself in the mirror. She thought of the many hours over the years that Mary or Abigail had helped her put her hair up while they'd talked and laughed. And now she could only see the long, white locks falling on the dirt floor around her while Mr. Sawyer laughed and ranted about how she would never forget that he was a man not to be crossed and how she was only beginning to see how he would ruin her for what she'd done to him.

Lily hardly recognized the rage rising inside of her until she swung hard with her bound hands toward Mr. Sawyer's head. There wasn't enough force in her blow to hurt him, but it did throw him off balance just long enough for her to get to her feet and take hold of the little table at her side—just as she'd practiced. Before Sawyer got his balance, she swung the table toward his head with every minuscule bit of strength she had—which was due only to some miraculous survival instinct surging through her. The blow of the table was enough to knock Sawyer to the ground, and the scissors fell out of his hand.

Barely thinking of what to do before she did it, Lily grabbed the scissors with her bound hands—but then she wondered what she might actually do with them. Her immediate conclusion was that she didn't have it in her to kill him—in spite of how much she wanted to—but she could make certain he wasn't capable of following her out of here. In a flash, memories flooded her mind as she recalled fending for herself against drunken men who believed she should offer them more than the drinks and food she'd served in pubs in order to make a living. More than once she'd been followed at night or simply accosted in the street. Her instincts took hold fully, giving her the knowledge that there was one thing a woman could do to a man that would make it impossible for him to do anything unsavory for a good long time, and it would certainly inhibit his ability to run or perhaps even walk for at least a few minutes. With all the force she could manage, Lily kicked him hard where a man was most vulnerable. Sawyer groaned and curled up on the floor in response to the pain, and she felt just slightly vindicated for what he'd done to her.

Through the span of only a few seconds, Lily told herself she was a good Christian woman and she would never seek vengeance or do harm to another human being. But she did believe in defending herself against someone's evil intentions. And her next thoughts were consumed with poor little Danny being subjected to this man and the horror she herself had endured while being dragged out of her home, then left here tied up and cold and frightened. And then she saw her hair on the dirt floor and an unmitigated sob erupted from her throat. It wasn't the literal loss of her hair that hurt her so deeply but rather that it represented *everything* this man had done to inflict pain and suffering on her and an innocent child. She recalled his reference to wooing more than one woman who had clearly meant nothing more to him than something akin to slave labor; Danny's mother had obviously been one of those women. For herself, for those women, for Danny, she tightened both hands around the scissors and struck Mr. Sawyer hard in his thigh. She couldn't kill him, but she was determined to make certain he would never be able to follow her in her escape, and she silently asked God to forgive her for actually feeling some satisfaction at seeing how much pain this man was in.

Lily tossed the bloody scissors to the ground, looked around quickly, and grabbed the blanket with her still-bound hands. She took one more sad glance at her discarded hair, as if to say a final farewell, telling herself firmly, *It's only hair. It will grow back.* Still, she sobbed as she made her way carefully up the cellar steps and out of the old, dilapidated house. The night air felt cold, and she maneuvered the blanket around herself while she attempted to get her bearings and head in the direction of home, wondering how long it would take her to get there, while in the same moment, she felt every bit of strength drain out of her, as if she were a lamp that had been given only enough oil to light her way out of Sawyer's imprisonment, and now the wick had been extinguished. The oil was suddenly and completely gone, and Lily was barely into a patch of trees before she collapsed and the symptoms of her illness overtook her like a wave crashing onto the shore in a storm. She could hardly move, paralyzed by severe aching, and her fevered shivering felt as if it alone might kill her. All she could do was pray that someone would find her—and soon. And that Mr. Sawyer was truly incapacitated enough to not come after her before she was found.

* * *

Frederick came awake in the dark and rolled over, surprised to find Lily gone. Knowing she hadn't been feeling well, he knew she couldn't have gone far, but he needed to make certain she was all right. He pulled on some breeches, not wanting to wander the house in a nightshirt, and quickly surmised that she wasn't in the sitting room, the bathing room, or the water closet. His concern rising, he considered that she might have gone down to the kitchen to get some tea or something to eat, although he intended to scold her for doing so in her condition. She could have awakened him, and he'd have gotten her anything she needed. In fact, he recalled telling her so just before she'd gone to sleep.

In the kitchen, Frederick found a lamp burning and evidence that someone had been preparing tea but had obviously been interrupted. And then he found that the outside door nearest the kitchen had been left wide open. He attempted to calm his pounding heart and told himself to be rational and not jump to conclusions. He even quickly asked God to help him think reasonably. And then he panicked. Within minutes he had awakened Max and Wally, as well as Mrs. Pilfer and Mr. Ingham, telling them his concerns and suspicions. They in turn woke the remainder of the staff, and the house was given a quick and thorough search, as were the stables and the gardens. By the time they had clearly established that Lily was nowhere to be found, the sky was beginning to lighten with the promise of dawn, and the carriage was harnessed to horses and ready to go. It had been Wally's thought that if their suspicions were correct and the wicked Mr. Sawyer had something to do with this, they would need the carriage to bring Lily safely home, as opposed to the men just taking horses.

Arriving at Mr. Sawyer's home, Frederick was ready to break down the door and search the house and that dreadful cellar with no heed to what Mr. Sawyer may or may not think about such an intrusion. In his heart *and* his mind, Frederick had no doubt that this man was behind Lily's sudden disappearance, and he would do whatever it took to get her back safely. He could only pray that it wasn't too late. If this man had done anything to harm her . . . He couldn't even think of that. But he couldn't *stop* thinking of the fact that Lily was ill. Her lack of strength concerned him as much as the idea of her not getting the care she needed. He feared this might push her illness into the complications that were known to more likely afflict adults who contracted the pox.

Frederick was surprised to find the front door of the house wide open, and he exchanged a puzzled glance with both Max and Wally, who were at his sides. They went into the house and quickly surmised due to its small size that no one was there, but the cellar door was also open. Frederick didn't want to go down there; he'd been haunted by thoughts of Danny being imprisoned there for years. But Max headed down the stairs, holding a pistol in his right hand, and Frederick followed him with Wally—also armed with a pistol—bringing up the rear. A lamp on the floor of the cellar illuminated the room with enough light for Frederick to see Mr. Sawyer on the floor, clearly alive but in pain, his hand pressed over a wound on his thigh, with blood oozing between his fingers. Frederick's eye was then drawn to the bloodied pair of scissors on the dirt floor nearby, and he felt certain Lily was responsible for this. He felt proud of her but also horrified over what might have preceded this happening. Then he turned to survey the remainder of the room, searching for any clues that might help him know what had happened and where he might find Lily now. He took in a faltering breath and couldn't let it go when he saw the long locks of white hair scattered over the floor. He grabbed Max's arm, both to bring his attention to what he was seeing and also to help steady himself.

Max muttered an expletive under his breath, then turned to look at Sawyer as if he might kill him. But before Max could move, Frederick bent over, took the collar of Sawyer's shirt into his hands, and hauled the man to his feet, not caring that it was obviously causing Sawyer pain. He shoved Sawyer up against the wall and snarled in his face, "What did you do to her, you filthy scum of a man?" When he got no response, Frederick slammed him against the wall again and shouted, "What did you do to her? Where is she?"

Sawyer called Lily some horrible names, blamed her for trying to kill him as if all of this was her fault, then admitted, "I don't know where she went. If I did, she'd be dead by now."

Frederick let go of Sawyer, who sank to the floor, exhibiting a complete lack of dignity in the way he whined about his injured leg. Frederick was surprised to realize Wally had gone upstairs and now returned with a few things in hand. He knelt down by Sawyer, tore open his pant leg, opened a bottle of liquor, and poured half the contents of the bottle over the wound, which made Sawyer squeal like a dying pig.

"There," Wally said with an anger that belied his efforts to help Sawyer. "That'll keep it from gettin' infected if you can manage t' keep it clean." He then pressed a rag over the wound and growled, "With any luck, that's clean. You'd do well t' keep some pressure on it until it stops bleedin'." Wally stood up. "I suspect it won't kill you; not that any of us would care if it did." With that, Wally hurried up the stairs, saying over his shoulder, "We need t' find her. He can fend for himself."

Frederick agreed and followed, as did Max. Although the way Max glared at Sawyer made Frederick wonder if Max would shoot him on his way out. Frederick almost wished he would. The parts of himself that had once been a vicar were nowhere to be found. He'd always considered himself to be a good Christian man, to be charitable and forgiving. But he felt none of that now. He felt only a deep, festering hatred toward Sawyer, fueled by his fears concerning Lily. Where was she? She'd gotten away, but she was ill. And she could have been injured. Hints of autumn had barely begun, but still, the early-morning air was cool, and he feared she was in grave danger of being completely overcome by the combination of her illness and such a traumatic event.

"She would have headed toward home," Wally said, pointing toward the wooded area not far off the road that led back to the manor. "We should move that way and spread out. It would have been dark when she left; she might have been disoriented."

Frederick only nodded, grateful for Wally's clear thinking but unable to speak. The three men fanned out and moved into the woods, each loudly calling Lily's name. There were no other homes within hearing distance, so there was no one else to hear them and no other logical place she could have gone in her weakened state.

*   *   *

Lily drifted in and out of a dazed consciousness, intermittently praying that her loved ones would find her and that she would survive whatever complications might be induced by the cold air and the drama she'd just endured with Mr. Sawyer. Recalling any detail of the incident made her shudder and sob until the shivering of her fever made it impossible to even find the ability to cry. She huddled in the blanket as best she could, grateful at least to have it, and she just kept praying.

When Lily heard a man's voice calling her name, her first thought was that God had answered her prayers by calling her home and she was on the verge of death. Her entire body hurt so badly that it wasn't difficult to imagine being at death's door. She heard the voice again and recognized its familiarity. *Wally.*

Lily drew all the breath into her lungs that she possibly could and exerted every bit of energy she had to call, "I'm here! I'm here!"

While she was struggling to find the strength to call out again, she realized that Wally was kneeling on the ground beside her, thanking God aloud that she'd been found. She heard him shouting, "I've found her! She's here!" He repeated the phrases more than once before Lily saw Max appear. She was finding it difficult to keep her eyes open, but when she looked again, she could see only Frederick's face close to hers, and she managed a little laugh of relief before she closed her eyes again.

"You came," she whispered. "I knew . . . you would come . . . for me."

"Of course I would come for you," he said with a trembling voice, and she believed he was trying not to cry. Lily couldn't prevent tears from leaking out of her own eyes when she felt Frederick lift her into his arms, knowing she was being carried away from the place in the woods where she had wondered if she might die. "The carriage is nearby, Lily. We'll have you home and in your own bed in no time."

Lily tried to hold on to him, but her arms burned with the ache of illness, and she had no strength to even move. The events of the night came back to her, and she murmured tearfully, "My hair, Frederick. He took . . . my hair."

"I know," he said, glancing toward her at the same moment she happened to open her eyes. Then he looked straight ahead while he continued to carry her in his strong and capable arms. "It doesn't matter. Whatever happened doesn't matter. You're safe now, and you're going to be all right."

As if his promise had given Lily permission to let go of any effort to remain strong, she drifted into oblivion.

Frederick panicked when they reached the carriage, and he said to Max and Wally, "She's unconscious! What if she—"

"She's ill and exhausted," Max assured him while Wally helped Frederick get her into the carriage.

"We'll get her home, and I'll head straight t' find the doctor," Wally said. "She'll be fine. She'll be fine." He said it as if he were trying to convince himself. Frederick didn't feel convinced either. He looked down at Lily's face, holding her in his arms as the carriage moved toward home. She'd always had an unusually pale complexion, which was strangely enhanced by her white hair. But right now she almost looked dead. If not for the evidence of her strained breathing, he would have feared that she *was* dead. He pressed a hand over her head, trying to become accustomed to the very little bit of hair that was left there. The haphazard lack of consistency in length was evidence of how Sawyer had cut it off sporadically and no doubt very cruelly—Frederick knew that worse things could have happened, but at this point he wasn't certain something worse *hadn't* happened. He could only pray that her hair was all that she'd lost. It *would* grow back—assuming this illness didn't take her from him, especially given the way it had just been exacerbated by this horrible trauma. He had feared repercussions for the way they'd taken Danny out of his father's care—or rather the lack of it. They had discussed it and had certainly shared concern. But in Frederick's mind, his concerns had been focused on the legalities involved. It had crossed his mind that Mr. Sawyer might become violent in some way, but he'd always imagined that it might involve him showing up at the house drunk and angry and that Lily would be protected by servants who were on guard and well versed on what to do if such a thing should occur. Never had he imagined something like this! He still couldn't believe it! He'd only been married to her for a few days, and already he felt as if he could never live without her. He'd become accustomed so quickly to sleeping beside her at night and waking up to find her there. He had come to rely on their conversations and discussions over every little thing that either of them might need to talk about. He loved her, he needed her, and now she had endured a terrible trauma heaped upon the fact that she was seriously ill. He could see hints of the pockmarks beginning to surface on her skin, and he could not allow himself to avoid the reality that—all things combined—she was likely to get extremely ill before this was over. But, God willing, she would actually survive it.

Back at the house, Frederick carried Lily up the back stairs while Mrs. Pilfer and Abigail followed him, at first asking questions, which he attempted to answer succinctly, and then informing him that water was already heating and they would quickly help get Lily into a bath to warm her up and clean away any evidence of her ordeal. The women were horrified over the way Lily's hair had been cut off, but they said nothing, and Lily was thankfully oblivious to their stunned expressions. Frederick was glad he was her husband so he could help the servants care for her instead of being banned from her rooms—which would have been the case if they'd *not* made the decision to become husband and wife not so many days ago.

Their wedding day seemed like a dream or a distant memory as he observed Lily now. She was conscious but dazed and clearly in a great deal of pain as they bathed her, put her into a clean nightgown, and tucked her into bed with a warmer full of hot coals placed near her feet.

Once she was settled, Frederick moved a chair very near to the bed and took her hand into both of his. She was shivering violently now, most likely from the worsening of her fever, and she looked at him with eyes that betrayed how traumatized she felt. He saw tears pool there and then fall, and he couldn't keep from crying himself. He had so many unanswered questions but didn't want to upset her further by pressing for answers.

"Thank you . . ." she murmured through her shivering, "for . . . coming to . . . find me."

"Did you think I wouldn't, Lily?" he asked, leaning closer to her. "I would move heaven and earth to keep you safe. I only wish . . ." his voice cracked, "I could have prevented it . . . that I could have . . . foreseen this somehow, and—"

"It's not . . . your fault," she insisted weakly. "But . . . how did he . . . get in? How did he know . . . I was in . . . the kitchen . . . at that time . . . in the middle of the night?"

"I don't know," Frederick said. "But we're going to do our best to find out. Right now you must try not to think about anything except getting through this illness." He kissed her hand, grateful that he didn't have to be concerned about contagion and he could remain close to her. "You must be strong, Lily," he muttered, his voice even more strained. "Please, be strong. I need you! We *all* need you!"

She nodded slightly, and he realized her shivering had worsened and she was finding it increasingly difficult to speak. Trying to reassure her, he pressed a hand to her face and said with conviction, "I only want you to think about being safe and warm in this comfortable bed and how every person in this house will be praying for you. We will all work together to care for you. Do you understand? Nothing else matters right now!"

Lily nodded again, and Frederick pressed a hand over her head, surprised by the feel of very little hair there. It had become a common habit for him to press his fingers through her hair, but he wished he hadn't done so now when he saw the expression on Lily's face. "My . . . hair," was all she managed to say, and new tears formed in her eyes.

"It will grow back," he assured her. "And you are every bit as beautiful as ever! Do you hear me? It doesn't matter." She nodded very slightly, as if she were trying to believe him, and he knew it would take time for her to come to terms with all that had happened. But questions haunted him, and while he didn't want to upset her, he needed to know—now, before she inevitably became more ill. "Nothing will ever change the way I feel about you, Lily. Nothing! Still . . . I need to know . . . Did he do anything else to hurt you? Anything?"

"No," she said quickly and with confidence, and he could see that she meant it.

Frederick's relief coursed through his entire body. He smiled and kissed her brow and murmured close to her ear, "I'm so glad you're all right." He looked into her eyes. "Everything is going to be all right. I know this is so difficult; I do. But I will never be far away, I promise. If I'm not right here, it's only because I'm taking care of the children."

She nodded with an expression that let him know that's exactly where she would want him to be, then she struggled to say, "Don't . . . let them . . . see me . . . this . . . way."

Frederick didn't know if she meant letting them see her so ill or if her plea was about her hair. Likely both. But it didn't matter. He simply honored her request and said, "I promise."

She seemed relieved, and a moment later there was a knock on the door and Mrs. Pilfer escorted the doctor into the room. Frederick was grateful the man was already aware of the situation with Danny, which made it easy to explain what had happened to Lily—and the terrible timing of it happening just as this illness had been taking hold of her. The doctor conducted a thorough examination before he assured Frederick that there was no evidence of any injuries beyond some mild abrasions from the ropes on her wrists and ankles. Her symptoms in regard to the chicken pox were all very normal, and he told them what to expect, how to best manage the illness, and what to watch for that might be an indication for concern. He promised to check back every few days and insisted they should send for him if she showed any signs of difficulty breathing, excessive coughing, a dramatic increase in pain, or anything else that seemed suspicious. He reminded Frederick that the illness had to run its course and little could be done to alter that course, but he also confirmed he would do everything he could to manage the symptoms properly in order to see her safely through.

After the doctor left, Lily fell asleep, and Frederick crawled into the bed beside her, holding her hand beneath the covers. He kissed the side of her face and thanked God for her safe return, and he fell asleep in the midst of begging God to carry her safely through this illness, certain he could never survive losing her. She was the best thing that had ever happened to him, and the very idea of not having her with him throughout the remainder of his life felt more devastating than he could comprehend.

* * *

Frederick spent the next day doing his best to move forward with lessons for the children as usual. Nellie was kind enough to spend stretches of her usual time off during the day to be with the children so that he could come and go from the classroom to check on Lily and communicate with the staff about her care and their observations of her symptoms. The pock blisters were worsening and growing in number, her fever was often making her delirious, and the aching in her head and body were readily evident. Frederick found himself engaged in a continual internal battle between getting caught up in fear and worry, and trying very hard to trust in God and turn the matter of Lily's life over to Him.

The household staff was aware of Lily's illness, and since they'd all been awakened to help search for her in the night, they were all aware that she had gone missing. But upon Lily's return, only those who were privy to Danny's presence in the home were allowed to know what had really happened. The entire household had been told days earlier that Mr. Sawyer might have cause to be angry with Lily, but they'd been led to believe it was due only to his negative response to her efforts to help him. They'd felt it was important to put the staff on alert should Mr. Sawyer show up. But until it was absolutely necessary, Frederick and Lily had agreed that no one else should know about Danny—which would make it easier to keep his being there a secret and therefore keep him safe. Not wanting the household to be alarmed now, those who knew the whole truth had been instructed to tell the others that Mrs. Woodstone had simply wandered off in her delirium and had been found not far from the house. Frederick figured that whatever repercussions might follow could be handled as they came up. For now he could only focus on being there for the children and praying that Lily would survive this.

Frederick checked in on Danny often enough to make certain the boy didn't feel neglected. He went over the child's school assignments with him and left him in Mary's care since she had bonded well with Danny and he seemed secure and relaxed as long as she was nearby. Frederick talked to Danny—as he had the other children—about Lily being ill, and he did his best to assuage all the children's worries and fears. He knew better than to promise them she would come through all right. As a vicar he'd learned not to make promises over things he couldn't control. He told the children that Lily was very ill, believing it was best to be honest with them, but he also told them truthfully that many people were working hard to take good care of her and they would all do everything they could to see that she got through this all right. He also prayed with the children and encouraged them to keep doing so, sharing with them his firm belief that God truly did hear and answer prayers, even if the answer might be that God would help them get through even if it wasn't His will for Lily to survive. Frederick believed it was better that the children be prepared for the worst outcome and still encouraged that all would be well. He only wished he could feel as much optimism as he'd managed to convey during their conversations.

That afternoon Max came to the classroom and asked if he could speak privately with Frederick. Nellie wasn't there, but Frederick knew he could count on the children to behave for a short while without supervision—and he told them so, reminding them that he would be in the hall and would be able to hear if they got too rambunctious.

Frederick stepped into the hall and closed the door, wondering about the reasons for Max's determined—and perhaps angry—expression. "I went back to Sawyer's place," Max began. "I confess that I woulda liked t' kill him, but I thought I should try t' behave like a Christian even if I didn't feel like it."

"I know *exactly* what you mean," Frederick said. "Go on."

"The old devil had managed t' get t' his bed, but that wound in his leg looked bad—not that he didn't deserve it." Max scowled and went on. "And I told him he deserved worse. He told me t' get out, but he couldn't very well chase me out o' the house. He made threats about tellin' the police that the lady had tried to kill him and how she'd stolen his boy. And I told him the police would probably be interested t' hear how he'd locked the boy up for years and that he'd kidnapped the lady and done her harm. He quieted down after that, and it makes me think we don't have t' worry no more about him even tryin' t' get the law on his side."

"That's good, then." Frederick felt a flood of relief.

"Once he stopped shouting at me, I cleaned the wound and bandaged it up as best I could and made sure he had somethin' to eat."

"That was *very* Christian of you," Frederick said, not certain he could have found it in himself to be so charitable—and he having once been a vicar.

"Seemed the right thing t' do," Max said, "although I must admit I had my motives." Now Max looked a little sheepish—even though anger was still evident in his eyes. "I wanted t' know how he'd done it—how he'd gotten the lady out o' the house right at that time. How could he have known she'd go t' the kitchen in the middle o' the night for some tea? I just couldn't settle myself t' relax a bit until I knew because I certainly don't want it happenin' again. We got t' keep the lady safe—and the boy."

"I agree," Frederick said, now impatient to hear if Max had gotten answers to these questions that had haunted him as well.

"Turns out he admitted that he's made himself a squatter 'round here. He's been hidin' in the stables and the carriage house, stealin' food, peekin' through the windows; not one of us noticed. He bragged about it, he did. He suspected right off that it was the lady that took his boy, and he's been watching ever since for a chance t' snatch her."

"I can't believe it!" Frederick sputtered.

"Nor could I!" Max exclaimed. "I wanted t' hurt him bad the more he told me what he'd been doin', but I wanted him t' keep talking more than I wanted t' hit him, so I s'pose that's good."

"Likely *very* good," Frederick said.

"I have t' say," Max put a finger to his temple, "there's somethin' odd about the way he talked about little Danny, but I can't quite figure it."

"What do you mean?" Frederick asked, his attention piqued even more.

Max shook his head. "Not sure, but . . . it just seemed t' me that he . . . wasn't so much unhappy about the boy bein' with us—not that I admitted he was—but it was more like . . . the boy might know things he didn't want no one else knowin'."

Frederick felt his brow furrow as he let that settle in. He needed to think about that some more, but he was glad to have enough information to help him be aware of the possibility that such a thing might be true. It could very well help them in nurturing Danny toward a normal and happy life—especially since the biggest hurdles to overcome were the boy's father and the fear that Sawyer had instilled in him.

"That's very insightful, Max. I'm so glad you told me. And I'm proud of you for helping Sawyer—even if part of your purpose was to get information. But we very much needed that, and your helping him truly was the Christian thing to do. I dare say you are a better man than I am."

"Nah," Max said and looked sheepish again. Apparently having said all he needed to, he walked away, saying over his shoulder, "I do hope the lady will come through the pox all right."

"I hope so too," Frederick said. "Thank you."

He stood in the hall for another couple of minutes, contemplating all that Max had told him. He felt angry to think that Sawyer had been lurking around here for many days and no one had noticed. He would certainly inform the staff of that—not for the purpose of scolding them; no one could have possibly anticipated such a thing. But he did want the entire household on a more keen alert. Mr. Sawyer would eventually heal, and he might very well continue to pursue his ludicrous quest in regard to his son. Whether or not he ever did, it would now become mandatory for the servants to be mindful and aware of anything unusual. Doors previously left unlocked would be locked at night, and certain areas of the house and outbuildings that were often overlooked would be checked consistently for evidence of any irregularities. Given that they had a houseful of adopted orphans, even the servants who knew nothing about Danny could be convinced that this was a reasonable precaution. As of now, the biggest concern was getting Lily safely through this illness. How they would explain the loss of her hair to the rest of the staff and the children was something they would discuss when she was feeling better, and Frederick only wanted to think of the day when she would be past the worst and would start becoming like herself again.

During the following days, Lily was utterly miserable. She felt too wretched from the aching and the itchy pocks to be able to sleep, and the fever only enhanced her anguish. As the illness worsened, she often slipped into a hazy delirium that was frightening to observe. The doctor came to check on her regularly and didn't see any cause for alarm, but he warned that it was still likely to get worse before it got better.

While he was still in the house following his most recent visit, Mary came to report that Danny was not feeling well. A quick examination made it evident he was getting a fever, and a few tiny pockmarks were showing up on his back. Lily had not been around Danny since she'd begun to feel ill, but she had spent time with him just a short while before that. The doctor told them that he'd seen evidence of contagion taking place even before a person felt symptoms. As much as no one wanted Danny to be ill, they considered it better that he endure the chicken pox while he was young, which made complications much less likely. Frederick hated the reference to possible complications in adults, recognizing that it was presently his greatest fear in regard to Lily. As for Danny, the doctor said he was in much better health than he had been when he'd first been rescued and had shown signs of being undernourished. He confirmed that Danny would be miserable for a week or more, but he should get through this just fine. And since everyone else in the house had already survived the disease, any fear of it spreading was laid to rest.

Frederick made a concerted effort to spend time each day with Danny during the course of his illness. He wanted to be at Lily's side every moment, which made him feel torn given that he'd grown to feel responsible for Danny as much as he'd grown to love him. Frederick was glad to be with the child when his fever reached its peak and he descended into a mild delirium. Danny's inhibitions fled with the fever consuming him, and Frederick observed in shocked horror as the child muttered about his fear of his father. When he recognized Frederick, who was holding his hand and trying to remain calm and offer comfort, Danny pleaded urgently, "Please don't let him find me. Don't ever let him find me. I'll do anything. Anything! I'll stay hidden. Please don't let him find me!"

"We won't," Frederick promised, praying it was a promise he could keep. "We'll keep you safe, Danny. I promise. Now rest. You must rest."

The same conversation went back and forth a number of times, and all Frederick could do was keep reassuring the boy while Mary kept bathing Danny's face and limbs with cool rags to try and reduce the fever. Mingled with his pleas for protection and safety, Danny muttered details of what his life had been like locked in the cellar of his home and being fed barely enough to remain alive. Mr. Sawyer had obviously done a great deal of shouting and screaming, which had terrified Danny. Sawyer hadn't struck the boy very often, but often enough that Danny had always lived in fear of it happening. It seemed the old man was holding on to a great deal of anger and he had daily taken it out on Danny in one way or another.

While the boy ranted and slipped in and out of consciousness, Frederick often exchanged concerned glances with Mary and saw his own horror mirrored in her eyes. But the maid remained kind and calm and helped Frederick do the same. When the fever finally went down some and Danny was able to sleep, Frederick thanked Mary and excused himself, hurrying to find a place where he could be completely alone. Closing the door to an unused guest room that was far from where he could be overheard, Frederick leaned back against the wall and slid to the floor, where he sat with his head against his knees, gasping for breath. He prayed to understand why he was so deeply upset. Logically his compassion and concern for Danny was more than enough to upset him, but he sensed something deeper—a turmoil rumbling inside of him that had just been dredged up for reasons he didn't see and couldn't grasp. He prayed for more than an hour, occasionally crying a few stray tears, well aware that his entire body was trembling.

When Frederick's back began to ache, he stumbled to a chair and hung his head in his hands, continuing to pray, not certain he could return to Lily's side and maintain his composure until he could achieve some kind of understanding. When an idea dawned on him, he drew in a harsh breath and had trouble letting it out. He pressed a hand over his pounding heart as if it might verify to him that the thought was true. He wanted to talk to Lily about it and mourned the depth of her illness and how far away she felt.

Frederick's mind went to his mother and the story she'd told him many times of how she'd fled from an abusive husband—his father, a man who had most often been drunk and full of senseless anger. He had physically hurt Frederick's mother many times, and she had feared that in time he would have hurt her son. Frederick had no memory of these events since his mother had taken him away while he had still been very young. But now Frederick wondered if somewhere in his subconscious mind those memories were stored and Danny's experience had stirred them up. Allowing the idea to settle in, Frederick felt a calm kind of peace that seemed to affirm the truthfulness of what he was feeling. His compassion for what his mother had endured deepened, along with his compassion for Danny. It became clearer to him that he and Danny were kindred spirits. No one could be a better father to Danny; Frederick knew that now more than ever, even if the actual reasons for it were not something he could consciously recall. It made sense in a strange kind of way, even if he would find it difficult to explain. He believed Lily would understand, but he couldn't talk to her while she had no awareness of anything going on around her. Frederick could only pray that she would come back to him and they could renew the love between them that was still so young. He missed her so much! Fresh tears overtook him as he considered the possibility that he might lose her. The thought was so terrible that he forced it out of his mind. For now he had to believe she would be all right. He needed her. The children needed her. The *world* needed her. She just had to be all right!

Frederick finally dragged himself back to Lily's side, grateful for Mrs. Pilfer's tender care of his wife while he'd been gone. He sent her away to get some rest so that he could be alone with Lily.

* * *

Lily drifted in and out of a strange kind of consciousness, sometimes bordering on delirium. Images of the people helping her were often hazy, as were the words they said to her. One truth stood out above all else: she'd never felt so miserable in the whole of her life! She'd endured illness before, but never like this! And to make matters worse, at the heart of her misery was the ever-present memory of being a victim to Mr. Sawyer's heinous behavior. Unable to sleep well, she spent far too much time recalling how it had felt to be accosted in her own kitchen and dragged out of her home, to be tied up in the dark cellar with the dirt floor, and to feel the stark fear that he might do her great harm or even kill her. And then there was the horrible memory of him coming at her with those scissors and maliciously cutting off her hair, all the while saying horrible things—words that screamed in her memory and somehow took her back to her childhood and youth when she'd been unwanted and struggling to survive.

The unrelenting march of her thoughts combined with the physical pain she was enduring left her consumed with a sense of loss and deep grief that seemed capable of devouring her. She felt as if she'd lost herself somehow; it was as if Mr. Sawyer had stolen her soul, even though she knew that no one could take away her inner self. It was her first husband who had taught her that; she'd come to this household initially as a servant, frightened and timid, lost and alone. And he had taught her that no matter what horrible things might have happened to her, no matter how cruel other people had been, no one could steal from her what he called the *true Lily*. With the help of his kindness and sound wisdom, she had gradually healed and had come to believe that what he'd taught her was true.

There was the woman inside of her that she'd been born to be, the woman who had nothing to do with her physical appearance, her worldly struggles, or the pain she'd endured. She had risen above so much to find joy and fulfillment in her life, and she believed that the true Lily still existed inside. But as consumed with pain as she was and as overcome so freshly by the trauma of what Mr. Sawyer had done to her, she was having trouble finding that Lily. Occasionally she put one of her weakened hands on her head to feel the absence of her once-beautiful hair, and she wanted to scream as much as she wanted to cry like a baby. But she was too drained of strength to do either. It was as if her hair somehow represented the true Lily, even if the concept was completely contradictory to the point that Mr. Broadbent had been making. Surely her hair had nothing to do with who she was inside, with her true character and identity. But she didn't feel capable of thinking rationally, and she knew her emotional reaction to what had happened was not rational at all.

Right now she felt as if the true Lily had been left on the dirt floor of Mr. Sawyer's cellar among the pile of discarded white hair. A part of her wanted to just die from this illness and never have to face the emotions brewing inside of her. It was only Frederick's regular appearance at her bedside, and knowing that he was in the bed beside her at night, that gave her any will to live. She often thought of the children and knew they would miss her, but hairless as she was, she couldn't imagine being with them and ever being seen the same. A part of her knew that her thinking was distorted, but she couldn't find her way past the distortion enough to truly believe that life was worth living. Frederick kept telling her to be strong, to hold on, and to get through this. The love in his eyes hadn't changed in spite of how she knew he was seeing her in such an awful state and so drastically changed in appearance. She believed that he meant it when he said the changes didn't matter, but still, she felt different. She felt scared, and she wondered if she would ever be able to find the true Lily again.

Chapter Ten
ON THE BRINK

FREDERICK BECAME UTTERLY TERRIFIED MORE than a week into Lily's illness when the coughing and difficult breathing the doctor had mentioned took hold of her. She was officially declared to have pneumonia—a common complication of the chicken pox, especially in adults. The doctor gave specific instructions to Mrs. Pilfer and the maids who were helping to care for Lily, and he began coming every day. Frederick gave honest reports to the children and did his best to put on his most brave and optimistic mask in order not to upset them during their time together, but inside he felt himself trembling with fear that Lily would just stop breathing and they would all lose her.

In the midst of his fears he had to contend with a growing anger toward Mr. Sawyer. He knew from Max's reports of having gone back every couple of days to take food and change the bandaging on the wound that this culprit of crimes against Danny and Lily was healing and coming along nicely—and was as foul tempered as ever. Frederick admired Max's charitable attitude about helping Mr. Sawyer, but a part of him also resented it. He became so consumed with his own anger that he found himself wishing the old man had been left to die of an infectious wound or starvation—whichever would have been the most painful. In Frederick's mind, the reasons for Lily's condition becoming so severe were directly related to her having been abducted, with all of the ensuing trauma and exposure to the cold. The doctor told Frederick that she very well could have been afflicted with pneumonia either way, but Frederick was convinced that Sawyer had pushed Lily closer to the edge of death, and he hated him for it.

A few days later, Lily was so ill that Frederick accepted Nellie's offer to take complete charge of the children so that he could remain with Lily continually. Other members of the staff eagerly offered their assistance with the children so that Nellie wouldn't be too overwhelmed. The children knew these changes were happening because Lily's illness was worsening, and it naturally created somber moods and emotional responses. Some of them were more prone to crying now and then, while others tended to act out with anger or bad behavior. But Nellie was close to each one of them, and with some guidance from Frederick, she had learned how to address each challenge with appropriate discipline and tenderness. Everyone in the household was afraid and sorrowful, but Frederick doubted that anyone could be more frightened and upset than he was. He recognized it was likely a selfish idea, knowing that the children relied on her so deeply and loved her so much, and losing her would be devastating to each and every one of them. If nothing else, Frederick considered his own grief to at least be equal to that of the children. He too felt like a lost child that she had taken into her home and her heart, and he couldn't imagine going on without her.

Frederick would have lost track of night and day if not for the maids who came into the room and opened the drapes to let in the sunlight. They brought him meals, but he could barely eat enough to keep his stomach from rumbling. He tried to sleep beside Lily, but he only drifted in and out of fitful slumber while his exhaustion battled with his keen awareness of her every labored breath. He'd lost track of how long she had been mostly unconscious from the effect of the fever and the infection smoldering inside of her. The pockmarks were far too many to count, and she unconsciously tried to scratch at them even in her delirium. The maids helped him try to keep calamine on them as much as possible to reduce the discomfort and hopefully help them heal faster. More than once while he was putting calamine on the pockmarks on her scalp, he wondered how they might have been able to do so if her hair was as it had been before. The idea didn't make him glad for the loss of her hair, but he was trying very hard to be optimistic. When he commented on it to Mary and Abigail, Mary suggested this could be used as an explanation as to why her hair had needed to be cut. Abigail added with a forced positive tone, "And when she's up and about, I can make the hair even, and she'll look utterly adorable."

Mary added, "She has some lovely scarves that can be wrapped around her head and pinned. I've seen ladies do as much simply for the sake of being fashionable. Surely that will help her feel less self-conscious."

"That's an excellent idea," Abigail replied. "And as we keep saying, hair does grow back. She'll have long, lovely locks again in no time."

Frederick just listened to their conversation, wishing and hoping and praying that a day would come when Lily would be up and about enough to actually be concerned about her changed appearance and how to deal with it in a way she could feel good about. He missed her so much already that living without her would simply be impossible. He missed her voice, her laughter, her kiss. And he hated seeing her suffer; he hated it more than anything he'd ever experienced. He tried to separate his growing negative emotions over all of this from what Sawyer had done to her, but in his mind the present situation, with all of its fear and grief, was inseparably connected to the horror of what a selfish, pathetic old man had done to his wife.

More days passed with a dark anguish hanging over Frederick. He barely ate and rarely slept, and he found it difficult to be away from Lily's side for even a few moments. He'd come to truly fear she would take her final breath and he wouldn't be there when she left. In some bizarre way he'd come to believe that if he *was* there, he could somehow prevent it from happening, that somehow he could keep death at bay and deny it entrance into the room. His mind was caught up in constant prayer, a continual pleading to God for Lily's life to be spared. He reminded God—as if He might have forgotten—of all the good that Lily did for so many people, and Frederick felt no shame in completely exposing his own utter love for Lily and his complete dependence upon her. The more he focused on constant prayer, the less he thought about Mr. Sawyer, and when he did think of the old man, he realized he no longer cared what he may or may not have done to contribute to Lily's present state. He didn't know if that meant he'd experienced forgiveness toward Sawyer or if he was just too preoccupied with Lily's survival to have the mental or emotional energy to devote to such inconsequential thoughts.

Frederick made a concerted effort once a day to pull himself together and not look as undone as he felt so that he could check on the children and do his best to offer them some hope and optimism. He knew they were all struggling, fearing they would lose their mother—even Danny had started calling her "mother" despite not interacting with the other children at all; as of yet, they were still not even aware of his presence in the house. Frederick had to remind himself every day that he believed in being honest with children; he knew they were sharp and could see through pretenses; and honesty—however difficult—was far better for them when all was said and done. If Lily didn't survive this, they would all grieve deeply. To lead them to believe that death was not a possibility would only make that grief more shocking and difficult to process. Frederick also needed them to trust him, and if he was foolish enough to promise them that Lily would be all right—and then she wasn't—they might never trust him again. He simply answered their questions as best he could, expressed compassion for their fear and their sorrow—which he encouraged them to talk about—and left them again in Nellie's care, grateful beyond words for her willingness to watch over them and for the way she did it with such efficiency and kindness. He was also grateful for every member of the staff who was putting in extra hours to help care for Lily and the children. If they hadn't felt like family to him before, they certainly did now. He'd never imagined that paid servants could be so thoroughly devoted to their employer. But then, he'd never imagined a woman like Lily.

With the passing of more days, Lily's pocks began to scab over and heal, and the women who helped care for her commented that they weren't likely to leave scars, which would surely please Lily. Frederick could only pray that she would survive this pneumonia-induced stupor so that she might actually have a chance to care whether or not the pocks had left scars. *He* didn't care. He didn't care if she was left scarred and hairless for the rest of her life. He only wanted her to live! She was beautiful to him no matter what! He knew her, he knew her heart and her spirit, and he loved her beyond any limitations of this physical world or any of its associated appearances or illusions.

Frederick grew so deeply weary—both in body and spirit—that he found it increasingly difficult to even hope that this waiting would ever end. He couldn't allow himself to even think that this nightmarish limbo might be concluded with her death, but neither could he imagine anymore what it might be like to have her recover and come back from the brink of death to once again be a part of their lives.

Frederick awoke on a rainy morning after a typical night of drifting in and out of restless dozing, remaining close to Lily, holding her hand beneath the covers, and listening to her strained breathing that was a result of the pneumonia. The room was barely light, but he couldn't tell if that was because the sun hadn't come up fully yet or if the drapes hadn't been opened. He knew the maids came in and out of the room often to check on Lily or just to sit with her, even while he might be attempting to get some sleep; therefore, he'd become accustomed to feeling disoriented over what might have taken place in the room while he'd been dozing. With his back turned to Lily, he listened for the sound of her breathing—a sound that had become his constant measurement of minutes and hours, offering him continual evidence that she was alive but also that she was ailing. Her difficulty in breathing had varied during her illness, and he listened now while still half asleep to try and assess her condition since he'd fallen asleep.

When Frederick heard nothing, he panicked and sat up, turning to look at her, his heart pounding as he expected to find her cold and dead. He heard a strange sound come out of his own mouth when he saw instead her blue eyes open and gazing at him. He couldn't even count how many days it had been since he'd seen her eyes open!

"Oh, Lily," he murmured and put a hand on her face, feeling no evidence of fever. "Oh, my sweet Lily!" he cried and pressed his lips to her brow.

"How long . . . have I . . ." she murmured, her voice hushed and raspy.

"Days. I don't know," he said. "Oh, I love you!"

Abigail came into the room at the sound of voices; she'd clearly been in the sitting room with the door open, close by in case she was needed. She exclaimed delightedly at Lily being awake and rushed out to have someone go for the doctor so that he could determine whether or not this was evidence of the improvement they'd all been praying for. He would have come later in the day anyway, but they all felt anxious for an earlier assessment of Lily's well-being.

Lily reported that she felt some difficulty breathing, but it wasn't painful. She was thirsty and even a little hungry, and Mrs. Pilfer brought her some broth, emphasizing that she needed to start out with something easy to digest and take it slowly. Lily was too weak to even lift a spoon, but Frederick was only too glad to help her, grateful beyond words to just have her conscious and talking. He prayed it was not just a temporary improvement, fearing that more complications might yet set in. But he kept that fear to himself and just enjoyed having his wife back.

Lily was too weak to say much, but her first concern was for the children. Frederick filled in for her inability to speak by offering detailed reports of their concern, their faith, their prayers, and all they'd been doing with schoolwork and projects, which had kept them busy and distracted from Lily's illness. She was glad to hear they were doing well, and saddened to know that Danny had also been afflicted with the chicken pox. But her concerned countenance lightened as Frederick reported that Danny had been miserable but was already improving and had gone back to working on his reading and other lessons because he'd become bored with remaining in bed.

"And what of Mr. Sawyer?" Lily asked between spoonfuls of broth.

"What of him?" Frederick countered, wishing it hadn't sounded so terse.

"Is he all right?" Lily asked with such genuine concern that Frederick was taken aback.

"Max has been checking in on him," Frederick reported. "Taking him food, helping him keep the wound clean."

"Good," Lily said with her eyes closed, as if it was exactly what she would have asked of Max if she'd been coherent enough to do so.

Frederick also told her, "I suppose it's good news that Sawyer apparently doesn't want to involve the police. He might have legal rights to Danny, but now that he's guilty of kidnapping, it seems he prefers that we keep each other's secrets. At least that's how Max put it to me. Max never admitted to him that Danny is with us, but I think it's obvious that Sawyer believes he is. I don't think it's wise to bring Danny out of hiding just yet, but perhaps there's hope that we'll be able to—eventually. For now, Sawyer is barely getting around but doing fine; I don't think he'll be keen on causing problems for us anytime soon."

"That's good then," Lily said, her eyes still closed. She reached for Frederick's hand, and he set the soup bowl on the bedside table to hold her hand in both of his. She turned her head slowly on the pillow and opened her eyelids to look at him. "I wouldn't do anything differently, my darling. You need to know that. Even when I was utterly terrified, wondering what Sawyer might do to me, I realized that I could have never left Danny in his care."

"I know," Frederick said, marveling freshly at the goodness of her heart. He'd spent many hours pondering the dilemma of Danny's well-being versus the danger Lily had been subjected to. He too could not imagine ever being able to leave Danny in such a situation. They had both grown to love the boy almost immediately, but even if they had no personal affection for the child, *no* child should be subjected to such neglect and abuse. Frederick was struggling a bit with negative feelings again concerning what Sawyer had done to Lily—and to Danny—but now was not the time to address those. He simply said to her, "I'm only glad that you're all right."

She managed a weak smile and closed her eyes again as if it were difficult to hold them open. She said lightly, "I don't suppose my hair grew back while I was lost in oblivion."

"I'm afraid not," he said, mimicking her light tone. "But having it so short did make it easier to put calamine on the pocks on your scalp. I'm glad to say that they've all scabbed over now and appear to be healing well."

"There were pocks on my scalp?" she asked, opening her eyes again.

"You don't remember?" he asked, knowing she had drifted in and out of consciousness, and it had been difficult to tell when she was actually conscious or when she might have been delirious with fever.

"No," she said, gingerly putting a hand to her head and making a disagreeable noise.

Trying to remain positive, he told her, "Abigail said that when you're up and about she will even up your hair, and Mary has some wonderful ideas about how you can wear scarves on your head in a fashionable way." He leaned closer and offered what he knew was important information. "Only those in the house that know about Danny being here are aware that you were even taken that night. None of the children or the rest of the staff have seen you while you've been ill." She nodded, and he saw tears glisten against her closed lashes. He tightened his hold on her hand. "We were thinking that having pocks on your scalp could be the explanation for why your hair was cut."

Lily nodded again. "I like that explanation," she said. "I'd wondered . . . what . . . I would say."

"Everything's going to be all right," he said and kissed her brow, figuring they'd talked enough about such things for now. "Get some rest."

She nodded again and almost immediately fell asleep. She would no doubt be very tired for a good, long time. But her breathing definitely sounded less strained, and Frederick felt increasingly hopeful that she had indeed come past the worst.

The doctor came about an hour later and gave Lily a careful examination, asking many questions of her. He reported that her lungs sounded better, her fever was completely gone, and he saw no reason they shouldn't expect a full recovery. He gave them careful instructions on how to slowly ease her back into health and cautioned them on how vital it was that she remain down until her body had a chance to gain some strength; they didn't want to take even the slightest risk of any setbacks.

Frederick was glad to be able to report to the children that their mother was going to be fine. They cheered and literally jumped for joy. He knew exactly how they felt. They all wanted to see her, but he told them she was still very weak and needed more time before she would be up to having company. He also knew she needed to feel ready to have the children see her looking so dramatically different with the loss of her hair. He distracted them by assigning a project of painting pictures and writing notes and letters to their mother. He assured them she would be thrilled to receive such wonderful gifts and they would lift her spirits. The children dug in enthusiastically and put great effort into their projects. The idea had occurred to Frederick days earlier, but it had seemed relatively pointless when Lily had been mostly unconscious or delirious, and if she hadn't come through, he'd feared that the children might have difficult feelings over their efforts never being seen by her. Now it was the perfect thing to keep them busy, and it was a project that could be repeated until Lily felt ready to see the children.

Within just a few days, Lily was sitting up in bed at regular intervals and spending more hours awake. She was still too weak to feed herself, but she enjoyed having someone read to her, and Frederick was only too happy to meet her every need and request, feeling nothing but gratitude that she was alive and doing better every day. She loved the children's written words to her and their art projects that brightened her room. The pictures were all tacked to the wall where she could see them, and he often noticed her glancing toward them and smiling.

Lily's desire to see the children soon overcame her self-consciousness about her hair and the pockmarks on her face and hands that were still healing. Now that she was getting in and out of bed with some help, she was able to sit in a chair long enough for Abigail to even up her hair so that it didn't look so haphazardly cut. Abigail also helped Lily carefully wash her head with rose-scented shampoo, which helped loosen and remove much of the scabbing from the pocks on her scalp. Lily's hair was rubbed dry with a towel and was sticking up all over her head, no more than an inch long. She looked at herself in the mirror and actually smiled, saying to Frederick, "I look like a dandelion when it's gone white and fluffy."

"So you do," he said, doing his best to adopt her positive attitude.

Mary tried wrapping some scarves around her head and pinning them, and Lily liked the way they looked and declared that when she was ready to leave her bedroom, she would likely take advantage of that option, but as for seeing the children, she preferred that they see her as she was. They'd been told that her hair had been cut off, which had made it easier to care for the pocks on her head. Frederick had been careful in how he'd worded it, not wanting to actually lie to them. He didn't say her hair had been cut *because* of the pocks but that it made caring for them easier. It was easy for them to assume that was the reason. And he'd done the same in reporting the situation to the staff. They were all thrilled with Lily's recovery, and even though most of them hadn't seen her since she'd become ill, they had all put in extra time and effort to care for her and the children. He expressed his gratitude whenever the opportunity arose, feeling more and more comfortable in his place at the head of this very large, diverse family.

The children were overjoyed about being able to see their mother. Frederick cautioned them to not overwhelm her and told them their first visit needed to be brief. But he couldn't hold back a laugh to see how Lily brightened when the little herd rushed into her room, all wanting to get to her bedside first. She hugged each one of them and laughed at the way they wanted to touch her fuzzy head. They all found a place to sit on the huge bed and asked her questions about her illness, which she answered directly. Frederick nearly cried to hear the children express—each in his or her own way—their gratitude that Lily was getting better. He had spent a great deal of time wondering how he would be a good father to them without Lily in their lives, and he was grateful that he didn't have to wonder about that anymore.

He could see Lily tiring, and he guided the children reluctantly out of the room so she could rest, but she was noticeably more content having spent some time with them. After she'd taken a long nap, Frederick brought Danny to see her, and their reunion was even more touching for some reason. They talked about how they'd both been ill. Frederick looked on, struck by the deep irony and poignancy of their relationship and the trauma Lily had suffered as a direct result of bringing Danny into her home—an event Danny would likely never know about. Frederick could only be grateful that they were both safe and sound and getting healthier every day.

When the household had quieted down for the night, Frederick crawled into bed next to Lily and turned onto his side where he could just look at her and gratefully savor the way she was looking back at him, alive and well and completely aware of her surroundings. He'd lost track of the hours that he had lain in this very spot and watched her coughing and struggling to breathe, delirious and drifting in and out of consciousness. But now she'd come back to him, and he could only gaze at her and silently thank God for granting him such a miracle.

"You look so tired," she said and put a hand to his face.

He smiled and closed his eyes, savoring her touch. "I confess that it was difficult to sleep when I didn't know if I'd wake up to find you dead."

"I'm so sorry," she said with a quivering voice, and he opened his eyes to look at her.

"Sorry? For what?" he asked.

"For putting you through that. If the situation were reversed, I . . . I don't know if I could have . . ." She bit her trembling lip and didn't finish.

"It's not your fault, Lily. It just—"

"But I was careless," she said, and tears glistened in her eyes. "I exposed myself to the disease without—"

"Hush," Frederick said and put his fingers over her lips. "You went into that situation the way you go into *every* situation—with courage and the best of intentions. It's one of the reasons I love you as I do, and I wouldn't want you to be any different. I admit I struggled with some feelings of anger when I thought that I might lose you, and if I had lost you it likely would have taken some time to come to terms with those feelings—but I always knew in my deepest self that I could never resent anything you did from the absolute goodness of your heart. And that includes the way you brought Danny into our home . . . and into our lives."

Frederick heard his own voice quiver and closed his eyes again, recalling far too well how deeply Danny's traumatic memories had stirred up such difficult feelings within himself.

Lily pressed her fingers into his hair before she once again cradled the side of his face in her hand. "What is it, my darling?"

Without opening his eyes, Frederick murmured, "I'm just . . . so grateful Danny is with us. I regret not being able to protect you from his father, but . . ."

"You mustn't be upset about that," Lily said firmly. "You came for me, and no damage was done that won't be undone with time."

A recently familiar anger rose inside of him that was so consuming he squeezed his eyes shut more tightly, as if doing so might prevent Lily from seeing how deeply it affected him. Still, he couldn't keep himself from saying, "Sometimes I'm so . . . *angry* with him that I nearly fear . . . I could do him harm . . . for what he did to you . . . and to Danny and . . ."

"Frederick, look at me," she said, and he did. "We must forgive him. We must. I'll not deny that what he put me through was terrible . . . and I too have felt angry, but my feeling that way will not make him suffer; it will not undo what's been done. If nothing else, having been so ill has made me even more appreciative of the gift of life, and it's certainly put certain matters into perspective. We must do as the Bible teaches us to do, Frederick; you know such teachings in your soul. I know you do. We cannot judge why Mr. Sawyer is the way he is, but—"

"The man is a monster!" Frederick spurted. "That's what he is!"

"Monster or not, it is not for us to judge. Jesus taught that principle with no room for doubt. Only God can judge because only He knows all. Perhaps Mr. Sawyer was treated badly by his own father and he knows no better. Perhaps he is harboring his own pain and simply doesn't know how to cope any other way besides drinking and being cruel. It's not for us to judge, Frederick. It is for us to forgive, to let it go, to give it to God. The best way we can stand up against such cruelty is to keep doing what we're doing. We will keep Danny safe, and we will care for him and all of the others who have also endured horrors and misfortune. And we will do everything we can to give them the skills and ability to live good lives and contribute love and charity to a world that is so in need of it."

Frederick took in her words as he took in a deep breath. "You always leave me humbled, my darling. I confess that I need some time . . . to come to terms with my feelings. But I know you're right."

She nodded and gazed into his eyes as if she were searching his soul. "Something else is bothering you," she stated with the confidence of knowing she was right—which she was.

Frederick struggled for long, silent moments to get past his difficult feelings and find the right words. "When Danny was the most ill . . . with the fever removing his inhibitions . . . he said things that . . ."

"That what?" Lily asked gently when he hesitated.

"That certainly fueled my anger toward Sawyer," he admitted, "but it also . . . stirred up something inside myself . . . that I'm struggling to understand."

"Tell me," she encouraged, making it easy for him to do so. He repeated all that Danny had said and how it had made him feel. He told her how he'd been so upset and had prayed to understand, and of the idea that had come to him—that Danny's experience had somehow tapped into memories Frederick couldn't consciously recall but seemed to be trapped inside of him somewhere. She agreed with his theory, which felt validating and strengthening. She also agreed that he and Danny were indeed kindred spirits for that reason, and she reminded him that each of the children had endured varying degrees of trauma prior to coming into their home. She believed this was further evidence that Divine Providence had brought Danny into their lives and that no one could be as good a father to them as Frederick could.

He was freshly humbled by her faith in him, but he couldn't deny that he agreed. Frederick also agreed that in order to set a good example for the children in overcoming the hardships of their past, he had to forgive Mr. Sawyer and put the matter into God's hands. In talking through his feelings more deeply with Lily, he knew he also had to forgive his own father. Even though he couldn't consciously remember anything of what his mother had told him, he knew it was a part of his own history, and he likely had held on to difficult feelings toward this man he'd never known who had made it necessary for him and his mother to live such a difficult life.

Frederick felt infinitely better after being able to share his deepest thoughts and feelings with Lily, and he fell asleep at her side, overcome with gratitude for having her in his life and for the miracle that had kept her alive. He couldn't imagine ever being without her. Ever!

* * *

Lily quickly became frustrated with the slowness of her recovery. She was grateful to be up and about some, but she couldn't walk farther than to the sitting room or Danny's room without feeling weak and out of breath. It was a joy to have the children come to see her, and story time was now taking place in her sitting room instead of the usual place. She was also glad to be able to spend time with Danny, although she had a growing concern for him. The boy's restlessness was becoming more evident. He'd recovered from his illness completely, and he was becoming understandably bored with his isolation. During all the years he'd been kept in solitude, he'd longed to see the outside world. It broke Lily's heart to realize that Danny didn't even know what grass felt like or what it was like to stand in the rain. He'd only experienced sunlight through windows—and this only since he'd come to Lily's home. She longed to have the other children know about him, and to be able to integrate him into their society, certain that his peers could do far more than the adults in his life ever could to teach him about social interaction and the basic lessons of life. But as long as she had any reason to fear that the law might intervene and send Danny back to his father, she simply couldn't risk having anyone else know that he was in their care. It felt like they had merely traded one "prison" for another; yet they all knew there was no comparison, and they looked forward to the time when Danny could be set free.

Following a pleasant afternoon with Danny, during which she'd avoided thinking about her dilemma, Lily sat at her dressing table and gazed at her reflection. She rubbed a hand over the short, downy hair that stuck up all over her head and fought back the temptation to cry. *It's only hair*, she told herself for the thousandth time. *It will grow back. It could have been so much worse.* Still, she felt self-conscious and wondered how many weeks it would take to have enough hair to feel feminine again. And it would surely take months or even longer for her hair to return to the length it had been.

Lily leaned closer to the mirror and examined the fading pockmarks on her face. They too could have been so much worse, and it appeared they would all heal just fine and not leave any scars. She sighed and told herself to not get caught up in any kind of vanity. She'd always had an odd appearance; she knew that and she'd adjusted. But now she looked even more strange, which made it especially difficult to feel pleased by her own appearance. She reminded herself that she was loved by many people, most especially Frederick. The children were quick to look past appearances and not care, and she couldn't deny that her husband was the same, as were the servants that had been helping her through her illness.

The bedroom door opened, and she turned to see Frederick enter the room. All of her self-consciousness and concerns over her appearance vanished with the way he looked at her and smiled. He made her feel beautiful; his *love* made her feel beautiful.

"How are you feeling?" he asked, bending over to kiss her brow.

"A little better every day," she said. "Still weak and slow, but understandably so."

"Yes, it will take time," he said and squatted down to face her. "But I think getting you out of this room is long overdue. I believe it's high time you joined everyone in the kitchen for supper this evening. Everyone's been so worried about you, and they miss you."

"But I . . . could never walk that far, and . . ." She said nothing more, but her hand went unconsciously to her head, and he guessed her thoughts.

"You are as beautiful as ever, but even if you weren't it doesn't matter." He stood and took her hand. "And I will *carry* you to the kitchen." He chuckled. "That's what husbands are for."

"Is it?" she asked, standing to face him.

"It is indeed," he said and kissed her. More seriously he added, "You'll feel better; I know you will. If wearing a scarf will make you feel more comfortable, that's fine. But I don't think you need one. No one will see you who isn't as good as family. It will only take half a minute for them to become accustomed to the new you. What do you say?"

"You've talked me into it," she said, and he immediately lifted her into his arms and headed out of the room and toward the back stairs, making her laugh as he occasionally jostled her in his arms.

It only took Lily a couple of minutes to realize Frederick had been right. She *did* feel better being back among the entire staff to share a meal in a way that had long been a comfortable part of her daily routine. And every one of them expressed nothing but gratitude over her recovery and their joy at seeing her again. Comments about her hair were light but respectful, and she was glad that it could be talked about matter-of-factly as opposed to having everyone pretend that nothing had changed. She was glad to know that the few people in the house who knew the truth about what had happened to her could be trusted to keep her secret. She was managing to come to terms with her difficult feelings about the incident; she didn't want others to now learn about it and have their responses open old wounds.

Lily was content to remain at the supper table long after the meal was finished, chatting and laughing with these people she loved so dearly. Having Frederick at her side made the experience all the better, and she realized that they had barely had time to adjust to being married before she'd become ill. But it was evident that Frederick had done well with managing the household in her absence. The respect everyone had for him was evident, and she knew him well enough to know that he had surely earned it with his natural humility and genuine concern for the well-being of others.

After Frederick had carried Lily back upstairs to their bedroom, he helped her get ready for bed since she'd used up all her strength, then he crawled into bed beside her and held her close, making her feel more safe, more loved, and more happy than she'd ever thought possible.

Chapter Eleven
THE HAND OF IRONY

THE FOLLOWING MORNING, LILY SHARED breakfast with Frederick in her sitting room, and she was pleased to note that her appetite was improving. They had barely finished eating when Abigail came to their room, looking a bit sheepish and very nervous. Her official reason for being there was to take away the tray of dirty dishes from their breakfast, but it was evident she wanted to talk to them about something, even before she said, "May I speak with you? I fear I have need to apologize to the both of you, and I would prefer to have it done because I don't want to have any ill feelings between us, and I've been praying that you'd forgive me for my indiscretion. I know you're both the forgiving kind of people, but I—"

"Please sit down, Abigail," Frederick said kindly. "There's no need to be so upset. Just tell us what you're concerned about; I'm certain we can work it out."

"But you don't even know what it is I've done," Abigail said, looking as if she feared being sent to the guillotine or something equally horrible.

"Then why don't you tell us and get it over with," Frederick said, "and we'll take it from there. I think I speak for my wife when I say that whatever the problem might be, we appreciate your honesty and humility in coming to us."

"Yes, of course," Lily said and offered Abigail an encouraging nod.

Abigail took a deep breath and drew back her shoulders, but she kept her eyes turned down as she spoke. "You know that Luca and I are very close."

"Yes," Lily said. "And you have intentions to marry, I believe—which is wonderful. When might the blessed event take place?"

"We're hoping to be married soon," Abigail said, looking at Lily since this topic had nothing whatever to do with what she was dreading to admit. "We haven't set a date yet. I was intending to speak to you about it near the time you became ill, and I didn't want to wait to bring it up until you were feeling better, but—"

"Well, we must talk about it soon," Lily said. "We'll plan a lovely celebration."

Abigail's eyes turned down again. "Perhaps you should hear what I have to say before you offer such generosity."

"And perhaps you should tell us and get it over with," Frederick said again with perfect kindness.

Again Abigail took a deep breath. "As I said . . . Luca and I are very close. With the amount of time we spend together, he couldn't help but notice my coming and going from this part of the house with no explanation of my reasons for needing to spend so much time here."

"You mean the time you've been spending with Danny," Lily said for clarification.

"That's right," Abigail said, and Lily could see where this was likely headed. "Luca became concerned when I couldn't account for my whereabouts, and I tried to explain without breaking the trust you put in me to keep Danny's being here a secret, but I must have said too much because he figured it out, and . . ." Abigail wavered into tears and hung her head further.

"With the two of you being so close," Lily said, "such a thing happening is understandable." She was relieved to realize this was not nearly as serious as Abigail believed it to be—although they did need to make some clarifications to be certain that Danny would remain protected.

"Do you trust Luca?" Frederick asked as if he'd read Lily's mind. "I assume that you *must* trust him if you're intending to marry him."

"Oh, I do!" Abigail said, lifting her head abruptly to look Frederick in the eye. "I confess that I finally gave in and told him the truth when he'd mostly figured it all out anyway. He swore to not tell a soul, and I know he'll keep that promise."

"Then I don't see that we have anything to be concerned about," Frederick said, and Abigail's eyes widened with surprise, as if she'd expected a good scolding—or perhaps even a dismissal from employment.

"I agree," Lily said, and Abigail turned her wide eyes toward the lady of the house. "If we'd given the matter more thought, I think we all would have agreed that secrets shouldn't be kept between two people who have devoted their lives to each other. Luca is a good man; we all know that well enough. If you trust him, then we do as well."

"Thank you for letting us know, Abigail," Frederick said. "There's no need for you to be upset or concerned."

"Oh, you're so kind," Abigail muttered on a loud sigh of relief. "I mean . . . you've both always been so kind, but still . . . I feared you would be unhappy over me breaking my promise like that."

"We understand," Lily said, and Abigail thanked them again before she collected the breakfast tray and left the room.

"Isn't she sweet?" Lily laughed softly. "Poor girl."

"I'm glad she's working for *you*," Frederick said, "and not some miserly beast who might have tossed her out over such a silly thing."

"No, she's working for *you*," Lily said with a smile toward her husband.

"Us," he said, returning her smile. Then he kissed her.

Not many minutes later, Mary came to tell them that a police officer was there who wanted to speak with the lady of the house. Lily took hold of Frederick's hand, wishing this could be corrected as easily as Abigail's drama.

"What shall we do?" Mary asked, wringing her hands. "Do you think he suspects we have little Danny? Do you suppose Mr. Sawyer has—"

"There's no reason to jump to any conclusions until we see what he wants," Frederick said calmly, even though Lily sensed he shared Mary's panic—and her own.

"Help me with a scarf, please," Lily said to Mary, preferring to cover her hair for the purpose of meeting a complete stranger. She was pleased with how quickly Mary was able to cover her head with a floral scarf that went well with the dark-red dress Lily was wearing. Mary pinned the scarf into place with a lovely brooch, and Lily tried to see a confident and innocent woman in her reflection. She prayed silently to be able to handle this well and was glad for the way Frederick took her hand, making it clear she didn't have to face this—or anything—on her own.

Frederick carried her to the bottom of the stairs so as not to consume her strength. Together they took a deep breath and entered the drawing room. A man who had been seated on one of the sofas came abruptly to his feet. He appeared to be near their own age; for some reason Lily had expected someone much older. He had dark-blond hair cut very short, and he wore an extremely plain dark suit, but he immediately held up his identification badge to prove that he was indeed from the police force.

"I'm Officer Paten," he stated, offering a slight bow. "You must be Mrs. Broadbent."

"Mrs. Woodstone," she corrected and motioned toward Frederick. "This is my husband; we were married not so many weeks ago."

"Ah," the officer said and nodded toward Frederick. "A pleasure, Mr. Woodstone."

"I understand you've been ill, Mrs. Woodstone," the officer said. "I hope that I'm not putting a strain on you to speak with you at this time."

"I'm doing much better," she said. "Thank you."

"What can we do for you?" Frederick asked and motioned for the officer to be seated.

Lily sat down on the sofa opposite the officer, and Frederick sat close beside her, as if he might be able to better protect her by doing so.

"I'll come straight to the point," Officer Paten said. "We've had a complaint filed from a Mr. Sawyer . . . who leases property on your estate, I believe. I would merely like to ask you some questions and try to set the record straight."

"Of course," Lily said with an even voice that disguised the pounding of her heart.

"You know Mr. Sawyer?"

"We do," Lily said.

"Not a very pleasant fellow," Frederick commented dryly, and Lily could easily imagine the torrents of ill feelings that were hidden beneath that tiny, benign statement. But her husband was appearing completely calm and indifferent, and she hoped they could get through the remainder of this interview without letting on to their complete lack of indifference in regard to Mr. Sawyer.

"I would agree with that," Officer Paten said with an expression that indicated great distaste. Lily took that as a clue that this man might very well have compassion for their position in the situation, but she would tread carefully, knowing that Danny's safety and well-being were at stake.

"What is the nature of Mr. Sawyer's complaint?" Lily asked.

Officer Paten leaned back slightly and narrowed his eyes as if he were setting himself to watch them both closely to see how they responded. Lily picked up on his manner and set *herself* to keep her expression steady and to measure her responses carefully.

"He claims that you assaulted him, Mrs. Woodstone, that you are responsible for the wound in his leg."

Lily exchanged a quick glance with Frederick, appalled that Sawyer would have the nerve to report such a thing to the police. Was he such a fool that he couldn't see how bringing this to the attention of the law could incriminate himself? Frederick's eyes told Lily that she should say whatever she felt was best and he would support her; she knew that he would. And it only took her a moment to know that she needed to be honest with Officer Paten—even though she was determined to test this man's attitude a little at a time; she wasn't about to spill everything all at once. But she felt comfortable saying, "Well, that allegation is certainly true, Officer Paten. I *did* stab Mr. Sawyer in the leg . . . with the pair of scissors he used to cut off my hair after he'd abducted me from my home and locked me in his cellar."

The officer's eyes widened. He glanced at the scarf wrapped around Lily's head as if to assess its presence as a piece of evidence. "Why would he do such a thing?" the officer asked, sounding more astonished than accusing. Lily assumed that Mr. Sawyer's character—or rather the lack of it—would have already left an impression on Officer Paten. She hoped that would work in their favor.

"Why, indeed?" Frederick countered. "And why do you suppose he would bring the matter to the attention of the police when he only incriminates himself? It's my opinion that he was either drunk or he's a bit mad."

"Perhaps both," Officer Paten said in a tone that indicated he was more on their side than against them, which helped Lily feel a little more relaxed with this conversation; she was glad to note that it felt more like a conversation than an interrogation. With any luck he would prove to be an ally in their predicament rather than the opposite. But she still couldn't be completely confident on that count. She uttered another silent prayer and waited to see what he might say next.

The officer went on. "Have you had any prior confrontations with Mr. Sawyer?"

Lily answered without hesitation. "I have many times left baked goods or other food at his home—as I do with many of my tenants when I have some indication they are struggling. My carriage driver is always with me, and more recently my husband has accompanied me on such visits. Mr. Sawyer has always been rude and cantankerous, but it appears that he's always made good use of the things I've left for him."

"I see," the officer said thoughtfully. "And is there anything else I should know about?"

Lily hesitated to answer, not knowing for certain what to say. She tried to weigh her instincts but couldn't deny that fear might well be influencing her ability to do so properly. She felt Frederick discreetly squeeze her hand and wished they could leave the room for a moment to talk freely about how to move forward, but that was impossible.

Officer Paten responded to the silence by stating, "I've been doing this job long enough to recognize when I don't know the entire story. I'm simply trying to ascertain whether or not there is any just cause for Mr. Sawyer to need the intervention of the law—or perhaps *you* need the intervention of the law. Right now I am certain of two things—one is that there is certainly more to this story than I'm aware of, and the other is that you're not telling me something. It seems logical to me that those two things are one and the same. Your hesitancy to speak implies that you know more than you're telling me. Would you be so kind as to help me understand the *entire* story, Mrs. Woodstone?" He looked directly at Frederick and added, "Feel free to contribute to the conversation, Mr. Woodstone."

"I will if I need to," Frederick said. "I trust my wife's judgment, and I will stand behind her in however she chooses to handle this."

The officer looked again at Lily. "Handle *what*, exactly?" His question was firm but surprisingly free of accusation. She sensed that he sincerely wanted to get to the truth more than he wanted to stir up any kind of unwarranted trouble.

"I am at a disadvantage, Officer Paten," Lily said. "I'm certain you came here with some knowledge of my reputation and character—so far as it might be perceived by the community. But I know absolutely nothing about you. I admit that there is a sensitive matter of a dispute between ourselves and Mr. Sawyer, but I don't know if the law would necessarily handle the matter in the best possible way. I believe there are good people who do their best to see that justice is well served, and I would like to believe you are one of those people. I do not necessarily believe that certain legal matters have been established and upheld in a way that truly serves justice. For instance, as a woman, I am keenly aware of the fact that my rights are dramatically different from any man's. As an unmarried woman my rights to my own inherited property were questionable; as a married woman, everything I own belongs to my husband. Thankfully, my husband is a good and trustworthy man, but such is not always the case, and I'm certain many women suffer from such legal injustice. I would very much like to know your opinion on matters of the law in regard to such things, Officer Paten."

He looked slightly taken off guard but deeply thoughtful. He said with apparent sincerity, "I agree that the letter of the law is often unjust. You said that you know nothing about me, and you're asking for my opinion. I consider myself a trustworthy man, and I strive to do my job well. I also tend to be a man who adheres more to the spirit of the law. My superiors are not always pleased with the way I do things, but I get the job done, so they've come to give me allowances in that regard; somehow I usually manage to maneuver what is fair and just into what is legal—if that makes any sense."

"It does, actually," Lily said, feeling relief over such a statement— especially when her instincts were telling her that he was being completely truthful, which aided her confidence in pressing forward. "If you know anything about me," she went on, "then you know that I have several adopted children. These children came from orphanages and equally hideous facilities where there is no law to protect them from unspeakable treatment and neglect. I've done my best to give them a good home and an education; they are safe here, and they know they are loved. The very idea of *any* child lacking in such necessities is very upsetting to me. I wish I could adopt them all."

"Your efforts are very noble, Mrs. Woodstone," the officer said.

"I'm not seeking compliments, Officer Paten. I'm merely trying to explain to you the kind of person I am. You asked for the missing pieces of this story. I confess that I'm hesitant to tell you because I do not necessarily believe the law would be on my side if the entire story were known. Can you understand my dilemma?" she asked and saw an enlightenment come into his eyes.

"I believe I can," he said and was thoughtful a long moment. "Perhaps you could speak to me . . . hypothetically . . . about the possible reasons for the situation."

"Perhaps," she said, again sharing a glance with Frederick, glad to see that he seemed in agreement with her approach so far. Gazing firmly at Officer Paten, she added, "Does the law not support that a man has the right to have possession of his children no matter how badly he might treat them?"

The officer took in an audible breath as the implication became evident. "But if we are speaking of Mr. Sawyer—hypothetically, of course—he doesn't have any children, so why would . . ." He stopped as if to think the matter through more thoroughly. "I've looked into local records. His wife and child died years ago."

Lily felt hesitant to respond, mostly due to the unexpected wave of emotion that was overtaking her as she recalled the condition in which they'd found Danny. She feared being able to speak without letting on, and she bit her trembling lip as she glanced at Frederick.

He picked up on her cue and was quick to say, "Hypothetically speaking, Officer Paten, what if the wife died and the child did not but was rather kept concealed, locked away, neglected, and abused?" Again the officer drew in a loud breath, his expression a combination of surprise and perhaps horror. "Would the law defend that a man has the right to maintain possession of that child in spite of such unconscionable behavior?"

Officer Paten was silent for several tense moments. Frederick put his arm around Lily's shoulders, and she leaned against him, feeling weaker than she had in days as she felt the weight of all that hung in the balance. This officer's attitude could determine Danny's well-being and safety; he also had the power to seek legal action against Lily and Frederick for removing Danny from his father's home. Mr. Sawyer was certainly guilty of kidnapping, but so were they.

"Hypothetically speaking, then," Officer Paten finally said, "if you became aware of the child due to your visits to the home and you took the child into your care, which angered Mr. Sawyer and provoked him to vengeance . . . which resulted in his abducting you . . . and his wound is a result of self-defense . . . then . . ." He sighed loudly. "Well, that certainly completes the story, doesn't it!"

"And how does the story end?" Lily asked.

"Well," the officer drawled, "as I see the facts, Mr. Sawyer's accusations included no mention of a child, and there are no records of a living child . . . therefore, unless he is willing to come forward and report an abduction, he is clearly in the wrong for having abducted you, Mrs. Woodstone, and threatening your safety, which means you were justified in your reasons for inflicting him with the wound he suffered. If he comes forward with further accusations, I will look deeper into the matter; otherwise it appears to be settled."

Lily took a deep breath of relief and felt Frederick do the same. But she had to ask, "And what if Mr. Sawyer *does* come forward . . . wanting his son back?" She realized that she had just as good as admitted to what she'd done, but she now truly believed that Officer Paten was on their side and would do his best to protect Danny if it came to that.

"I wouldn't worry too much about that," the officer said. "If he had the nerve to admit that his son was missing, he would have to admit to having kept him hidden all these years, and I doubt he would do so. *If* that happens, I will do everything I can to help you. I hope you can believe me in spite of our barely being acquainted."

"We're very grateful to know that," Frederick said.

"Knowing the whole story," the officer said, "hypothetically at least . . . I would be very glad to know that such a child might be in your care." Officer Paten stood up. "I will certainly inform you straightaway if anything else comes up in regard to the matter."

"Thank you," Lily and Frederick said at the same time as they also came to their feet.

Once the officer had left, Lily turned to her husband and practically collapsed into his embrace, overcome with relief as much as weakened by the strain of what had just taken place. "Oh, praise heaven!" she murmured. "I pray this man is as good as he seems, that he will help keep Danny safe."

"Amen," Frederick said and just held her in a way that filled her with strength.

* * *

Frederick shared Lily's relief over both having spoken to Officer Paten and having his support in their desire to keep Danny safe and in their care. He felt hopeful that in time they could ease Danny into a more normal existence, and he and Lily talked often about the hope and peace they felt over the matter.

Lily's healing took a giant leap forward, which Frederick attributed to be at least partly due to being free of the fear—or at least the majority of it—she'd been feeling on Danny's behalf, and also partly due to the hope and joy she felt in regard to Danny being a part of their family permanently. Their private conversations were often centered around the welfare and progress of each of the children, as well as their mutual desire to have Danny remain safely in their care and become a part of their family.

Frederick was filled continually with gratitude for Lily's recovery, and he marveled at her ability to be so forgiving toward Mr. Sawyer. She readily admitted that difficult feelings sometimes surfaced, and she had to consciously focus on remembering that it was not her place to judge either the heart of this man or his intentions. Frederick agreed with her wholeheartedly about knowing it was not his place to judge Mr. Sawyer's actions, but he was not finding it as easy to be forgiving as it seemed to be for Lily. Each time he thought of this man's deplorable actions and the hurt he'd inflicted on both Danny and Lily, Frederick fumed inside, sometimes feeling as if a fire were literally burning inside of him that might consume him. He had no difficulty admitting his feelings truthfully to Lily. She was compassionate concerning his anger and completely confident that in time he would come to terms with it. Frederick had difficulty sharing Lily's confidence over the matter and was continually amazed at her own charitable nature and ability to forgive. She had a way of leaving him feeling humbled and wanting to strive to be a better man; if only to earn her respect, he put forth a conscious effort each day to attempt to let go of his hate and anger. He'd devoted a great deal of prayer toward that end, and he'd certainly tried to replace his raging thoughts with an attitude that was more Christian in nature. But at moments he wondered if his efforts were futile. He just felt so *angry*! And he was reminded of the reasons for his bitterness every time he looked at Lily's short hair or when he spent time with Danny and saw evidence of how the boy was still struggling with so many simple facets of life. The child was making progress with his reading and writing, with social skills among those with whom he interacted, as well as basic etiquette. But in every regard he was dramatically behind for a child his age.

Frederick did well at concealing any negative feelings when he spent time with Danny, and he tried to remain positive around Lily. But he knew she suspected how difficult this was for him. When she'd ask how he was doing, he would simply tell her that he was working on it. That was the best he could give her for now, and he was grateful for her patience and understanding. He often wondered why he was having more difficulty than Lily when *she* was the one who had been abducted and subjected to the cruelty of this monstrous man. Frederick wondered if it had anything to do with the helplessness he felt in thinking of how he'd not been able to protect his wife from such danger, or if it had more to do with his own childhood and the trauma his mother had spoken of. Perhaps both. Whatever the reasons, he knew he needed to find peace with this, or he feared it would eat away at him like a raging cancer.

* * *

On the first morning Lily had walked down the stairs on her own to share breakfast with the staff, Frederick noticed that Max seemed distracted and agitated throughout the meal. Frederick didn't want to draw attention to it in front of everyone, but he kept a discreet eye on Max, determined to speak with him privately before he left to see to his work. When Max stood to leave, Frederick stood as well, but he was surprised when Max approached him and asked quietly, "Could I speak with you and your good wife when it's convenient?"

"Of course," Frederick said, glad he didn't have to try and convince Max to share whatever might be bothering him. "We'll meet you in the east parlor in a few minutes . . . just as soon as we're finished here."

"Thank you," Max said without looking at him—which was not his usual manner—and Frederick felt genuinely concerned.

Max left the room, and Frederick discreetly waited for Lily to finish her breakfast. He escorted her into the hall and said, "Max wants to talk with us. He seems upset; I'm not sure why."

"Oh, dear," she said, and he knew she likely shared his most promi-nent suspicion over what this might be about. Max had been the one to help Mr. Sawyer when he'd been wounded, and he'd kept an eye on him. But he'd not reported anything to them since Lily had turned the corner into recovery.

They entered the parlor to find Max pacing while he wrestled with the hat he held in his hands.

"Please . . . sit down," Frederick said, motioning to a chair.

"Thank you, sir, but I'd rather stand if it's all the same."

"Of course," Frederick said. He guided Lily to a chair before he stood to face Max and asked, "What's the problem, my good man? I'm glad you asked to speak with us. I could tell you were out of sorts."

"It's Mr. Sawyer," Max said, coming straight to the point.

Frederick felt some panic, wondering if this man would cause them more trouble. A quick glance at Lily showed him that she shared his concern. But Max dispelled that worry when he added, "The old man is ill, very ill."

"What's wrong?" Lily asked in alarm.

"It's the pox, my lady," Max said, and Frederick exchanged a long gaze with Lily as the irony settled in. If Mr. Sawyer had never contracted the illness as a child, then he would have been susceptible to catching it from Lily when he'd abducted her. There seemed no reason to verbalize their thoughts, and they both turned again to Max, silently asking for more information, which he readily gave. "I kept checkin' in on him whenever I was passin' that way goin' into town. I figured you would have left your baskets for him if you'd been up and about," he said directly to Lily. "And since you was laid up, I figured I would do it for you. I figured it's not up to me to judge if a man deserves help when he's down and out." He nodded toward Lily. "You taught me that, my lady." Max cleared his throat. "Once the old man was up and about after that wound was gettin' better, I just left things for him every couple of days, and he usually came out to yell at me the way he always did before. Then he didn't come out, and I felt inclined to check on him. I found him ill and offered t' get the doctor, but he wouldn't have it. I confess I've been going there a couple of times a day and spending some time trying to ease his suffering as best I could. I didn't want t' bother you with it." He looked at Frederick then Lily then Frederick again. "With the lady doing so poorly and the boy ill too, I thought it best I handle it on my own. I spoke t' Mrs. Pilfer, and she agreed with me. She helped me know what t' do, and fixed some things for me t' take that helped."

Max's nerves increased as he apparently drew close to whatever had changed to cause such urgency in him.

"Go on," Lily encouraged.

"The thing is he's gotten so much worse the last day or so. I think the doctor should be brought, but I was also thinkin' that's not really up to me, seein' that I couldn't pay the fee and given all the upset old Sawyer has caused. I just . . . thought I should be talkin' t' the both of you. And now that the old man's gotten so much worse, I'm thinkin' I shoulda talked to you days ago; maybe I waited too long. It's just that I didn't want to cause any distress, and he got so much worse real sudden, like just early this morning when I went t' check in on him."

"You mustn't blame yourself," Lily said. "You've done a good thing by being so kind to him. But you're right, the doctor should be sent for. And of course we will take care of his fee."

"Thank you, Max," Frederick said, as humbled by Max's charitable efforts as he was by his wife's sincere ability to forgive. "You did the right thing, looking after him . . . and coming to talk to us. You go for the doctor, and I'll go and sit with him." Frederick heard the words come out of his mouth and wondered what might have prompted him to make such an offer. He had no desire whatsoever to even be in the same room with this man he could barely tolerate thinking about. There were others in the house he could easily send to be with Mr. Sawyer, but now that he'd said it, he would only sound like a fool to back down. And perhaps he needed to just follow the example of Max and Lily and show some charitable compassion toward someone in need, instead of being so focused on his own strained emotions.

"I'll go for the doctor, then," Max said and hurried from the room.

Lily stood and took Frederick's hands. "I should come with you," she said, and he knew she was concerned about his difficult feelings toward Mr. Sawyer.

"No, you should not!" he insisted. "I don't ever want you to go back to that place—ever! I'm glad Max has shown him such kindness; I really am. But you need to stay here and take care of yourself. I'll see that all is well."

"But you're . . ."

Lily hesitated, and he could guess what she didn't want to say . . . that he was struggling with hate and rage toward Sawyer. He forced a smile and said with conviction, "I promise to be kind. I promise." He took her shoulders into his hands. "I promise," he added more softly. "Since he got this illness as a result of having contact with you, it seems he's enduring severe consequences for his actions. I must say I find it ironic that *you* became ill because of your *kindness* in trying to help someone with sick children." He kissed Lily's brow. "I will send word with Max or come back myself as soon as we hear what the doctor has to say."

Lily nodded, and Frederick left quickly before he could talk himself out of it. Already he felt sick with dread; he didn't want to get anywhere near the Sawyer home, let alone go inside and offer kindness to the man who had caused so much pain for the people Frederick loved—and for himself. Still, he rode quickly to his destination, finding it odd that he actually felt some genuine concern for the old man. Perhaps he wasn't nearly so uncharitable as he'd believed.

Approaching the house, Frederick had to force his anger and hatred down deep into himself where they wouldn't threaten to erupt. He dismounted and tied the reins of his horse to a fence rail, where it could graze. Trudging toward the door, Frederick told himself over and over in his mind that he needed to think like a vicar more than he ever had even when he'd actually been a vicar. He needed to focus on all that he knew about the teachings of Jesus that he'd learned from fierce study of the Bible: don't judge, be kind to the sinners, love one another, forgive. He was a little startled to have a phrase jump into his mind seemingly out of nowhere: *Love your enemies, bless them that curse you, do good to them that hate you, and pray for them which despitefully use you, and persecute you.*

Frederick took the memory of these words into his spirit with a deep breath, freshly amazed at how well his sweet wife lived such teachings with her whole heart. He pressed one hand over the center of his chest as if that might ease the tightening he felt there, and with the other hand he turned the knob and pushed open the door. The dingy front room had only a little light coming through dirty windows. Frederick quietly closed the door behind him and moved toward what he could see was a bedroom. He took a step and thought of Danny locked in the cellar here for years. His stomach smoldered, and he forced the thought away. He took another step and saw a clear image in his mind of Lily held captive and having her hair cruelly cut off while Old Man Sawyer cursed at her and uttered horrible threats. He forced that away, too, and repeated in his mind the words from the Bible that he knew so well. He knew the principles were true; he'd seen them work miracles in the lives of others. But never had the need for such teachings been so pertinent in his own life. He knew that his mother had forgiven his father and had found peace. He'd never felt any anger toward his father, perhaps because he'd never known him, and his mother had more than made up for the absence of a father in his life. It occurred to him as he took yet another slow and careful step that perhaps he *did* feel anger toward his father; perhaps his mother's stories of him *had* left more of an impression than he'd believed. And perhaps that was the very reason that Mr. Sawyer's behavior was proving so difficult for him to forgive. He wondered if having the idea come so clearly to his mind was some kind of answer to his prayers. He'd like to think so.

Another two steps and Frederick was in the doorway of a bedroom that looked much more tidy and free of dust. He suspected that Max might have had something to do with that if he'd been checking in here regularly and trying to help the old man. The subject of so much trauma in Frederick's life lay on his back in a narrow bed beneath a worn blanket. He might have appeared dead if it weren't for his raspy breathing and the way his chest rose and fell with strain. His helplessness and misery helped soften the hardness of heart Frederick had been wrestling with.

"Mr. Sawyer," he said and gently put a hand on the old man's shoulder, but he got no response. Sawyer was clearly too ill to be aware of his surroundings. That alone let Frederick know his condition was very grave. Recalling Lily's struggle to survive the same illness, Frederick wondered if Sawyer would have the strength to get through this, taking into consideration that he was much older than Lily; and with his drinking habits, he had likely not been in very good health to begin with. A horrible thought sprang into Frederick's mind: what if Mr. Sawyer had become ill or had died without anyone knowing there was a child locked in the cellar? The very idea sent a harsh shiver over Frederick's shoulders and down his back.

Frederick considered the deepening ironies as he sat in a chair that had been left near the bed. Observing the placement of the chair, he wondered if Max had spent time sitting here with Mr. Sawyer. And he also wondered how much grumbling and complaining the old man had done prior to his becoming too ill to speak. Frederick touched Sawyer's brow with the back of his hand, not surprised to find it hot with fever. He went in search of cool water and some rags.

Finding rags that had been laid out to dry in the kitchen, he saw evidence that Max had also been doing his best to help calm the fever during the time he had spent here. He wondered how much Wally had been covering Max's work at home so that Max could be here and how much time Max had actually spent caring for the old man secretly because he hadn't wanted to upset Frederick or Lily. Frederick sighed at the thought of the giving nature of these two good men, which added to his own humility as he filled a basin with cold water, gathered the rags, and went back to the bedroom, where he scooted the chair closer to the bed so that he could reach to place cool rags on Sawyer's brow and neck and arms.

Minutes ticked away while he sat there and found himself wondering *why* this man had become the way he was. What factors might have contributed to his becoming so cruel and selfish? Frederick was glad to know that only God had the right to judge any person's actions, because only God knew the entirety of any given life. Had Mr. Sawyer been treated by his father the way he had treated his son? Did he not know any better? Was he so deeply unhappy or afraid or in pain that it made him unable to think clearly? Frederick understood such concepts, given his work as a vicar, but he'd never made the effort to sincerely consider them in regard to Mr. Sawyer; his mind had been too clouded by the suffering this man had caused. But now, seeing him so weak and helpless, Frederick's thoughts were shifting, and subsequently he felt his heart softening. Perhaps his impulsively volunteering to come here and sit with the old man had been the answer to his prayers—or at least a portion of that answer. He'd been actively seeking to find peace and forgiveness. He couldn't say that all of his ill feelings had magically vanished; he felt certain that if Sawyer were conscious the old man would be full of hatred and rage. Frederick knew he was guilty of those same feelings, even if he knew he would never act on such feelings by hurting someone else. Still, there was certainly more to this man—and this situation—than Frederick could ever understand.

Glancing around to take in the details of his surroundings, Frederick found the room stark and bare albeit surprisingly clean, all things considered. He thought of how Danny had come into their home with evidence of fairly good hygiene; apparently for all of Sawyer's faults, he considered cleanliness a priority. The room had no evidence of anything personal or sentimental, and there was certainly no warmth in the decor; there was nothing at all to add any charm or appeal. Was the man's life so devoid of anything personal? Then Frederick's eyes were drawn to a very large old book on the bedside table, which looked completely out of place. Frederick picked it up, surprised by its weight until he realized it was a family Bible. It took several minutes of just holding the Bible in his hands to try and make sense of its presence here in Mr. Sawyer's home. It was common for families to have such a Bible when they held to Christian beliefs; not only was it the source of spiritual learning and guidance, but it was also used to keep family records. Births, marriages, deaths, and other important dates were recorded in these books; therefore, their value was priceless for multiple reasons. However, the actual *cost* of a Bible such as this was no small thing. He knew well enough that the poor most often didn't have the luxury of owning such a Bible, and many of them were illiterate and would not even be able to read it or record their own important events. Generally the only way someone of poor means had possession of such an expensive book was if it had been inherited, passed down from prior generations. He recalled Mr. Topp having such a Bible, and he wondered if the kind, humble man had made any progress in overcoming his grief. Frederick made a mental note to check in on him at the soonest possible opportunity.

Frederick considered the evidence that, for all of Mr. Sawyer's mean disposition, he had come from a Christian background. Of course, Frederick knew well enough that even practicing Christians could behave very badly in their personal lives. Believing in Christianity or attending church with a congregation often did not equate with people actually behaving like Christians. Still, Mr. Sawyer had in his possession a very fine and old family Bible. And it was clearly the most valuable thing in the house; in fact, Frederick doubted there was *anything* else in the house with any value. There appeared to be barely enough dishes and bedding for him to function, very few clothes, and little of anything else at all. Frederick wondered if Max might have been reading from the Bible while he'd sat in this chair; given the placement of the book, within easy reach, it was a natural conclusion. It also occurred to him that perhaps the Bible didn't belong to Mr. Sawyer. Could it be Max's family Bible? Frederick opened it just long enough to glance at the handwritten records and saw the name Sawyer there. So the book belonged to the man who had caused so much pain for the people Frederick loved, the same man who could now be dying—as a direct result of coming in contact with Lily when she'd been ill. The ironies continued to mount.

Frederick closed the Bible and set it back on the bedside table, wondering if there was anything else he could do to help the old man. He dipped the rags in cold water and wrung them out to refresh them and make them cooler before again placing them against Sawyer's skin, where they would hopefully help bring down the fever. Other than that, Frederick had no idea how he could help. He'd spent many days wondering the same thing at Lily's bedside. There was little to be done except to allow the symptoms to run their course. He would be glad to have the doctor check on Mr. Sawyer and offer a more professional view on how bad the situation really was. But Frederick was taken aback by his preeminent thought that he might prefer having Sawyer die as opposed to the possibility of him recovering to once again return to his cruel and ornery self, and to potentially cause difficulties in regard to Danny. Frederick felt selfish and uncharitable as he admitted to himself that he truly preferred the idea of this man dying. He hung his head and prayed silently for more compassionate thoughts and for forgiveness.

Chapter Twelve

MISTAKEN IDENTITY

THE DOCTOR FINALLY ARRIVED WITH Max. He'd been delivering a baby and had needed to be certain mother and baby were well before leaving to attend to Mr. Sawyer. After an adept examination, the doctor declared what Frederick had suspected after sitting with the old man: his condition was extremely grave, and it was much more likely that he was near death than there being any chance for a miraculous recovery.

"All that can be done now is to try and keep him comfortable so that he doesn't suffer as he struggles to breathe. I'm going to leave some medicine with you." He set a bottle of brown liquid on the bedside table and told Frederick and Max his dosing recommendations. "I would suggest," the doctor added, "that he not be left alone; I doubt he'll hang on more than a day or two at most."

"No one should die alone," Frederick said, looking at the stricken man while he considered the pathetic state he was in and the fact that Mr. Sawyer had lived his life in such a way that the only people who were willing to be with him when he died were practically strangers whose only interactions with him had been linked to horrifying events directly resulting from Sawyer's deplorable actions.

After the doctor left, Frederick felt strangely overcome with a need to remain with Mr. Sawyer and sort out his own strained thoughts and difficult emotions. All of his stewing and fretting over the need to forgive this man took on a whole new perspective with the reality that he was likely dying. And for reasons Frederick didn't fully understand, he had a bizarre sense of urgency to find peace with Sawyer before he passed on.

Attempting to think clearly, he said to Max, "I'm very grateful that you've been kind enough to be here for Mr. Sawyer—as much as he would let you."

"He's not been protestin' so much since he got too sick t' get out o' bed." A sadness hung over Max's countenance, and Frederick wanted to ask him about what he was feeling and why. Before he could, Max glanced toward the ailing patient and said, "It don't make no sense, but I've gotten attached t' the old man—in a strange kind of way. I do believe there's good in him somewhere. I'm wantin' t' think that when he's gone on t' wherever it is we go after this life, he'll be able t' find his way back t' that goodness." He chuckled uncomfortably. "You was once a vicar. Maybe that sounds like crazy talk t' you, but that's how it feels t' me. Or maybe that's just how I want t' think it would be."

"It doesn't sound crazy, Max. I agree with you. I believe that God loves all of His children and that He is merciful. A merciful God would surely give us another chance to make things right—especially when this life is far too unfair to be the basis of any kind of fair judgment."

"Yeah . . . that makes sense . . . I think."

Frederick sighed and said, "I'd like to stay. Would you please take word to Mrs. Woodstone of what the doctor said, and tell her I'm going to stay here for the time being, but I would prefer that she remain at home and see to her health. If you could bring back something for me to eat when it's convenient, I'd very much appreciate it."

"Glad t' help," Max said. "I've got some work t' see to, but I'll come back as soon as I'm able."

"You do what you need to do," Frederick said. "I'll be fine. Thank you again for all of your efforts."

Max nodded, seeming a bit uncomfortable at having attention drawn to his kind acts. His humility in giving of his time and patience once again warmed Frederick and left him feeling ashamed of his own anger toward Mr. Sawyer. He reminded himself of what he'd often told those of his congregation who had come to him seeking advice on matters of forgiveness: it isn't something that occurs magically in a single moment simply because we want it to. Forgiveness often takes time and a great deal of effort. In truth, not that much time had passed since Mr. Sawyer had been so cruel to Lily; and having Danny in their care was still fairly new in terms of the grand scheme of life. Frederick gave himself credit for at least consciously making an effort to forgive this man and give the matter over to God. And he also knew that forgiveness does not equate with trust. It is entirely possible to forgive someone and never trust them, knowing that many people were likely to never change their bad behavior. But if Mr. Sawyer was truly on his deathbed—as it seemed—trust was no longer an issue.

Frederick sat down again in the chair by the bed. He checked Sawyer's face and still found it very warm. He freshened the rags with cool water and put them on the man's face and arms, feeling that his efforts were futile, but he wanted to do *something* that might at least seem helpful. Again Frederick noted that if it weren't for the old man's strained breathing, he would already look dead. He had shown no sign of consciousness since Frederick had arrived, which was perhaps the reason that Frederick felt confident speaking aloud to him, knowing it might be his only chance to say what he wanted to say without Max or anyone else around.

"I can't begin to understand why you are the way you are. I know nothing of your life before you ended up here. I only know that your wife died and you were left with a child that you deplorably hid away. Your treatment of Danny has made me very angry." Frederick heard the depth of his own anger in the way he spoke, but now that he was gaining some momentum, he went on. "Only God can judge why you did what you did, but I believe God knows *why*, and that's something I could never comprehend. I'm glad to be able to turn the matter over to God, and that's what I'm doing. The same goes for the way you took my wife from our home and the unconscionable way you treated her. I confess that I actually had thoughts of wanting to kill you, and I've *never* felt that way before about another human being. Now that it seems you're dying, I guess I won't ever have to find out if those feelings would have continued to tempt me." He chuckled in a feeble attempt to ease the harshness of his own words. "I never would have done it, you know; it's not in me. But you should know I *did* feel tempted. What you did is . . . atrocious and . . . beyond appalling . . . but it's done; it's in the past. I want you to know that my wife is a strong woman—and a very forgiving one. Whether you live or die, you will never harm her again, and she will not be undone by your cruelty toward her. I also want you to know that Danny will never be allowed into your care again. We will fight to protect him; we will do whatever it takes. If there is anything good in you at all, you will just let him go and allow us to raise him the way a boy should be raised."

Frederick sighed and assessed the fact that he was in essence talking to himself, but he couldn't deny feeling somewhat better for having stated exactly how he felt. More calmly he added, "I don't know if you realize that this illness that may very well take your life was contracted from my wife . . . because you chose to steal her from her home while she was contagious. Oh, the ironies of life! I don't know if you can appreciate the irony of this, but I certainly can. Strange that I might actually feel some sorrow over your condition and the likelihood that this is the end for you. I have no idea why. Still . . . I used to be a vicar. Did you know that? I don't know if I was a very good one; I suppose that's why I decided to be a teacher instead. Teaching children is more to my liking, and it was something I believed I could do well, as opposed to perhaps being a mediocre vicar. But . . . for what it's worth, I truly believe you're going to a better place . . . and perhaps there you will have an opportunity to repent of your wrongdoings . . . and to heal from whatever harshness occurred in your life to make you the way you are."

Frederick remained silent for several minutes, contemplating everything he'd said aloud and the way it had helped purge the darkness from him. He felt lighter and more able to think of moving beyond all that had happened. Unable to think of anything else to say that would have any relevance, he picked up the Bible from the bedside table and settled the heavy book onto his lap. It occurred to him that if Mr. Sawyer passed, this book would have value to Danny, perhaps not right away . . . but someday when he was stronger and he'd had years to heal and get beyond what his father's neglect and abuse had done to him. For all that Danny's early childhood was nothing but horror and tragedy, this Bible still held the records of his family.

Frederick flipped through the pages of scripture, searching absently for some of his favorite passages in the New Testament. He found the chapter where Matthew had recorded the profound teachings of Jesus about love and righteousness and forgiveness. He began reading to himself for only a moment before it occurred to him that if he could talk to an unconscious man, he could also read to him. It might not do Mr. Sawyer any good on either count, but reading aloud Jesus's words helped Frederick feel better. He couldn't say in that moment his forgiveness was complete, but he'd certainly come a long way. Seeing Mr. Sawyer in this helpless, pathetic state had given him an enormous perspective on the plight of the human condition and the stark need to not judge the actions of others. Instinctively he believed this man had likely endured his own horrors early in life and he'd never known any better than to behave badly as a result. Of course, Sawyer—like all people—had the agency to choose how to behave, and he would be accountable to God for his choices. Still, Frederick believed God *would* be merciful. No human being was without imperfections and weaknesses, and without God's mercy we would all surely be lost. Reading from the Bible brought that fact home to him more deeply than it ever had.

Frederick stopped in the middle of a sentence when he heard a faint mumbling and realized Mr. Sawyer was trying to speak and had turned his head slightly on the pillow. Frederick closed the book and set it down, leaning closer to the old man and instinctively taking hold of his hand, surprised to feel Sawyer weakly squeeze his fingers.

"What did you say?" Frederick asked. "Did you say something?"

Sawyer's eyes flickered open slightly and stared toward Frederick. "You came back," he mumbled in a quiet, raspy voice that Frederick could barely hear. "I didn't . . . think . . . I would ever . . . see you again."

Frederick didn't know who Mr. Sawyer believed he was, but he thought it best to not try and protest. The man was surely delirious. "I'm here," Frederick said, figuring that was a true statement.

Sawyer closed his eyes as if it were too much effort to hold them open. But he continued to speak in a gravelly whisper. "I . . . hurt your mother; I know I did. It's . . . good that . . . she went. Better . . . that she went." Frederick just listened, wondering if Sawyer believed that he was somehow a grown-up version of Danny, whose mother had died years ago. That idea was squelched by Sawyer's next comment, which made no sense to Frederick, given what he knew. "Your brother . . . your brother . . . I hurt your brother . . ." Frederick actually saw the glisten of tears in the corners of the old man's eyes while he wondered how Danny might have had a brother. It had been said that Sawyer's wife and child had died; they'd assumed that the child hadn't died but had been shut away in the cellar. But if Sawyer had kept Danny a secret since his wife's death, was it possible there had been more than one child and the other one *had* died and was buried with his mother?

Frederick desperately wanted to ask questions, but intuitively he knew he wouldn't likely get any comprehendible answers. Sawyer turned his head away from Frederick as if in shame, and the tears leaked over his temples and into his hair. "I . . . never thought . . . God would . . . hear the prayers of . . . a man like me . . . but I still prayed . . . hopin' you might come back to me. And you did. Maybe . . . there's hope for me . . . just maybe." With great difficulty, Sawyer turned his head back to look at Frederick and opened his eyes just slightly. "If . . . I could hope . . . that you'd forgive me . . . for all I done . . . then maybe . . . just maybe . . ." He didn't complete the sentence, as if he either didn't have the strength or didn't know what to say. But Frederick understood the implication. If he believed that Frederick was his son and was hoping that God might have heard his prayers, then perhaps he believed that if his son could forgive him for his terrible deeds, then maybe God could forgive him too.

Frederick actually felt a little choked up to hear this man admit to praying and to hoping that God might grant him some form of mercy. He found it remarkably easy to pretend to be whomever Sawyer believed him to be, but the words he spoke were his own when he said with full purpose of heart, "I forgive you, and you must know that God *is* merciful and He loves you."

Mr. Sawyer showed the tiniest hint of a smile as he took on a more peaceful countenance. "You've become . . . such a fine . . . man. So much . . . like your mother." He closed his eyes and sighed. "It was good she went," he said again, then began to cough so fiercely that Frederick feared he'd never catch his breath again. He helped the old man sit up and supported his shoulders while he coughed and coughed, and the evidence of how poorly his lungs were working became starkly clear. The coughing finally settled into the strained, raspy breathing that had been evident earlier—but now it sounded much worse.

Frederick helped him take some of the medicine the doctor had left, followed by some sips of water. As soon as Frederick guided Sawyer's head back to the pillow, it was clear that he'd drifted back into unconsciousness; their conversation—strange and bizarre as it had been—was now over. And Frederick doubted that Mr. Sawyer would ever regain enough consciousness to be able to speak again. It seemed a miracle that he'd been able to speak at all, but perhaps it was the miracle Frederick had needed in order to finalize his own forgiveness toward this man. And perhaps it was what Mr. Sawyer had needed as well in order to be able to leave this life with some measure of peace. Even though Frederick couldn't begin to understand what Sawyer had been referring to or how the pieces of this man's life fit together, he believed that the words spoken had been important to him—even if he'd not actually been speaking to whomever he'd believed Frederick to be.

Frederick leaned back in his chair and sat in contemplative silence, listening to the rhythm of Sawyer's breathing, well aware that his strained breaths were becoming more difficult and further apart. Given his experience as a vicar, it wasn't the first time he'd sat with someone as they'd passed from this mortal life into whatever lay beyond death. But never had it felt so personal to him, and he wondered why. This man had done nothing but cause grief in his life, and the hurt he'd inflicted on Lily and Danny was still close to Frederick's heart. Nevertheless, the raw pain in his heart had been soothed and replaced with peace—a peace that passed all understanding. Frederick marveled at the miracle and offered a prayer of gratitude for experiencing God's grace in his life over this crucial turn of events, and he prayed that Mr. Sawyer's journey into the next life would bring *him* peace.

Max returned with some food and a few other supplies for both of them on the chance that their vigil with Mr. Sawyer required one or both of them to stay. He offered to take over for Frederick so that he could go home, but Frederick felt the need to remain. With Max's report that all was well with his wife and children, Frederick declared that he preferred to stay with Max—who also was determined to stay with Mr. Sawyer. They talked a little as they settled in more comfortably to watch the old man's breathing become more and more strained.

Frederick lost track of the time and ate very little while he and Max mostly remained silent and just waited. Sometime in the darkest part of the night, Mr. Sawyer finally ceased struggling to breathe and left this world. Frederick was surprised to feel a few stray tears trickle down his face. He attributed them mostly to the tenderness he'd always felt to observe the magnitude of someone passing from this life to the next, but deep inside he knew it was more. Somehow in the past several hours, he had grown to feel a great deal of compassion and even warmth for this strange old man who had impacted his life in ways he never could have imagined.

Max went for the doctor, who would need to verify Mr. Sawyer's death, and also the undertaker, who would take care of the burial. Frederick waited with the body, strangely mesmerized by the look of peace on the face of the deceased. When the others arrived, Frederick spoke with the doctor to thank him for his efforts and to verify their agreement that Frederick would cover his fees. Frederick also spoke with the undertaker and made some specific requests regarding Mr. Sawyer's burial, assuring him he would be paid for whatever it might cost for a decent coffin, a respectable burial, and a headstone to mark the grave. Frederick considered it a tangible way to finalize his forgiveness toward Mr. Sawyer, and even if he hadn't been blessed with the good fortune of being married to a very wealthy woman, he knew he still would have done the same, using whatever was necessary from his salary to see that Mr. Sawyer wasn't buried with the impoverished and unremembered of this world.

Before Frederick left the house, it occurred to him that Danny's father had just died, and for all that Danny had no experience or memory with his father that was even remotely good, Mr. Sawyer was still his father. He looked around the little house for anything that might be of value or significance to Danny, finding nothing except the family Bible. He felt no qualms in taking it on Danny's behalf, certain that this record of the boy's family would one day mean something to him.

Frederick arrived home just as the sky was beginning to show a hint of light from the forthcoming dawn of a new day. He removed the saddle from his horse and settled the animal into its stall before he lumbered into the house, exhausted in body and spirit, and overcome with a plethora of emotions. He plodded up the back stairs and went quietly into the bedroom. Lily immediately sat up in bed, and he knew she either hadn't been sleeping or her sleep hadn't been very deep.

"Are you all right?" she asked.

"It's difficult to say," he muttered and set the heavy Bible down on the bureau before he removed his coat and boots and curled up on the bed, putting his head in Lily's lap.

"Tell me," she encouraged gently. "Is Mr. Sawyer going to be—"

"He died," Frederick said and heard Lily gasp; a moment later he heard her sniffle and knew she was crying. He might have questioned her reasons except that he'd experienced his own strange sadness over the passing of the old man.

Lily cried for a few minutes before she said, "He died because of the illness he got from me."

Frederick turned to look up at her in the early-morning light. "He was exposed to the illness because he *abducted* you from your home. I too feel some sorrow at his passing . . . or at least some tenderness over it, but this is a result of choices *he* made, Lily. He has no one to blame but himself."

"And yet his terrible choices have now taken him to a better place," she said. "Perhaps he will be able to find peace and healing now."

"That is my hope," Frederick said and relaxed again. "There is a great deal I want to tell you," he added, "but . . ."

"But you're exhausted."

"I am," he admitted. "I can't even think clearly right now."

"We'll talk after you've had some sleep," she said, pressing her fingers through his hair in a way that relaxed him further. "Do you need something to eat first?"

"No . . . thank you," he said. "I just need to sleep." He lifted his head and asked, "Are you all right? I didn't even ask."

"I'm fine," she said and kissed him. "Get some sleep, and we'll talk later."

* * *

Frederick eased himself under the covers, and Lily watched her husband drift into deep slumber within a couple of minutes. She sighed and just watched him sleep, grateful to have him back safely. And while she felt strangely sad over Mr. Sawyer's passing, she knew that this meant a new freedom for Danny. She was too tired to consider details of what that meant exactly, but she would be lying to herself to say that she didn't feel some relief that Mr. Sawyer could no longer pose a potential danger to Danny or anyone else.

Having slept very little in Frederick's absence, she snuggled up close to him and quickly fell asleep herself, blanketed in a warm gratitude and a peaceful hope.

Lily awoke to find the room bright with sunlight. She turned over to find Frederick in the bed beside her, sitting up, leaning back against pillows he'd propped against the headboard.

"Good morning, my love," he said when he realized she was awake.

"Good morning." She moved her head to his shoulder. "Although I suspect it's afternoon."

"It is, actually," he said. "Mary brought some food a while ago. Max told the staff what happened, so they let us sleep. Mary assured me that the children are fine and everything is under control."

"Oh, that's nice," Lily said and eased closer to her husband. "We are very blessed."

"We are," he agreed. "And sometimes I wonder why."

"Why what?" she asked, looking up at him.

"Why I am so blessed," he said, his eyes distant. "I've felt a strange kind of connection to Danny ever since the night we brought him here. We've talked some about the possible reasons. But I felt it more than ever last night . . . sitting with Mr. Sawyer . . . watching him die. I realized that if it hadn't been for my mother's courage and sacrifices, I could have ended up being raised by someone very much like him. What kind of man might I have been if that had been the case? Why was I blessed enough to be set free from such a situation when so many are doomed to live that way?"

"We can't possibly understand such things from our limited mortal perspective," Lily said. "Only God can fully see and comprehend the journey of each life."

"I know," he said, "but I suppose there are moments when a person just has to stop and consider that very thing . . . the fact that only God can see and comprehend . . . and therefore understand the need to trust that God will see that all things are made fair in the end."

"I do have my own opinion," she said, "about you and why you have been blessed with the opportunities you've been given."

He looked down at her, his brow furrowed. "And what might that be?"

"I've wondered the same about myself, Frederick; why I would be lifted out of such a dreadful life and planted into this one. I can only believe it gives me the opportunity to do some good in this world and gives me the compassion that only comes from personal experience. The same applies to you, my darling. You are a good man with a good heart; you have so much to give." She sat beside him so she could look into his eyes. "I believe you were destined to come here, Frederick—for many reasons."

He touched her face and smiled at her, but there was a distinct sadness in his eyes. "I believe it too," he said and sighed. "Did I ever tell you *why* I came *here*? More specifically, my reasons for coming to this area to look for work."

"Not that I recall," she said. "May I ask why this is coming up now?"

"I'm not sure." His eyes became distant again. "I just . . . found myself thinking about it . . . while I was sitting there with Mr. Sawyer, knowing he would die. I wondered how I had ended up here, feeling so right about everything in my life. I've never felt so at peace . . . so content. It's as if I was meant to be your husband . . . to be a father to Danny and the others. And I suppose . . . given the fact that Mr. Sawyer is the boy's blood father, being with him, knowing he would die . . . left me thinking about what that meant for Danny and my place in his life. I can't even bear the idea of my having ended up anywhere else; the very thought of never having known you or the children is simply . . . unbearable. And then I was thinking that if it was destiny . . . or God's hand . . . that brought me here, then perhaps I was somehow meant to be with Mr. Sawyer when he died." He looked at Lily again, his eyes vehement. "A strange kind of healing took place inside of me while I was there, Lily. It's difficult to explain, but . . . seeing him that way . . . my heart was softened. I was able to forgive him, and in a bizarre, outlandish kind of way, I found myself forgiving my own father even though I don't know if I've ever consciously recognized that I had harbored ill feelings toward him. I don't even remember him, but I knew from my mother's stories that he behaved deplorably, and my mother was forced into terribly difficult circumstances in order to simply protect herself and her child."

Frederick sighed again and went on. "And what is even more strange, I believe that somehow Mr. Sawyer found healing as well."

"What do you mean?" she asked, her attention piquing even more.

"Mr. Sawyer was conscious for only a short time," Frederick said with a kind of reverence. "He spoke to me. It was if he were a completely different person. He didn't know who I was; he talked to me as if I were his son. And he said that he'd prayed I would come back, and he asked for my forgiveness."

Lily trembled inwardly, sensing the enormity of such a miracle. She squeezed Frederick's hand to encourage him to continue.

"It's almost as if he believed I was an older version of Danny or some-thing equally strange. He said that it was better that my mother went, that he knew he'd hurt her. His attitude was complete contrition; again, he was nothing like the man we've come to know. He also spoke to me—assuming that I was whomever he believed me to be—about how he'd hurt my brother. It made me wonder if he'd had another child, and per-haps *that* child had died and been buried with his mother. I don't know; it doesn't matter, I suppose. But I believe he passed feeling some hope for redemption on the other side, and he died believing he'd been reunited with someone he loved; he asked for my forgiveness, and I freely gave it. When I told him I forgave him, I spoke it from my heart in regard to my own difficult feelings toward him. Even though the conversation was not exactly what he believed it to be, it seemed a miracle for both of us."

Lily heard her husband's voice crack as he spoke the last, and she could do nothing but agree with him. "Oh, it is a miracle," she mur-mured and wrapped her arms around him.

They were both silent for several minutes, allowing the enormity of such strange happenings to settle over them.

"I suppose," Frederick finally said, "the next thing for us to do is tell Danny that his father is gone. I wonder if he will feel any sorrow at all. The most natural response for him will be relief, I think. I can't deny that *I* feel relief. I'm very glad the end was good for Mr. Sawyer, that he found some healing and peace—and that is a miracle for me. But it doesn't change the results of all of his bad behavior, and I won't feel any guilt for acknowledging that his death is a miracle for us in regard to Danny."

"Oh, it is a miracle!" Lily said again, this time with more enthusiasm as it dawned on her that this meant there was no longer any need to hide Danny and there was no fear of Mr. Sawyer causing any problems for them. She looked directly at her husband and said, "But . . . we must consider the best way to go about it. Even if Danny feels a great deal of relief, this man was still his father, and at best he will likely experience some confusion. We will need to handle the matter carefully."

"Yes, of course."

"And . . . we must still tread carefully in regard to any legal matters. We don't want anything to go wrong in our being able to make him a part of our family. We don't ever want to lose him now that we've come this far."

"I agree on all counts," he said. "And I think we're both very overwhelmed with far too much to think about at the moment. Let's give the matter some time, and of course we should pray about it." He glanced at the clock. "Right now, I think we should go and rescue Nellie and Abigail from the children, and check in on Danny. Mary's been looking after him, but he needs to see us."

"Of course," she said and got out of bed to prepare herself for the day while Frederick did the same.

Only a few minutes later, they were standing side by side in front of the long mirror to make certain they looked presentable. A thought occurred to Lily, and she asked, "What of Mr. Sawyer's burial? We should take care of that and—"

"I already did," he said and kissed her. "Max went for the doctor and the undertaker, and I made arrangements with both of them to see that their fees were taken care of and all the arrangements would be made for a proper burial."

"Aren't you clever," she said and kissed him again.

"Not . . . clever," he said, wrapping her in his arms, as if doing so might help settle his overwhelming emotions. "It was just . . . the right thing to do, what needed to be done." He looked into her eyes. "It's what *you* would have done, and you are my greatest example in all things."

"I believe it's the other way around," she said.

He let out a scoffing laugh, but its tone indicated a lightening of his mood as he took her hand and they headed to Danny's room to check on him. He was doing well, and they said nothing of what had transpired, wanting to wait until they'd decided the best way to approach the matter, although Lily knew they couldn't wait too long.

Lily and Frederick then went to the playroom, where the children were all engaged in different activities, some of them much louder than others. Nellie and Abigail were mingling among them to keep them from misbehaving. As soon as they all noticed that their parents had entered the room, the children came running, eager for hugs, which always created a wave of laughter among the little brood.

After a short while of just visiting to see how everyone was doing, Frederick took them to the classroom to at least get a little bit of school time in. Lily found Mrs. Pilfer and sat with her in her little office near

the kitchen to go over the usual report of the household. Because of
the closeness they shared, Lily also talked to her about the death of Mr.
Sawyer—which she'd already heard about from Max—and the impact it
would have on Danny. Lily told her trusted friend and housekeeper that
she needed to pray about how to best handle the situation from here on,
and Mrs. Pilfer expressed her own commitment to praying on behalf of
Danny—and all the children. They shared a warm hug before parting,
and Lily felt renewed gratitude for this good woman and all she did to
bless the lives of everyone who lived here.

After leaving Mrs. Pilfer's office, Lily went to her own and wrote a
brief letter to Mr. Key, which she sent off right away in the care of Zed,
who would personally see it into the solicitor's hands. Ever since she'd
recovered from her illness, she'd been wanting to check with Mr. Key
and be certain that Frederick's adoption of the children was in order. But
now she also felt inclined to discuss Danny's situation with him and to
get his legal advice. With Mr. Sawyer dead, the need for secrecy was no
longer an issue—even though she knew Mr. Key would always honor her
confidentiality. She would speak with Frederick about the matter before
they spoke to Mr. Key.

Lily went to the library to read, knowing that Frederick would look
for her there when lessons were completed. She tried to read but couldn't
concentrate as she considered the ironic turn of events that had ended in
Mr. Sawyer's death. She believed she had done well at forgiving him for
what he'd done to her—and to Danny. But she couldn't deny her relief
in no longer having to fear any possible future intrusion upon their lives
from this difficult man. Her heart was warmed once again by the miracle
that had taken place just prior to his death: Mr. Sawyer had expressed
an indication of healing within himself, and Frederick had been able to
finally forgive him and let go of the anger that had been haunting him.

When Frederick arrived, he reported that the children were doing
well and he'd left them with an assignment to complete under Nellie's
supervision, which he hoped would allow Nellie some time to just be able
to read while she kept an eye on them until it was completed. He greeted
Lily with a kiss and sat close beside her, holding her hand while they
revisited all they were feeling and thinking. He agreed that they should
discuss Danny's situation with Mr. Key and get his legal advice, and

Frederick was glad she'd sent word for the solicitor to come whenever it was convenient.

They were just wrapping up their conversation when Luca knocked at the door and came in to report that Officer Paten had just arrived and would like to speak with them.

"Thank you, Luca," Frederick said. "Make certain he's comfortable, and we'll be there straightaway."

Luca left and closed the door. Lily said, "Oh, my. I suppose we should have expected this, but I didn't even think about it."

"He will surely know of Mr. Sawyer's passing. But given our last conversation with him, there's no reason to think that he won't be in favor of our keeping Danny safe and cared for. Perhaps he can also give us some advice on the best way to handle the situation."

"I do hope so," Lily said and held tightly to her husband's hand as they left the library to go and speak with Officer Paten.

Chapter Thirteen
INTRODUCED TO THE WORLD

WHEN LILY AND FREDERICK ENTERED the drawing room, Officer Paten turned from where he'd been looking out the window.

"Good day to you both," he said. "I apologize if I've arrived at an inconvenient time."

"Not at all," Frederick said. "Please . . . sit down."

"Thank you," the officer said and took a seat while Lily and Frederick sat across from him.

"I assume," Frederick said right off, "that you're here regarding Mr. Sawyer's death."

"I am, yes," the officer said. "I spoke with the doctor, who informed me of the circumstances of his illness. I must say that I find it ironic that he likely contracted the illness from you, Mrs. Woodstone."

"Yes," she said, "that irony has certainly struck us very deeply. Of course, his passing is poignant at best, but you know—or have at least assumed—enough about the situation to know that it puts us in a better position—or at least we hope it does."

"We're very glad you've come, actually," Frederick said. "Now that Mr. Sawyer is gone, we no longer see the need to pretend that we don't have his son in our care. We believe we can trust you to help us and to consider the boy's best interests. We hope that's the case."

"You *can* trust me," Officer Paten said with zeal. "In fact, my greatest purpose in coming is to simply assure you that there is nothing for you to be concerned about in regard to my knowledge of the situation. I've told no one what you shared with me—hypothetically, prior to now—and I've had some thoughts on how to proceed from here."

"We would very much like to hear your advice," Frederick said, exchanging a glance of overt relief with Lily. It seemed their prayers were being answered.

"Well," the officer said, leaning his forearms on his thighs and clasping his hands, "I confess that I've thought a great deal about the entire situation with Mr. Sawyer's son. I looked into local records more thoroughly, and the child is considered to have officially died at the same time his mother did. Mr. Sawyer reported to the police that they had both contracted an illness and he had built the casket and buried them himself in the woods. I found it a little surprising that the police apparently did no investigation since that is not the customary way to handle such a situation. The doctor was never called in to verify the deaths; no one actually saw the bodies. Considering Mr. Sawyer's reputation, I myself would have felt some suspicion. But that's all in the past now. I'm only very glad that you discovered the child's presence there and brought him into your home. Given that the boy is legally considered dead, I've had the thought that perhaps you should simply adopt him as you have your other children. There are no other relatives whatsoever according to the information I was able to find. If he's comfortable and safe here, then this is where he should stay."

Lily's heart quickened to hear this man suggest the very thing she'd hoped for. Frederick's hand tightened around hers, and she knew he was feeling the same elation. Still, she said, "I agree completely, and that is our hope. I'm just not certain how to go about it. We can discuss the legalities with my solicitor—a man I trust implicitly. But . . . only a few members of the staff even know that Danny is here. We've kept him hidden, not wanting any chance of idle gossip endangering him. And we couldn't expect the other children to lie or keep his being here a secret."

There was a stretch of thoughtful silence among the three of them before Officer Paten said, "Perhaps . . . if you could get him out of the house without being seen . . . you could take him away for a few days and return with him as if you'd just brought him from an orphanage. Is that not how you acquired custody of your other children?"

Lily couldn't even speak. The idea was so perfect that she completely lost her breath.

"I do believe you are an inspired man, Officer Paten," Frederick said, sounding a little breathless himself. He turned to Lily and said, "I think it would be very good for Danny to have a few days to go out into the world and experience some things he's never done before—and for us to spend more personal time with him. And we can bring him back as if he's never been here before. He's a good little actor. I think he'll be able to do it. What do you think, my dear?"

"It's perfect," Lily said, unable to keep her voice from betraying just how perfect it really was.

They discussed their plans a little more with Officer Paten and thanked him for his kindness and for keeping their secret for the sake of Danny's welfare. He assured them that he would take care of everything that was within his power and that there was no reason that anyone in the valley would ever know anything at all about Danny's existence or Lily's difficult experience with Mr. Sawyer.

After Officer Paten had left, Lily turned to Frederick and wrapped her arms around him, holding him tightly as a silent expression of her relief and gratitude. The way he returned her embrace let her know he felt the same. They had real and tangible hope that all would be well with Danny, and they had a plan on how to make it happen. Together they returned to the library to discuss their feelings and the details of all that would need to be taken care of before they left with Danny for a few days.

By the time they got there, Lily was overcome with tears of joy to think that Danny could officially become their son and all of this secrecy and worry could come to an end. Frederick urged her to sit close beside him on one of the couches, and he just let her cry. She heard him sniffling a little himself, and once they'd both composed themselves, it was easy to express all they were feeling. She found it tragic that they could actually feel joy over events that had been put into motion as a result of Mr. Sawyer's death, but neither of them could deny that he had caused a great deal of grief before he'd reached his unexpected repentant attitude at the very end.

At Frederick's suggestion, they decided to wait to tell Danny anything at all until after they'd spoken to Mr. Key. They didn't want to get Danny's hopes up on the chance that there was some legal snag that might be problematic. While neither of them could imagine what that might be, they wanted to be absolutely certain before they discussed their plans with anyone else.

Lily had trouble sleeping that night; she was as excited and nervous as she'd ever been in her life. She was admittedly relieved that Frederick too was restless, which made it possible for them to talk through all that had happened and all that they hoped for in the future. Their conversation felt healing to Lily, and Frederick said as much in regard to his own coming to terms with such enormous changes in their lives. They both marveled at how it actually hadn't been so many months since he'd first come here in the spring. Autumn was just beginning to really settle over the valley, and neither of them could comprehend that when winter had departed last they hadn't even known each other. But Lily had no regrets, and she was glad to know that Frederick had none either. They both knew they were exactly where God wanted them to be, and they had a long, wondrous life ahead of them, working together to shepherd their large family.

The following morning, Lily was relieved to receive a message from Mr. Key, letting her know he would be coming to see them that very afternoon. He was always efficient in responding to her needs as quickly as possible, but he often traveled for business and sometimes couldn't be reached for many days. She considered it one more miracle that he'd been available and would be able to offer his advice right away. Lily couldn't imagine having to wait an indeterminate number of days to know how they might proceed. Now that she knew Danny could officially be their son, she felt intensely impatient to make it all right and legal—and especially to get Danny out of hiding.

When Mr. Key arrived, he jumped directly into informing Lily and Frederick that he had been glad to receive her message since he'd been intending to visit them soon anyway. He wanted to let them know that all of the legalities had been completed in regard to the changes that had taken place as a result of Frederick and Lily getting married—and the children had now all been officially adopted by Frederick. He emphasized that it had taken some effort for him to make certain all related matters were recorded with legal documents, but given the fact that the law was so in favor of men having control and power regarding property and all things related—including custody of children—there had been no opposition in making certain that Frederick had all rights transferred to him upon his marriage to Lily.

Lily felt great joy at the news—and she could tell that Frederick did too—but she still appreciated Mr. Key's perspective when he said, "I'm so glad this has worked out so well for the both of you, but I still find it very frustrating to see how the law favors men over women this way when I know many an undeserving man who has simply inherited great wealth and power—or acquired it through marriage. I can only say how glad I am that in your case it's such a good situation."

"Amen," Lily said and felt Frederick squeeze her hand.

Mr. Key sighed and offered a broad smile as he added, "That's the best kind of news I can deliver in my profession."

The solicitor went on to explain that he'd legally added the name Woodstone to each of the children's names in their official records, adding it to the name Broadbent, which had previously replaced whatever their prior surnames had been. Since all of the children had been neglected, abused, and abandoned by their birth parents, the change had seemed fitting. But having them keep the Broadbent name honored all that Lily's first husband had made it possible for her to do on behalf of the children, and now they would take on the name of the man who would be their father from this time forward.

"Now," Mr. Key said, handing Frederick copies of all the legal documents, "you sent for me. What else might I do for you?"

"Well," Lily began, "we have a somewhat sensitive matter to deal with . . . and it will take some explaining. I hope you're not in a hurry."

"I've got all the time you need." Mr. Key leaned back in his chair.

Lily turned to Frederick, hoping he might get this story started. She was grateful when he picked up on her cue and began with the day that Lily had unwittingly exposed herself to the chicken pox and then gone to leave some things for Mr. Sawyer, where she had heard a child crying out for help. Once Frederick had gained momentum, Lily helped fill in some details, and she found it easy to admit to the fear and anger they'd experienced on Danny's behalf and the relief they now had in being able to move forward in making this boy a part of their family.

"But we need your help," Lily said.

Frederick added, "Officer Paten told us he'd be glad to help you in any way he can to make the matter legal. He has access to local records that indicate the boy has no other family, and of course, he's believed to be dead."

"Well, I must say," Mr. Key said, "this is by far the most unique adoption case I've ever handled, but I see no reason it can't be taken care of appropriately. I think your plan is excellent, and I'm glad to be a part of it. However, given the unique nature of the situation, I can't promise that it won't take some time . . . and perhaps some careful maneuvering on my part." This made Lily a little nervous, but she reminded herself to exert some faith and to remember her convictions in regard to making Danny a part of their family. She was relieved to have Mr. Key add, "However, I promise I will do everything I can to make it happen. If he has no other relatives and he is safely in your care, then clearly this is the right course of action. I'm very glad to have the help of this officer, and I will meet with him as soon as I can fit it into my schedule."

"Thank you," Frederick said. "We can never adequately express our gratitude for your support."

"Oh, you'll get the bill," Mr. Key said with a little laugh and a wink. Lily knew he always put in far more effort than the money he made would ever warrant, but she was glad to know that they had the means to compensate him properly. Without someone with Mr. Key's professional expertise—along with his compassion and trustworthiness—she wondered if they would ever have the hope of being able to adopt Danny legally.

Lily was relieved to hear Mr. Key go on with a declaration of his beliefs that in spite of his respect in honoring the law, sometimes the technicalities of it did not work in favor of those who most needed its protection, and he was more than willing to carefully maneuver the parameters of the law in order to make certain that Danny's future was protected. Now that Mr. Sawyer was dead, the matter of officially taking on the care of his orphan son was not terribly complicated and was within the parameters of the law—as long as no one became aware of the means by which the boy had come to them in the first place. And that was the part that made Lily nervous. It could be difficult to produce legal evidence of where the child had come from when he'd been declared dead, but Mr. Key assured them he would discreetly take care of the legalities, and even though it would take some time, they should move forward with taking Danny away for a few days so that they could bring him back home officially and allow him to begin a new life. Even though there was no reason to think that anyone would become suspicious and seek out proof that Danny was legally in their care, Lily would still feel much better when she knew it was properly taken care of.

Once Mr. Key left, Lily pushed away any concern about possible difficulties that might arise, deferring to her convictions that Danny was meant to be their son. She focused instead on the positive aspects of the situation and couldn't get to Danny's room fast enough, even though she still had a tendency toward shortness of breath because of her illness, and she had to take it slowly. Frederick finally just picked her up to carry her to their destination, and they laughed together as they speculated over how Danny might respond. Of course, this also meant that they had to deliver the news of Mr. Sawyer's death, and they weren't certain how that would go. They needed to tread carefully, but they were both confident that Danny would be pleased with the plan that had been set in motion on his behalf.

While they were still a short way from Danny's room, Lily said, "Wait, we need to talk before we do this."

"What are you thinking?" Frederick asked, gently setting her on her feet.

Lily took a long moment to sort her thoughts. "I believe there are two things I'm concerned about. First of all, we don't know how he's going to react to news of his father's death. There's no reason whatsoever that Danny would feel anything positive toward his father, which makes me suspect he will mostly feel relief—but simply given the concept of how we often think of how we *should* feel, relief could come with—"

"Guilt," Frederick said with perfect accuracy. "Yes, I've felt some of that myself, and I know that I can't comprehend the depth of Danny's experience."

"So . . . we need to just . . . what? You're an expert with children, Mr. Woodstone. What should we expect?"

"I don't think we should *expect* anything. We just need to give him permission to feel whatever he feels and deal with it accordingly. He needs to know that it's all right to have a mixture of emotions and that anything he feels is valid."

"Oh, that's good," Lily said and took a deep breath. "I knew you would have the answers."

"I fear your faith in me might not be entirely realistic," he said.

"You've never let me down so far." She smiled and kissed him quickly.

"I can only pray the trend continues," he said and smiled back at her. "What else are you concerned about?"

"Well . . . we're involving him in this ruse, asking him to lie about how he came into our lives. Are we handling this the best way?"

"Lily," Frederick said, taking hold of her shoulders, "I grew up pretending to be someone I was not. Woodstone is not even my real name. I don't know where my mother came up with it; it doesn't even make sense. Wood and stone are opposites. But the only thing that matters is that my mother did what she did for our protection and preservation. We're not being dishonest for the sake of personal gain or greed; our intentions are noble. And we need to help Danny understand that. He spent years pretending that he wasn't upset by his father's neglect and violence in order to avoid more violence. I think he'll be fine in being able to manage this. We need to propose our ideas and allow him to contribute *his* ideas and feelings, and we'll work it out the best we can. It's not ideal, but it's what we have to do to keep him safe and well."

Lily nodded, once again assuaged by Frederick's logic as well as his confidence. They clasped hands and went to Danny's room to find Mary there with him; they were reading a book together. The boy was excited to see them and jumped to his feet, throwing himself into Lily's arms for a hug and then turning to Frederick for the same. He'd certainly come a long way since they'd first brought him here.

"Let's sit down," Lily urged after Mary had left the room, and Frederick situated chairs so that the three of them could sit close together and all see each other's faces. Lily took hold of Danny's hand, saying, "We have some very important things to talk to you about; some of it might be upsetting, but some of it is very grand—at least we think it is." She glanced at Frederick then back to Danny. "We hope you will think so too." Danny looked concerned, and she hurried on; now that this conversation had begun, she wanted to be done with it. "Danny, my dear, your father has died. He got very sick, and he died."

Lily watched the boy closely, wondering if he would respond with some kind of outburst—either a manifestation of some strange kind of grief or perhaps great relief. They allowed time for Danny to take in the news, and he finally said, "I don't feel sad. Am I supposed to feel sad?"

"Your feelings are your own, Danny," Frederick said. "It's not for anyone else to tell you how to feel. We have talked about it, and we both understand why you might not feel sad, and it's all right."

"And if I'm glad he's dead . . ." Danny said, his voice cracking in concert with a quiver in his chin, "is that all right too?"

"If that's how you feel," Lily said, "then it's all right. When big changes happen in our lives, we can feel all sorts of things, and sometimes feelings change along the way. The important thing is for you to be aware of how you're feeling and to know that you can talk to us about it . . . no matter *how* you feel."

Danny nodded and bit his lip as if he were trying not to cry—but from what he'd said, Lily assumed his emotion was based more in relief than any kind of sorrow. He gave up on trying to hold back tears, and they fell down his gentle face as he asked, "Does this mean I have to leave here? Do I have to—"

"No, no, Danny," Lily said. "This means that you will *never* have to leave. We want to be your mother and father, just as we are to the other children. And we want to—"

Lily was halted midsentence as Danny flew out of his chair and flung his arms around her neck, crying uncontrollably.

"Oh, my darling," she whispered and eased him onto her lap. Frederick scooted his chair closer and wrapped his arms around both of them. "You're going to be our son now," Lily said, unable to hold back tears of her own. "And nothing could make us happier. It's all going to be taken care of—legally and officially." Danny drew back to look at her, and she said, "Do you understand what that means?"

"Sort of," he said.

"You don't need to understand anything," Frederick said, "except that no one will ever be able to take you away from us . . . and you don't have to remain hidden anymore."

Lily was glad to hear her husband say that, but she would certainly be more relieved when it was all official so that she'd never have to wonder if a problem might arise.

Danny laughed while he kept crying, and they laughed with him. The boy finally said, "But I don't want anyone to know . . . who my father was . . . or that I've been hiding here. I want to . . . pretend it never happened."

"That's very good," Frederick said, winking at Lily, "because we have a plan that we believe will make it possible for all of us to have a brand-new start, a whole new life for you. No one will ever know except those of us who already do, and we can trust all those people to never talk of how your life was before we started over again. What do you think about that?"

Danny nodded with enthusiasm and sniffled. Frederick handed him a handkerchief, and he wiped his face with it.

"We've made a plan," Frederick added with enthusiasm. "Would you like to hear about it?"

Danny nodded even more enthusiastically, and Frederick began to tell him of the adventure they would embark upon, which would begin by sneaking Danny out of the house very late at night. He and Lily took turns explaining their plan in detail, how Danny would need to return to the house in a few days pretending he'd never been there before and that he didn't know Max and Wally, Mary and Abigail, and Mrs. Pilfer. But he wouldn't have to pretend very long because once he'd been back for a few days he would get to know them all over again. Danny liked the plan very much, and he was completely confident about being able to do his part. They reassured him that if difficult feelings ever came up about his life before now or his having to keep certain things a secret he should always come and talk privately with them, that they would always do everything they could to help him be happy.

They allowed Danny time to ask them any questions he might have and promised that they would have some wonderful time away on their little vacation—time in which they could talk through all of their feelings and discuss their plans for the future in more detail.

With Danny well prepared for the upcoming adventure, Frederick and Lily went their separate ways in order to see that everything was taken care of so they could leave that very night. Frederick went to the classroom to finish up lessons with the children, while Lily went to find Mrs. Pilfer. The housekeeper was thrilled to tears over the plan, and she reassured Lily that those who knew the truth would put on their best acting skills to make everything go smoothly upon the trio's return. While Mrs. Pilfer went to find Abigail and Mary to speak with them, Lily went in search of Max and Wally to catch them up on everything that was taking place and to enlist their aid; the two men would be going with them for their little holiday since they didn't want to have to depend on hired coaches. In reality they wouldn't be traveling terribly far, and the two men would actually be able to have some holiday time of their own. They were both delighted with the plan and with Danny being able to become a permanent part of the family. And Lily felt more content than she had since she'd first heard Danny's cries for help. At last, he would be hers and Frederick's to care for, and that was all that mattered.

* * *

Frederick was pleased to find the children doing well under Nellie's supervision. During the course of Lily's illness, Nellie had become very proficient at keeping the children occupied and disciplined. Frederick had been able to give her suggestions on how to do so without having to exert a great amount of physical effort, and since the children knew there would be consequences if they misbehaved while in Nellie's care, they'd become much better behaved in her presence than they had been before Frederick had come into their home.

Frederick thanked Nellie for her help and told the children to continue reading while he spoke with Nellie in the hall. He told her what the other servants would be told—that he and Lily would be leaving for a few days since Mrs. Woodstone was determined to adopt yet another child. Nellie was pleased and only too happy to watch over the children for the next few days, knowing that Mary and Abigail would be helping her. Now that they didn't have to keep Danny hidden and see that he was cared for, the two maids would be freed from their responsibilities with him.

That evening when it was story time for the children, Frederick told the children that instead of a story they had some news to share. Between them, he and Lily explained that they both believed strongly there was another child who needed to be a part of their family so they would be traveling to an orphanage to get that child. Since each one of the children had come into Lily's care through the same means, they all knew exactly what that entailed, and they had very few questions. Lily came right out and asked if any of them had any concerns about adding a new brother or sister; Frederick knew she put it that way because in every case she'd not made the decision of which child to adopt until she'd gone to a particular location and had met the children living there, and she had chosen by what she called *a spiritual nudging* that had let her know the child that she believed God meant to be a part of her family. None of the children seemed concerned at all, as if they knew exactly how this would work, and they apparently had enough faith in Lily and Frederick to believe that there would always be plenty of love to go around no matter how many children came into the family.

After a long discussion, Lily gave in to the children's pleading for her to read a story anyway. She chose a very short one, and then they were all tucked into their beds with the promise that all would be well while Frederick and Lily were gone for a few days. There was some speculation over whether they would get a new brother or a new sister and what that person's name might be. Frederick felt a secret delight to think of how it would be when they returned with Danny and how good it would be for him to spend time with the other children—even if it inevitably meant there would be some challenges in the adjustment. But Lily had dealt with such things many times before, and they both felt confident that it wasn't anything they couldn't handle—especially since they already knew Danny well and he had expressed many times how lonely he felt and how much he wanted to be around other children and feel like he was a part of the family. It all seemed meant to be.

Danny barely came awake when Frederick lifted the boy into his arms, keeping a blanket wrapped around him as they made their way quietly down the back stairs to the waiting carriage, where the boy quickly relaxed against the pillow left on the seat and fell back to sleep. With the luggage already having been loaded, they were soon off on their little adventure. Frederick held tightly to Lily's hand and couldn't hold back a little laugh.

"Is something funny?" she asked.

"Not at all," he said. "It just seems too good to be true."

"That is surely evidence that God's hand is involved," she replied.

"I'm certain it is," he said and relaxed with his head against the inside of the carriage.

In what seemed only minutes later, Frederick lifted his head and gasped. It took him a moment to realize he'd been dreaming. He turned to see Lily sleeping with her head against the other side of the carriage and Danny still asleep on the opposite seat. He was glad to know he'd not disturbed them, but the memory of his dream was haunting, and he felt cold from the inside out. He'd dreamt that he was sitting at Mr. Sawyer's bedside while the old man had been dying, but instead of the brief, tender conversation they'd shared prior to his death, Sawyer had been shouting at Frederick, threatening him and cursing him. Frederick knew it was only a dream and it was likely only his mind's way of releasing all of the traumatic residue that had accumulated through his interaction with Mr. Sawyer. Still, he felt unsettled and found it difficult to go back to sleep. Recalling the memory of the old man's death in detail, his unrest deepened so much that he had to force himself to not think about it all. He was finally able to drift off again, glad to awaken with light coming through the carriage windows—and a terrible cramp in his neck. But Danny was sleeping peacefully, and considering how bad off the child had been when he'd first come into their care, Frederick could only feel gratitude for how far they'd come and for what this little holiday would bring about.

* * *

Lily had experienced joy many times in her life, although she couldn't recall ever feeling it prior to Mr. Broadbent rescuing her from a miserable life to give her opportunities she never could have imagined. Following his death she'd made a choice to move her life in a direction that would offer her more opportunities for joy in direct proportion to what she was willing to give of herself to help others find the same. Mrs. Pilfer had once pointed out to her that when she'd become a widow, Lily could have chosen to lock herself away and never do anything that wasn't about her own comforts; many women with an abundance of wealth certainly lived that way. Lily wanted to believe that the goodness in her life was a result of her own choices, but in her heart she felt far more blessed than she'd ever believed possible, and it seemed that she'd been given far more joy and peace than seemed proportionate to what she'd been willing to give. Still, she could recognize her own joy and acknowledge its source. And she could also appreciate the fact that she'd never felt such extraordinary joy as she did in observing Danny's introduction to the world. Holding Frederick's hand in hers while they watched the child running across a grassy field, just taking in the sunlight and laughing, she felt utterly in awe and quite simply speechless. Frederick muttered that it was a miracle; beyond that, he too was speechless.

Lily and Frederick had discussed Danny's possible reactions to experiencing facets of life he'd never been exposed to. They'd been prepared to have him be excessively timid or even afraid of certain things. But he thrived on being outdoors; he loved the rain as much as the sun, and the weather was kind enough to oblige them with both during their brief holiday. Danny also did well going into a crowded pub, where they enjoyed a fine meal, which the boy gobbled down voraciously. They stayed at three different inns in different locations, encountering many people as they wandered through shops and among street vendors, exploring and observing Danny's wide eyes as he took in everything with great wonder. It quickly became evident that he wasn't shy at all, and the timidity that had resulted from his father's abuse had apparently been forever banished. He talked openly with people they met, and evidence of a sharp sense of humor came through in the way he often made people laugh. They purchased some new clothes and shoes for him since he'd only been wearing used clothing up to this point. His excitement over having new things heightened Lily's joy. They also bought him some new books that thrilled him due to the mere fact that they belonged exclusively to him. And they purchased a little porcelain bird that caught his attention. He was apparently quite taken with birds and was noticing them frequently. Given that, they were pleased when Frederick found a book about birds in one of the bookshops they visited, and he was eager to purchase it for Danny.

On the final night of their time away, the three of them were sitting near the fire in the room they were sharing. As with the other places they'd stayed, the innkeeper had brought a comfortable cot into the room for Danny so that he had his own bed.

"Do you feel ready to go back?" Frederick asked him. "Your brothers and sisters can be kind of loud and crazy sometimes."

"I can't wait to meet them," Danny declared, and Lily couldn't believe this was the same child she'd found in Mr. Sawyer's cellar. "You said that even though they don't get along sometimes, they love each other and help take care of each other. I want to have brothers and sisters like that. I feel like I love them already; I hope they can love me too."

"I'm certain they will grow to love you very quickly," Lily said. "You all have one remarkable thing in common; you have all come from circumstances where love and safety were *not* a part of your lives. In that way you can all understand each other."

Lily noticed as a shadow fell over Frederick's countenance, and she wondered what he was thinking about. In fact, he'd had many moments recently of becoming rather distant, as if his thoughts were very far away and were distracting him. He'd reassured her that it was nothing and he was fine, but the expression she saw on his face now was less subtle, and she knew something was troubling him. Knowing she couldn't bring up her concern for Frederick with Danny present, she focused her attention on the boy.

Danny asked with excitement, "And I'm really going to have my own bed in a room with some of my brothers?"

"That's right; just like we talked about," Lily said. "You'll have your very own bed and a bureau with drawers that is also your very own, where you can keep your clothes and books and whatever else belongs to you. One of the rules is that no one else is allowed to use or take anything you keep in or on your bureau without your permission."

Danny sighed and looked as if he were being given a huge fortune. Having gone through this process eleven times before, Lily took Danny's hand and asked, "Is there anything you're concerned about? Anything you would like to discuss? Of course, you can come to speak with either of us at any time if you need to, but I'm wondering if there's anything right now that you want to talk about."

Danny became deeply thoughtful, as if he were searching his mind to see if there were any thoughts in there that might need to be expressed. His expression became very serious. "There is something I haven't wanted to say out loud, but since you're my mother and father now, I think that I should say it. Since Mr. Sawyer is dead . . ." He hesitated, gathering his words, and Lily considered how quickly and vehemently he'd come to call his blood father by his name rather than using any term that identified him as a father. Thus far, Danny had done well at apparently being able to let go of his father's horrible behavior and to understand that most people were not like the man who had caused him so much grief. She prayed that he would continue to be able to heal and progress in that respect, and she waited to hear what he would say. "Well . . ." Danny went on, looking down, "I was very little when my mother died, but . . . I remember it, and . . ."

"What is it, darling?" Lily encouraged, sensing that this was becoming more difficult. Frederick too became more attentive and put a supportive hand on the boy's shoulder.

"I know he told the police that she got sick and died . . . and he told them I died too . . . and that he'd buried us together in the woods.

I was hiding when the police came; I heard what they said." Danny looked up at Lily then at Frederick, as if to gauge their reactions so far. He then looked down even while he drew back his shoulders as if he were gathering courage. "But she didn't get sick. They were fighting . . . the same way they did every time he drank too much, and that was nearly every day. He . . . hit her; he hit her hard. She fell and hit her head." Danny began to get emotional, and Lily wrapped her arm around him. "I was hiding under the table, and I . . . I saw her fall. I saw the blood; her head was bleeding. And he . . . Mr. Sawyer . . . he told me that if I ever told anyone . . . he would kill me too."

Lily gasped as so many things became clear. Mr. Sawyer had likely hidden the boy to keep him from telling the truth about what had happened. The death of Danny's mother might have been seen in some ways as an accident. Mr. Sawyer had been drunk, and even though he'd struck her, he likely hadn't intended for her to hit her head and die. Still, he was responsible for his wife's death, and Danny had been the unwitting witness and had been locked away as a result. Lily felt sickened at the thought, but she just held Danny closer when she realized he was crying. He'd been holding his secret inside for years—it was likely one of his earliest memories.

"It's all right, darling," Lily muttered and stroked his hair. "You never have to be afraid again."

"I'm so glad you told us," Frederick said, gazing at Lily over the top of Danny's head, his eyes filled with a combination of horror and compassion.

When Danny calmed down, they talked about how good it was for him to not have to carry the burden of those memories alone, and they assured him that if he ever needed to talk about the memories in the future, both Lily and Frederick would always be there for him. Danny seemed relieved and pleased, and he began talking again about his excitement to return home and be a part of the group of children. He was well prepared to play the game of pretending he'd never been to the house before and that he didn't know the servants there who had come to know him well. He also repeated what they had discussed with him previously—that it was good for him to talk to his new brothers and sisters about his own story if he chose to. Except for any details that would connect him to the recently deceased Mr. Sawyer, Danny could talk about his past truthfully. Frederick and Lily had both spoken to him about how all of the children had difficult circumstances from their past, and they'd been encouraged to share them with each other, which helped them become closer and brought out the common bond they shared. Danny had practiced by telling them how his father had kept him locked in a cellar while everyone had believed he was dead, and then his father had died and he'd been found. He repeated the story again for good measure, gaining confidence that he would be able to share it, and he became less emotional each time. Now he included what he'd just told them—about how he'd witnessed his mother's death.

Lily couldn't help feeling overcome with all this child had been through in his young life, but she'd felt this way about each of her children, and she felt confident that Danny was firmly on a path of healing and that he had a good life ahead of him.

After Danny had gone to sleep, Lily crawled into bed and put her head on Frederick's shoulder. They talked for a few minutes about their hopes that returning home with a clean slate for Danny would go well, and they shared their amazement and horror over what Danny had revealed to them this evening.

"It certainly explains a lot," Frederick said.

"It certainly does," Lily agreed. "But why do you suppose the police didn't look further into the situation? Does it not sound terribly suspicious for a man who is known to be violent to declare that his wife and child died of illness and he buried them himself? Is it not required for a doctor to verify a death or—"

"I don't exactly know what the law is regarding such things, Lily. And perhaps Mr. Sawyer was just mean enough that the police simply didn't want to rile him. It's difficult to say. I think it's likely best that we just leave the past in the past and move forward."

"I agree completely, but . . ."

"But what?" Frederick asked when she didn't finish.

"I get the feeling quite a lot lately . . . that your thoughts are much more in the past than you want them to be."

His silence implied his surprise that she'd noticed something amiss, and he didn't know how to respond.

Lily leaned on her elbow and looked toward his face in the darkness. "Something's troubling you; I wish you'd tell me what it is."

"I would if I knew," he said. "I just . . . keep thinking about Mr. Sawyer . . . about the things he said when he was dying. I don't know why I can't get it out of my head. I've even dreamt about it a few times . . .

although my dreams are more like nightmares; he ends up shouting and cursing at me before I wake up." He sighed deeply. "I don't know why it just keeps . . . haunting me."

"Perhaps it will simply take time," Lily said. "He stirred up a great deal of trauma in our lives, including some difficult feelings for you. Given the brief amount of time that's passed, I believe we've all done fairly well at being able to forgive him and move on—even Danny has done brilliantly at understanding the need to forgive his father."

"I know; the boy is remarkable. I feel such a deep bond with him. I do believe I've come to see him as somewhat of an example for me . . . of how I *should* handle the difficult feelings from my own childhood that have been stirred up. And perhaps that's all it is, and as you said, it will likely take time. I just . . . need to keep praying . . . and I'm sure I'll be fine." He reached up a hand to touch her face. "We have so much to be grateful for, my darling, and tomorrow we will take Danny home and work on settling back into a normal life. I look forward to getting the children back on schedule with their lessons, and just living life to its fullest with all of you."

"How lovely," Lily said and put her head back onto his shoulder. "And we'll have a dozen children." She laughed softly. "Would you have ever dreamed when you came looking for work that within months you would be the father of twelve?"

He laughed with her. "Never! But I couldn't be happier. A dozen seems like a nice, round number. We shall all live happily ever after."

"I agree with the happily ever after," she said, her heart quickening as if to prompt her to tell him something she'd been needing to say, but the right moment had eluded her. "However, I don't believe stopping at a dozen will work."

Frederick laughed softly once again. "Do you intend to keep searching orphanages for more little lost souls?"

"No, I can say with confidence that I feel complete in regard to adopting any more children."

"Then what do you . . ." he began, then hesitated and took a sharp breath. It was now Frederick who leaned up on one elbow to look at her. "Lily, what are you saying?"

"Our next child will come to us through the conventional method," she said with a little giggle and guided his hand to her belly. "I only became certain the day we were getting ready to leave with Danny."

"Oh, Lily," he said and pressed a hand to the side of her face. "Really? A baby?"

"Really," she said and laughed again.

"But . . . it's not been so long since you recovered from your illness, and—"

"I've been feeling very well," she reminded him. "We will have the doctor come as soon as we get settled in at home, and I shall take very good care of myself. I promise."

"Oh, Lily!" he said again with more enthusiasm and the hint of a quiver in his voice. "Seeing Danny blossom as he has, I thought I could never be happier, but this . . . this is . . ." He laughed again with a delightful ring to it that expressed the depth of his joy. Lily wrapped her arms around him and felt his joy seep into her, mingling with her own.

Chapter Fourteen
FAMILY CIRCLE

FREDERICK AWOKE THE FOLLOWING MORNING to find Lily sleeping beside him, looking like an angel with her fluffy white hair against an equally white pillow. He watched her sleeping and tried to imagine what it would be like for them to have a baby. The very idea left him in awe, which made him all the more unsettled to have thoughts of Mr. Sawyer invade his mind. He pushed them away when he realized that a harsh wind was beating rainfall against the windows of their room at the inn. They'd enjoyed pleasant autumn weather the past few days, but now it seemed the elements were boldly declaring that winter was at the threshold. He got out of bed to stoke the fire so the room would warm up, and the noise woke both Lily and Danny. He hugged his new son and asked, "Are you ready for your big day?"

"It's going to be a wonderful day," Danny said with a grin before he yawned. Frederick ruffled his hair and kissed the top of his head before he went back to the bed where he and Lily had slept, and kissed his wife.

"Good morning, Mrs. Woodstone," he said. "How are you feeling?"

"I'm fine," she insisted and sat up to hug him. "I'm more than fine."

They packed up their things while Lily and Frederick both engaged Danny in a conversation which made it increasingly evident that he was more than ready to start over and return home with what they'd come to call the *new story* of his life. In the dining room of the inn, they shared breakfast with Max and Wally. The two men had accompanied them on some of their adventures the past few days, and some of the time they'd gone off to have some holiday time of their own. Danny talked easily to them regarding his excitement about returning home, and they joked about how well they'd gotten to know Danny since they'd picked him up at the orphanage the previous day. The pleasant rapport among them increased Frederick's comfort over all that was unfolding, and the joy on Lily's face was priceless.

They were soon on their way home, and Frederick felt perfectly content—until familiar, haunting thoughts forced their way into his mind. He wanted to scream and tell his mind to stop thinking about Old Man Sawyer, to just let him go and move on. The future before them had every promise of being good; he saw no reason to dwell in the past at all—not his own childhood nor his experiences with Mr. Sawyer. But he just couldn't get his mind to move beyond these strange thoughts which evoked an unsettled feeling he couldn't shake.

Throughout the carriage ride, Frederick prayed silently to be able to find peace, and he was relieved with the way Danny talked and talked of his excitement about being a part of their family and his hope that his brothers and sisters would like him. The boy found it amusing to think of how he would pretend not to know Mary or Abigail or Mrs. Pilfer but how he expected they would become very good friends within a few weeks. He said it as if it were a very funny joke he'd come up with, and he laughed about it in a way that made Frederick and Lily laugh as well.

They stopped for lunch at a pub that was about an hour from home, but lunch would have been served at the house before they arrived. Danny grew quieter and a little nervous as the carriage neared their destination, but Frederick and Lily both offered some final reassurances, and they even said a prayer together that all would go well. If nothing else, Danny's nerves helped aid the ruse that he'd never been here before. When he stepped out of the carriage and looked up at the house from a view he'd never seen, it was easy to believe he had no idea where he was or what might happen.

Ironically, the three women that Danny already knew were just inside the door, waiting to greet him. But Frederick wondered if they'd planned it that way. Abigail, Mary, and Mrs. Pilfer all did well at pretending to meet Danny for the first time, even though no one else was around. But Mr. Ingham soon appeared, and he introduced himself to Danny as if the boy were royalty and it was a great honor to have him there.

Frederick and Lily escorted their new son up the stairs and to the schoolroom—which they found empty. They went to the playroom and could hear the children being noisy on the other side of the closed door.

"Are you ready?" Lily asked Danny, and he nodded firmly in spite of some obvious apprehension in his demeanor.

Frederick went into the room first and was overwhelmed with the usual onslaught of hugs that occurred when he'd not seen the children for a while. "Are you ready to meet your new brother?" he asked when he got them quieted down a little. They all responded with enthusiasm, which included a few lighthearted comments from a couple of the girls that they might have preferred a sister, but it was all in good fun. Frederick then motioned toward the door, and Lily came in holding Danny's hand.

"This is Danny," she said to the children, who all spoke a haphazard chorus of hellos. The children all hugged Lily in greeting while Nellie looked on at the scene with tenderness. It wasn't the first time she had witnessed a new child coming into the home, and she had no idea that Danny had been a part of their household for a while now.

Frederick had everyone sit down on the rug and be still before he told them a little bit about Danny's history, and then he invited Danny to tell the children a little bit more about himself, which he did with some genuine nervousness but not without confidence. The children were then invited to ask him questions, and each of them was given a turn to tell Danny their name and a little bit about themselves. Once the official introductions were complete, the children were given permission to play, and a few of the boys immediately invited Danny to join them in building a fortress with blocks. Frederick and Lily sat and observed, occasionally exchanging a warm glance as it became evident that Danny was going to do just fine. He appeared to be a little in awe and overwhelmed—but in a good way. It was as if he'd been meant to be part of a large family and he had truly, finally come home.

Within a few days, Danny had settled so well into the household routine that it was difficult to imagine him not being there. Frederick had expected to deal with some challenges, knowing how the children could vie for attention and sometimes act out by picking fights or causing other problems. But they were all amazingly compassionate toward Danny, and the boy was thriving on simply being a part of the group. He took to school time like a bird to flight, and he loved sharing meals with his new siblings. On Sunday he went to church for the first time in his life, blending in with his brothers so well that Frederick doubted anyone even noticed there was an extra child. At Sunday dinner when everyone had their turn to share the highlight of their week and something they'd learned at church, everyone at the table expressed how glad they were that Danny had joined their family. When Danny's turn came, he said with enthusiasm that it had been the best week of his whole life; he loved his new family, and he had learned at church that even though he'd never even heard about God until he'd learned about Him from his new parents, he knew that God loved him because he'd been given so many blessings.

Frederick felt choked up to hear Danny say such a thing; glancing toward Lily, who sat at the opposite end of the long table, he saw her dabbing at her eyes with her napkin. He thought of how she was going to have a baby, and his happiness threatened to explode inside of him. And then those blasted, unwanted thoughts of Mr. Sawyer burst into his mind, and he wanted to curse aloud. He couldn't recall *ever* cursing aloud. His mother wouldn't have allowed it, and then he'd become a vicar at a very young age. But he wanted to do it now. If not for needing to be a good example to his children, he might have done it. Why couldn't the old man just leave him in peace?

* * *

Less than a month after bringing Danny into the family, Frederick was pleased with how well Lily was doing. The doctor had declared her to be healthy and strong, and her pregnancy symptoms were minimal. Now that Danny had settled in well and all was going smoothly, they told the children one night at story time that they were going to have a new baby—that a new brother or sister was coming to their family. They were prepared to have the children express concerns that having a baby might make Frederick and Lily love their adopted children less, but the children were easily reassured that nothing would change, except that their family would grow and they would all have a baby to love. Frederick observed how easily the children accepted the promise that they would always be loved and cared for, and he knew that Lily had proven to them over time that they could believe whatever she promised them; they trusted her, and they knew she loved them. He believed they knew the same of him, but it was Lily who had taught them true love and trust; he had simply been blessed enough to be allowed to become a part of their family.

As autumn settled fully into winter, Abigail and Luca—who had been romantically involved since before Frederick had come into the household in the spring—finally made an official announcement that they would soon be getting married. They didn't want a big fuss, but Lily insisted that the household would celebrate, and she thought it appropriate that all who lived on the estate as tenant farmers or in leased houses should also be invited—since most, if not all, of them were acquainted with Abigail and Luca. With a party being planned, there was a buzz of excitement in the household, and since the children all knew both Abigail and Luca quite well, they were especially excited to be involved in the forthcoming celebration of their marriage.

While Frederick left the party planning to his wife and the servants, he oversaw a dramatic remodeling of the home where Mr. Sawyer had lived so that it could be leased to someone else. Even though the overseer of the estate handled the details well and the work was being taken care of efficiently, Frederick kept feeling drawn to the place, wishing the visible improvements to the house might help him feel some kind of healing within himself. He continued to pray to understand why he was having trouble letting go, but the reasons eluded him. He often wondered if a part of him hadn't truly forgiven Mr. Sawyer, and therefore the things he'd done were eating away at Frederick. But with time, he came to know that wasn't the case. He believed it had more to do with unsettled feelings over his childhood, but since he couldn't consciously remember anything about his father, he found it difficult to understand why he was being so strangely affected by the entire situation.

He discussed it freely with Lily a number of times, and she agreed with his theory, but she had no new insights, and they just seemed to be having the same conversation over and over. She mentioned more than once that she wished his mother was still living; she would likely have some answers that might help him. But that was not an option, and as far as he knew there were no other relatives who would know anything. Even if he did have living relatives, he wouldn't begin to know where to find them. Throughout his entire upbringing, he'd not once met any other family members, and his mother had told him there was no one beyond the two of them. He wondered sometimes if there might have been someone else, but perhaps they had been people she preferred to avoid for reasons similar to her need to remain hidden from his father. Frederick also wondered if these feelings might be leading him to try and find his father, that perhaps what had happened to Mr. Sawyer was urging him to be able to find the man that his mother had run away from and somehow try to make peace with him. This too he discussed with Lily, but again he had no idea how to go about such a thing. He didn't know where he and his mother had lived prior to their escape, and he didn't even know his father's name.

When Frederick had a nightmare about Mr. Sawyer that was so intense that he woke Lily, she suggested that perhaps he should at least try to find some information about where Frederick had come from. She mentioned how Officer Paten had talked about his access to records that had made it evident Danny had no other family, and Mr. Key likely had connections and knowledge that could possibly be of assistance. Frederick pondered that idea for a couple of days and decided that it couldn't hurt to ask them, just to see if they might be willing to at least give him some direction. The very idea of being able to actively do something to help solve this problem already made him feel better. Was that what God had been trying to tell him all along? That he needed to search for his father? Was it possible to find the man and make peace with him? The very idea seemed impossible and even absurd. But when Frederick considered all of the miracles he'd witnessed since Lily had come into his life, he had to admit that nothing seemed too impossible or absurd—especially when putting the matter into God's hands.

A letter arrived from Mr. Key to let them know that in spite of having had some obstacles to overcome, Danny's adoption was now complete and official, and copies of the documents were enclosed. They showed the papers to the children, who were all excited, but none more than Danny, who behaved as if he'd always been a part of the family. Each of the children recalled the day their own adoptions had been made legal, and it was always cause for celebration. Some of their school lessons were cancelled, and instead they all played games together, and Mrs. Maddox made a special cake for dessert to celebrate the occasion.

With the wedding celebration only a few days away, Frederick noticed that Lily's pregnancy was beginning to show. Everything seemed perfect except for his own nagging feeling that he needed to find his father. Now that he'd taken time to fully settle with the idea that this was the course he needed to follow, he went to the office after the children were all asleep and sat down to compose letters to Mr. Key and Officer Paten, requesting their assistance at a time that suited their convenience. He wrote in both letters what little information he had, which was little more than his and his mother's names and birth dates—with the explanation that she had changed their surname in order to remain safe. It was very late when he sealed the letters and had them ready to be posted. He left them on the desk and went up to the bedroom, where he found Lily sleeping soundly. He knew he should sleep, but he felt restless and instead just sat in the dark, pondering once again everything that had led him to this intense desire to find his father. But he wondered if it was even possible.

Turning his mind to prayer, he begged God to guide him so that he could be free of this continual unsettled feeling. The thought of sharing this burden with the men to whom he'd written those letters gave him hope that he was finally on the right path, and he wished that he had taken this step weeks ago. Feeling a need to read from the Bible—as he often did when he needed to calm his mind—Frederick lit a lamp, taking care to remain quiet so he didn't disturb Lily. He was about to pick up the lamp from the bureau and go get his personal Bible out of the drawer in the bedside table when his eye was drawn to the family Bible that he'd brought here from Mr. Sawyer's house. He'd become so accustomed to seeing it here—right where he'd left it—that he'd stopped noticing it. The absence of dust on it was evidence that the maids had dusted it, along with all of the other objects that were always on the bureau. Frederick knew that the Bible belonged to Danny, but he and Lily had both agreed that they should wait until he was more settled and comfortable before giving it to him, since it might provoke some mixed emotions.

Frederick picked that Bible up instead of going in search of his own. He sat down and placed the lamp close enough that he could see sufficiently to read, and he began searching for one of his favorite passages in the Old Testament. He felt frustrated when he couldn't find it, especially when he knew the Bible so well, and he certainly knew the order of the books and the chapters that were most dear to him. With an exasperated sigh, he lifted his hands, and the book fell open on his lap to the pages at the beginning where significant family events were recorded. Something caught his eye that seemed completely out of place and entirely out of context. His breathing sharpened before his mind could even process what he was seeing. He looked at it again and again—certain he was hallucinating due to lack of sleep and his own fragile emotional state. Then he cried. He cried for all the lost and neglected children of the world, he cried for Danny, and he cried for himself. When his tears settled into a numb shock, he knew he needed to talk to Lily—even if it meant waking her. This couldn't wait until morning. He squeezed his eyes closed to try and connect with God through a feeble attempt at prayer, which was all he could muster the strength to do.

A quiet noise startled him, and he opened his eyes to see Lily standing beside him. "Are you all right?" she asked.

He reached for her hand. "I'd like to be able to say that I'm sorry if I woke you, but I'm not. I was about to wake you anyway."

"You *didn't* wake me," she said and sat close beside him. "I had a strange dream; that's what woke me. Then I realized you weren't in bed."

"What did you dream?" he asked, not certain where to begin telling her what he'd discovered.

"As with most dreams, I couldn't recall most of it once I woke up. But you were in it; you were . . . rescuing Danny from some kind of danger . . . or helping him in some way . . . or something like that. I don't remember. I'm sure it's nothing."

"Or maybe it's something," he said, twitching slightly from a sudden chill that rushed over his shoulders and down his back.

"Are you cold?" she asked, putting her arm around him.

"No," he said and shifted the heavy Bible onto her lap. "But . . . I found this." He pointed to the names and dates written there. "Did you know that Mr. Sawyer was married before . . . before Danny's mother?"

Lily gasped softly. "I just remembered. When he had me in the cellar . . . he talked about the women he had wooed. That's what he said, *women*—more than one. I'd forgotten."

"Well, there it is," Frederick said, putting his finger on the page as he read aloud. "Eartha Jane, his first wife. Not a very common name." He heard himself speaking in a calm voice that felt completely detached from what he was experiencing inside. "Notice how there is no death date for her prior to Sawyer marrying Danny's mother, which is recorded farther down the page. Nor is there a death date for their son . . . Eartha's son."

"I see that," she said, but she did little more than glance at the page; she seemed more concerned about *him* since she'd obviously picked up on the fact that he was upset—even though he was trying not to show it outwardly.

Frederick looked into her eyes and just said it. He had to say it. Until he said it he could never believe it was real. Was it a miracle? Or a nightmare? Perhaps once he got through this nightmarish feeling, he would be able to more fully accept that it couldn't be anything *but* a miracle—a great many miracles, in truth. "Lily," he began carefully and cleared his throat to give himself another few seconds to put the words together on his tongue, "Eartha Jane . . . is my mother's name." She gasped but looked thoroughly confused, as if she couldn't begin to imagine how that was possible; he knew how she felt. "And see here." He drew her attention back to the page in the Bible where he was pointing. "Her son . . . is Frederick Quentin."

Lily gasped more loudly before she put a hand over her mouth and stared at what was written, her eyes wide with disbelief. She was his wife; she knew his middle name. She also knew his birthdate, but just to be clear, he added, "And you'll note the date of his birth . . . is the same as mine." He heard Lily sob even though her hand was still over her mouth. He felt compelled to state what was obvious. "He is the man my mother ran away from." The words came out on the wave of a sob of his own, but he forced himself to keep speaking; he had to get it out— as if the information would eat him alive if he couldn't say it. "That is why . . . I've been haunted; that's why . . . I haven't been able to let go." He sobbed again, and Lily looked into his eyes. The tears he saw running down her cheeks were somewhat validating. "He knew, Lily," Frederick cried. "Somehow he knew. On his deathbed . . . when he spoke to me . . . I thought he was hallucinating; I thought he believed me to be someone else. But he knew it was me; he said that he'd prayed I would come back. He said that it was good my mother went, that he knew he'd hurt her. He asked for my forgiveness. I gave it . . . metaphorically; I mean, at that moment I *did* forgive him—for what he'd done to you and to Danny. But he was speaking literally . . . about what he'd done to me and to my mother—and I had no idea what I was saying. How could I have forgiven him for that," he cried, "when I didn't know? How could I have known? And how did *he* know it was me? I've always been told I look very much like my mother. Did I look so much like her that he knew? And if he knew . . . what did he make of my being there?"

Frederick knew he was rambling, but he couldn't stop; he had to cleanse his mind of all its racing thoughts. "Did he believe that I'd come there because I'd been searching for him? Because I didn't; I never wanted to find my father. It didn't even occur to me that God might want me to until very recently . . . and God knew I'd already found him. I came to this area because I felt drawn here; I had no idea my mother had come from here because she never told me. How is all of this possible, Lily? How? I believe in miracles; I do! For me, the miracle in coming here was finding you! And the children! And Danny! Oh!"

Frederick wrapped his arms around his middle and lowered his head abruptly as he became dizzy and felt a sudden tightening in his stomach. He was vaguely aware of Lily setting the Bible aside and wrapping her arms around him. "Oh, Danny!" Frederick said through a growing amount of tears. "I tried to talk you out of rescuing him."

"And then you admitted straightaway how glad you were that I'd ignored you. And you felt a bond with him right from the start."

"But how could I have known?" he cried. "How could I have ever imagined such a thing?"

"You couldn't have," Lily said gently. "But the truth is undeniable, my love. And it *is* a miracle. Danny is your brother, even though he is young enough to be your son."

Hearing the words spoken aloud heightened Frederick's emotion, and he moved his head into Lily's lap, where he cried like a lost child; he *was* a lost child. For all that his mother had loved him perfectly and guided him well, he'd always known that he had a father out there somewhere—a father who was cruel enough to hide from and be afraid of. His mother had told him over and over that it didn't matter, and he had always forced any curiosity or ill feelings out of his mind, but he could see now that it had always been held at bay in his spirit. Learning to cope with the loss of his mother had been the most difficult thing he'd ever faced, but he'd found a new home with Lily, and he'd believed that his every prayer had been answered in the life he now shared with her and the children. Now he knew there had been a prayer buried deeply inside him that he'd never even thought to consciously utter; he never would he have asked God to help him find his father, to help him make peace over the missing pieces of his family circle. But God had known that this discovery would bring him peace, that it would heal an ache in him that he'd not even consciously realized existed until he'd sat at Mr. Sawyer's bedside—his father's bedside—and had watched him die. It *was* a miracle, just as Lily had said. In fact, it truly was too many miracles to count. And he felt confident that once he found his way through this haze of shock and grief, he would be able to more fully appreciate the remarkable measure of God's hand in guiding him to this discovery. For now, he could only hold tightly to Lily and cry for the fatherless boy who had been forced to live in anonymity for the sake of his own preservation. The ironies were too many to count, the enormity of the situation too incredible to comprehend. For now, he could only cry.

* * *

Frederick could barely remember Lily urging him to bed and the way she'd held him while he'd cried himself to sleep. He'd slept fitfully, easing in and out of slumber, surrounded by a montage of strange dreams and even stranger thoughts and memories that kept circling around in his mind. He came fully awake to an awareness that it was daylight, but the drapes were closed. The growling of his stomach alerted him to the fact that it was likely well past his usual breakfast time, and perhaps he'd even missed lunch. Mixed into his memories of drifting in and out of sleep, he recalled hearing Lily tell one of the maids that he was not feeling well and to make certain the children were looked after while she remained with her husband. Frederick was grateful once again for a houseful of people who loved the children and were more than happy to pitch in to make certain the children were safe, cared for, and kept busy while he and Lily dealt with the dramas of life. He felt certain they'd seen more than their fair share in the relatively few short months they'd been together, and he hoped that life would now settle down and go more smoothly. He hoped even more that this new discovery—which had shaken him to the deepest caverns of his soul—would reconcile itself into his spirit and he could finally be at peace with himself and the life he'd been blessed to live.

"How are you?" he heard Lily ask just before he felt her ease onto the bed beside him. He turned over to look at her, feeling more love for her than he ever had. It was as if having his most inner self so open and raw—and sharing that experience with her—left him more keenly aware of what a beautiful and remarkable gift she was to him. Impulsively he sat up, took hold of her chin with his fingers, and kissed her in a way that he hoped could somehow express all he was feeling.

"What was that for?" she asked with a little laugh when their kiss ended.

"Do I need a reason?" he countered.

"No, but . . . given the present situation . . . it's not the greeting I expected."

"I love you, Lily," he said, still holding her chin and looking into her eyes. "I'm so grateful to have you here with me . . . to be here with you; to know that whatever we might face, we will be together. How could I ever go on without you?"

"There's no need to wonder about that," she said and kissed him in a way that fully reciprocated all he was feeling. "This is very nice," she murmured in a dreamy voice. "But . . . I've been very worried about you. It was a difficult night; what we learned is shocking. I need to know how you are . . . really."

Frederick did a quick assessment of what he'd discovered and how he felt about it. He hesitated to answer her question until he could answer it honestly. "In truth," he said, "I'm much better than I expected to be. Perhaps I've already wrestled with the issue enough that I only needed this piece of the puzzle in order to understand . . . in order to make peace with him and with myself." He sighed and wrapped her in his arms. "I'm certain it will take time, but . . . I'm all right, Lily. I really am." He shifted to lean back against the headboard, holding her hand in his. "Now that the shock has settled, I'm quite overcome to look back and realize that I was with my father when he died . . . and that he knew me. The conversation we shared is very clear in my memory. I can recall it now and realize the enormity of the miracle that was taking place— even though I never could have imagined it at the time. To me it seems tangible evidence of God's love and mercy."

"I couldn't have said it better myself," Lily said. "I've had similar thoughts. It *will* take time to feel settled with something so . . . unbelievable. But we *will* settle with it; we'll talk about it as much as we need to, and we'll go forward." She squeezed his hand. "I have to ask, though . . . what about Danny?"

"What *about* Danny?"

"Should we tell him? That he's your brother?"

Frederick was surprised at how easily he knew the answer, and he felt calm and confident over it. "Yes . . . but not yet. We'll know when it's time to tell him. Right now I think he just needs to grow into the family and feel the love and unity we all share for reasons that have nothing to do with the connection I share with him. It doesn't make us feel any differently about him; in spite of knowing what I now know, I don't love him any more or less than I did yesterday. Someday we'll give him the Bible, and he'll be mature enough to understand the miracles that brought us together . . . and he'll know by then that the love in this family has nothing to do with whether or not anyone shares the same blood."

Lily let out a contented sigh and smiled at him. "Once again . . . I couldn't have said it better myself."

Frederick smiled back, amazed by how calm and peaceful he felt when last night he had been falling apart from grief and shock. "You and I have always had a tendency to think very much the same. Have we not?"

"Indeed we have," she said and kissed him. "It's one of the countless things I love about you."

She put her head on his shoulder, and he put his hand over her belly, where their child was just beginning its tender life. The circle of their love felt perfectly right and complete with the knowledge that the circle expanded out to the twelve children who were every bit as important to them—and every bit as loved—as any children they might have in the future. And the circle extended beyond that to every member of the household, a group of people who were full of goodness in their hearts and commitment to a common cause, which in essence was an integral part of the very fabric of what it meant to be a family. Frederick marveled at the miracle and just held Lily close, silently thanking God for bringing him home.

Epilogue

FREDERICK LEANED BACK IN HIS chair and let out a long sigh, which was the only sound in the empty classroom. Just a few minutes earlier, the children had left with Nellie at the close of another day's lessons. Frederick had listened to their chattering and laughter as it had slowly faded away, and now he could hear nothing. The silence was a stark contrast to spending the majority of his time in the presence of twelve children, and even though he was glad for time to be able to do other things that needed his attention, he definitely preferred the noise and chaos of having the children around. He glanced at the clock, looking forward to joining Lily and the children for their supper—even though he and Lily ate very little during the meal, since they also made a point to share what they called their second supper with the servants, recognizing the value of spending time with them in order to be involved in their lives on a personal level. He thought of the friendship he had gained with many of them and the fulfillment he'd found in being able to help some of them gain skills in reading and writing, which was expanding their horizons and opportunities.

Frederick put a halt to his daydreaming and focused on reading through the children's writing assignments, then he went over his lesson plans for the day after tomorrow so that everything would be ready. Tomorrow there would be no school, and they were all looking forward to celebrating the marriage of Abigail and Luca and the festivities that had been in the making for weeks.

When Frederick had finished all he needed to do for the day in his role as a teacher, he idly wandered to the back of the classroom to view what had been declared—just today—the conclusion of the children's visual study of nature. They had been drawing pictures of the stages of plants and flowers since he'd first come here in the spring, and those drawings had been tacked to the wall so they could be observed and compared. The most recent excursion to the garden had shown that the leaves had lost their autumn color and fallen to the ground, and all the foliage had darkened and retreated due to the cold of winter. In class they had talked about how the flowers and plants would hide through the winter, getting ready for the following spring, when the warm air and sunshine would bring them back to life and the cycle would start over again.

Frederick looked at Danny's drawings—which had only begun recently since he'd not been among the other children for long—and he smiled to think of how well the boy was doing. He felt a deeper warmth as he did each time he stopped to ponder the knowledge that Danny was his brother and one day they would be able to talk about that. For now, everything was as it should be. Frederick's contentment deepened as he recalled Danny raising his hand in class earlier today when they'd been talking about how the plants would be hiding until spring, and he had easily and with confidence compared it to the years he'd been kept hidden in the darkness and then been brought here and he could bloom like a flower in the spring. The other children had liked his comment, and Frederick marveled that they could all talk so freely of such horrible things; it truly was evidence of the healing taking place in their lives. They were all such shining examples of faith and forgiveness and hope. And he loved them all.

The following day was filled with a bright, cloudless sky. Even though the air was cold outside, it was a perfect day for a wedding. The children all did very well at behaving themselves at the church during the ceremony, and now Frederick was sitting with Lily at the edge of the rarely used, huge ballroom in the house. He held his wife's hand while the children played some unique version of tag they'd just made up. Whatever the rules might be, they were managing to remain relatively quiet, and thankfully the room was large enough that no one seemed to care what the children were doing. There were several other children playing with them who belonged to the families of wedding guests, but they all appeared to be getting along.

With the children all playing together and having a good time, Frederick turned his attention more to the bride and groom and all of the wedding guests. They *all* appeared to be having a good time. Abigail and Luca were clearly very much in love, and everyone was glad for them—and especially glad that they would both remain here and continue to be a part of the family they'd found among their peers. All members of the staff appeared to be enjoying themselves with laughter and conversation and even a little bit of dancing. The food had been carefully planned and prepared ahead of time so that not much last-minute work was involved, which meant that everyone could help do what little still needed to be done, and everyone could have a relaxing and enjoyable day.

Every person who lived on the estate—including tenant farmers and those who were leasing homes—had been invited to the wedding, along with some people who lived in town and were friends and acquaintances of Abigail and Luca. Frederick liked the fact that he'd come to know every person here—thanks to the way his wife took him with her on various visits. He was especially pleased to see Mr. Topp here with his children, looking so much happier and more at peace than when Frederick had first met him when he'd been consumed with grief. The evidence of healing he saw in Mr. Topp resonated inwardly with Frederick as he considered his own journey of healing during the months since he'd come here and how his life had changed in ways he never could have foreseen.

Frederick heard Lily laugh and turned to look at her, smiling at the way she was caught up in observing Luca and Abigail teasing each other. As always he was struck by her unique beauty, and he'd grown accustomed to the unconventional style of her hair, which actually suited her well. She was just beginning to actually *look* pregnant, which also suited her well. Overcome with just how precious she was to him, he leaned over and kissed her cheek before he whispered in her ear, "I love you dearly, Mrs. Woodstone."

She laughed softly and turned to look at him. "And I love you, Mr. Woodstone." She glanced again at the bride and groom. "I do believe they'll be very happy together."

"Yes," Frederick said, "but no happier than we are."

"Never!" Lily said and laughed again. Thoughtfully she added, "We didn't have a wedding cake . . . or a party."

"Do you regret that?" he asked.

"Not at all!" she said fervently. "Our wedding was perfect!" She gave him a quick kiss. "However . . . I would really like some wedding cake *now*, but I don't feel at all like getting out of this chair."

"I think I can take care of that," he said and stood, but before he could walk away, she grabbed his hand.

Frederick looked down at her, surprised to see warm sincerity in her eyes as she said, "You're very good at such things, you know."

"At getting you a piece of cake?" he asked, laughing.

"At all the big and little things that make me so very happy—and at doing the same for our children."

"It's the easiest thing I've ever done, Lily," he said, leaning over to kiss her again. "You're all very easy to love."

He'd barely said it when they heard the sound of children arguing loudly. They both laughed, and Frederick said, "I will go take care of whatever *that* is about, and *then* I will get you some wedding cake."

Lily gave him a smile of self-satisfaction, as if to say his doing so proved her point, but she seemed oblivious to the fact that he felt the same way about her. She was so good at doing every big and little thing that made him perfectly happy—and she was such an amazing mother. As he headed toward the arguing children, he had a brief thought pass through his mind that his own mother would be so pleased with where he was now, and he could easily imagine her watching over her grandchildren like some kind of guardian angel. He smiled at the thought, then he stopped walking when his next thought appeared so abruptly in his mind that it took his breath away—and somehow he knew it was true; somehow he knew that the same applied to his father— that he was very proud of Frederick, and of Danny, and that he too was watching over them.

Frederick blinked back the threat of tears, took a deep breath, and hurried to intervene with whatever had caused discord with his children. It only took a minute to ask some questions and to get the children to calm down and apologize to each other. Even that was evidence of the progress they'd made. Then they all went to get some wedding cake.

About the Author

ANITA STANSFIELD HAS MORE THAN fifty published books and is the recipient of many awards, including two Lifetime Achievement Awards. Her books go far beyond being enjoyable, memorable stories. Anita resonates particularly well with a broad range of devoted readers because of her sensitive and insightful examination of contemporary issues that are faced by many of those readers, even when her venue is a historical romance. Readers come away from her compelling stories equipped with new ideas about how to enrich their own lives, regardless of their circumstances.

Anita was born and raised in Provo, Utah. She is the mother of five and has a growing number of grandchildren. She also writes for the general trade market under the name Elizabeth D. Michaels.

For more information and a complete list of her publications, go to anitastansfield.blogspot.com or anitastansfield.com, where you can sign up to receive email updates. You can also follow her on Facebook and Twitter.